HUNGER

Also by Eve Langlais,
Kate Douglas, and A. C. Arthur

Growl
Wild

HUNGER

Eve Langlais   Kate Douglas   A. C. Arthur

St. Martin's Griffin ❧ New York

HUNGER. Copyright © 2017 by St. Martin's Press.
Alpha's Mate by Eve Langlais. Copyright © 2017 by Eve Langlais.
Dangerous Passions by Kate Douglas. Copyright © 2017 by Kate Douglas.
Bound to the Wolf by A. C. Arthur. Copyright © 2017 by A. C. Arthur.

All rights reserved. Printed in the United States of America.
For information, address St. Martin's Press,
175 Fifth Avenue, New York, N.Y. 10010.

www.stmartins.com

The Library of Congress Cataloging-in-Publication Data
is available upon request.

ISBN 978-1-250-07860-5 (trade paperback)
ISBN 978-1-4668-9107-4 (e-book)

Dangerous Passions by Kate Douglas and *Bound to the Wolf*
by A. C. Arthur were originally published in e-book format under
the title *Claimed by the Mate, Volume 3,* in January 2017.

Our books may be purchased in bulk for promotional, educational,
or business use. Please contact your local bookseller or the Macmillan
Corporate and Premium Sales Department at 1-800-221-7945, exten-
sion 5442, or by e-mail at MacmillanSpecialMarkets@macmillan.com.

First Edition: May 2017

10 9 8 7 6 5 4 3 2 1

CONTENTS

HUNGER

ALPHA'S MATE

Eve Langlais

CHAPTER 1

The fresh air presented a nice change after the time she'd spent getting bounced around in the confining, and somewhat stifling, trunk of the car. However, getting to vacate her vehicular coffin didn't mean her situation improved, as she found herself heaved over a shoulder with less care than a sack of potatoes. How rude, but then again, she really couldn't expect much manners given she was in the midst of a kidnapping, her own, to be exact.

Certainly not how I planned to spend my evening. But more exciting than the catching up on the DVR programming she had planned.

One tall lamppost lit the surroundings, but this was the only sign of civilization. The sounds of the city didn't penetrate the gravel-packed parking lot. Night had fallen, and the hum of crickets from the shadowy forest filled the air as opposed to the buzz of flies in dirty alleys. A city girl at heart, she didn't often find herself in such lush green places and, given the mosquito that buzzed looking for a spot to land, with good reason.

Logical deduction put her in some kind of conservation area, a guess she made because of the glimpse she got of a placard reading: PLEASE STICK TO THE MARKED TRAILS. And KEEP OUR PARKLANDS CLEAN. DON'T LITTER.

Does dumping bodies count? She idly wondered what kind of fine that would entail.

The jouncing journey on her kidnapper's shoulder proved short, her landing abrupt, the splintered, weathered wood planks she hit not providing the most cushiony of landings.

"Would it hurt you to be gentle?" she grumbled.

"Shut up."

She took that to mean yes, it would.

"Should we kill her now?" a gruff voice asked.

She frowned. That seemed kind of drastic, especially given she didn't even know these thugs, although they'd certainly targeted her. They'd lain in wait in the parking garage of the building where she worked. Like an idiot, she never even sensed them until they'd conked her on the head.

"How should we kill her? I'm not too keen on getting blood on these shoes. I just broke them in." The shoes in question were some type of patent leather. Not a great loss if he tossed them.

Thug Number Two replied, "We could strangle her, but I've heard them forensic folk can sometimes lift prints."

"So use gloves." Said with a duh-like sigh that she wanted to echo.

"Did you bring some?"

Judging by the silence, her kidnappers came ill prepared. Just her luck she'd gotten nabbed by incompetents. That boded well, for her at least.

"Fuck the gloves and killing her by hand. The river will take care of her for us."

Death by drowning? Uh no. This conversation about ways to bring about her demise needed to end. She cleared her throat. "Excuse me . . ." *Asshats? No, too aggressive. Gentlemen? Ha, say that with a straight face.* "Guys, you really don't want to do this."

"A hundred Gs says we do," retorted the one who advocated drowning.

A hundred grand? Damn, for that money she'd want to kill herself, too. "Who's paying?"

"The guy who wants you dead."

Well, that wasn't the answer she hoped for. A name would have been nice since the list of people who disliked her was rather extensive. "Murder for money. Is that really something you want on your conscience?"

"Murder?" The one who had carried her snorted. "How is it murder if you fall in the river and drown? I hear this stretch has a pretty decent current. Not our fault if you can't swim."

As if she could swim given the way they had her bound. Not only were her hands tied in front of her, but her feet were tethered as well. Overkill if you asked her and not exactly an ideal scenario. It probably explained why her heart pounded, putting rumors to rest by those who said she had none.

"That's not very sporting. I mean the least you could do is untie me." She batted her lashes, but they didn't fall for it.

"Untie you? Not a chance. I am not risking our payment just in case you actually manage to get out of this alive."

"Maybe we should kill her before we dump the body in the water," the other one whined. "What if she doesn't drown?"

This discussion of her demise was really getting old. "Listen, gentlemen," she said, even if, to her mind, they were little better than petty thugs, "perhaps we can negotiate. If it's money you want then—"

"Shut your trap."

The open-handed cuff snapped her head. She bit her lip, hard enough to taste blood.

Instead of making her cower or zip her lips, it annoyed her. "Well, that wasn't very nice," she retorted.

"Like we give a damn," snarled the guy closest to her.

"Who are you?" *Tell me your name so I know upon whom to exact my revenge.*

"As if we're going to tell," Jerk Number Two said from behind her. She really should put a face to the voice for when she managed to escape and needed to find him again. She craned for a peek, only to receive another slap to her noggin.

Her head throbbed, and a hint of fear tried to weave its way around her confidence, attempting to strangle it.

Never. Giving up would cost her life. Since she didn't have it scheduled in her agenda, death would have to wait. She had too many appointments to keep, too much still to experience.

"Didn't your mother ever teach you to not hit girls?" she muttered.

"Yeah, and then our father told her to shut up with his fist." The pair of thugs snorted at their poor jest, entirely too pleased with themselves.

Since she couldn't seem to dissuade them, she tried to stall and gather other info as her fingers worked at the duct tape keeping her hands bound. Damn them for buying the good stuff. "Who hired you?" A hundred Gs wasn't chump change, but it was also kind of an insult. *Surely my death is worth more.*

And what was the ultimate plan? Why kill her here, in this spot? Which was where exactly?

A glance around showed her seated on some kind of weathered wooden dock that jutted out over a span of water where the occasional whitecap glinted as the current rolled past.

"You talk way too much," grumbled the hired killer.

"I told you we should have taped her mouth, too. But oh no, you said we had to keep her breathing until we got here because dead bodies stink up the car."

"Shut up or I'll slap you, too. Let's get this over with."

"You'll regret this," she threatened.

"Yada. Yada. Say hello to the underworld. I hear it's warm this time of the year."

A snort of laughter accompanied the rough hands that gripped her arms, and despite herself, fear swamped her confidence. She couldn't help but struggle, squirming and twisting in their grasp. She used everything she had, even her teeth, managing a satisfying chomp.

"Ow! The bitch bit me," complained the thug who dropped her.

A minor victory, and she used it to inchworm her way across the dock, not very far, though.

A booted foot made contact with her poor head, and she gasped in pain, then struggled for consciousness as dark spots made her blink.

And blink.

And—

The cold slap of the water stole her breath, and she sank, much like a rock. No amount of wiggling or thrashing stopped her descent. It didn't take long before her lungs burned, the pressure of holding her breath urgent.

She breathed out a few bubbles. It didn't change her situation. It just meant she lived a few seconds longer.

I'm going to die.

That totally blew.

She didn't want her life to end. She didn't want to feed the fishies.

Apparently, fate didn't want her to pollute the river either, because something caught hold of her.

It's a gator. It's a fish. It's a . . . man?

She caught only a glimpse of his features, the scant starlight providing more shadow than illumination. Yet who cared about his looks? He'd saved her!

Their heads broke the surface of the water, and she drew in a much-needed lungful of air. As she fed her abused lungs, she caught a glimpse of her rescuer. Perhaps he was a merman. He certainly appeared as if he belonged to the water elements with his hair slicked back. However, his eyes, vivid even in the darkness, were lit as if from within with a golden fire that screamed, *I am not human!*

But he certainly was attractive. He held her with a dependable strength as he trod water for both of them. A savior from the shadows.

She couldn't help but whisper, "Who are you?" And then her brow creased as her mind hit a wall, a wall she could have sworn hadn't existed before, and she exclaimed, "Who am I?"

However, her identity issues would have to wait, because it seemed the splashes of water all around them weren't rocks falling from the sky. They were bullets.

Someone is shooting at us!

CHAPTER 2

Villains don't save damsels.

Hadn't Fabian written the memo? Didn't he preach the word? Then what the hell possessed him to play the part of hero?

What idiot dove, in the dark, in a river with a decent current, to save a bloody stranger?

Apparently, he was just such an idiot, and if he survived this stupidity, he'd give himself a proper reaming.

If he survived.

Splish. Splosh.

Those assholes are shooting at us!

Fabian could have kicked his own ass once the bullets began to fly, peppering the river's surface with their deadly impact. Yet, given the slight female in his arms would have surely drowned if he'd not acted, he couldn't completely say he wouldn't do it again.

Who would have thought a hero lurked beneath his jaded veneer?

A hero he'd deny existed if anyone remarked on it. He did have a reputation as a badass to maintain after all.

"Who's shooting at us?" the woman squeaked.

Answering a question at a time like this was stupid, so

he did the only thing he could think of to shut her up. "Hold your breath."

Not much warning, but then again, they didn't have much time. He yanked them both under the water's surface that served a dual purpose. First, the murky river would act as camouflage, making it harder for the gunmen to spot them and, second, because the thick liquid would slow the impact of the bullets.

Not that he really cared if he got hit. He'd survive. As a werewolf, and a powerful one at that, he possessed an amazing constitution that mocked most injuries. But his amazing ability to heal didn't stop one crucial thing.

Getting shot sucked. He knew this from experience. He also knew another thing. *The woman could get hurt.* Humans were fragile that way.

We must protect her.

The altruistic thought didn't come from him. *Pesky inner beast.* It seemed his wolf half-harbored irritating concepts of honor and duty. It enjoyed helping others, even if it made Fabian's villainous reputation so hard to maintain.

Ignoring his Lycan side, which whined at the whole swimming-underwater thing—*must find a patch of dirt to roll in*—he kicked his feet while keeping his arms wrapped around the woman. The current helped move them away from the scene and out of reach of the gunmen.

While his lung capacity meant he could have swum a while longer underwater, he kept in mind the woman he held was human. She needed to breathe.

He popped their heads above the surface and heard her take in a gasping breath.

"*Shh,*" he hastened to whisper before she could speak. "We have to remain quiet."

She nodded and didn't say a word. However, she might as well have shone a beacon given how noisily she sucked in air.

In the distance, he heard shouting.

"Where the hell did they go?"

"I'm pretty sure I hit them," boasted the other.

Wishful thinking, Fabian thought with a smirk.

The current took them farther downstream, deeper into his territory, and that meant it was less likely the thugs would continue their pursuit.

The gurgle and rush of the water as it carried their bobbing bodies, held aloft by his scissoring legs, filled the silence between them.

She was a woman, so of course it couldn't last forever.

"I'm cold," she said through chattering teeth.

"But alive, so stop complaining. We can't exit the river yet. We've not gone far enough."

"How would you know?"

"Because I own these lands." Said not without a little bit of pride. He'd worked hard to get where he was today.

"I want to go to shore."

"What part of 'not yet' did you not understand?"

"You can't tell me what to do. Let me go." She squirmed in his arms, not that it did her any good. He was much stronger than her.

"How about we first untie your hands? Or is this a new fashion statement?" What kind of coward tossed a bound woman into water? It was a cruel way to kill with no honor.

Given he held them both afloat, he had to quickly tear the sodden tape in two before she sank. But separating her hands wasn't enough, apparently. He had an irrational need to see the tape gone. "Hold on to me with one hand while I get it off."

She braced a hand on his shoulder while holding out the other to him.

As his feet trod water, he peeled the sticky binding from her wrist, swiftly, ignoring her gasped, "Ow! Couldn't you have been more gentle?"

"Don't whine. Tape is like a Band-Aid, best yanked off quick. Switch hands now so I can get the other."

While she might have protested at his methods, that didn't stop her from offering her other wrist to him.

She clenched her lips tight as he ripped the tape away.

"Done. Was that so hard?"

A glare was her reply.

He chuckled. "Your gratefulness is overwhelming me."

"Smart-ass."

"Will you stop whining if I kiss it better and promise to get you some ice cream?"

"I'd prefer if you freed my feet."

"I can do that if you float on your back so I can reach them."

Except she didn't know how to float very well, apparently, which meant he ended up ducking underwater for a second to tear at the tape holding her ankles together.

As soon as he broke the surface of the water, she started in on him again.

"Let me go. I want to go to shore."

"Can you swim?" he asked.

"Of course I can. I think." She said the last bit on a higher note.

"Suit yourself."

He released her and let her sink like a cement block a few feet underwater before reaching under and yanking her back up.

She spat out water and invectives: "Bloody hell, I can't swim."

"Just how many other things do you not remember being able to do?" He couldn't help a smug grin, his expression pure *I told you so.*

She glared at him, her evil stare visible even in the feeble starlight. It made him smile only wider.

"You are not funny," she stated.

"I wasn't trying to be a comedian, merely practical."

"Well, you suck," she wheezed, still trying to catch her breath.

Feisty. He kind of liked it. It wasn't often he came across people with the balls to talk back to him. Being a man of power meant most people feared him. As he was alpha of the wolves and a small contingent of cats, his position meant people obeyed him—and trembled if he turned his displeased mien their way—and women tended to simper in his presence and do their best to seduce him in the hopes of becoming Mrs. Garoux. They all wanted to become a powerful woman in the shifter underworld and beneficiary of his immense wealth.

He couldn't have said what prompted him to say, "Yes, I do suck. And lick. I'm also partial to nibbles. I'm a man of many talents, vixen."

"You can keep those talents to yourself."

"Such ingratitude for the man who saved you."

"You're right. I should show some manners. Thank you."

"That's it?" He said the words teasingly, and to his surprise, his prickly, waterlogged lady chuckled.

"How's thank you very much?"

"You forgot to add a cherry on top."

How about a kiss?

An odd thought to have, given he didn't know the woman and she was hardly attractive soaked in river water that proved quite odiferous.

"Cherries are overrated. I prefer ooey, gooey caramel."

Yes. Caramel, licked from her lips.

Bad wolf.

At least, he wanted to blame his wolf, and yet he was the one who pictured himself caressing her full, if slightly purple, lips.

Perhaps it is time to head for shore.

The temperature of the water truly affected her, much more than him.

If the thugs planned on pursuing, they'd have to enter his lands, and if they did . . . Surprise, they wouldn't make it out alive.

And, no, he didn't exaggerate to maintain his reputation. Some things just weren't allowed in his world. Shooting at him was one of them.

Feet scissoring, he kicked them toward shore, aiming for the faint lights he glimpsed in the rising mist. Unless the landscape for his property had changed, that glow came from the solar lights bolted to the dock he maintained. Not that he boated. Wolves weren't sailors, but he did enjoy fishing.

And this time I caught the biggest prize of all.

Using the current and traversing at an angle, he managed to guide them to the dock, then past it, as it didn't have a ladder and he doubted she'd have the upper body strength needed to hoist herself up.

He dragged her toward the shore until her feet touched the bottom. He found his footing and steadied her as she stumbled clumsily upright.

"About time," she muttered, yanking herself from his grip. Head held high—her regal attempt making his lips twitch—she slogged away from him through the shallow current.

Fabian followed behind and, being a man, took a moment to admire the way her ass moved in her wet leggings, her hourglass shape clearly delineated by the clinging white blouse. A curvy handful with some cushion at the hips and butt, an indent at the waist, and short, dark, bobbed hair that revealed a tempting—*oh let's bite it*—neck.

Bite it?

No. Fabian did not mark women. Any women. Not the ones he slept with. Not the ones he dated. And definitely not a water-soaked woman conveniently suffering from amnesia with thugs looking to kill her.

There would be no biting. Ever. Because everyone knew what a good chomp meant. Lycan tradition had males claiming their mates in a very permanent and scarring fashion.

It was archaic. Barbaric. It also meant a man had to limit himself to one woman the rest of his life. Talk about major commitment.

Fabian wasn't sure he'd ever make the plunge, and before anyone tried to tell him he'd not have a choice, that once the mating urge struck it would prove relentless, he said, "Ha!" Strength of will would be his armor against the ultimate collar around his neck. Determination and an ability to resist temptation would—

Ooh. Nice. Mine. Want.

His train of thought derailed as the woman strode a few yards away from the shore and then turned to face him, hands on her hips.

The white blouse clung to her upper torso, outlining her very full breasts. Even though she wore a bra, as the cool night air touched the wet fabric covering the tips they puckered and poked.

A man of his experience shouldn't have to clamp his jaw lest he slobber.

Look away. Look away! He knew how to fight her siren temptation, and he would have, fought it, that was, if she'd not caught him with her gaze just as a sliver of moon lit the shoreline. Bright blue eyes snared his, their expression quizzical and appraising.

How did he appear, striding from the water—Neptune rising from the sea or, in this case, a river? He thrust out his chest and wondered if she noted his musculature through his soaked garment. While just a hair over forty, he didn't look it. He was in prime shape, and it wasn't vanity that said he was good-looking. His mirror told him every day.

If she did notice his fine physique, she didn't openly admire it. On the contrary, she wrinkled her nose. "You've got a weed caught in your hair."

As he tugged the offending greenery from his soaked crown, he scowled. "You really need to work on your thanks to the man who saved you."

"I already said thank you."

"And?"

"And what? What else would you like me to say or do?"

Good question. What did he want her to do?

Do me.

No, he wasn't going to coerce her into having sex for his doing the—*ack!*—right thing.

But speaking of the right thing, time to rein her back in before she went too crazy.

"So any idea where the closest phone is? I should probably call the police and—"

Involve the fuzz? "Whoa there, vixen. I don't know if you want to call the cops."

She paused midsentence and blinked wet lashes at him. "Why not? Someone, two someones actually, just tried to kill me. They would have killed you, too, if their aim was any good."

"But they didn't, and for the moment, they're probably assuming you're dead."

She peeked down at herself, which had the effect of drawing his gaze.

We really should peel her out of those wet clothes and warm her up.

Before he could suggest it, she spoke. "But I'm not dead."

"No, you're not, but if you go to the cops, they'll make some kind of public announcement, which means those guys will know they failed and they might try again."

"Or the cops will catch them."

Fabian snorted. "Catch who? Can you describe them? Do you know their names? The make or model of their car? Their motive? Anything?"

The more he fired questions at her, the more she stiffened and her lips tightened. "I know nothing. Not even my own damned name." She kicked at the loose pebbles on the shore.

For a moment, chagrin touched him at the way he'd verbally hammered her. However, in this situation—violence, death, and cops—he truly knew best. And best was her taking his advice whether she liked it or not.

A flash of predator eyes from the shadowy coverage of the woods let Fabian know they weren't alone. He held up a hand meant to convey, *Stay where you are.* No use letting this stranger see more than necessary. Not everyone could handle the appearance of wolves, even tamed ones.

Yet she is handling the wildest wolf of all with ease so far. And, no, it wasn't arrogance that made him think that. Fabian was the biggest, baddest Lycan around.

As alpha and boss of these lands, he could command her to obey, but the manners his mother had instilled won the day. "Why don't we continue this discussion at my house, where there are dry towels, a shot of brandy, and a fireplace to chase the chill from our skin?"

"You live close to here?"

"Yes, about a half mile or so from the river. There is a path we can use."

When it seemed as if she would hesitate, he strode past her, head held high and imperiously, an appearance ruined by the squelch of water in his sodden Italian leather loafers.

Instead of arguing further—a miracle—she followed, followed the big bad wolf to his secret lair.

Awoo! Ahem, he meant, *Excellent!*, with an evil twiddle of his fingers of course.

CHAPTER 3

Cold and wet, with no memory of who she was, no idea of where she found herself, meant she followed the broad back of the man who'd rescued her. *A nice back,* she should add, but, still, that of a stranger.

She didn't know him or his motives. What did he plan? And why did he risk his life for her?

Yet, despite her questions, following his advice about not calling the police was probably the most prudent thing she could do. After all, what did she know of surviving a murder attempt?

But the more worrisome question should be: What did he know? And how?

Something about the man who saved her seemed off-kilter. Had she imagined the goldenlike glow of his gaze when they bobbed in the water? There was no denying the fact that he spoke and acted like a man used to getting his way—and not getting any argument.

Well, guess what, I am not going to play the part of sub-servient maiden. She might not recall her identity, but somehow she knew meekness was not something she allowed.

What apparently did seem allowed was an admiration for the male who moved with uncanny grace before her on the shadowy path. The feeble moonlight along with scattered solar lamps let her catch glimpses. Despite her sodden and chilly state, what she saw warmed her.

Apparently, I haven't forgotten what I like in a man. And she did like the width of his broad shoulders, the height of him as well, at least a foot taller than her own frame. His pants clung to a tight rear, and as she let her gaze rove upward from it she noted the play of his muscles, outlined by his damp, clinging shirt.

As for his face, sharp cheeks, piercing eyes, a strong jaw, and lips that needed softening.

By a kiss.

She shook her head at the startling thought. Then winced. Her poor skull throbbed, the end result of the blow to it. Odd how she remembered what had recently happened and yet everything before it . . . just a blank slate in her mind.

Who am I?

It belatedly occurred to her she should check her pockets. Perhaps she had some form of identification, a wallet if she was lucky, maybe a phone. If she had pockets. Patting herself, she noted her outfit and made a moue.

Leggings with an oversized blouse meant no hidden recesses with a driver's license. While the outfit might prove comfortable under normal circumstances, she couldn't wait to shed it. The cold and wet fabric clung to her skin, and it was all she could do to not let her teeth chatter.

She couldn't have said how long they walked, in silence since he didn't seem in a hurry to start a conversation and she was too miserable to bother.

When he did finally speak, she almost stumbled.

"You'll be able to see the house around the next bend," he announced.

A house, he says?

As they came around the corner in the path, the foliage that previously blocked their view thinned. She gaped at the mansion, and her steps slowed as they approached.

Lights illuminated the exterior, a Southern-style plantation home with white columns, wide double doors in gleaming carved wood, and a multitude of windows.

"You live here?" A note of incredulity seeped into her query.

"Yes."

"With your wife?" Okay, she honestly couldn't say why she'd asked that.

His lips twitched as he caught her gaze. "I'm not married."

Excellent. Although why she cared she couldn't have said.

"Surely you don't live here alone."

"I have staff. Some of them have quarters in the attic. A few have cabins. I tend to host many visitors. So while I technically live alone, I am never truly without company."

As they approached the front step leading up to the porch, a sweeping wide affair that wrapped around the mansion, the double doors were flung open with a flourish, and a balding gent, properly dressed in a suit, stepped forth, holding out some towels.

How did he know we needed some?

"Hot from the dryer, milord."

Milord? Before she could giggle at the title, the warm, fluffy towel was draped around her shoulders. She couldn't help a sigh of delight. *So this is what butlers do. Hand out warm towels when their boss goes for a midnight swim. Handy.*

Also handy was the mug thrust into her hand.

"A warm toddy for the lady?"

She stared stupidly at the steaming liquid. She had no idea what a toddy was, but it smelled like cinnamon. Given her trembling body and the cold nestled deep within, she probably needed it. She sipped and gasped as the alcohol burned its way down.

Her sodden rescuer chuckled. "As my father likes to say, fire in the hole!"

Fire indeed. She took another gulp and peeked around as the butler and his lord—snicker—had a chat in low tones.

If the outside of the house proved grand, the inside appeared even more opulent. Whoever this man was, he had wealth. Lots of it.

But I'm just as rich.

I am?

The certainty didn't leave, but it also didn't give her any memories or facts to support her belief.

The marble floor gleamed, and she stared at her feet, still clad in sandals, the leather straps holding them firmly to her feet. Brilliant red polish adorned her nails while a French manicure showed on her fingers. No thick calluses on the pads of her hands. *I obviously don't work in a labor-intensive field.*

Because I'm the boss.

She was? Boss of what?

"Follow me."

Distracted from her inner thoughts, she lifted her head

and saw her rescuer stood on the first step of the sweeping staircase.

"Where are you going?"

"Follow me and I'll show you to a room."

She didn't move. "What happened to talking about what happened and what to do next?"

"Wouldn't you prefer to do that after a shower and a change into dry clothes?"

It sounded so tempting. She took a step forward but halted before taking a second step. "Why are you doing this?"

"Doing what? Offering you basic hospitality?"

"Yes, that and the whole saving-me thing. I mean who dives into a river to save a drowning woman and then acts so blasé about the fact that someone is shooting at them? Who are you?"

"I am Fabian Garoux."

She snickered.

"I'm sorry, you find something amusing?"

"Did your parents not love you?"

"I'm not following."

"Who saddles their child with a name like Fabian Garoux?" She laughed again. "I mean, it sounds like something out of a cheesy romance movie or novel."

How indignant he appeared. His chin rose, his chest, if possible, widened, and his tone held a degree of imperial cool as he replied, "It is a name that makes people shiver."

"With repressed mirth."

"I am beginning to think I should have let you drown," he grumbled as he turned and headed up the stairs.

"Oh please don't tell me you're going to mope. I hate it when men mope."

"I do not mope," he grumbled, shooting her a dark look over his shoulder. "I brood."

"Because that's so much better, *Fabio*."

"It's Fabian."

"Whatever."

"Says the river rat."

Her grin faded. "Excuse me?"

"Well, since you can't remember your name, we need something to call you by. Since you look like a drowned rat and I pulled you from the river . . . I'd say it should be self-explanatory."

How nice of him to point out she looked less than presentable. "You suck."

"I thought we'd already ascertained that I did. Although I would prefer if you bathed before I place my lips on your skin."

"There will be no lips placed anywhere on my body," she announced, even if said body shivered in response to his words.

"We'll see," was his enigmatic reply. "Here is your room." He twisted the handle of a door and swung it open before sweeping his arm in a grand gesture.

She entered what could only be termed a suite, a large one by any standards. Thick carpeting of a creamy color offset the dark wood of the furniture. A patterned gray comforter piled with varying shades of pillows garnished the king-size bed.

Fabian strode to the fireplace in the room and ran his fingers under the mantel. Flames erupted in the hearth, and she couldn't help but be drawn to their promised warmth.

"There is a bathroom through there." He gestured to

another door. "Clothing is being gathered as we speak and will be left on the bed as you bathe. We will speak once we've both refreshed ourselves."

"Speak or do you mean you'll order me around some more?" She didn't say the words with any true vehemence. Rather, she peered at him through thick lashes with her lips curled in a partial smile.

"I doubt anyone can order you around, vixen." With a smile that did warm and decadent things to her, he turned and left, the soft click of the door a signal to release the breath she held.

Alone. At last. Yet a part of her wished he'd stayed. She couldn't have said why. It wasn't as if she was in danger and in need of him for protection.

Who was to say he wasn't dangerous in and of himself? He certainly wasn't a rich yuppie, not with that physique, manner, and brash self-assurance.

He'd faced down danger without a qualm. Only the truly brave—or stupid—showed no fear. But she doubted anyone could call Fabian stupid.

Sexy yes, though.

But she had more important things to worry about than a handsome man who made her pulse flutter.

Someone tried to kill me. Someone had also given her a wicked shiner, she noted as she entered the bathroom and caught sight of herself in the bathroom mirror.

She raised fingers to the colorful swelling that ran the length of her cheekbone and truly popped around her eye. It went well with the bird's nest known as her hair and the mascara that ran down her one unblemished cheek in dark rivulets.

Pretty. Pretty ugly. And to think Fabian had still flirted with her. It could mean only one thing. He probably flirted with every woman he met.

She let out a big breath, surely not of disappointment. Upon inhaling, her nose wrinkled. She sniffed.

Oh, eww. That stench came from her. No wonder he'd suggested she bathe. She reeked.

A hot shower later—a long one that she luxuriated in where she scrubbed herself, twice—she smelled a lot better. She also looked better, given there was a hair dryer in the bathroom along with a brush that she used to tame her unruly mop.

What she didn't find, though, was clothes. But hadn't he said someone would leave some in the room for when she was done?

Leaving behind the wet towels, she stepped from the bathroom, the steam of the shower billowing out with her, but the shock of warm skin meeting cooler air wasn't what made her nipples tighten.

Desire slammed her, hard and furious as she met Fabian's smoldering gaze.

She took a step toward him. He took one back. Did he fear her? It almost seemed that way. Yet he couldn't stop staring.

Another step forward. He hit the bed and could go no farther. She entered his space and waited for him to do something. Anything.

Nada. His eyes moved from her body to her face. His lips tightened, and his eyes flashed. Way to remind her she was less than perfect at the moment.

Stung, she snapped. "Take a picture. It will last longer."
Or take me and let's remember this moment forever.

CHAPTER 4

Take her. She's ready, and mine. All mine.

Oh fuck.

Hell no.

And a whole lot of other dark and nasty words that did nothing to stop what happened next when she got too close.

The mating fever hit him, hard, without mercy and with a lot of lust.

Cock-hardening. Toe-tingling. Blood-boiling. Lust.

He could have perhaps explained the reaction being a result of catching sight of her naked body. Creamy smooth skin covering curves. *Fuck me, those curves.* Rounded hips, indented waist, and plump breasts topped with fat pink nipples.

Suckable nipples.

Please tell me I'm not drooling. It wasn't seemly in a man his age or of his status.

Yet he really craved a taste of the sumptuous feast before him, but that wasn't what brought on the certainty this woman belonged to him.

Before, he'd wondered at his wolf's strange interest in the woman, especially its desire to protect. That was when she reeked of the river, with all its myriad strong scents.

However, now she didn't have that stench to mask her. Now her musk—sweet ambrosia—wrapped around him, a snug noose and decadent pleasure at once.

The scent of her awoke the primal side of him, the wild half. This half recognized his mate.

The jaws of fate tried to catch him in its grip.

No! Not without a fight. A coward might have whirled. Out of sight, out of mind. But turning away wouldn't hide her scent.

And I am not afraid.

"Did you forget something?" Arching a brow, he sought to command the situation, only to have her once again try to snag control from him.

She peeked down at herself, and he barely restrained a groan as her nipples hardened into peaks begging for his lips. "Well, I didn't shave, but that was only because I didn't see a razor."

"I was talking about your nudity."

"What about it?"

"It's indecent." And yes, he got the irony of his statement, given most shifters placed little stock in nudity. Actually, until this moment, he'd never batted an eye. But that was before now.

She laughed, the sound throaty and low. "Oh please. Indecent?" She pitched the word high. "Don't tell me you've never seen a naked woman before."

Did she have no shame? Nope. She tilted a hip, placed a hand on it, thrust her breasts out, and her very stare taunted him.

He gritted his teeth. "I've seen many naked women." He relaxed and smiled. "Most of them my lovers. Is this your way of gaining my attention?"

Now it was her turn to look uncertain. Not for long. Her chin tilted. "Hardly. As you might have guessed, I wasn't expecting company. Most gentlemen would have knocked before entering a lady's bedroom."

"First off, I'm not a gentleman." *Try more like a wild animal.* "And second—"

"Don't you dare say I'm not a lady," she threatened with narrowed eyes.

"I was going to say 'my house, my room,' which means I see no reason why I should knock."

"How about common courtesy?"

"Common courtesy is for others." He smiled. "I make my own rules."

"Speaking of rules, I noticed this room didn't have a phone," she mentioned as she stepped even closer to him.

He didn't move, just watched her with only the barest grip on himself. How he wanted to sweep her into his arms and embrace those lips into compliance. To strip off his own clothes and feel the silkiness of her flesh against his.

She got right next to him. So close. So—

She leaned around him and grabbed at the garments he'd brought before stepping away. Before he could stop himself, he reached out to grab her.

Bad hand. He slapped the misbehaving appendage down and had both hands tucked behind his back before she whirled and shot him an inquiring look.

"Did you just slap yourself?"

"Mosquito." Said completely deadpan.

She bought it or at least didn't mention it further, a good thing, too, because he might have temporarily lost his ability to speak as she did her best to drive him insane.

No, seriously, she did it on purpose. What woman bent

over, ass toward him—*bare ass,* he might add, which meant he got to see the pinkness of her sex, the hint of dark curls— as she tugged on soft flannel pants.

His pants.

When Fred, his butler, had run into Fabian in the hall with a stack of clothes, Fabian took one sniff of another wolf's scent on them and decided he didn't want her wearing them. At the time he'd not questioned his irrational need to have her wearing something of his, something with his scent.

Something that shows she's mine.

Now it made all too much sense. It also provided a form of torture as the fabric touched her skin and hide her bountiful assets. The matching flannel top did its best to camouflage her splendid breasts, but the image of them was burned in his mind.

The overly large garments did not fit her well at all, the sleeves too long, the pant legs needing several rolls so she didn't step on them. Still, though, in that moment, she outshone all the women he'd ever known.

It both exhilarated and frightened.

Fear? He feared nothing. Especially not one human woman who didn't even know her name.

A woman whose face bore the mark of a coward. He couldn't help but scowl at the bruise marring her face.

She noted his interest and raised a hand to cover it. "Not very pretty, is it?"

"Have you remembered anything yet?"

"If you mean do I know who I am . . ." She shook her head. "Nothing. Which is so weird because I remember those guys talking about killing me on the dock. I even recall

being annoyed at their nerve. But my name, address, everything else that would tell me who I am, is like this blank
spot in my mind. It's frustrating."

Nice to know he wasn't the only frustrated one. Of course,
his was easily fixed. A few steps and a seductive kiss would
help him regain his footing.

But only a jolt to her memory would help her.

So jolt her then.

Alas, sex wasn't the answer to everything. Pity.

"I've got my men searching the area where they dumped
you. Maybe they'll find a clue that will either help us iden-
tify you or at least lead us to the men who tried to kill
you."

She frowned. "You've got people hunting them down?
Isn't that a job for the police?"

He made a face. "Trust me when I say you're better off
letting me handle this. The police are fettered by too many
rules and bureaucratic shit."

"You're not above the law."

"Actually, in many respects, I am." Did he allow himself
a smug smile? Yes. As alpha of the shifters in this city, he'd
earned it.

"Are you a criminal?"

"Would it matter if I was?"

"No." Funny how she looked so surprised when she answered. Her brow knit. "I mean, yes. I mean . . . Oh hell, I
don't know what I mean. It's like I already have all these
opinions on stuff, and yet no background to put them in
context. While I know I should be advocating calling the police and doing things right, legal-like, another part of me
is . . ." She bit her lip.

"A *bad girl*?" Said with way too much pleasure.

"You wish." She might have uttered it with indignation, but her smile took the sting from it. "So what happens if your men don't find anything? How long do you plan on keeping me prisoner here?"

Forever.

Wrong answer. "You are free to leave at any time. If you want, I'll have my man call you a cab. But let me ask you, where will you go?"

Her mouth opened and shut a few times, the gears in her mind turning as she mulled his question. "I don't know."

"Exactly. Since you have nowhere to go, and I have all this space, why not stay here until we find answers?"

"What if those killers are still looking for me? Won't that put you in danger?"

Extreme danger. Just not the type she thought. "Danger is my middle name."

"That is so cliché."

"Very well, my true middle name is Eugene." Why he admitted it he couldn't have said, but he did enjoy her tinkle of laughter.

"Oh my God. Did your parents not love you at all? Fabian Eugene Garoux?"

"It's better than that. Try Fabian Eugene Larry Garoux Junior."

The bright sparkle in her eyes, and the way her lips parted in a throaty chuckle, proved more than he could handle. Before he realized he'd moved, he held her forearms and growled, "Stop laughing."

"Or else you'll do what, *Junior*?"

Dared? Challenge accepted. She continued to laugh, and

he stopped the sound with the press of his mouth against hers.

Uh-oh.

What had he done?

CHAPTER 5

What is he doing?

Kissing me, idiot.

And kissing her very well. Make that thoroughly with a dash of pleasurably and a whole lot of give-me-more. Except someone wasn't on the same wavelength.

He mumbled, "No, I must resist," and tried to pull away.

Excuse me? Sorry, but she wasn't letting him escape so easily. He'd kissed her first. He'd lit her blood on fire and, now, too bad. He wasn't stopping until she said it was done. However, she couldn't have said in that pulse-pounding, panty-wetting moment where done would end up.

Crazy, but, then again, no crazier than this entire evening. Her desire for him was probably the only thing that made sense right now. Attractive man rescued her from certain death. In relief, they cling to each other in passion and a need to reassert their link to the living.

Blah, blah, blah.

Psychology mumbo jumbo. She kissed him back because it felt damned good.

Better than good. Right.

Such an odd thought to entertain, given, how would she

know? She didn't recall any past embraces or lovers, so how could she be so certain this was the best kiss of her life?

In a sense, though, wasn't it?

It was the first kiss she remembered feeling—hot and melting.

The first touch she recalled—sizzling her nerve endings.

The first, and only, man she ever desired—*the only man I want . . .*

While he might have initially resisted, he caved at the sensual demands of her tongue. His mouth opened at her insistence, but while she might have initiated the next step in their embrace, he quickly tried to take over.

Their tongues met in a sinuous duel, each determined to provide the most sensual slide, the most decadent suck, the most anything of everything.

Her fingers weaved through the strands of his hair, tugging and pulling at the thick and dark mass. She traced the hints of silver at his temples that enhanced his rugged looks rather than detracted from them.

While she pegged him in his forties, he was fit. Solid. A man who took care of himself and his body. She could feel all this as she pressed herself against him. Could feel the true hardness of him—and she should add largeness—as his hands cupped her bottom and partially lifted her that he might grind himself against her mound.

Liquid heat pooled between her thighs. Hot, decadent desire. She barely felt her back hit the wall as he pushed her against it. She eagerly parted her thighs and loosely wrapped her legs around his waist so that he might properly rub against her.

The layers of clothing did not take away from the erotic

sensation at all. On the contrary, the fabric raised her level of awareness. The friction had her gasping as he ground himself against her, the erect promise elevating her arousal.

His lips left off the plundering of her mouth, traveling the line of her jaw to her neck, then farther downward to other treasures.

Her breathing hitched as his hand cupped the swell of her breast and his thumb stroked over the erect nipple that protruded through the material.

"So perfect." The words were spoken low, husky. Words meant for her.

She gasped as he dipped his head and caught the erect nub. He teased it with his lips, moistening the fabric, tugging at the nipple, each suck sending a jolt of pure pleasure to her sex.

She cried out. She clutched at his shoulders and arched her back to silently beg him for more. His hands skimmed under the hem of her shirt, sliding over her skin, upward toward her breast until he cupped her, skin on skin. He dropped down in a crouch and let his lips follow the path of his hand. Fiery kisses on her tummy, up her rib cage, his warm breath tickling her breast. His mouth sliding toward her—

Knock. Knock. Knock. The rap at the door took a moment to process. *Talk about inopportune.*

She wasn't the only one to think so.

The mouth that had almost reached its treasure was torn away—*sob.*

"This better be fucking important," Fabian snapped as he righted himself, his eyes again emitting that odd golden glow.

"Milord, the men you sent searching have returned and are ready to report their findings."

How nice that his men were on the ball when it came to tasks. However, someone needed to talk to them about their terrible timing.

While a part of her wanted to hear what they had to say, another part wanted to yell, *Go away!* so she could finish what she and Fabian had started.

For a moment, she thought Fabian might actually do that. He seemed so torn, his eyes riveted on her lips, which throbbed still from their intense kiss.

Instead, with a strange growl of frustration, he turned away from her. "We shall discuss this later."

Discuss? She had a better idea. "Or finish it."

Did he shudder? *Good.* There was something powerful and primitively pleasing about knowing she affected him.

Before she could drag him back and see if she could change his mind, he crossed the room quickly—almost too quickly—and opened the door.

"Where are they?" he asked the butler, who apparently didn't sleep.

"In your office, milord. Would you like me to tell them to wait?"

"No. I want to talk to them."

"Me too," she said, pushing away from the wall, hoping her wobbly legs would hold her.

"I'll give you a report in the morning. Get some rest," he ordered without a backward glance. He left and closed the door behind him.

Like hell. She wanted to hear what his men had found. Except that wasn't part of the plan, apparently, she soon discovered, as the knob under her hand refused to turn.

He'd locked her in.

"You son of a bitch!" she yelled. "Let me out this instant."

Apparently, he lingered in the hall, because he replied, "Sweet dreams, vixen."

Screw his dreams. She was about to become his nightmare.

CHAPTER 6

Fabian might have wished her sweet dreams, but he was plagued by disbelief.

I can't believe I lost control and kissed her.

And then his tempting vixen kissed him back.

How could any man retain control faced with her passion? He certainly couldn't. The more he tasted, the more he touched, the more he wanted.

Mine. All mine.

He'd almost claimed her. Thank goodness Fred had interrupted, because a few more minutes and Fabian would have probably been sheathed in her body, thrusting and pounding, racing to nirvana—and kissing his bachelor life good-bye.

We should kill Fred for stopping us, his inner beast grumbled. His wolf had no problem tying his fate to one woman.

Slow down. Fabian wasn't ready for that yet. Lust for a woman was no reason to lose his head, the sweet taste of her lips not a reason to change his life.

Time to concentrate on the more important things right now like finding out who she was and who wanted her dead. Once he fixed both problems, then he could get her out of his life, out of his mind, and go back to the way things were.

Oh yeah, smart-ass, if you're so determined to rid your-self of her, then why lock her in her room?

Because. Just because, and no, he didn't need to explain, even to himself, any further.

Entering his office, he ignored his staff until he'd taken position behind his desk. If he'd learned one thing about ruling, appearance meant a lot.

To be powerful, act powerful. The confident ruled the world for a reason.

Sitting in his massive leather recliner, he leaned forward and placed his fingers in a steeple on his desk. He fixed his best hunters, two of them wolf shifters, the third a lioness, with a stare. "Report."

"Not much to report, boss," said Jeremy, the oldest of the three. "We went to the public launch by that picnic ground just outside the property where you told us to. There was nobody there."

Of course not. He'd hardly expected the killers to stick around.

Myrna rolled her eyes and echoed his sentiment. "Well, duh. Like those dudes were gonna stick around. They did the dirty work and left."

No, they'd failed in their task and run away before he could mete out punishment.

"Surely you've more to report to me than the obvious?" He let his gaze land on the last of the trio, who'd yet to say a word.

Dean, the quietest of the three, peered at him through long bangs. "It was bears. Two of them. Judging by their prints, average-sized guys, at least compared to us. Size fourteen shoes on the one and at least a sixteen on the other. They drove a car. Judging by the wheelbase, a sedan, an older model. The tire tread was getting real thin. They've got a slow leak, too, from the oil pan."

Great, he knew a ton about a fucking piece of junk but not what he really wanted to know.

"Did any of you find anything that might tell us who the woman is?"

The three of them shook their heads.

Myrna said, "We got a faint whiff of her while we were scouting. She wore some kind of fancy perfume. But that was all we found. No purse or wallet. Nothing. Sorry, boss."

Sorry, however, didn't solve the mystery of who she was. It didn't tell him who wanted to kill her. It most definitely didn't answer why he wanted her so fucking bad.

Because she's our mate.

The simple reminder from his wolf didn't appease him. Surely there was more to it than this. How could he base his whole future on a feeling?

Trust.

Trust in the intangible? Trust a virtual stranger? Fabian hadn't gotten to where he was by putting blind faith in people he'd just met. No matter how much he wanted to fuck them.

But there's more to it than me wanting to sink my cock into her. He couldn't help a protective streak when it came to her. The thought of her in danger filled him with anger, and a determination to keep her safe. The thought of her sleeping in a bed upstairs made him grip his desk, tightly, lest he take the stairs two at a time to join her. He wanted to be with her. Now. This instant. He wanted more of her spunky attitude and bravery.

He wanted her.

Ugh.

Thankfully, his minions left and no one else was around to see him bang his forehead off his desk and growl, "Fuck me. Fuck her. Fuck everything." If someone had borne witness, they would have been shocked. Fabian wasn't one to lose his composure, especially not over a woman.

Then again, he'd never met one so determined to drive him mad.

He couldn't have said how long he sat there, doing his best to ignore everything about her and failing miserably. But hey, at least he didn't go running to her.

And she didn't come running to him. *Probably because you locked her up, dumbass.*

Oh yeah. He winced. She probably wouldn't be too happy about that. Was it sick of him to admit a spurt of anticipation at what would surely prove a fiery rant on her part?

Make-up sex rocks.

No. No sex. What happened to keeping his distance, playing it cool?

Playing it cool wouldn't fix his blue fucking balls. *Sigh.*

A rap at the door had him straightening. It wouldn't do for his staff to see him like this.

"Who is it, and what do you want?"

The door opened enough to let Fred stick his head through. Did the man never sleep? "Milord, I am sorry to disturb you. However, something has happened."

"What now?"

"It seems your guest has left the premises."

"Excuse me? Are you talking about the woman I brought home earlier?"

Fred bobbed his head. "Yes, her. It is my regret to inform you that our hospitality did not suit her. She seems to have picked the lock in her room, borrowed a set of keys from the board in the kitchen, and absconded with your BMW."

She did what?

Any other man might have ranted and raved about the nerve of her stealing his car. A part of him should have wanted to say good riddance, one less thing to worry about.

But Fabian wasn't just any other man.

He was a wolf, and his vixen had escaped. She'd run.

Or in Lycan terms, she'd invited him to chase.

Awoo.

CHAPTER 7

Keep me locked in a room, will he?

The nerve of him still had her simmering even though she'd escaped. The anger helped her to avoid the more intriguing questions of why a part of her wanted to stay and the more baffling one: *Why the hell do I know how to pick locks?*

This inquiring mind wanted to know. Just who and what was she in her real life? And the answer to the more pressing question: How could she find out?

Despite Fabian's heavy-handed tactic, she would grant him one thing. He was probably right that she was still in danger. But why? Why? *Why?*

Nothing made sense, especially not her reaction to Fabian.

The man had locked her in a room, supposedly for her own good. He'd hinted he wasn't the hero his saving implied. He was arrogant. Commanding. So convinced of his superiority and sexiness. She should hate him. Yet, when he'd kissed her, she'd liked it. Make that *loved* it. As a matter of fact, if he were to appear in front of her right now, she'd probably think about doing it again.

A speck appeared in her rearview mirror. A fast-moving blob, which turned out to be someone on a sport bike.

Her pulse ticked up a notch. It could simply be someone sharing the road with her, even at this early hour. She didn't change her speed, but she kept a close watch on the rapidly approaching motorcycle.

It roared right up to her bumper, the figure driving hunched over, head encased in a visored helmet.

The big headlamp on the bike flickered. On. Off. On. Off.

Someone wanted her to either stop or move faster.

She slowed down. If the asshole wanted to pass her, then go right ahead. The road ahead was clear.

As for stopping . . . like hell.

The motorcycle veered into the oncoming lane and sped until it came alongside her. She couldn't help but peer sideways and noted the driver of the bike doing the same. But who was it? Friend, foe . . . the man she'd escaped?

He made no other gesture. Rather, he sped ahead, passing her with ease. He kept going, putting a little distance between them, and she let out the breath she held.

False alarm. Just some jerk wanting to—

"Shit. Fuck. Damn." She cursed as she spun the wheel of the car she'd borrowed—a really nice luxury sedan with leather seats and a kick-ass sound system. Bon Jovi's "Living on a Prayer" blasted from the speakers, revealing another fact about herself. She liked hair bands, or so she surmised, given that was the rock channel she'd stopped on when she browsed the satellite-radio channels.

However, who cared if she knew all the words and played a mean drum on the steering wheel? Apparently, she lacked the nerve to run vermin over.

The car skidded as her foot slammed on the brake and lurched onto the gravel shoulder. For a moment, she clutched the steering wheel, heart pounding, and with reason.

The rising dawn light partially blinded her and cast the figure straddling a motorcycle in the middle of the road in shadow.

What did he want? And it had to be a he given the width of the shoulders in the black leather jacket. Gloved hands tore off the helmet, and despite the sun partially blinding her, she recognized the driver.

Fabian. He'd come after her—to her pulse-quickening disgust and pleasure.

But she refused to allow herself any giddy-girl enjoyment in the fact that he couldn't let her go. Especially since she could have run him over. Thank goodness the morals she'd forgotten wouldn't allow her to do so. Still, he couldn't have known that when he pulled that stunt.

"What is wrong with you? You could have gotten yourself killed!" she yelled as she exited the car. She flung her arms wide as she gesticulated. "What kind of idiot sticks himself in the middle of the road? You do know that's how roadkill happens, right?"

A big shoulder rolled in a shrug, his nonchalance as maddening as her reaction to him. "It got your attention, didn't it?"

"I could have run you over." Who knew what she was capable of? Lock picking, car stealing, vehicular manslaughter . . . perhaps she was a super spy in her real life.

He arched a brow. "I trusted you wouldn't perpetrate the false myth that women are terrible drivers."

"It wouldn't have been a lack of skill that killed you. You

should have been more worried that I'd be tempted to run over you on purpose."

"Is that any way to thank the man who saved you?"

"You lost all rights to thanks when you locked me in that room."

"For your own good."

She rolled her eyes. "How would you know what's good for me? I don't even know what's good for me." Not entirely true. She knew his kisses were yummy for her libido, but that wasn't knowledge he needed to know.

"I was trying to find out more about you when you so rudely absconded with my car."

"I planned to return it." Once she was done using it. Eventually.

"Exactly what else did you plan, other than racing off in the middle of the night in my pajamas driving a stolen car with no license or money?" He fixed her with a stare as he poked holes in her brilliant escape.

"You suck." A phrase she was quickly learning was her reply whenever things didn't go her way.

"I did. As a matter of fact, I can still recall the feel of your nipple in my mouth."

Her mouth rounded in an O of surprise. She found herself speechless, not just from his audacity but also because he so vividly reminded her of the heat. The passion. The—

He growled his pet name for her. "Vixen. You know, I have to say I really love that look, although, I must say, your mouth would look a lot better with something in it. A pity we don't have time for that, nor is this the place."

"There won't ever be a place or time. These nipples"—she

slapped her hands over both breasts—"are off-limits to you. As are these lips." She clamped them tight.

He laughed. "Is that a challenge? Are you deliberately trying to tempt me?"

Was she?

He took a step forward, then another, and she stood stock-still. Surely he wouldn't dare to try after she'd just said no.

To within a foot of her he came, his big body blocking the dawn's blinding rays. His eyes as mesmerizing as before. His lips curled in a smirk.

She tilted her chin. "You can't intimidate me."

"Who says I was trying to?"

"Then what are you trying to do?"

"Oddly enough, save you from yourself."

But who will save me from you? "I don't need your help."

"On the contrary, I think you do. Until we have an idea of who you are, and how you ended up getting tossed off that pier, like it or not, I'm your best bet."

"You're nuts if you think I'll go back to your house so you can lock me up again."

"What if I promise to not do so? I can admit, because I am a big man, *everywhere*"—and yes, he winked—"that perhaps I might have been hasty in my actions. In my defense, I'm not used to people ignoring my orders, hence my decision to restrict your movements."

An apology? She got the impression it wasn't something often given. While she hated to admit it, he also had a point. She'd fled half-cocked with no idea of where she was going other than away from him. But she hadn't fled him out of fear, more annoyance.

Yes, let's get annoyed at the guy who saved your life and

wants to help you. There was a name for girls like her—too stupid to live—and in the movies they usually died. Still, though, if she went back then, "How do I know you're telling the truth? How do I know you won't lock me up again?"

"You don't. But how about I promise you this? The next time I do keep you from going anywhere, it will be in my bed, tied to the four posters with neckties so I can have my wicked way with you." The sensual grin he shot her didn't hold any hint of a joke. He meant what he said.

A smart girl should have run at that moment. Surely she wouldn't go back with a man who had just stated his intent to tether her and torture her erotically? Actually, the fact that he stated his intention made up her mind—or, should she say, her body decided for her?

"Fine. I'll go back, but if you try any of this heavy-handed business again, I am out of there, and"—her turn to wink—"I'll be keeping the car."

His laughter warmed her more than it should have, as did the light kiss he dropped on her lips. "Race you to the house," he dared.

"You're on." She turned to return to the car and was just about to pop into the driver's seat when the hum of an engine, in bad need of muffler maintenance, reached her. While mostly desolate this time of the morning, the road was a public one, so why did she feel a sense of unease?

Apparently, that trepidation was shared, because as she tossed a look over her shoulder, she noted Fabian doing the same.

The still-cresting dawn sun blinded them. She tossed a hand over her eyes to shield them but still had to squint.

The approaching vehicle slowed and stopped, but a few

yards back, making it impossible for her to make out any details.

She didn't need Fabian's shouted, "Get down!" to realize something was amiss.

Quickly she ducked, using the open car door as her shield. A good thing she moved fast, as a projectile hit the glass and exploded it. Most of the tempered pieces tinkled harmlessly to the ground, her crouch behind the door panel and head duck having saved her from more serious damage, but given someone was shooting at her, she needed better cover.

Someone is shooting at me?

Let the shock of it sink in later. Right now, she needed to protect herself.

Another bullet hit the door, this time passing straight through, and she gaped at the hole it left behind, the daylight streaming through it testament to the deadliness of the person attacking.

But what of Fabian? He stood out in the open with nothing to shield him.

"Drop your gun."

Had her idiot hero seriously ordered the murderer to do that?

"Fuck you and die, dog."

Gunfire cracked again, and this time, it didn't hit the car she hid behind.

Fabian!

A crash sounded, and she might have wondered at it if she'd not seen Fabian's helmet bounce into view.

The oddest sound occurred next, almost like the ripping of fabric. Which made no sense. And neither did the growl she heard next. A very caninelike growl.

What the hell? Had someone brought a dog to the attack party?

She peeked over the edge of the door and blinked.

Um. No. That can't be right.

Closing her eyes for a few seconds, she took a deep breath before opening them again. Nope, she still saw a giant black dog standing on the hood of the gunman's car, his weight leaving dents in the metal.

That's one big fucking dog.

Awoo.

Or was that a wolf?

The crack of a firearm had her ducking again, but if she couldn't see, she could hear. The creak of a door as it swung open, the muttered, "Die, asshole."

Hey, I know that voice.

The voice of the man who'd tried to kill her. He had come back, apparently to finish the job.

Crouching down, she leaned over to peek around the side of the door. The wolf still stood on the other car, his dark silhouette a unique hood ornament.

While one thug had exited the vehicle, the other remained within, shooting at the windshield.

She couldn't tell if the bullets hit the wolf. If they did, he certainly didn't yelp or run away.

Luckily, the thugs seemed to have only one gun, and she couldn't help cheering for the wolf as he lunged at the cracked windshield, snarling at the occupant.

One of the missiles went wild, or so she assumed since it hit the glass in the door she hid behind. She barely managed to duck her head. Leftover glass showered her head. She took a moment to shake most of it loose.

Meanwhile, what had happened to the wolf? For some reason, she wanted to know.

Back over the sill she peeked and then wondered what the hell kind of drugs she was on because, as if a wolf wasn't enough, a bear had now joined the fight.

Things had gotten much too whacky for her to handle, so she looked for a point of sanity. In other words, Fabian. In all the commotion, she'd not looked to see what had happened to him. Was he shot and bleeding on the ground? Was he, at this very moment, dying or, gulp, already dead?

Or was he nowhere to be seen?

Nothing except a leather jacket tossed to the ground and a road littered in tattered fabric.

Had the wolf mauled him before turning on the other men?

Possible, she guessed, except she saw no body, no trail of blood.

Don't tell me he fled.

With his previous actions and words, she'd not taken him to be a coward. Then again, what good was a man against bullets—and wild animals? Could she blame him for escaping. After all, this wasn't his fight.

Still, a part of her found itself disappointed. Apparently, she'd expected him to pull the hero card again, even though he'd made it quite clear that he was more villain than knight in a slick Armani suit.

Guess I'll have to save myself.

While the wolf and the bear engaged in a tussle, she took stock. The car she used as a shield was still usable, if damaged. She hopped into the driver seat and cranked the key. The radio immediately blared—Iron Maiden's "Run to the Hills," which was ominously apt—and the engine purred to life. However, she'd no sooner put it into gear than the guy with the gun got out of the car.

Shoot the wolf. Or the bear. Either of them worked for her.

She wasn't so lucky.

He strode toward her with grim determination on his face.

A face that seems somehow familiar.

Yet she'd wager if she did know him in her past life, they weren't close friends, given he raised his weapon and fired.

Sonofabitch. He shot at me!

But missed.

Well, missed killing her at any rate. The windshield, however, took the brunt of his attack. The radiating hairline cracks distorted her view but not enough for her to miss him taking aim again.

Dammit.

She dove out the driver side door just as he fired again. The windshield shattered, honeycombed glass falling everywhere as she hit the pavement hard.

There went her nice manicure and some of her skin, ouch. She scrabbled to her knees and squeaked as something penetrated the door and went zinging past her head. At her current height level, she could see under the door, and what she saw were feet clad in black combat boots coming her way.

Not good.

Furry paws landed in the gunman's path. A vicious snarl erupted.

Had the wolf come to her rescue?

She peered around the side of the door and first spotted a big furry hump on the road. *Bye-bye, Mr. Bear.* The wolf had won, and now he seemed intent on a new target. So long as it wasn't her, the oversized dog could eat anything he liked.

Except the gunman wasn't in the mood to offer himself up as dessert. He aimed his weapon at the wolf.

Poor thing. The beast didn't know how deadly that would prove, else he probably wouldn't have stalked the thug with slow, measured steps.

Then again, the wild creature wasn't entirely defenseless. *Just look at his teeth.* Great big fucking teeth exposed in a snarl that made her wish she had some doggy snacks or a steak, a great, big, juicy red one, just in case he turned that yellow gaze her way.

"Eat my bullet, mutt!" snarled the guy with the weapon. This close, there was no way he could miss. She almost shouted a warning to the wolf. After all, if not for his intervention, she'd probably already be dead. Then again, given the choice between her and His Hairiness?

Self-preservation won. But that didn't mean she watched the coming carnage. She prepared to make her escape.

Click.

Click.

Forget running, she wasn't the only one frozen in disbelief as she realized the killer was out of bullets. Of course, her mien was probably nothing compared to his.

"Fuck!" He tossed the gun at the wolf, who handily ducked it, but then, instead of running, the gunman . . . stripped?

And the wolf patiently waited.

Whatever. She wasn't sticking around while Mr. Wolf's dessert peeled his outer wrapper. Already on her feet, she scrabbled to the motorcycle, wondering if she even knew how to ride one.

Apparently, she did. As she straddled the bike, her feet automatically went to a pedal—*that's the clutch, idiot*—and she turned the key. It roared to life just as a more bestial roar erupted behind her.

Don't look. Don't look.

Yeah, she didn't listen to herself. She couldn't help a peek over her shoulder. The *Twilight Zone* song played in her head as she noted another bear had joined the party. Of the guy stripping, only a pile of clothes remained.

Where did he go?

Why did she care?

Big bad wolf was busy with the new brown bear, and she needed to leave.

Trusting her body knew what to do, even if her mind didn't, she put the motorcycle into gear and twisted the handle. *Throttle, you boob. It's a throttle.*

Whatever the damned thing was called, it shot the bike forward, and she almost fell over in surprise. Almost. She caught herself, and while the bike wobbled, it soon righted itself as she applied speed.

Whee.

She might not remember much of her past, but the wind in her face felt familiar and nice. As she moved away from the fighting beasts, she didn't care that she drove toward Fabian's house. Drove toward the home of the man who'd abandoned her and left her to survive on her own in a world gone completely freaking mad.

Still, who could blame him? It wasn't as if she was going to stick around and see what happened next. She'd rather take her chances within his solid walls and hope that the butler had a gun. A big one.

However, she didn't go far before she noted vehicles

coming toward her. Upon spotting her, the drivers veered sharply and stopped in the road, the vehicles' bulk effectively blocking it and her escape route.

Not knowing if they meant her harm or not, she played it safe. Without even thinking of it, she hit the brake. The ass end of the bike lifted, and she crouched low and held on tight to the bars.

The back end of the bike swung, and she executed a pin turn. As soon as the rear wheel hit the ground, she throttled the bike and shot forward.

I might not remember riding a motorcycle, but damn, I'm good at it.

It didn't take her long to approach the car she'd ditched and the animals snapping and snarling at each other. Lucky her, they didn't seem to pay her any mind as she drove toward them.

As she passed, she watched them, her head turned to the side, unable to prevent a macabre fascination.

The wolf had once again proved dominant, or so it appeared, given he stood over the bear, his jaw clamped tight.

Without losing his grip, the wolf raised his golden gaze her way.

Saw her.

Marked her.

Shit.

She whipped her face forward and applied more gas to the bike. She gathered speed and hit a curving bend, leaving the disastrous scene behind, but she couldn't escape the chilling howl that rose into the brightening dawn sky.

The cry of a hunter.

Wanna bet he's hunting me?

Except four legs couldn't catch up to the massive horsepower of a bike.

Unless the wolf took a shortcut—which, with her luck, of course he had.

The many weaves and bobs of the road meant a wolf cutting through the woods could emerge ahead of her and plant himself on the road, a big shaggy mass with an intense stare.

He could stare all he wanted. She wasn't about to stop.

She hunkered down and kept her aim straight. A game of chicken with a wolf.

Except . . . what was happening to the wolf?

Between one blink and the next, fur receded, skin emerged, pale and covering defined muscles. Paws turned into hands and feet. As for the muzzle, holy shit, it was gone to give way to the man.

Fabian to be exact.

What. The. Fuck.

Since he didn't seem inclined to budge, she clamped on the brake and jerked the handlebars at the last moment so she wouldn't hit him. Unlike with her previous maneuver, the bike didn't like this at all and toppled, sending her flying, right into a set of arms.

She peeked into a face, one that was now 100 percent human if she ignored the yellow glow in his eyes.

Questions jumbled in her mind, but none could make her frozen mouth work.

His lips quirked into a half smile. "I don't suppose you like dogs?" he asked.

CHAPTER 8

Fred met him at the door to his house with a fluffy navy-blue robe, but Fabian ignored it for the moment, more intent on barking orders.

"There's a mess a few miles up the road. I need a cleanup crew sent out right now to help the boys scrub the evidence of the fight." He didn't have to say what fight. By now, his men would have found the bodies and the cars and reported in.

"Already being taken care of, milord."

Of course it was. Fabian didn't run a sloppy operation. The pack knew what had to be done to keep their secret safe.

A secret that his vixen now knew.

She knows I'm a wolf. What he didn't know was how she felt about it. Then again, the fact that she didn't say a word, not even to protest his carrying of her, he imagined meant she was still in a state of shock.

Given the front hall wasn't exactly the place to ask, with his vixen in his arms, Fabian headed to his office and placed her on the couch. She didn't move as he stepped away, nor did she look at him. Then again, given a certain part of his anatomy was at eye level, perhaps it had nothing to do with his secret identity and more about the fact that his extreme virility intimidated her.

Modesty wasn't something he subscribed to.

To put that possibility to rest, he finally accepted the robe from his manservant. She didn't move at all from her spot on the couch as Fabian slipped his arms into the sleeves and belted it shut.

What was going through her mind?

The good news? She'd not run screaming from him yet.

Better news, she hadn't flinched when he'd told her to hold on tight when he drove his bike back to the house. Did he enjoy the cheap thrill of having her arms wrapped around him? Totally. The outright snickers and amusement on his men's faces as he rode past them, stark naked, not as much.

As to the bad news, she had yet to say anything. At all. She just stared. And stared. And stared some more, making him just a tad self-conscious.

It was, frankly, driving him a little crazy.

"Are you going to say anything?"

She cocked her head, lips pressed tightly.

He raked a hand through his hair. "Seriously? I couldn't get you to shut up before, but now, you find out I'm a Lycan and you are giving me the silent treatment?"

"What should I say?"

"Halle-fucking-lujah. She has a voice."

"Don't pull that sarcasm stuff with me. I'm not talking, because what is there to say? I'm obviously having some messed-up dream, and I am not feeding it by acting as if it's real. I am going to wake up any minute. Probably in my own bed. Knowing my damned name. This"—she swept a hand— "you. Everything that's happened to me so far isn't real."

"You're kidding, right?"

"No, I'm delusional, because men turning into wolves—"

"And bears. I also know some lions and tigers."

"—just doesn't happen. Memory or not, even I know that."

"Except what you know is wrong."

"Says you."

"Knows me. Or would you like me to show you again?"

"Don't bother. I am going to wake up any second and—"

It took him only a scant moment to reach her and haul her from the couch. He could hear the change in her heart rate. It sped up, but not in fear. He could tell. The smell emanating from her matched the heat rising from her skin.

"What are you doing?" she asked somewhat breathlessly.

"Proving I am real." He mashed his lips to hers, the contact igniting the passion that seemed to constantly simmer between them.

She started out stiff in his grasp, her body ramrod straight, her lips pressed tightly and unyielding. However, the more he softened his embrace, slipping and sliding, lips nibbling and tasting, the more she softened. Her mouth parted, and their hot breaths mingled.

Her arms wound around his neck and . . . she yanked his hair and pulled them apart.

"What the hell?" he yelled.

"Just because my dream self has made you into a fabulous kisser doesn't make this real."

"Then why stop?" he asked with a grin, a grin because she couldn't hide the musk of her arousal. She liked his kiss, and that, he would wager, was why she'd stopped.

"Isn't there some kind of law about getting frisky with animals?"

"I am a Lycan, and those laws don't apply to my kind."

"That is seriously arrogant."

"But true."

"I can't believe I'm arguing with a figment of my imagination."

And he couldn't believe she was denying reality.

He gave her a sharp slap on the ass.

"Ow!" she yelled. "What was that for?"

"I'm sorry. Did you feel that?"

She glared at him and probably would have harangued him, except there was a knock at the door.

"Come in."

Brody, one of his main minions, stepped in and spared his vixen only a glance before focusing his attention on Fabian. "We ran the plates on that car with the two guys. Small-time thugs from the next state over. Bears, as you already know, but no clan affiliation."

"What were these loners doing in my territory?" Other than the obvious part, which involved fucking with the wrong wolf.

He couldn't help but glance at his vixen. She had moved away from him at the interruption.

A scowl crossed her features. "Don't look at me. I don't know who they are or what they want."

"We know what they want. You. Dead." Which didn't please him at all. The mating instinct roared through him full force.

The need to protect her and to smite her enemies, now his enemies, made him more rash than usual.

"I want answers. And I want them yesterday. I want everyone working on this. I want to know exactly who these fuckers were. Who hired them? Where were they staying?

What they fucking had for breakfast. I will know who dares attack my woman and me. And when I find out who is behind this, then by hell, if it's a war they want, then a war they shall fucking have."

Silence met his words, along with a drop-jawed Brody. "Um, okay, boss." His minion backed out, head slightly bowed, knowing better than to rile Fabian's bristling alpha side.

Someone else still in the room didn't know better.

"Good grief. Is that how you talk to your staff? It's a wonder they don't all quit."

"They can't quit, because they belong to my pack."

"Pack? Pack of what? Henchmen gum?"

He whirled on her. "Now is not the time to push me, vixen. I am feeling a touch unbalanced." More than a little out of control.

But she didn't heed the warning.

"Unbalanced? Welcome to my world, Fido."

"Don't mock me." He took a step toward her.

"Or else what? You'll turn me into your chew toy? Give me fleas? How about I find a ball and toss it for a while so you can work off that extra energy?"

"Your taunts are not amusing."

"They weren't meant to be. If this isn't a dream, or nightmare, or major hallucination, then shit in my life has just gotten seriously messed up. While you're freaking out about people daring to attack you, I'm freaking out because the guy I was making out with last night is a fucking werewolf." Her face paled, and he could almost predict her exact next words. "Oh shit. Does this mean I'm going to turn furry and howl at the moon, too?"

Stupid legends. They got only part of it right. "No, you're safe from the virus. It only affects men."

"No dog collar or Milk-Bone treats for me?"

He grimaced. "No. And for your information, Lycans don't appreciate dog humor."

"So what are you going to do about it, Fluffy?"

No missing the daring taunt in her eyes. She did it on purpose to provoke him. Why?

"Why? Why are you doing this? It's like you want me to lose control. When really"—he moved too quickly for her to evade him and pulled her into his arms—"all you had to do was ask."

"I don't know what you're talking about." She denied, and yet her eyes told another story. Her tongue wetted her lips, and Fabian breathed deeply, the musk of her arousal scenting the air, as did the more coppery scent of her blood.

"You're hurt."

He, remarkably, wasn't. Just because the enemy had a gun didn't mean they could shoot it worth shit.

Most petty thugs relied on intimidation. Only rarely did they actually fire because bullets meant forensics, forensics meant cops, and no one skirting the law wanted the fuzz sticking their noses into their business.

But Fabian also owed his lack of injury to luck. A jostle of the car at just the right time when the killer had fired the gun. A lack of bullets when face-to-face. The few scratches and contusions he'd incurred had already healed, appearing days old instead of hours.

"I scraped my hands, and knees." She held the damaged palms aloft, and his anger simmered anew.

He clasped them in his hands and almost yelled for his

butler. But really, what could Fred do? The abrasions needed cleaning. That was something Fabian could do himself.

He tugged her toward the door.

"Where are we going?"

"We need to wash these out."

"I'm fine."

"You are not." Because he was not fine. The beast simmered just below the surface.

An attempt to pull away had him just tightening his grip. "I can take care of it myself. Just point me to the nearest washroom."

The nearest washroom, though, wouldn't wipe from her garments and skin the stench of gunfire, fear, and his failure to protect.

Without asking for permission—because it just wasn't done and because he was sure she'd argue; she did: "Put me down!"—he tossed her over his shoulder. He exited his office and took the stairs in threes, his long stride getting them to the second floor before she could call him every name in the book. Although she did her best. He especially liked her use of "fucktard" and "douchebag."

"I thought we discussed you not acting high-handed anymore," she grumbled from her dangling spot down his back.

"No, you discussed. I merely agreed."

"You mean lied."

"I meant it at the time." But old habits died hard.

"I demand you put me down."

This time he complied before turning his back on her so he could shut the door.

"Hold on a second. Where are we? This isn't my room."

Turning back to face her, he let a slow smile stretch his

lips. "No. It's not. It's my room." He might have said *ours*, but he figured that might be pushing it. "The shower is through there," he said with a hand gesture to his left.

"I don't need a shower. I'll just rinse my hands."

"You will strip and bathe."

"Oh no I won't."

She crossed her arms over her chest, and her expression turned stubborn.

Utterly adorable.

He copied her and arched a brow to raise things a notch. "Oh yes you will, or else."

"Or else what?"

"I was hoping you'd say that." He stalked toward her.

But she didn't cower before him. She held herself straight, chin tilted. "I don't know what you're planning, but I'm pretty sure my answer is 'don't you dare.'"

"I know, which is why I'm not asking." When he was close enough, he darted a hand forward and clasped the fabric of the flannel top she still wore.

She gasped as buttons pinged. Clasping the ends, she hugged the shirt around herself and glared. But, he should note, it wasn't a peeved glare. Heat smoldered in her gaze, and the tips of her nipples pushed at the fabric.

The undeniable attraction between them simmered. She might not understand the draw of her mate, but she also couldn't fight the pull. Just like he couldn't fight it.

Was it only a day ago he'd sworn to never let a woman put a collar around his neck? Funny how things could change so fast.

As he looked at the woman before him, her eyes sparking and her entire body rigid with a feisty spirit that nothing could tame, he couldn't help but anticipate the future.

Things would never be boring with his vixen. And he already knew the passion was worth killing for.

"Take it off." His order emerged low and gruff.

For a moment, he thought she might argue again. But with a smile that promised evil things, she let go of the shirt, the loose flaps exposing a line of skin and a hint of cleavage. She didn't shed the top first. No, she was more wicked than that.

Never losing his gaze, she hooked her thumbs into the pants and tugged them over her hips. Once they reached her thighs, they fell without aid. She stepped out of them.

He swallowed.

While the shirt came down fairly low, it gaped, in just the right spot. Gaped enough for him to see the dark curls covering her mound.

"I think I understand how Little Red Riding Hood felt," she remarked.

"Scared of the Big Bad Wolf?"

"More like wondering if you'll eat me all up." Such a sassy retort that matched the naughty shed of her shirt, which left her standing only in all her naked glory.

And she was glorious. Heavy breasts begging for a grab. An indented waist he could grip to hoist her. Creamy thighs perfect for wrapping around his waist.

An ass that begged for teeth marks as it sashayed past him to the bathroom.

He took a moment to breathe, striving for control. His arousal raged much like a wildfire within him. Out of control. Wanting to consume.

She was right to compare him to the Big Bad Wolf. He did want to eat her. And mark her. And claim her.

Do it. Do it now.

Primitive instinct said he shouldn't wait. However, the more civilized side of him said that perhaps he should take his time and ease her into the concept. Given her strong personality, she might not take well to having him unilaterally make a decision that affected the rest of her life.

Pussy.

It wasn't even his inner wolf that insulted but himself. What had happened to the man who ruled the city pack with an iron fist? Who was this hesitant coward? She was his woman. His. She would have to accept it. Accept him.

Awoo.

He stripped off the robe before even entering the bathroom. She'd left the door ajar, and he took that as an invitation. She already stood under the steaming shower with her head tilted back. The water made her skin slick and tempting.

She didn't move as he stepped into the large glass enclosure with her, but she did say, "You know, you could have just said you wanted sex. You didn't have to pull the I-am-the-boss-hear-me-roar."

"First off, I don't like to state the obvious. We both want this." He crowded close, fitting her against his body, her round buttocks cushioned against his thighs, her head tilted back and leaning into his shoulder. "Second, I don't roar. I growl." Head dipped, he nibbled on the smooth column of her exposed throat.

She sighed as he explored the skin, and while the water sluiced away the musk of her passion, he could tell by her body language that she desired him.

He spun her into his arms and claimed her lips. She met him for passion, her tongue restless and eager to explore his mouth. Her arms wound around his neck, drawing him close.

The skin-to-skin contact proved electric. His cock, trapped between their slick bodies, throbbed against her lower belly. The tips of her breasts poked his chest.

So many sensations, each of them fueling his desire. He grabbed her arms and raised them above her head as he pressed her against the glass wall of his shower. She didn't seem to mind this mastery of her. On the contrary, she regarded him through eyes at half-mast, lips swollen and parted on a breathless, "Yes. Touch me."

Oh, he'd touch all right. He left the sweetness of her lips for another goal, one interrupted earlier. His lips blazed a trail to her breast, the firm plumpness of them inciting nibbles. The nipple, so erect, begged for a suck. How could he disappoint?

He latched on to the peak, tugging it with his mouth, enjoying the sensation of it and, even more, the cries she emitted as he teased the hard nub.

As he toyed with her luscious breasts, he inserted a hand between her thighs. The slick moisture he found wetting her nether lips had nothing to do with the shower. He sawed a finger back and forth, feeling the quiver of her sex. His own cock hardened in response.

Impatience rode him hard. He so wanted to take his time, to taste her sweet ambrosia, but a need to sink into her demanded satisfaction.

Fabian wasn't one to give in to demands, and with her, selfishness was not an option. Forget his need. She came first.

And he meant that quite literally.

He dropped to his knees, an unusual position for him. For once, he was the supplicant. Eye level with her sex, he could see the honey on her pink lips. "Put your leg over my shoulder."

"With pleasure," she practically purred. At least in this she didn't argue.

Her thigh rested on him, with the added benefit of exposing her more fully to him. *Perfect.*

He took a moment to savor her as the water from the shower pounded his back. Inching close, he could smell her arousal.

Taste it. Now.

A flick of his tongue and he groaned. Her flavor exploded in his mouth, and he hungrily went back for more. He lashed her sex with his tongue, dipping between her nether lips and feeling the pulse of her excitement. Her flesh swelled as her pleasure mounted, but he wanted her more than just aroused. He wanted her to come.

His tongue located the swollen nub of her clit, and as he toyed with it he inserted a finger into her tight channel.

"More," she whispered.

More? As his vixen demanded. In went a second finger, making it even tighter than before. The flesh of her sex quivered around him, and he could feel the mounting tension in her body.

His lips tugged at her pleasure button, stimulating it, and her pants grew harsher. Her fingers dug into his scalp as her hips ground against his face.

"Fabian!" she screamed his name—*Mine!*—when she came, her glorious climax rocketing through her with a force that made him swell in masculine pleasure.

He'd done this to her, made her cry out in ecstasy.

An ecstasy that wasn't yet done.

He kept working at her clit, and she practically sobbed as she shuddered. He soon had to leave off fingering her sex to hold her as her knees buckled.

She was ready for him, and he was more than ready for her.

As he stood, he claimed her lips. She panted against his mouth, her breathing ragged and hot. Given the difference in their height, he let his hands span her waist so he could lift her. She understood his plan, and her legs went around his waist while her arms circled his neck.

The shower helped support her, enough that he could spare a hand to grasp his thick shaft. How it throbbed. It ached with need.

The head found the entrance to her molten core. The heated flesh sucked at him, the tight entrance making him strain as he sought to not just pound into her.

Slow. Take it slow. Control yourself.

So hard. And he wasn't just talking about his cock. Inching his way into her was a form of torture. How tightly her sex gripped him. How wetly her honey bathed him. How perfect it felt.

As to when he was finally fully fitted? He paused and allowed himself a moment to enjoy it.

She didn't want to wait, though. "Fuck me," she demanded. "Stop being so gentle and take me."

Her sex squeezed around him. *Holy fuck.*

A groan was heard. Him. Her. Maybe both? He couldn't have said. All he knew was he couldn't hold back anymore, and she had, after all, demanded.

In this, he was her slave.

He pulled out, only a few inches, and then pushed back in.

Ah.

Out then slam back in.

Oh.

Grind and push as he pumped back and forth.

Her nails dug into his back, and her head went back against the wall as she panted, "Yes. Yes. Yes."

Harder he thrust, striving to hit that sweet spot that made her breathing hiccup each time he struck it. Faster he rammed, the edge of his pleasure there.

He gritted his teeth, trying to hold on. Just one more thrust. A few more seconds.

This time her scream was practically silent, the intensity of her orgasm too much. He didn't waste another second. He buried his face against her neck, sank his teeth into the skin, and bit, hard.

She screamed again, not in pain, but in pleasure, as right on top of her current climax a bigger one hit just in time to welcome his own.

"Mine!" He might have howled the word as he came. He certainly thought it as his seed bathed her womb.

He'd marked her. Claimed her.

Made her his.

Slowly he let her slide down his body, and she shivered, the stimulation of their lovemaking still too fresh.

He held her loosely cradled in his arms and placed a gentle kiss on her forehead.

The moment was intimate. Special. It humbled even a man like him. There were no real words he could think of that applied at this moment. Other than perhaps, "Thank you."

To which she replied, "No problem. Mind passing the soap so I can wash off?"

What?

CHAPTER 9

He stiffened against her, and a part of her felt guilty. Asking for soap wasn't the most romantic thing, not after the explosive passion they'd shared, but what else could she say?

Hey, thanks for the best orgasm ever? Because missing some memories or not, she doubted she'd ever experienced anything so intense. Even his bite, a rough bit of play she'd not expected, proved pleasurable.

Thing was, though, while she enjoyed herself immensely she doubted he felt the same. Fabian was a man of the world. A man who probably had a dozen girlfriends or lovers—*give me their names and they'll die.*

Such a bloodthirsty thought. However, she couldn't stem the spurt of jealousy. For some reason, she thought of Fabian as hers, which made no sense. She still barely knew the man. They'd met what, a day ago? Not even.

Maybe it's love at first sight?

She could have scoffed at the very concept. Surely she wasn't some ninny who believed in that rubbish, but how else to explain the instant connection she felt to the man, a connection she wanted to deny and would certainly never admit?

He'd mock me for sure if I claimed we were soul mates.

Hence why she sought to put some distance between them, to play down what had just happened.

While she could sense his displeasure radiating, he nonetheless handed her the soap. The suds made her all too aware of the abrasions on her hands. She hissed at the stinging burn as the cleanser hit the broken skin. She raised them in front of her to rinse them in the shower spray.

A low growl left him. Was he about to go rabid? He turned her in his arms and grasped her by the wrists. He peered at her palms. "Bastards."

His vehemence pleased her, but his word also reminded her of the fight on the road. "Don't you mean bears? Because I am assuming that's what they were?" Her eyes rose to meet his.

"Yes, they were Ursan, which makes this whole mess surrounding you even more mysterious. Who are you? And why are some shifters determined to end your existence?"

Wouldn't she like to know? "Maybe I'm a secret bear princess." Her lips tilted as she teased.

"As I mentioned already, women can't be shifters."

"Well, that sucks. Talk about sexist." She pinned him with a glare.

He held his hands up. "Don't blame me; blame biology."

"So no chance at all I'll start going after picnic baskets?"

He shook his head, bursting her theory. Not that she'd truly believed it. Her shock at discovering Fabian and those other men weren't a hundred percent human had rocked her too thoroughly. Surely if her real self knew about the masks some men wore she wouldn't have reacted so strongly. Then again, was her reaction normal? After all, knowing he could go furry hadn't stopped her from having sex with him.

And without protection, too! *Dammit.* "We didn't use a condom," she noted.

"My kind are not plagued by the usual diseases. While we might have certain strengths and weakness of the body that vary, and we do eventually succumb to age, we are a healthy bunch."

"What about babies, though? Can you impregnate women?"

"Yes."

"Aren't you worried that we might have, you know? I mean we have no idea if I'm on the pill or anything. What if you knocked me up?" For some reason, the idea didn't frighten her like it should have. In her normal life, could she hear her biological clock ticking?

"You aren't in a fertile cycle, which means you're safe."

"I am not going to ask how you know that." Because the answer would probably freak her out. "So what happens now, oh growly one?"

"Now we figure out who those men were working for. Eliminate the threat. And find out who you are."

"Eliminate, as in kill. Just like you killed those thugs." For some reason, the fact that Fabian had nonchalantly announced fatal violence didn't bother her. As a matter of fact, she felt a certain satisfaction in knowing he was a man of action who didn't take threats sitting down. He took care of them just like he took care of her.

But how long could she expect him to keep doing so? How long before he tired of protecting her and putting himself at risk, not only of injury or death, but of the police?

She spent the next few days wondering about that, as lead after lead turned into a bust.

"How can nobody be looking for me?" she grumbled on

the fifth morning over breakfast—which meant a heaping plate of fluffy eggs, crisp bacon, savory potatoes, freshly squeezed orange juice, a glazed donut, and strawberries sprinkled with sugar. That was just for her. Fabian ate all that plus a few pancakes as well. "Doesn't anybody give a damn I'm missing?" Surely someone in her old life cared?

"I'm sure your disappearance had been noted, but for some reason, they are keeping it on the down low."

"Why would they do that?"

"There could be lots of reasons. Maybe they're waiting for a ransom notice. They could have a fear that a public outcry could lead to your demise."

"Or we could subscribe to Occam's razor and go back to the simplest theory. No one gives a damn."

"I give a damn."

The words warmed her, but then again, what about Fabian didn't heat her?

While her days might be spent in frustration as their investigation failed at every turn, her nights were anything but.

Since their passionate session in the shower, she shared the master bedroom with Fabian. He wouldn't take no for an answer, and she was more than happy to indulge him. At least their erotic interludes managed to distract her from the big question of "Who am I?"

More and more, she wondered if it mattered. With Fabian, she found herself happy, and really, what more could a person ask for?

How about not getting killed?

It was that very question that wouldn't allow her to relax in this new life. For all she knew, danger lurked, waiting for her to lower her guard. Or was she being paranoid?

Surely if someone wanted her dead, they would have tried something else by now. Then again, only a brazen idiot would infiltrate Fabian's property. She'd seen the cameras outside the house. Noted the men patrolling. And heard the howls at night.

So did no attack mean she was safe, or were more killers waiting for their chance?

Only one way to find out.

While Fabian had demanded—in bed while nibbling on her tender bits—to not leave the property and the security measures he had in place, playing it safe meant they didn't know if she was still being watched.

Fabian was useless to discuss it with. As soon as she made any mention of going into the city, he shut her down.

"No leaving the property until I know you're safe."

So cute, but impractical, which was why when Fred tried to stop her from getting into the Lincoln Town Car—whose key she filched from the board in the kitchen—she snapped. "Listen. I appreciate what Fabian's trying to do. But I can't live like this."

"Milord is simply trying to keep milady from coming to harm."

"Which is totally appreciated, but I feel like a freaking prisoner."

"Milady has free rein of the house."

"Bingo. The house. I can't even go for a walk outside unless he's with me. And only an idiot would attempt something with him there. The only way we'll really know if the threat is gone is if I leave this place."

"It is perhaps not my place to point this out, milady," and, yes, Fred insisted on the title despite the fact that she'd told him not to. Then again, given the only other name she had was the nickname given by Fabian of Vixen, she couldn't really give Fred another option to call her. Although she was certain he must have thought, *Bitch,* on more than one occasion, like now. "But while your desire to assess the threat level is understandable, leaving without a proper escort is foolhardy."

Wince. Fred sure knew how to insult while sounding utterly polite. Probably learned that skill in butler school. "What are you suggesting, that I pack this car with bodyguards while I go shopping? How the hell is that supposed to tell me anything? Only an idiot would go after me with a ton of guys in tow."

"Milady is correct. However, there are other options."

"Such as?" She regarded the older gent, as usual properly dressed in slacks, the seams pressed, a white shirt, and a vest. No coat. His bald pate gleamed, and she wondered, not for the first time, if Fred purposely waxed it to get that shine.

"Say a group of guards were to leave at random times, with the knowledge of milady's whereabouts. To ensure no suspicions, you would take one man with you when you depart the premises."

"And these other guys that you send out in advance would what, skulk around the stores I'm going to hit for some clothes?" Because while Fred meant well, the stuff Fabian had him order wasn't her style or the right fit.

"They would discreetly place themselves so as to keep an eye on you at all times."

"What about on the drive over? The last time they hit me, I was still on the road."

"Milord has taken precautions, which means that no vehicle now comes within a mile of this place without being tracked. But in case our surveillance is compromised, then your choice of car should protect you."

"How?" It looked like a car to her, a nice one, but still just a dark four-door sedan.

"This is a custom vehicle sporting bulletproof glass and shielded panels for the body. As milord said when he ordered it, it would take a fucking bomb to open it."

Good to know, and yet she couldn't help but ask, "Why does it seem like you're giving me permission to do this? Aren't you afraid of pissing Fabian off?"

"Milord knew that you would eventually attempt to leave."

"He predicted this?"

Fred allowed himself a twitch of the lips. *Gasp!* He almost cracked his implacable mien. "I don't think your actions were too hard to predict. As such, he left me with orders that, if I couldn't stop you, to at least ensure you did not, and please note these are his words, not mine: 'Do something stupid that will get her fucking killed.'"

She scowled. "Is it possible to like and dislike someone at the same time?"

"Absolutely, milady."

A laugh bubbled its way out. "Fred, if there is an award for most awesome butler ever? You deserve it."

"I am glad to hear you say that, milady. I shall ensure you receive a ballot when the secret society of impeccable manservants has its vote."

She could have swallowed a fly, her mouth hung open so wide. "Fred, did you just make a joke?"

"I would never dare, milady. I take my duties quite seriously."

And he did. In short order, Colin was behind the wheel

of the Lincoln, she was in the back—*As is proper for milady*—and teams had been sent ahead and would follow behind, none of them ever too far out of reach should her route into the city become compromised.

She wasn't sure if she should be happy or annoyed when they made it without mishap downtown.

Is it over? Had the person who wanted her dead given up?

One road trip and five days since the last attempt was hardly evidence the threat no longer existed, but it did give her hope.

As she browsed the shops, enjoying the credit card Fred had bestowed upon her that had no limit—*Ka-ching*—she found herself relaxing and enjoying herself. Especially awesome was the grimace on Colin's face when, after three hours of shopping, and an armful of bags, she paused in front of a lingerie store.

"Ooh, look at that push-up bra. I just love the lace edging. But what color should I get it in? Pink or the mauve?"

"You do realize I feel my man card disintegrating in my pocket," Colin grumbled as she grabbed the door handle to the store's entrance.

"Is big, bad Colin afraid of a women's lingerie store?"

"Yes."

He didn't even try to lie.

She laughed. "What if I promise it's the last store we need to hit?"

"I'd say hooray, except I fear I won't survive the taunting by my packmates."

"Poor baby." But he did have a point. Dragging him inside where she planned to snag some practical items like underpants and bras seemed cruel. Not to mention

embarrassing, especially since a few of the sexier items—
that she could totally picture Fabian peeling from her later
on—had caught her eye.

"Listen, why don't I pop in and get started while you drop
that load off at the car?"

"I'm not supposed to leave you."

"You aren't entirely. You can see the shop door from the
car. If any guys go in, then make sure you wag your furry
tail back here pronto."

"I don't wag."

"Fine, you slink with rabid purpose. Whatever. I don't
see any big, bad thugs inside." She pointed through the
window where they could see a cashier ringing up a purchase for a woman, plus a few other feminine occupants
browsing.

His brow furrowed.

"Oh, come on. Nothing's happened. What's the worse
that could happen to me in there? Someone attacks me and
strangles me with a G-string?"

"Promise you won't skip out the back or take off."

"I promise." Where would she go? The only place she
wanted to be now was in Fabian's arms.

Another glance through the window, his forehead still
creased as he studied the shoppers, Colin sighed. "I won't
be long."

But he was. And she got her answer as to whether or not
someone was still after her only a minute after she entered
a cubicle with an armful of sexy garments to try.

It wasn't the muttered, "Arms up where I can see them,"
that made her wish she'd stayed home or the embarrassment as the flimsy nighty she held meant she stood there
buck-ass half-naked in only a pair of underpants.

It was the gun aimed at her head by the blond woman who appeared under the change-room partition that made her utter, "I guess that answers one question."

Problem was, would she live to answer any others?

CHAPTER 10

What the hell am I doing?

Oh yeah, hunting down his vixen. And no, it wasn't pathetic that Fabian was excited he'd get to see her.

Okay it was, but he'd punch the first idiot who said anything to his face.

According to the latest text from Colin, they were right around here somewhere. Here being downtown where his vixen wanted to do some shopping.

Fabian didn't like it, but he'd expected her to do something rash before now. At least she'd listened to reason and taken a guard while Fred ensured others shadowed their movements. Still, nothing beat hands-on. His hands.

And mouth.

How he'd missed her when he had to leave. However, while a good portion of his business could be conducted from home, there were times he needed to hit his official office and play the part of corporate mogul, times like today. But even bigwigs in the business world—even those with questionable business dealings—were allowed to stop for lunch.

Given Fabian knew she was in the area, he decided to track down his vixen and take her to lunch—then maybe back to his downtown office where they could *consult* behind closed doors.

If nothing happened in between now and then. So far, so good. No attack. Not even a hint. Good, right? Except he didn't trust it.

As he walked the few blocks to their last location, he couldn't help but mull over the frustrating lack of information. Everywhere he turned, he ran into a dead end. No one had heard anything about a missing woman, either in the shifter world or human, and it wasn't for lack of trying.

His friends in law enforcement ran searches for him. No one matching her description popped up. Fabian had Brody tapping the shifter grapevine for rumors.

Everything came up empty. For all intents and purposes, it was as if she didn't exist. And if he couldn't figure out who she was—*She's mine*—then how was he supposed to take care of whoever wanted her dead?

Must protect.

Indeed, he had to, but protect her against what? He couldn't kill what he couldn't find, if there was still someone to find.

Perhaps whoever had a grudge against her had decided to let it go. But what if they hadn't?

The possible threat to her still worried him, and yet, at the same time, he couldn't keep her a prisoner in his mansion forever—even if he would make her stay most enjoyable by keeping her entertained with sensuous delights. However, his vixen, a name that now seemed rather permanent, would end up chafing at the restriction eventually. Maybe even resenting him.

While he wasn't averse to the occasional fight and ensuing make-up sex, this curtailment of her freedom couldn't last forever, not if he wanted her to stay with him.

Argh. In the olden days, a man could have locked his woman in a tower and no one would have batted an eye at his protective instinct. Nowadays people would call it forcible confinement and call the cops.

Society and its damned rules, rules even he had to follow.

Hence, his orders to Fred. *If you can't stop her from leaving, then at least make sure she is well protected.*

Except her protection was currently on the sidewalk beside the car, playing pretty eyes with a curly-haired redhead whose skimpy shorts and tight tank top left nothing to be discovered.

As soon as Colin saw Fabian bearing down on him, his eyes widened. "Boss, what are you doing here?" The redhead who'd been chatting Colin up slipped away.

"I thought I'd surprise my woman with lunch. What I'd like to know is what you're doing here outside without her." Where the hell was his vixen?

"Your lady is over in that boutique. I've been watching the door the entire time. No dudes have entered, and Johan is watching the alley behind it to make sure no one sneaks in the back."

That should have eased his mind, and yet unease nagged him.

"I'm going in."

Colin smirked. "Brave man. All that lacy shit and bras is emasculating if you ask me."

"A real man can handle a lingerie store, especially when he knows he gets to peel the goods off his woman later," Fabian said with a smirk. He also lied. He did find the idea of entering such a feminine domain daunting, which was why he added, "If I'm not back in ten minutes, come find me."

Off he strode, the urge to run strong—stupid gut feeling wouldn't go away—but Fabian kept his pace measured. Upon his entering the shop, nothing untoward jumped out at him—unless that negligee with the strategically placed holes counted.

The overwhelming girlishness of the interior battered at his masculine defenses. Pink walls, painted red hearts, and mannequins wearing flimsy articles all over.

He wasn't quite sure where to look lest someone accuse him of ogling the plastic dolls. How he wanted to escape, even if a part of him snickered at his cowardice. He should be better than this. He knew men bought lingerie for their girlfriends and wives all the time. He certainly loved seeing the end result. However, the sheer abundance of frilly under-garments made him want to scratch his man parts.

Of more concern than his masculinity was the fact that he couldn't spot his mate. Given the racks displaying the wares only rose a few feet high, he should have seen her. Where had she gone?

His visual scan located an employee, so he headed in her direction. "Excuse me."

The young woman turned his way and bestowed upon him a perky smile, a smile that widened as she took him in. "Well, hello there. Are you shopping for yourself or some-one else today?"

"Me?" He practically choked. "No. I'm not shopping at all. I'm looking for my wife. She came in here a little while ago. She's about so tall"—he held his hand up—"with short, dark hair and a decent set." He cupped his hands.

The salesperson didn't bat an eye at his gesture. "I

remember her. She hit our change rooms with some stuff. Very sexy stuff, I might add. You're a very lucky man."

"Yes, I am." He started to move away, but the woman stepped in front of him.

"I'm sorry, sir, but you can't go back there."

"But that's where you said my wife is."

"Yes, but she's not the only person trying on things. We have a policy about not allowing the opposite sex in the woman's change area. It makes them nervous. Now if you were to try something on yourself, then we do have a male-only area. Just installed last spring for the man who likes to pamper himself." She smiled brightly.

"No." *And no.* "Listen, I understand your policy. I'm kind of glad of it actually." No men allowed in the change area meant no one he'd have to kill for seeing his woman. "But see, I was hoping to surprise her. It's our anniversary," he lied with impunity, adding in a wink for good measure.

He could see the clerk wavering. Ducking his head, he whispered, "I'll be very discreet, and as a thanks that you're looking the other way just this once, let me buy you dinner." He slid a hundred-dollar bill into her hand.

"I don't know—" Two more bills magically appeared. The eyes of the salesgirl widened. "You promise to be quiet?"

"Like a mouse." Which really made no sense. Those long-tailed rodents squeaked pretty damned loud when chased.

"Okay, but don't tell anyone I let you."

"Promise." He let her bask in the charm of his smile for a moment before heading once again toward the change room. He didn't run, barely.

Unease nagged at him. He didn't smell anything untoward. Didn't hear or see anything, yet he couldn't shake the sense that something was wrong.

Someone threatens our mate.

Problem was, what was a man to do when the threat was a woman? And one smaller than him?

As he went through the curtain that led to the change rooms, he was startled to see his vixen, shirt untucked, hands laced behind her head, being prodded by a petite blonde wielding a gun.

Do something.

Like what? Not only was it against his moral code to hit a woman, but this one also held a firearm that, if fired, could kill his vixen.

His mate's eyes widened when she spotted him. "Fabian!"

"Stay back or I'll shoot." The blonde took aim in his direction, and in that moment of inattention a fist flew.

Smack.

And no, it wasn't he who punched the blonde holding the gun. His vixen had whirled on a heel and snapped out a perfect left hook that hit the threat in the jaw and sent her to the floor, out cold.

"Nice shot," he remarked with a hint of surprise.

"I can't believe I did that," she replied, looking from her fist to the woman on the floor.

"Just another hidden skill, my delightful vixen. Now let's see how you are at smuggling a body out."

"What?" Her brow furrowed.

"This woman is our first living clue. Hence we need to take her for questioning."

"I understand that, but we can't just waltz out of here with her. I'm pretty sure the saleswoman will notice. The saleswoman is why my attacker made me get dressed before she forced me out of the cubicle."

"Which is why we'll send her out the back. Or did you not wonder where she was taking you?"

"I was kind of distracted by the whole she-wants-to-kill-me thing."

Was that him who growled? More like his wolf, who didn't like the reminder of the threat. "The whole she-wants-to-kill-you thing is why we need to get her out of here and fast before someone notices anything."

"But—"

"Do you want to know why people keep trying to kill you?" As he asked, he knelt down and took a peek at the space under the stall doors, looking for feet—in other words, witnesses who might require handling.

"There's no one else here. And, yes, I want answers." Lips in a tight line, she bent down and grabbed the feet of the gunwoman. "Let's go before I realize what a stupid idea this is."

"I never have stupid ideas," he remarked. Rash ones, violent ones, and, sometimes, regrettable ones—such as the rat tail he sported in high school—but a true man never admitted to stupidity. Unless a woman pointed it out. "And no need to dirty your hands. I don't need any help carrying her."

Thunk. She let go of the feet.

"So what exactly am I supposed to do?" she asked.

"You act as lookout in case that saleslady comes snooping."

"How did you know I was in danger, anyhow?" she asked as they went through the door marked: EMPLOYEES ONLY. "Did your super Scooby sense go off?"

He glared at her. She didn't pay it any mind.

"I did have a gut feeling, yes, and it had nothing to do

with my Lycan side." He did not mention the part where he was only here because he'd missed her. Some things a man did not admit.

"Colin's not going to get in trouble, is he? It's my fault I ditched him. And I really didn't expect any trouble. Who knew they'd use women killers?"

Fabian should have known, given his cousin Megan was an assassin for hire. Or at least used to be. Since she'd gotten hooked to Gavin—Mr. Strait-laced himself—she tended to avoid the use of deadly force.

What a waste of talent.

"Women are just as capable of violence as men."

"Apparently," she mused, peering at her fist as if she didn't recognize it.

She shoved at the metal push bar on the door at the back of the storage room marked EXIT in big red letters.

Before he could tell her to stop, she'd stepped out.

"Get your ass back here. We don't know if it's safe."

She poked her head back in. "Stop bitching. This was your plan. And for your information, the only thing in this alley is a little red smart car. You'd think a hired killer would drive something a little cooler." And out she popped again.

"Idiot," he grumbled as he quickly followed, the blond killer still deadweight in his arms.

His vixen was correct in that the alley was empty, at first glance. At second, Johan stepped from behind a Dumpster and blinked at Fabian. "What the hell, boss?"

"The hell is you and Colin didn't think to make sure the women entering the shop were clients or hired assassins."

Johan's blue eyes widened. "For real? Damn. And here I thought your cousin was the only hot chick with a gun. Is your mate okay?"

"Yes, but no thanks to you."

Figured that she would catch his slip of the tongue. "'Mate'? Is that some wolf term for 'girlfriend'?"

Before Johan could explain, and because Fabian wasn't ready, he shoved the limp body at his minion. "Take the assassin back to the house and secure her. I'll want to question her when she regains consciousness."

"Right away, boss."

His vixen snickered.

"What's so funny?"

"You. Your henchmen. Have you ever thought about growing a mustache and twirling it when you give them tasks?"

"You are not funny." Actually, she was, but he didn't want to encourage her. Fabian tugged her back into the storage area.

"What are you doing?" she asked. "Shouldn't we be going with Johan?"

"Not yet. We've got something more important to deal with first."

"What could be more important than getting information on who I am?"

Several things, such as reassuring himself that she was safe. He could think of one very good way to ease that panic. Not that he'd truly panicked. Real men didn't succumb to that emotion. Or so he'd been told. He now had to wonder if that was true.

"A certain salesperson told me you were trying on some sexy lingerie," he said as he closed the alley door behind them.

"I was, until a certain crazy lady pointed her gun at my hooch."

"We shouldn't let a paltry thing like a failed murder attempt keep you from the important things."

"But—"

He drew her into his arms for a quick, yet scorching, kiss. "I insist."

"Well, in that case then"—she smiled—"wait until you see the stuff I grabbed."

He couldn't wait. First a quick peek through the employee door. Spotting no one, he dragged her back into the cubicle, which, while spacious, wasn't meant to accommodate a male his size. But he didn't care once he spotted the lacy negligee hanging from a hook.

"Put that on," he demanded, his voice low and husky.

"You do know this is nuts. I just escaped getting killed by some midget blonde, and now you want to ogle me as I dress in a fancy nightgown."

"Ogle. Touch. And taste. So strip, or I'll strip you."

CHAPTER 11

Strip.

The word shouldn't make a woman shiver. It did.

She should have told him no way. Who wanted to try on clothes after escaping death? . . . except a strange urgency possessed her.

I almost died. Again.

And while she'd ultimately saved herself, with a surprise pugilistic skill, if not for Fabian's intervention things might have ended very differently.

Was it crazy to want to celebrate the fact that she lived with the man she loved?

Loved?

When the hell had that happened?

Or, more important, did she recall a moment when she didn't? Had it happened the first night he'd saved her? Perhaps love had struck during their first kiss?

Did the when matter? She couldn't claim they were strangers anymore. Over the course of this week, they had spent every moment they could together discovering each other and, in an odd sense, discovering herself.

She liked seafood. Hated broccoli. Loved action flicks, made gagging noises during the emotional parts. As Fabian explored her, body, mind, and soul, she learned not only about herself but also about him. And in the process, she'd fallen in love.

The how and why really didn't matter. The end result was the same. She loved this guy, furry split personality and all, and if he wanted to ogle and touch and taste her in a change cubicle where she'd have to remain silent lest they get discovered, then so be it.

Why make him wait?

Having him crowd the space made her ability to strip interesting. Facing him, she raised her arms and smiled as he stripped the shirt from her, leaving her clad in an ill-fitting bra that had her breasts hanging out over the cups.

"Those poor beauties," he murmured as he cupped them and stroked a thumb over the peaks. Reaching around to her back, he undid the clasp, freeing them.

Next went her pants, which proved a tad more difficult given they were a size too small. Unsnapping them first, she shoved them down past her hips before she sat on the bench in the small room. He crouched before her and pulled them off the rest of the way. That left only her panties.

Rip. Nope. Those were gone, too, leaving her naked to his view. But she didn't feel cold, not when the heat of his gaze seared her skin.

He stood and grabbed the silky undergarment from the hook. She went to her feet, and he draped it over her head, silent, and yet did he really need to say anything when the fire in his gaze said it all?

She put her arms through the armholes so that the delicate negligee hung by spaghetti straps. The silky fabric hugged her skin, molding her curves, especially her erect nipples.

The heat between them practically set the air on fire.

She leaned back. She had no choice. She needed the wall to brace herself because her knees no longer wanted to work. His hungry gaze made her tremble.

"So beautiful." He breathed the word, admiration not only clear in his eyes but also in the impressive bulge at his groin.

Words were cheap. Actions, though, actions led to bliss. "Show me."

For a moment, she thought he might kiss her. She knew by now that he was a man who loved to nibble. But he surprised her by dropping to his knees again.

There was something extremely powerful in his actions, a supplicant before her. A man who wasn't afraid to worship.

His big hands clasped her thighs, spreading them, exposing her wet sex to his gaze. She trembled and more liquid honey moistened her nether lips.

"Mine." His possessive claim was followed by a determined lick.

"Oh." Her soft moan seemed too loud. She had to be quiet lest someone come knocking. Was it bad to find that thought arousing?

Biting her lip, she fought to not to cry out again, but he didn't make it easy, not when his tongue did such decadent things to her.

He spread her sex and explored with his tongue, lapping at her juices. She probably hurt him, so tightly did she grip his hair, but she couldn't help it. She needed to hold something.

Deeper he pushed his tongue, thrusting it into her channel. Wild and wicked. But not as wild as when he shoved two fingers into her and then gripped her clit with his mouth.

That wrenched a cry from her before she could stop it.

He teased her nub, each flick of his tongue and pull of his lips spiraling her pleasure higher and higher.

"Fabian. Please." She couldn't help but beg.

And he listened.

He turned her around with a gruffly whispered, "Hands on the wall."

She did as told and closed her eyes as she heard his zipper lower. The light fabric covering her buttocks lifted, and a moment later the thick head pushed at her sex.

"Tilt your ass toward me," he ordered, and she obeyed, so hot for him she would have done anything. Anything to have him sink into her.

Again he rubbed against her moist slit. She could have sobbed with need.

Then the waiting was over. He thrust, sheathing himself into her, stretching the walls of her channel.

She couldn't stop a gasp as her fingers clawed at the wall, searching for purchase but finding none. She rested her forehead against the wall and made soft grunting sounds as he penetrated her, over and over, the thickness of his shaft filling her so perfectly. The length of him just right, just long enough to butt against her sweet G-spot.

She couldn't help how tightly her channel squeezed, making it harder and harder for him to shove in and pull out. But he didn't seem to mind. His cock thickened. Throbbed.

Over and over he slammed into her, taking her to the brink of ecstasy. With a growled, "Mine," he exploded, the final deep thrust and burst of liquid heat enough to send her over the edge.

She might have screamed his name. She didn't really know or care, not with the waves of pleasure shuddering through her body.

For a moment they stood, panting, the aftershocks of their lovemaking making their bodies pulse.

She squeaked when a knock came at the door.

"Um, is everything all right in there?" asked a tentative voice.

All right? She couldn't help but giggle. "Everything is great."

And it was. Even if she wanted to kill Fabian when he dumped all the items she'd brought into the change room on the counter and said, "We'll take it all. Plus add in a few dozen pairs of panties, too, would you? I seem to have a habit of tearing them."

It wasn't just the saleslady who blushed. Heat suffused her cheeks, too, but in her case, it wasn't embarrassment but recollection that did her in.

But as it turned out, it was a sound choice. He did play havoc with her undergarments, to her screaming delight.

CHAPTER 12

"We will make you scream if you don't answer." Fabian sat behind his desk, feet propped, impeccably dressed in a suit and tie, the complete image of nonchalance.

For those who wondered, it wasn't feigned. The prospect of violence didn't bother him, and while he might have a problem hitting a woman himself, there were other ways to make the opposite sex talk.

His mate, however, didn't know this. His vixen, who insisted on being present, frowned. Leaning down, she whispered into his ear, "Um, you're not really going to torture her, are you?"

He didn't bother to modulate his voice. "Damned straight I plan to torture her. She had no problem in attempting to kill you. Do the crime, pay the price."

"I thought that term was used by law enforcement when talking about criminals."

"It applies to anyone who dares to do something they know might get them punished. In this case, Blondie over there"—who wasn't looking so tough tied to a chair—"thought she could come into my territory and attempt to murder someone in my care."

"In your care? You make me sound like someone's pet hamster."

Snagging her around the waist, he yanked her onto his lap. "I was being polite. Would you have preferred I said this bitch dared to try and kill my lover and now her ass is grass?"

"Yes."

A grin stretched his lips. "So sorry then."

"You should be." Primly said, but he could see the glint of mirth in her eyes. "What are you going to do to her?"

"If she were a man, I'd probably bounce her face off my desk a few times. Break her nose. Make it bleed. Then hit her a few more times for good measure to make sure that nose never goes back straight. Then I might think of removing an ear, or two. For some reason, that really bothers people."

Her eyes widened. "Are you serious?"

"Yes. But I might add, I only do that in the most dire situations. One of the reasons my kind has flourished is because we don't purposely draw attention to ourselves. Killing people and maiming them tends to have the opposite effect."

"Weak," muttered the blonde.

"Try 'smart,'" Fabian corrected. "There are other ways to make a point, subtle yet powerful ways. Ways you're about to discover."

A knock at the door saw Fred entering bearing a plastic grocery bag. "The items you ordered, sir."

"Thank you. Please place them on my desk."

"Do you require me to apply them, milord?"

"No, I think Vixen and I can handle it from here."

"Very well, sir." Depositing the mysterious bag on the desk, a bag his vixen eyed, Fred turned around and left.

"What's in the bag?" his mate asked.

"Why don't you take a look?"

She rose from his lap—a shame, he did so enjoy it when she sat there, especially when she wore less clothes. As she walked away to circle around his desk, he admired the shape of her ass.

Dressed in one of her new outfits—a pencil tube skirt, white blouse, with a black bra peeking through the silk— she presented the image of the perfect businesswoman. A woman he could have tossed on his desk to have his way with that moment, if they didn't have pressing business at hand.

He found her choice of attire interesting. Whether she realized it or not, her subconscious had guided her when shopping. The end result told him that his vixen was a woman used to dressing for success. A woman in charge. A woman who should have made waves when she went missing.

Stopping on the other side of his desk, she peeked into the bag. For a moment, she stared, then laughed. "Seriously? These are the tools you plan to employ to make her talk?"

"I wouldn't scoff. I assure you, they will be very effective. Would you like me to demonstrate?"

"Actually"—his vixen grinned wider—"I think I'd like to give it a whirl."

While his mate might have seemed somewhat squeamish a moment ago at the prospect of bloody torture, she at least understood the need to get answers.

Seating herself on the desk, legs crossed, her height

asserting a level of dominance, his mate spent a moment staring at the assassin.

The captured killer stared right back. No remorse or chagrin in her expression. Yet.

His vixen braced her hands on the edge of his desk to maintain her balance when she leaned forward to ask, "Why?"

Simple, and to the point. He liked it.

"Bite me."

His mate stood and circled around to the back of the blonde. "Is that your final answer? Because, it should be noted, you are not in a position to throw insults."

"Your man just said he won't kill me. Too messy. Pretty little princess might get his soft, pencil-pushing hands dirty."

An insult to his face? The nerve. Apparently, he'd have to lay down the law in the less-than-savory circles and bring back the respect and prestige a man in his position was due.

And for her information, while he might have soft hands—Fred insisted he lotion them every day—he was most certainly not a pencil pusher. On the contrary, Fabian was the one pushing around those toting the pencils.

"Fabian isn't afraid of getting dirty. I would know." His mate shot him a look that was several shades of naughty promise. "But he's right. Violence isn't always the answer, even if it is sometimes fun." Grabbing the hair of the blond assassin, long tresses that probably took hours to blow-dry, his vixen yanked her head back, hard enough to earn a squeak.

If he didn't love her before, he certainly did now.

In a cool, modulated tone, his mate said, "Listen, I don't

know who you are, hell, I don't know who I am, but I can tell you right now that I am annoyed, feeling kind of irritable, and apparently I am willing to go fairly low to find some answers. If I were you, I wouldn't push me on this. You will tell me everything you know."

"Boo-fucking-hoo. Someone lost her memory. I don't give a fuck, and I ain't telling you nothing," spat the blonde.

"Were you dropped on your head as a child?" his vixen asked. "Is this why you're so deliberately stupid now?"

"Trying to hurt my feelings?" taunted the killer. "Like I fucking care what you have to say."

"You tried to kill me."

"Yup. And if your boyfriend here hadn't come along, I'd have succeeded, too. Hell, when I escape, even if there's no money involved, I'm going to decimate you just as a matter of principle."

Wrong answer. Fabian didn't bat an eye when his mate popped the mouthy killer in the face. He did, however, hope the blood from her dripping nose didn't ruin his rug. Cold water did not remove all stains. He knew from experience.

"Fucking bitch!"

"I somehow doubt that's the name I was given at birth," his vixen remarked. "Want to try again? I'm pretty sure you can fix that broken nose, but you might look kind of funny if I shave your eyebrows."

His vixen released the prisoner but only so she could shove her hand in the bag and pull out a razor, a cordless electric one.

Without warning, his vixen braced a forearm against the blonde's head, pushing it against the seat back.

Buzz. Buzz. Buzz.

When his mate stepped back, it was to the sound of the

blonde cursing. "You crazy, fucking cow. You shaved off my eyebrows!"

"I did. But at this point, that's pretty easy to fix, and they'll grow back. Now I'm going to ask you again. Why am I being targeted? And by who?"

"I won't tell. It's part of the code. Just ask your boy-friend."

Fabian raised his hands and shook his head. "Hey, don't throw this back on me. You're the one being asked to answer for her actions. I should also mention that, while I am interested in those answers, it is not me you need to worry about but the one wielding a weapon of hair destruction."

For emphasis, his vixen let the razor whir. He fought not to smile. Who would have expected he'd have such a grand ol' time. Could he truly be so lucky as to have a mate who would truly be his partner? What would it be like to rule his kingdom with her by his side?

An alpha king and his queen, a queen who wasn't done getting answers or playing with her prey.

His mate reached out to grasp a hank of the blonde's hair. She held it up and then let it drift from her hand. "How long did it take you to grow your hair? I'm wagering years. Lots of years." *Buzz. Buzz.* His vixen got the little motor of the razor whirring and held it inches away from the blonde's prized locks. "You know, I hear reverse Mohawks are all the craze."

"You wouldn't dare." The blonde narrowed her eyes.

Wrong answer. While a certain brash assassin screamed, his vixen shaved a strip, right up the middle. It proved too much hair for the poor razor to handle. With a grinding sound, it stopped.

"Oops. Did your tool fail?" the assassin cackled. "So you

shaved a bit of hair. Like you said, it will grow back. Besides, I was thinking of changing my look."

"Well, I am glad to hear that because I've got just the thing to help you get started." His mate dropped the razor on his desk blotter and reached into the bag. She pulled out the next tool. This one also made a buzzing sound but resembled a thick pen. "Forehead or chin? And what should the message be? Sucks dick? Loves anal? Or do you want me to surprise you?"

The blonde visibly shrunk. "You wouldn't dare."

Buzz. The tattoo pen hovered in front of the killer's face. "At this point, I would dare pretty much anything. I'm tired of this crap. No more screwing me around. Either talk or forever walk around with a tramp stamp on your face."

Would his vixen really do it?

Apparently, today wasn't the day he'd find out. The blonde grimaced, not a pretty sight given the blood dripping off her chin from the nose his vixen had smacked. "Fine. I'll fucking talk. It's not like I have much to tell you. I got this job anonymously via text only a few hours ago."

"And do you always take anonymous jobs?"

"Is she for real?" the blonde asked him. "What other kind are there? No one is going to send me a business card and say, 'Hey, mind killing so-and-so?'"

"How do you know it's not someone setting you up?"

The killer shook her head. "You don't, but those who have my number are few."

"If they're few, then how can you not know them?"

Fabian cleared his throat. "In the assassination field, there are usually middlemen, brokers if you will. Men with connections in the underworld. A client contacts them and expresses their need. These middlemen hook them up without either side knowing about the other."

"That is seriously messed up," she said with a wrinkle of her nose.

Fabian shrugged. "Perhaps, but that is how things work in the underworld. So you see, her story isn't out of the ordinary. Chances are she does know nothing."

"And I don't give a shit who pays me. So long as I get half of the money up front, I'm your girl."

"Okay, so you got the job via a text? What did the message say?"

"Said if I wanted to make an easy hundred Gs to get my ass down to the shopping district and kill you."

"So you know who I am?"

"Nope. Never heard of you before today."

Fabian saw her deflate at the news.

"How were you supposed to find and kill me if you never met me?"

"Easy. The buyer sent a pic."

"An image of me?" His vixen perked up. "I want to see it."

His mate turned to him, and Fabian held up the phone they'd confiscated from the killer. "Sorry, vixen. I went through her texts. Nothing there. She must have deleted it."

The blonde rolled her eyes. "Of course I deleted it. Only an idiot keeps that kind of evidence on their phone. Anyhow, I knew what you looked like and where you were supposed to be. The orders were to kill you and dump the body if I could on Fabian Garoux's property or, if I couldn't get you there, then at least make sure I planted the cuff link that was couriered to me in your hand or on your person."

Ah yes, the cuff link, lost a few weeks ago, and not

something he'd thought much of until it turned up in the hired killer's pocket. The plot thickened.

"Why does your client want me dead?"

"How the fuck should I know? I'm just paid to do a job. I don't care what the reason is."

"Why try to implicate Fabian then? What would be the point?"

The point was obvious to Fabian and to the killer, who rolled her eyes. "So he'd get the blame."

His vixen looked troubled as she asked, "But why kill me specifically? Wouldn't anybody have worked?"

It was in that moment that Fabian connected the dots and wondered how he'd not seen it before.

"Because you're obviously related to someone important and your death, supposedly sanctioned or done by me, would start a turf war or, if the cops got involved and arrested me, leave my organization in disarray allowing someone else to step in."

The question was, who was brazen enough to challenge him?

And just who was his vixen related to?

CHAPTER 13

"I've got a plan."

Since they lay spent and sweaty on his silken, woven bamboo sheets, she could be fairly sure his plan didn't involve another way to make her scream her way to ecstasy. Then again, if any man could wring an ounce more of pleasure from her body, Fabian could.

"Is it a devious plan?" she asked as she rolled to her side so she could see him. She never tired of staring. His rugged looks were sexy, but it was the intelligence behind that truly intrigued her. Businessman meet criminal mastermind. The ultimate bad boy, at least in her books.

And he's mine. At least for the moment. They'd yet to talk of the future, although he did make remarks to the effect that he expected her to stick around for a while. Like when he asked her opinion on what color scheme to use in the dining room. She laughed when her first suggestion— medieval dining hall with a large wooden table, benches, and intricate tapestries for the wall—made him wince but still agree with a sighed, "If that's what you want."

Lucky for him, her tastes ran to more contemporary styles, something they had in common.

Just one of many things they shared, such as their love of billiards, which they played almost nightly with fanatic enthusiasm.

Like this evening's game.

"If I win, you give me mind-blowing head."

"And if I win?" she'd asked with a smile.

"I give you toe-curling licks."

"Is it me, or do you win either way?"

His smile held devilish promise. And so they played. She got the first shot. The tip of her cue cracked the white ball hard and sent it careening into the pile. Colors shot off in all directions.

She chose striped. Sank the green. Then the red. And then, while holding his gaze, sank the eight ball. "Oops." A technical loss, and yet, as her sated body could attest, she wasn't a loser.

"You've got that look in your eye again," he said, drawing her from the erotic reminder.

She also had a tingle in her pussy. But it would have to wait, as he'd woken her curiosity. "So what is this plan of yours?"

"We are going to throw an engagement party."

"For who?" she asked.

"Us, of course."

She blinked. She then stared at him. He stared right back. "Um, I think I misunderstood."

"No you didn't. We're going to announce to the world that you and I are engaged. We'll have a picture sent to the papers. I'll have my media consultant—"

"You have a media consultant?"

"Of course I do. Image is everything. How is the world supposed to know I'm badass if no one announces it? Anyhow, like I was saying, we'll get the news out and invite everyone in the shifter and underworld to the party. Friends and enemies alike."

"You are going to invite them all here? Are you insane?"

"Not according to the tests they made me take in college."

"Okay, let's say I go along with this plan, one problem. I don't have a name."

But in the end the name didn't matter, not once his marketing team was done with it. Pictures were taken, invitations sent out, and it didn't take long before everyone was frothing to meet Fabian's mysterious fiancée.

However, the real question was, would someone who recognized her come forth, and would the person who wanted her dead show up?

Fabian was banking on both. She hoped his plan worked, but of more interest to her was the fact that her lover treated the engagement as if it were real.

Just look at the giant rock on her finger, a beautifully cut diamond that he presented to her during dinner.

Of course, he didn't attempt anything so pedantic as getting on a bended knee. He had it delivered to her on a silver platter, domed of course, the lid of which Fred swirled off with a flourish. The black velvet box screamed, *Open me!*

She did and couldn't help a pleased, "Oh my."

Since she didn't have anything for him, she made him later groan, "Oh my," her tight hand around his shaft catching glints from the overhead light making the ring sparkle.

But a ring didn't make their engagement real, and while she might find herself outspoken on many subjects, asking him if it meant anything more proved impossible.

Because I'm scared. Scared that the man she loved would tell her it truly was only a sham.

For the moment, she'd rather pretend it was real and she was truly engaged to this intriguing male who really tempted in his black tux with its crisp white shirt.

"Do we really have to go downstairs?" she asked as she minced toward him in her mermaid gown, the shapely fit flattering but definitely not conducive to taking big steps. She ran a finger down his chest. "I could think of other things I'd much rather do."

He caught her hand before it hit his belt buckle. "Don't tempt me. You look good enough to eat in that dress, and I look forward to peeling it from you later. The keyword being 'later.' Right now, we have a killer to unmask, an identity to reveal, and a party to host. Are you ready, vixen, to dazzle the movers and shakers of the under- and animal worlds?"

With him at her side, she could do anything. However, that confidence didn't mean a certain trepidation didn't grip her as they made their grand entrance. While Fred announced them, in his snootiest tone, they stood at the top of the stairs leading to the large foyer, which opened on to the massive living and dining room, a perfect backdrop. Hand tucked into his arm, she adopted a cool, composed mien, one that didn't show the inner tremble.

For his part, Fabian appeared utterly relaxed, to those who might not know him. But she knew him now, knew him quite well, and she noticed his rapier gaze as it sought out anything untoward in the guests milling below.

As to personal introductions? He smoothly countered those by saying he would formally introduce her shortly.

He seemed intent on simply having her see as many people as possible in the hopes of triggering a memory. Anything.

About an hour into the party, his plan worked.

CHAPTER 14

Fabian knew he was taking a risk in having such a public event. The throngs of people, so many of them in his home, would be hard to keep track of. He'd engaged every measure of security he could in the hopes of keeping his vixen safe.

He hoped that, after tonight, he could relax his guard.

Their engagement, which he'd yet to admit to his mate was real, at least in his mind, served more than a few purposes. She knew of the top two—answers to her identity and, they hoped, a flushing of the person behind the assassination attempts.

But it also served a more subtle purpose. It let the women know he was taken. Off the market and settling down with one fantastic lady. It let the men know she was his. *Mine. Touch her and die.*

It also more firmly entrenched her in his life, a life he believed she was adapting to.

Then why not ask her to marry you for real?

Surely the big, bad crime lord wasn't afraid she'd say no?

"You no-good, flea-ridden, mangy cur."

Fabian turned and couldn't help but smile at the insult.

Striding across the room, people parting before his stride, was the lion king himself, here to pay his disrespect.

It had been some time since Fabian had seen the asshole, and time had taken its toll. The once-thick mane of golden hair had faded to an almost pure white—which had to drive the feline crazy, given his youthful obsession with his hair. However, while the face might bear more lines, the eyes were as piercing as ever—and annoyed. Some things never changed.

Did Fabian enjoy needling the lion every chance he got? Yup. Not that it was often. Their respective jobs as leaders of large cities kept them busy. But every few years, when they ran into each other, they exchanged polite barbs.

"I see you're still trying to recapture your youth with that strawlike mop on your head. You really should do something about those split ends."

"My hair is perfectly fine. You should worry more about your skin, especially since you won't be wearing it for long."

The older man seethed in front of him.

Had Fabian found the culprit behind the attacks? The one who wanted to drag him down?

"What's got your knickers in a knot? Did your favorite seafood restaurant get shut down? If you want, I can arrange to supplement your diet with the rats we like to catch here in the city. I've got a blond one in the basement for starters."

"What the fuck are you talking about? You've got a lot of nerve insulting me after what you've done."

"What I've done? I threw a fabulous party, and this is how you treat your host?" Fabian employed his most aggrieved tone.

"Don't you aim those puppy dog eyes at me. You crossed a line when you stole from me."

"Stole from you?" Fabian snorted. "You wish. You have nothing I want."

"Liar. The evidence is standing right behind you."

"Daddy?"

At the querying word, Fabian froze and turned. Say it wasn't so. Not his vixen. She couldn't be related to the lion king. He would have known. He would have sensed it.

Oops. He hadn't.

One look in her eyes was all it took to realize the truth. His supposed perfect mate was his enemy's daughter.

CHAPTER 15

Memories of who she was crashed upon her in a tidal wave, rocking her in their wake.

I'm Vivienne. Twenty-eight years old. Daughter of the lion king. Superbitch in the business world. Mate of my father's enemy.

Damn.

"I swear I didn't know," Vivienne said as she saw the blank mask drop over Fabian's features. But he didn't reply. Not one word. He didn't need to say anything.

Fabian walked away, feeling betrayed even if she'd never lied.

Acting as if what had happened between them didn't matter. Yet it did.

Taking his wounded ego and leaving.

Hell no.

Placing two fingers between her lips, she let out a strident whistle. Instant silence fell upon the room, and that meant her words carried. "Don't you dare walk away from me, Fabian Garoux. We're not done."

"I have nothing to say to the daughter of my enemy."

"No, but I have plenty to say."

"There's a surprise." Cue the heavy sarcasm. He turned away again.

She might have whispered the word, but she saw his back stiffen. "Pussy."

"Excuse me?" He pivoted on one foot and fixed her with his most fierce stare.

She smiled. "You heard me. Only a pussy would toss what we've discovered together out the doggy door just because my dad happens to be a badass crime lord."

"I'm badder." His chest swelled, and the audience, as if on strings, turned to her, waiting for her retort.

"Prove it."

"A real man doesn't need to prove his worth. Just like a real man knows when to walk away."

"Don't you dare."

But he did, his pride having taken a blow, and she allowed it, for the moment, but only because her father would not shut up.

"The nerve of that bastard. This is war!" he exclaimed.

"No, it's not, Daddy. Fabian is not at fault here. He only ever tried to protect me." And love her. How easily she could see her fear that he didn't care was groundless. A man who didn't care for her would never have gone to such lengths or worshipped her body with such decadence.

Neither would a man like him let something like finding out his lover was the daughter of his enemy stand in his way. The Fabian she knew would smirk and taunt. He'd toss their mated status in her dad's face.

Which meant Fabian's exit was a ruse, and she could think of only one reason he'd leave the party, making sure everyone saw his displeasure with the feline pride.

He's setting himself up as bait!

CHAPTER 16

Standing at the window in his office, Fabian stared out into his well-cultivated garden and yet saw nothing. At least nothing that mattered.

Within his mind, there was only one image, that of his flummoxed vixen—who did her best to hide a pang of hurt—as he walked away. *Except she has a real name now.* Vivienne.

It suited her. A pity she had to be the daughter of that damnable furball feline, but lucky for her, he wouldn't hold it against her. Something he'd explain later if she let him.

She seemed kind of pissed when he walked off, but in his defense, he had good reason.

At the discovery of who she was, he'd had to improvise as certain clues came together. His quick mind quickly devised a plan to tempt the culprit. Now he only hoped someone took the bait.

Much like a kitty with a catnip-drenched toy dangled in front of him, a certain lion couldn't resist the temptation Fabian offered.

No knock announced their arrival, how rude. The interloper simply opened his door and entered, not bothering to hide their presence.

Fabian didn't turn around, even when a gruff voice said, "Meddling fucking dog. You just couldn't let her die, could you?"

As a matter of fact, no, he couldn't, just like, despite the fact that she was the daughter of his enemy, he couldn't let her go. "Finally, the culprit behind the acts shows his cowardly face. About time you came out of your hidey-hole to do the dirty work yourself."

"That's what I get for sending bears and humans to do the job. Fear not, though; while they might have lacked the skill to finish, I won't miss."

Turning on a heel, Fabian gave the man a once-over. Fabian wasn't impressed with what he saw. Jowly cheeks, red bulbous nose, and the ponderous frame that his suit strained around said it all. Except for his name. "Who the hell are you? Not that I really care, but I would like to send flowers to your widow and congratulate her on ridding herself of an idiot."

"You've got a lot of balls for a man who is going to die."

"The biggest," he boasted, not the most conducive thing to do, given the gun trained on him.

Showing fear, however, was never an option. Insouciance, however, Fabian was master at that. He dropped into his leather chair, frowning at the creak of the springs. Fred would need to see it got oiled—and if he saw any pamphlets suggesting he join a gym, heads would roll.

Leaning forward, Fabian opened a box on his desk, pulling forth an aromatic cigar. He ran it under his nose and inhaled. Fresh and hand-wrapped, only the best would do.

"What the fuck do you think you're doing?"

"Having a cigar of course. I'd offer you one, but it would be wasted on a dead man." He snipped the tip and put the uncut end in his mouth. He allowed himself a smirk at the consternation mixed with anger on the lion's jowly face.

"Arrogant fucking dog. With your death, blamed on my dear brother-in-law, I'll finally get what I want."

"An appointment to be neutered? A lifetime spent in a cage at the zoo?" Fabian smiled. "I think you messed with the wrong woman."

Indeed, someone had. Vivienne, the idiot's niece, had entered in utter silence. "I told Auntie June you were a jerk." And with that, his lovely vixen Tasered her uncle.

Fabian almost applauded. He couldn't imagine a more perfect woman to spend his life with.

But back for a moment to the idiot who wanted to start a war. As the electrical current jolted his body, he dropped to the floor, his body twitching, his eyes rolled backward so only the whites showed, and he uttered an incoherent, "Uh. Uh. Uh."

Paying her uncle no mind, Vivienne stepped over him and strode toward Fabian. Irritation marked her features.

"How dare you run away from me. I wasn't done with you."

"I should hope not."

But she went on as if she hadn't heard him. "You are such an idiot. Does it really matter who my father is? I want you. And before you try and lie to me, I know you want me, too. Now that I have my memories back, I know what this means." She placed her hand on her neck atop the spot he'd bitten. "The question is, are you going to let a little thing like who I am push me away?"

"You're the idiot if you believed that act out there." He smiled at her. "I don't give a damn who your father is. I don't care if keeping you here with me starts a fucking war between my pack and your pride. You. Are. Mine."

"What the hell is going on here?" her father exclaimed as he pushed into the room. "And what happened to Larry? Why is he drooling on the rug?"

Ew. Fabian made a note to tell Fred to get it steam-cleaned.

"Larry is the traitor who tried to have me killed," Vivienne announced.

"Why would he do that?" her father asked.

"Because I found out he was embezzling family money."

The lion king frowned. "But why? And how did you find out? You've been overseas for the last few years setting up our expansion offices."

"One of our company accountants contacted me while I was abroad with his suspicions. I immediately made plans to return and confront Larry, which is why you didn't know I was coming home. But somehow, my *dear uncle*"—she kicked the limp body—"found out. I was waylaid coming out of the airport."

Fabian took over. "But killing you to protect his secret wasn't enough. Your uncle wanted to divert your father's attention, hence the plot to try and pin the blame on me, and start a war between our packs."

"Why, that bastard!" Her father glared at the prone figure on the rug. "Is he dead?"

"No, he's just unconscious. However, I am letting you know right now that as an apology for not protecting your precious, delicate daughter—"

Fabian snorted while the lion leader blustered, "But I knew nothing about his machinations."

Vivienne fixed her father with a shriveling stare. "That's

no excuse. So you will fix this. I will expect to receive an invitation to his funeral within the week. And please note, I will be bringing a guest. My fiancé." She shot Fabian a look, which he met with a smile and arched brow.

"So the engagement is still on?" Fabian asked.

"You aren't escaping me that easily, Fido. But I will warn you right now, there will be a wedding. A big one."

"Over my dead body," growled her father.

"That can be arranged," Fabian announced, but glancing at Vivienne, he amended it to, "I mean, perhaps we can come to a mutually beneficial arrangement between our clans."

"But—"

"Daddy, if you don't leave now, I will be forced to post those pictures I've been hoarding."

"You wouldn't dare."

"The wolf is mine. Deal with it." Apparently, the look she shot her father was enough to convince him that he wouldn't win.

With a bit more posturing, and grumbling, the lion king took off but not before ordering his entourage to bring his new living room rug with them.

And they said the wolf packs were a strange lot.

"Shall we return to our engagement party?" he offered as their guests, and many of his guards, spilled into the room and out in the hall, exclaiming over the drama.

"No. I'm not going anywhere," she stated, and then she said the magic words that made him decide to ditch the party, too. "I think we should celebrate, *by ourselves.*"

CHAPTER 17

For a moment, she thought she'd miscalculated, that Fabian would want to return to the party, triumphant. It was what her father would have done. But Fabian wasn't her daddy.

"Out." Fabian spoke the word softly, but he might as well have shouted it, given the powerful echo behind it. The voice of an alpha, a man who wielded power, not by brute strength, not by fear, but by sheer charisma and intelligence.

His commanding aura had been sexy when she didn't understand it with her memory loss and even sexier now because she knew he was a rare type of leader.

And an awesome lover.

In moments, the commotion had disappeared, leaving Fabian alone with her. About time. She shut the door and locked it. *Click.*

Turning around, she leaned against the heavy portal and stared at her man. *My mate.* The male who'd marked her as his own without ever asking permission.

"You know, with all that's happened, there's one thing you seem to have forgotten," she said as she stalked toward him.

"What's that?"

"You never technically asked me to marry you."

He grimaced. "Ask? Why would I do that? You're mine." He smiled. "And you should know by now, if I see something I want, I take it."

Some women might have found his words arrogant, perhaps even offensive. Vivienne, however, smiled. "That's funny because that's exactly how I deal with things. Why do you think my father's business has been such a success? You are looking at the brains of the operation."

"How come I never met you or heard of you then?"

"The men in the pride tend to take the credit and I prefer to stay out of the limelight."

"That will change when you come to work with me."

"What makes you think I want to work with you?" Vivienne asked with a coy smile.

"Because I want a partnership, vixen. I want us to form an unstoppable duo, both in the bedroom and out. Are you up for that?"

How could his words bring such heat to her body? If she'd not already loved him, she would have in that moment. "A partnership? I guess we could negotiate something."

"Negotiate?"

"Minor details that we can hammer out later. In the meantime, I think we should celebrate. What do you say we seal the deal with a kiss?"

"Come here." He patted the desk in front of him.

Giving orders again, was he? "I thought we were partners."

"We are. But right now, I am asserting my husbandly rights."

"We're not married yet."

"But we are mated, and your man is saying to get your sweet ass over here." He didn't say it with any real heat, and that was why she teased him by saying, "And if I don't?"

In the blink of an eye he'd vaulted over his desk and stood before her, the wild shine of his primal side glowing in his eyes. The beast lurked, and so did passion.

Given her gown was too tight to have any real fun, she gave him her back and said in a husky voice, "Mind helping me out of this dress?"

"My pleasure."

She couldn't help but shiver as his fingers dragged the zipper down. The expensive evening gown pooled around her feet. Not that she cared. The air between them sizzled with erotic anticipation.

Fabian swept his desk, sending papers and pens as well as many other odds and ends flying. His unbridled desire for her was addictive.

She didn't need prompting to lie back on the cold surface. She did, however, smile when he growled and fingered the garters holding up her sheer black stockings.

"If I'd have known you were wearing these, you would have never made it down the stairs."

Reaching upward, she grabbed the lapels of his jacket and yanked him down. "I was saving them for later. I had a fantasy of seeing my legs up around your shoulders while you fucked me."

"Funny, I had a similar fantasy, especially when I saw you in those sexy heels," he said with a smile as he rubbed the head of his cock against the moist fabric covering her sex.

"You do realize we're made for each other," she whispered against his lips before biting the lower one.

"Mates for life," he agreed.

"I will not share," she added.

"Good, because I'm a jealous man and the alligators in the nearby swamp can only handle so many bodies."

She laughed. "I can see doing business with you will be interesting."

"But awesome. Especially since your working with me, building my pack riches, will drive your father mad."

"You say the sexiest things," she purred. "But I'd prefer if you acted."

Her legs hugged his waist, drawing him close. However, he didn't give her what she wanted.

"Not so quick, vixen. Didn't you just say you had a certain fantasy?" Arching a brow and giving her his most wicked grin—which never failed to warm her and arouse—he pulled out of her grip, only so he could push her legs high, high enough to rest on his shoulders.

It proved an erotic sight. Her thighs, clad in sheer hose, along with her new position opened her wide for him, made her vulnerable, but she trusted Fabian. Trusted him with not only her life but also her love.

"I will always," he said, thrusting into her exposed sex, "give my mate"—slide out, slam back in—"what she wants."

In. Out. In. Out. Hard and fast. His erotic onslaught had her gasping for breath and clawing at the smooth surface of his desk, but she couldn't escape his fierce passion, nor did she want to. He pounded into her willing body, bringing her to the edge of ecstasy. She hovered on the brink, panting for air. When his fingers found her clitoris and pinched it, he tossed her over the edge.

As her orgasm rushed over her in pleasurable waves, she couldn't help but shout, "I love you!"

"Of course you do," he grunted as he kept plunging his cock deep within.

She grabbed him by the hair and, human or not, growled against his lips, "Don't you want to say something, too?"

"You are mine, vixen. Forever." And as he came, the heat of his seed bathing her womb, he howled it for the world to hear. "I love you!"

And in the aftermath of their joining, they shared a chuckle as a large feline in the vicinity let out a mournful roar.

In all ways now, she was the alpha's mate.

EPILOGUE

Was there anything more incongruous than a wolf playing horsey? Yet that was exactly what Fabian, alpha leader of the wolf pack, did for the amusement of Gavin's son while his wife, Megan, watched with a smile.

Vivienne's own round belly promised that next year's Fourth of July picnic would have more than one small voice clamoring for a ride. According to building permits filed at city hall, by this time next year Fabian's property would also have a moat, an electrified fence, and a host of other security measures to keep the baby girl growing in his wife's womb safe.

While Theo gripped the hair of his uncle and squealed, Gavin flipped burgers on the barbecue while Megan did her best to reassure her daddy, who'd popped in for a visit, that Lulu, Broderick's wife, wasn't a narc out to arrest him.

Broderick didn't partake in the drama, as he was currently in the pool with his cop wife trying to convince her to remove her bikini top. And then, when she made to do so, he dove on her and said, in a voice that carried, "Don't you dare show my boobs to anyone else."

How interesting life had become in this pack. A pack that was now more than just people who worked for Fabian and the shifters in this city. A pack made of family and friends. The bonds they'd built strong and, dare he say, enviable?

As Cole spied through his binoculars and listened via the bugs he'd planted when he posed as a plumber, he couldn't help but wonder if perhaps it was time he thought of settling down. Perhaps offering his services to this alpha leader who knew how to balance strength with compassion.

When Cole had first encountered this group, he'd been simply a hired killer, doing a job, a job he found himself reluctant to complete. Working for money was fun until you realized money didn't buy happiness.

All his life he'd scoffed at the idea of a true mate, but now, seeing these once-confirmed bachelors settling into family life, and so obviously happy, made him wonder if perhaps there was something to be said for finding the one.

Would it ever happen to him? How would he know when he met the one?

A car rattled its way down the road, its muffler in dire need of repair, and that was probably why he never heard her approach. But he did hear the distinctive click of a hammer being cocked.

"Care to explain what you're doing in this tree?"

Apparently falling, so great was his shock at his bear's announced, *Mine.*

The End . . . Or is it?

DANGEROUS
PASSIONS

Kate Douglas

CHAPTER 1

Saturday, midday in late September, Trinity Alps, Northern California . . .

Darnell Deya stared through the dusty windshield, fully aware she'd made a horrible mistake. There was no denying the obvious—this was definitely not the road to Feral Passions. The one and only other time she'd been anywhere near the Trinity Alps, she'd flown up from LA and, once they'd gotten the rental car, Darnell had spent the twisty mountain drive out to the isolated resort hanging out the back window trying not to puke.

She'd done okay on this trip, to some extent. All the way to the north end of California from LA, turned west in Redding after spending the night in a nice motel, turned north again at a wide spot in the road that appeared to be Douglas City, and drove to Weaverville. Then she'd gone west again, following her lying GPS, and turned right. Only this didn't look like the *right* right, because it wasn't anything like the road that had led them to that beautiful resort hidden back in the woods.

The one with all the hunky guys. Well, with one guy in particular. If she could have gotten Evan Dark out of her head she wouldn't even be here, but months of lusting after a guy she hadn't even had sex with was so not fair. Now, if she could just find a wide enough place to turn the car around, she'd head back into town and find someone who could tell her how to find Feral Passions Resort.

Home to wolves and really gorgeous guys, and the most unique vacation she'd ever had in her life. Who could have imagined a resort where wolves roamed free and interacted with guests? The wolves were amazing, but not nearly as amazing as the men of Feral Passions.

She'd tried. Really she had, but she couldn't forget Evan. Somehow, he'd gotten that sexy smile of his lodged tightly inside every memory she had of her week in paradise.

A smile that, even now when she was totally lost in the boonies, had her squirming in her seat. Darnell drove slowly, looking for something—anything—familiar, but so far all she saw was wilderness. She was so not used to country like this. Empty country. Lots of nature, no people. Maybe around the next turn she'd find a spot to turn the car without falling off a frickin' cliff or running into a mountain. Weaverville wasn't much of a town, at least not compared to LA, but it did have people. And a couple of really nice-looking hotels.

Ah. Wide spot. There. Just ahead. She swung wide, made the turn, and was congratulating herself when the back end of the car shuddered and sort of shifted. She pulled to the side of the road, and as much as she'd hoped to see signs of humanity, this wasn't the best spot to look.

There wasn't enough room to pull over and get entirely off of the road.

She glanced in the rearview mirror and then looked forward and hoped anyone who might be coming her way was paying attention. Parking as far off the asphalt as she could,

Darnell set the brake, got out, and walked around the back of her Honda Civic. She glared at and then kicked the fucking flat tire hard enough to bruise her toes, but damn it all, she'd never changed a tire in her life. You called road service for something like that. She'd be lucky to get a signal on her cell phone out here in the middle of nowhere.

She dug the phone out of her purse and stared at the screen. *No service.* Well, crap.

She kicked the tire again, just because.

Pack alpha Traker Jakes and his pack mate Evan Dark stood in front of the Feral Passions lodge and waved as the last carload of female guests pulled out of the parking lot and headed for the main road. Smiling, waving, the men remained until the car was out of sight.

Trak turned to Evan, shaking his head. "Damn. I thought they'd never leave."

Laughing softly, Evan slapped him on the shoulder. "C'mon. Drew's got Growl opened. How about I buy you a beer?"

"Before lunch?" Trak raised one eyebrow.

"So I buy you a sandwich to go with it."

"That works." The two turned away from the resort. Unfortunately, not fast enough.

"Hey, Trak. I need a minute."

Cain Boudin. Trak sighed and turned. "What's up?"

Cain laughed and glanced toward the road leading to the main highway. "I thought they'd never leave."

At least Trak could agree with Cain on that one.

Cain turned and focused on Trak, lowering his gaze at first, as was befitting a submissive member of the pack.

Cain was damned good at the submissive role, always carefully masking his dominant side. It had taken Trak a long time to accept that Cain honestly wanted nothing more than to be a member of the Trinity Alps pack, not its leader. It wasn't easy, believing an alpha as strong as Cain wasn't going to challenge him at some point. He still didn't quite trust the guy.

"You were talking about wanting a pack meeting," Cain said. "You two up for a lunch meeting at Growl? We don't want to meet at the lodge because Cherry's working, though she said she'd man the phones and forward anything important to you at the bar. Thing is, the guys and I are anxious to find out what's next and Lawz is going to be here for a couple of hours."

Startled, Trak focused on Cain. "What's he doing in town? Isn't he building a bridge somewhere?" Trak's older brother was a successful engineer with a number of projects along the north coast under his belt. He didn't make it back to their home base nearly often enough. As convoluted as their relationship could be, Trak missed the guy. Mostly.

"Darian's got a story she's working on that brought her to Weaverville. He's hanging out down at the bar while she's meeting with some folks in town."

"That's good, then. Really good. It's better to meet when we can get everyone together. Can the rest of the pack be there in half an hour?"

"Sooner, if you like. Brad's already got sandwiches made."

Nodding, Trak turned toward the road. "Evan and I are on our way down there now."

"I'll get the rest of the guys." Cain tipped a salute and headed back to the lodge.

Trak watched him go. Then, shaking his head, he followed Evan toward the bar. One of these days, he really had to start trusting the guy.

Darnell kicked the flat tire on her car one more time, as if that might somehow convince the blasted thing to inflate. She stared at her phone, at the lack of bars and *no service* symbol that hadn't changed since she'd been stuck out here, and figured it was probably all she could expect in this godforsaken wilderness. What in the hell had made her think she could actually find the stupid resort on her own?

Not a single car or pickup truck had passed in over an hour. She glanced at her phone again, grabbed a bottle of water, turned on her emergency blinkers, and hoped no one would run into her car. Then she locked the doors and checked the road as far as she could see in both directions, which wasn't nearly far enough. Sticking her keys in her pocket, she started hiking up the hill that stretched above the car. If she could get above the steep hillside, she might find a signal.

She had the number for Feral Passions, but what if Evan didn't remember her? He'd had plenty of women come through—a new group every single week—all summer long. How the hell had she hoped to stand out?

She'd never been attracted to any man the way she had to Evan. He was a big, solid guy with broad shoulders and some amazing tattoos that absolutely fit his personality. Muscular without being overbuilt, he looked like he could probably lift her car with one hand and change the tire with the other one. But the one thing that had attracted her the most? He made her feel safe. He was protective and gentle, but she knew he would never let anything hurt her.

She'd grown up in East LA. She knew what it was like to be afraid. That was a time she preferred not to dwell on, though the dark memories were always there, lurking.

She preferred her memories of Evan.

He'd filled her dreams day and night. Of course, Evan probably had women calling him all hours of the day or night.

She was such an idiot, coming up here like this, no warning, no invitation. They'd spent a lot of time together that week she was at the resort, but in spite of all the teasing, even a few quite memorable kisses, they'd never taken that next step. Maybe he wasn't serious about wanting her. Maybe it was all part of the Feral Passions promise of a good time.

Maybe she was being a complete idiot and a coward to boot.

She was sucking air by the time she reached the top of the hill, but when she checked her phone she had two bars. So what should she do? Call road service or call Evan? She thought about it just long enough to tap on the number for the resort. She'd put it in her favorites before they left that final day but wondered if she'd ever use it.

This was as good a time as any. As much as her one short week in paradise had cost, someone had damned well better come out here and change her frickin' tire.

"Feral Passions Resort. May I help you?"

Wow. The woman picked up on the first ring. Darnell didn't remember any women employees when she'd stayed there. This one sounded familiar.

"Cherry? Is that you?"

"Yes. Who's calling?"

"Darnell. Darnell Deya. Remember me? I was at the resort the same week you were there."

"Of course I remember. Wow, it's good to hear from you. What's up?"

"Well . . . ya see, that's why I'm calling . . ."

Drew was bartending today, but he put a "Closed" sign up on the bar and the whole pack of them took over the small dining area. It was rare when they were all available to meet like this. Trak took the beer that Drew handed to him and grabbed half a sandwich off the big tray in the center of the table. Last time they'd had a serious meeting, none of these guys had yet found mates. Now all but he and Evan had someone to call their own. In that respect, Feral Passions had been a huge success—the whole point of the resort had been to give their pack of single werewolves a chance to meet women.

Except that Trak and Evan were still unmated and the season was officially over. It was time to figure out where they were going with this.

Trak nodded to Tuck and then to his older brother, Lawz. "We don't often get the two of you to show up at the same time. Glad you could make it." Lawz was usually off on a job somewhere, and Tuck was the only vet covering a large section of the area west of Weaverville, though now with Elle, his new mate and able-bodied assistant, he was able to handle a lot more cases in less time.

Lawz took a sip of his beer and grinned at Trak. "Sorry, little bro, but you can't get a rise out of me today, not when I've got Darian in the same county with me for once. That girl's been following stories up and down the north coast since she took on the news job. I think she's found her true calling. But you, dear brother? You need to find a woman. We going to give this resort business another year?"

Trak laughed. "I really wasn't trying to get a rise out of you, Lawson. I hate to admit it, but I've missed you." Then he shook his head and glanced at Evan. "Might feel differently if I had a woman, but Evan and I are the only two left. Evan, unless you want to give it another shot, I hate to keep everyone tied up with the resort when you and I are the only ones here who couldn't manage to find anyone during an entire season. On the other hand, we've built a really nice little retreat out here, sunk a bunch of money into it. It's got to be good for something. What are your feelings about it?"

Evan merely shrugged. Before he said anything, the phone rang.

Brad answered, listened for a moment, said, "Yeah, babe. He's here." Cupped his palm over the receiver and added, "It's Cherry, Evan. You might want to take it outside." Brad handed the portable phone to him. Then he winked.

Frowning, Evan grabbed the phone, saying hello to Brad and Cain's mate, Cherry, as he walked out of Growl and shut the door behind him.

"Where the hell is Evan going?" Trak stood at the front window, watching as Evan's truck peeled out of the parking lot, headed toward the main road. He'd taken the call far enough from the bar that none of them could hear Cherry's side of the call; then he'd stepped back inside, tossed the phone to Lawz, and was gone before they'd had a chance to ask him what the call was about. Trak turned to his brother and held out his hand. "Let me have the phone."

Lawz tossed it to him. Trak dialed the lodge. Cherry picked it up on the first ring.

"Where's Evan headed?"

"Well, hello to you, too, Mr. Alpha." Cherry laughed.

Trak knew better than to think she was insulting him. He also knew to wait her out. Cherry couldn't not respond. It hadn't taken him long to figure out the girl hated empty air space.

She laughed again and caved. "Okay. I give. Darnell called. Remember her? She was the Hollywood makeup artist who was here the same week I was. She's not all that far from here, stuck on the side of the road with a flat tire. I just sent Evan to the rescue."

"What's she doing up here?" He remembered Darnell. Cute little thing with a wacky sense of humor. Couldn't hold her booze, though.

"I think she's looking for Evan." Cherry laughed again. "Trak, I'll lay you ten to one that you're going to be the last man standing."

"Well, shit." He thanked Cherry—for nothing—and hung up. Handed the phone to Brad and realized everyone was staring at him. With their wolf hearing, they'd obviously heard the entire conversation, but the least he could do was confirm. Shrugging, he said, "It appears that the young woman who came up with the group from Hollywood—remember the makeup artist?—has come in search of Evan."

Cain and Brad high-fived each other. Everyone else was laughing.

Manny stood up, swept one arm out, and made an impressive bow. "All hail to Traker Jakes, the last man standing."

"Eat your lunch," he said, sitting back down at the table, though he couldn't help but smile. If anyone deserved a mate it was Evan. He was a good man with a lot of love to give some lucky woman, but he needed a female willing to run the show, something the guy freely admitted.

Trak had no idea what he needed in a woman. He'd always figured he'd know when the right one came along, but in spite of the dozens of women he'd met after a fully booked season at the resort, not a single one had caught his attention. He took a bite, chewing slowly, but that delicious roast beef sandwich Brad had fixed for him suddenly tasted like dust. He forced another bite and listened while the guys talked, and he got the feeling that the novelty of running a resort had sort of worn off.

A good alpha paid attention to the mood of the pack, and the men had worked their tails off to make the resort a huge success. They all had women of their own now, and if Cherry and Manny were right Evan would soon be with Darnell and Trak quite literally would be the last man standing. There really wasn't any point in continuing with the resort if it was just for him.

Closing down made sense. The resort was a lot of work, and since the guys now had mates, it wasn't nearly as much fun as when they were still looking. Trak had pretty much given up about midway through the summer. He hadn't clicked with any particular woman.

"So, Trak. What do you think?"

Raising his head, he realized everyone was gazing expectantly in his direction. "About what?"

Cain raised his eyebrow. "We're talking about ending the resort business and doing as Zach and Meg suggested, turning Feral Passions into a wedding venue. Weekdays would be mostly free, weekends a bit hectic, but we could offer the cabins for wedding party members and there're enough hotels and motels in the area to take care of overflow. For that alone, you know it would go over well in town."

Trak leaned back in his chair. He actually sort of liked this idea. "Well, we'll get an easy trial run with Zach and Meg's wedding next weekend. Meg hired a wedding planner to handle all the details, including the food. We just need to watch what they do and learn how to do it."

The door to Growl opened as he finished his comment. Cherry stepped into the bar. "Not gonna be all that easy, Trak."

"What happened? You okay, Cherry?" Cain headed across the room to his mate.

It was obvious she was fighting tears. "Meg just called. Their wedding planner took the money and ran, quite literally. She and her boyfriend skipped last week. They didn't show up at a wedding they were supposed to do today in Portland, and Meg said word is they've left the country with deposits for at least a dozen weddings."

"That's horrible." Brad reached Cherry ahead of Cain. He pulled her into his arms as she lost her battle with the tears. She and Meg had gotten to be really close during the week Meg and her friends were here.

"I hope I didn't make things worse." She took the handkerchief Cain grabbed out of his pocket. "I told her we could take care of everything. I know you and Cain can get the food together, but what about flowers? Or someone to help the wedding party get it together?"

Trak caught Tuck's eye. "You go into town more than any of us, Doc. Is there a florist in Weaverville?"

Tuck nodded. "I think there is." He checked his wristwatch. "I've got to go in and check on a patient. Elle and I'll see what we can find."

Evan knew exactly where she'd be. Cherry'd given him the information along with Darnell's cell number, but she said the girl had asked directly for him and, if she was back at the car, probably wouldn't have a signal. Damn. He'd never thought he'd see Nellie again. He didn't even know her last name, and she had no idea he'd always thought of her as Nellie because . . . well, Nellie suited her. Darnell was a city girl name and that was sort of intimidating.

No way in hell could he ever forget her. He'd spent time with a lot of very fine women over the summer, but not one had made an impression on him. Not a single one had made his heart rate soar at the mere mention of her name; none had kept him awake at night, thinking of all the possibilities, if only he'd taken the first step.

Nellie had.

And they'd never once made it to the bedroom. Well, except for the night she decided she really wanted to try a Long Island Iced Tea. He'd immediately given up hopes for some action because the drink had hit her hard and he wasn't like that. No way would he have sex with any woman who wasn't in complete control of herself, but she'd gotten so plastered he'd been afraid to leave her alone.

He'd spent the night on her bed, not in it—on top of the covers, checking on her all night long to make sure she was okay. But now she was here, almost to Feral Passions except for a wrong turn along the way.

Did she have any idea how much he'd thought about her this summer? Everything about Nellie had ruined any other woman for him. There was just something about her, something that warmed his blood and filled an empty spot in his heart, and if he'd been a little more confident, maybe not such a coward about speaking to a beautiful woman, he would have let her know.

Except he wasn't real good at that sort of thing, but Nellie was. She took charge. She'd come all the way from LA, and when she called she'd asked for him. That had to mean something, didn't it?

He took a left, heading out the first road east of the resort. She'd turned too early, and then she'd driven a lot farther than she should have before figuring out she was lost. He hoped she wasn't afraid. These hills could seem really lonely if you weren't used to the wilderness.

CHAPTER 2

Saturday afternoon, Weaverville, California
Chelo adjusted the roses in the arrangement she'd just put together in the front window. She'd only been open a couple of weeks, and already many local businesses in town were displaying her flowers in their stores and hotel lobbies. Of course, bargain prices never hurt, but she'd made certain everyone knew these were introductory prices.

She took her broom and went outside to sweep the walk, mainly so she could look at the sign on the front window. "Chelo's Flower Basket." Maybe not the ritziest name, but better than the one on the last store she'd had. Naming it Los Lobos Flowers had been stupid, like putting up a big arrow for her bastard of a brother-in-law to find her.

She wasn't going back. Never. She'd barely gotten away as it was, but she'd lived with an abusive man for way too many years, and she'd actually rejoiced when he was killed in that bar fight. Until his brother showed up, claiming Chelo as his.

Rube was crazy—crazier even than Jorge had been. No way in hell was she going with him. Not while she drew breath.

"Excuse me. Are you open?"

Chelo spun around with her hand over her heart. She'd been so lost in being pissed off that she hadn't even heard the customer approach. That was dangerous. "I am," she said, laughing.

"I didn't mean to startle you. I'm Elle." She was a large woman and tall—at least six feet to Chelo's five three. She had ebony skin and her long, dark hair, shimmering with burgundy highlights, was caught back in a ponytail. Even in blue jeans, hiking boots, and a gauzy shirt, she looked absolutely regal as she held out her hand.

Chelo wiped hers off on her jeans and shook hands. "It's a pleasure to meet you. I'm . . ." Their hands touched. She raised her head and stared into dark brown eyes with gold flecks. Shivers raced over her skin. "I'm Chelo," she said. "Please. Come inside."

Smiling, Elle followed her into the store.

It took Chelo a moment to catch her breath. "I need to talk to you," she said. Then she locked the door, flipped the sign to "Closed," and led Elle past the cold room she'd just had installed to keep her flowers fresh, to the small office in the back. Once they were both inside, Chelo shut that door as well.

Elle merely smiled, folded her arms across her chest, and waited. Chelo's mouth felt dry. She'd hoped for this day, had moved here in hopes that the rumors she'd heard had been true, but she'd never planned far enough ahead to know how to act once it happened. Her heart pounded in her chest and she knew the woman standing just feet from her could hear every beat.

"It's okay, you know." Elle hitched herself up onto the work counter and sat there, dangling her feet. "I can tell. Can you talk about it?"

Chelo nodded, sucked in a sharp breath, and swallowed back the nervous jitters that had her hands shaking. "You're a shifter, aren't you?"

Grinning broadly, Elle nodded her head. "That I am. And so are you."

Evan spotted the blinking lights and the shiny red Honda as he rounded a sweeping turn. That had to be the red car Cherry had told him to look for. A long hill sloped down to the right, a fairly steep hillside went up to his left, but as he drove slowly by the car, looking for a place to turn his truck, there was no sign of his Nellie.

He had to go almost a quarter mile before he found a spot wide enough to turn his big Chevy pickup. He liked the club cab when he wanted to take the guys somewhere, but it was a pain in the butt when he had to make a U-turn. He finally got the truck turned around and pulled up behind the little red Honda. Yep . . . right rear tire. He wondered if Nellie would think he was funny if he pointed out it was only flat on the bottom.

He got out and immediately picked up her scent, but he didn't see her nearby. "Darnell? Where are you?" What if she'd gotten a ride into town with someone? She shouldn't be too far—she'd only called about half an hour ago. He heard a sound on the hillside above him and she was right there, coming down the steep hill with a big smile on her face.

She waved, took a step, and her foot went out from under her. Evan was in motion before her butt hit the dirt. He leapt over the front of the car and hit the hillside a good ten feet beyond, landing about six feet from Darnell, who stared at him like he was some kind of monster. Ignore it, he thought. If I just ignore it she'll think her eyes were playing tricks on her.

"Evan?" Wide-eyed, she stared at him.

Before she could ask, he shot her a big grin. "Are you okay?"

She nodded, still staring.

"Well, let's get down there so you can unlock the car. Your spare should be in the trunk."

He'd helped her down to the asphalt before she turned to him with a stricken look on her face. "'Should' being the operative word," she said. "Damn it. I'm sorry, Evan. I don't think the spare is in there."

"I can't believe you made that long trip without a spare tire." At least he was laughing.

"I remembered my suitcase. Does that count? And my makeup supplies. I never go anywhere without them. You never know when a job opportunity might arise." She gave him a cheeky grin that she really wished he'd kiss right off her face, but they hadn't gotten that far. Yet. He'd hardly touched her.

"Actually," he drawled, "you almost forgot to get your stuff out of the car before we left."

"Don't remind me." Then she laughed. "You must feel like my babysitter by now."

He leered. At least she thought it looked like a leer. "Not even close."

She gave a soft whimper and leaned a little closer, but the cab of this blasted truck was just too wide for him to take advantage of the opening she gave him.

They were almost to the road to Feral Passions. Evan had told her he'd call for a tow truck once he got a decent signal, which he'd done, and they'd already met the tow truck driver at the main road to give the keys to him so he could haul the car into town and fix the flat.

Darnell glanced at Evan out of the corner of her eye. She was usually so levelheaded. She never did stupid shit like this, but she sighed and admitted it. "I totally forgot the spare and I feel like an idiot. I hauled some stuff for my neighbor and needed the room. The spare's in the garage back home."

She expected him to say something about how stupid she was, but instead he smiled at her. She loved his smile. She hadn't quit thinking about that smile ever since she'd last seen him, and that had been over four months ago.

"Don't worry about it. I'm just glad that if you had to have a flat, it happened up here."

She watched him, and Darnell could have sworn he was blushing, but . . .

"I'm glad you're here, Darnell." He shot a quick glance her way. "You left so suddenly that last morning, I never got to say good-bye to you, though I can understand your not wanting to hang around."

"That's an understatement." As much as she hated to remember that horrible morning, there was no avoiding it. The woman who had organized the week at the resort for Darnell and one other friend had turned out to be an absolute bitch. The last night of their vacation, she'd made some cruel comments about Cherry and her weight that Cherry had, unfortunately, heard. Humiliated, Cherry had sneaked out of the resort before anyone was up, taking her sister and her sister's girlfriend with her.

Darnell sighed. "I felt just awful when I found out what Fred said about Cherry. I've wished ever since that I could apologize to her. That was so cruel and she's one of the nicest people I've ever met."

"She is. You'll see her once we get to the resort."

"I know! I couldn't believe it when she answered the phone. I thought she sounded familiar, but I was still shocked when she said it was her. All I was thinking about was asking if you were available."

Evan gave her a quick grin.

"Available to come help me, Evan." She bit back a laugh when he sighed and turned his attention back to the road. "What's Cherry doing here?"

"Brad and Cain weren't playing her, like Fred told everyone. They love her. After she left so suddenly and we found out what happened, the guys went to San Francisco and brought her back to the resort. She's with them, now."

"You're kidding! That's so cool about Cherry." She shrugged. Wondered what might have happened if she'd stayed on . . . or at least had said something.

Evan merely laughed. "There've been a lot of changes since you were here. More new faces, all female. You'll meet them once we're there."

Wow. She wasn't sure how to take that. Had more women gone after their guys? If so, at least now she didn't feel nearly as weird about pursuing Evan, even if it had taken her all summer to work up the nerve to make this trip.

Mainly she just felt stupid for waiting so long, and she really wished the front seat of his truck weren't so honkin' wide. He might as well be in another room.

He slowed the truck for the narrow road that led through the woods to the resort, and it was even prettier than Darnell remembered. She glanced at Evan and wondered if he was the reason the view was improved. There was something about him—his manner, the way he watched her. He made her feel safe, as if nothing anywhere could hurt her, that bad things could never touch her.

She'd felt that way when she'd been at the resort. Felt safe with him. Probably the reason she'd gotten stupid drunk, because she knew it would be okay if she was with Evan. She'd trusted him to watch over her.

Growing up in a rough neighborhood had taught her at a very young age that bad things could happen to anyone. Could happen so unexpectedly that only the strong or the quick survived. Or the ones who had a strong person watching over them. She'd been on her own, but at least she'd been quicker than most. She'd lost some friends and the memories hurt.

Evan carefully negotiated the narrow hard-packed road running through a forest of cedar and pine and the occasional oak, driving with his right arm over the steering wheel, his left resting on the open window frame.

Every once in a while he'd sneak a look at her and grin. "I'm thinking of all that's changed since you were here," he said. "It's been a lot. A bunch of the guys went into the summer single, and most of them are paired up. Sort of like *The Love Boat* on steroids."

She laughed. "I didn't think anyone remembered that old show, but it sounds like Feral Passions has been a busy place. Is it something in the water?"

Evan laughed. "Might be. You never know."

Darnell laughed, but honestly, her heart wasn't in it. She studied Evan a moment, and an icy flash of fear sent chills down her back. What if . . . ? She glanced at his ring finger. "What about you? Have you found someone special?"

He stared at her for a long time before smiling that lazy, sexy smile of his. "I sure hope so, darlin'. And I am so glad you're finally here."

What did a girl say to something like that? Smiling like an absolute fool, Darnell watched the road ahead and forgot all about her car and flat tire, somewhere with a mechanic in Weaverville.

Elle's tea had grown cold while she sat in Chelo's small office and listened to her horrifying tale. Tuck had called about an hour ago and Elle had sent him off to his next appointment, said she was busy talking flowers with the proprietor.

Chelo hadn't mentioned so much as a rose. Instead, she'd told a story that Tuck was going to have to hear. Tuck and Traker Jakes, because Chelo was going to need the pack's protection whether she wanted it or not.

Elle was certain Chelo wanted it. It wasn't healthy for a shifter to live alone. Rogues were rarely successful, and Elle had never heard of a female rogue. Once mated, pairs generally stayed together for the remainder of their very long lives.

Elle was surprised Chelo had stayed with her bastard of a mate as long as she had.

"I'm going to need to call my mate," she said. "I want him to come here and meet you, but then I want you to come with us out to the resort. My pack has a vacation resort called Feral Passions. It's a long story why the guys built it, but we're in the process of turning it into a venue for weddings. That's why I came here—to talk to you about doing flowers for a wedding Sunday after next, if you're up to it. We have a couple of really good human friends who want to have their wedding at the Feral Passions Resort."

"A wedding? I would love the chance." She paused, took a deep breath. "You have human friends? They know about us?"

"They do, but it's an unusual situation. I'll explain it on the way out to the resort."

Chelo nodded, but she looked apprehensive. "Okay. But why do you want me to come with you?"

Elle knew she had every reason in the world to be afraid. "I'm still new to the pack," Elle said, "but I'm learning a lot of their protocols. You should check in with our alpha, let him know you're here, but most of all, I want him to hear your story in your own words. It's not my place to tell him. Are you willing to do that? Trak, our alpha, is a good man. He's honest, and most important, a very gentle, compassionate man. We're nothing like your old pack. Not at all."

Chelo stared at Elle for what felt like a long time, but then she nodded. "I'm essentially through for the day. Let me turn on my answering machine and put the displays back in the cold room."

"Good. I'm going to call my mate. Tuck's amazing, but I'm guessing you're not real comfortable around large men. My guy is huge, but he's gentle as a lamb. Quite literally. He's a veterinarian and his patients—and their owners—love him."

Chelo nodded, though she still didn't look convinced, but she went about closing down the shop. Elle called Tuck, and when he answered she laughed. When Chelo came back into the office, she caught Elle heading out to the showroom. "He's outside. Been sitting in the truck waiting for me. He'd already scented you and knew I was with a shifter, so it's been driving him nuts. I figure that's a good thing to do to my man every once in a while."

She waited while Chelo locked up the shop. Tuck was leaning against the hood of his pickup but pushed away from the truck and walked across the road to meet them. He winked at Chelo and then grabbed Elle up in a very hot hug and a kiss.

It always happened this way when she and Tuck had been parted for even a brief time, though not usually in front of someone who was essentially a stranger. Blushing furiously, Elle finally broke the kiss. When she glanced at Chelo, the other woman was smiling.

"That's the way it's supposed to be, right?" Holding out her hand, she shook Tuck's big mitt. Her fingers disappeared in his grasp. "I'm Consuela de los Lobos. It's very nice to meet you. Please, call me Chelo."

"It's a pleasure to meet you, Chelo." He glanced at Elle, and she nodded. They'd only been mated a short time, but already it was as if they read each other's minds. "Are you able to come out to Feral Passions with us now? And don't worry, one of us will give you a ride home."

"I guess now's as good a time as any."

Chelo didn't sound all that certain she believed what she was saying, but then Tuck smiled at her, and Elle wanted to hug the big man when he laughed. "Don't worry, Chelo. I know it's got to be scary, coming into a strange pack's territory, meeting the alpha and the rest of us, but it's a good pack, and I know they're going to be really excited to meet you."

Opening the back door on the club-cab pickup, he cleared some boxes and a cat carrier off the backseat, brushed the leather seat to make sure the dust and papers were cleared away, and then helped Chelo into the cab. "Sorry," he said with a quick glance at Elle. "Elle's always telling me my housekeeping is impossible. I don't think she means it as a compliment."

"I don't," Elle said, climbing into the front passenger seat. She fastened her seat belt but turned around to look at Chelo as Tuck pulled away. "But you have other redeeming qualities so I plan to keep you, anyway. If it's okay with you, Chelo, I want to call the pack office and let them know we're coming in with a shifter. This isn't something you want to spring on the guys, but it's merely a formality. We'll bring you back after you meet everyone, or I'm sure we can find a place for you to spend the night if you want to stay."

Chelo looked a bit dazed. Blinking rapidly, she nodded. "Thank you. I apologize if I seem a bit out of it, but this is more than I'd hoped, to meet other shifters somewhere, to have the chance to plead my case and not immediately be run out of their territory. Or worse."

Tuck glanced over his shoulder after he pulled onto the main road. "I can guarantee that's not going to happen. We're a small pack, but we look out for each other. We've managed to avoid a lot of the issues that bedevil other packs. Strong leadership is the reason. You'll like Trak. He's one of the best."

Trak scooted his chair into the shade on the deck and looked over the paperwork Cherry'd dropped on the table in front of him. She'd been such a find—the girl was a whiz on the computer and seemed to grasp everything about how to successfully run and promote a business like Feral Passions. She'd already put together plans for a new Web site should they decide that the wedding destination concept was the direction they wanted to take.

Plus, she kept both Brad and Cain smiling all the time, something any alpha enjoyed seeing in his pack. The phone rang inside the lodge. He waited to see if Cherry would take the call and relaxed when she did. But a moment later she was standing out here on the deck, handing the phone to him.

"It's Elle," she said, but she was smiling, so it couldn't be anything too bad.

He held the phone to his ear. "Trak here. What's up?"

"Tuck and I are coming in with a female shifter who's left the Rainy Lake pack from northern Minnesota. Just wanted to let you know we'll be there in about fifteen minutes."

His heart actually seemed to skip a beat. Women never left packs. What could have sent her here? Was she leaving her mate? Running away from a bad situation? He didn't know much about the Rainy Lake pack. They summered on the Canadian side of the border, came south to an area southeast of International Falls in the winter. A tough breed of wolves who clung to the old ways, from what he'd been told. He wasn't really sure—he'd never met any of them.

Well, he was about to.

"Excellent," he said, hoping he wasn't making a mistake. He'd have to trust Tuck and Elle on this one. "Please tell her she has my permission to enter pack territory."

"Will do. See you in a bit."

He got up to take the phone back inside to Cherry. Both

Brad and Cain were in her office, and the three of them were laughing when he handed the phone over.

Cherry took it and set the thing back in its cradle. Then all three of them stared at him.

"What?" he said, folding his arms across his chest.

Cherry laughed. "We heard your conversation, you know. It sounds as if it's a female shifter we're waiting on. I'm just wondering if I'm going to have to take back my 'last man standing' comment."

This he could handle. Trak merely shrugged, as if he hadn't already had the same thought himself, though he'd never admit it. "As Cain can tell you, whenever any wolf leaves their pack there's some kind of trauma involved. We don't know anything about this woman, why she's a rogue, how long she's been on her own, what the circumstances are that brought her here. Once we find out, see what she's like and if she wants to stay, what she'll need to help her assimilate into our pack, then you can start teasing me. But not until, okay? I don't want to do anything to add stress to a woman who's already in a stressful situation."

Cain hugged Cherry close. "Trak's right. When I joined this pack, I was literally at the end of my rope. Trak made it work, when I'm sure a lot of the guys would rather have had me just go away."

Trak laughed. "Including me, more often than not." And there were still days, but . . . "The thing is, Cain, when someone saves your life, it's really poor manners to treat him like a pariah."

Cain's green eyes twinkled. "There is that." He glanced toward the door. "Is that them already?"

Trak spun around. "Shouldn't be. Nope. Looks like Evan's truck. Crap. He's got Darnell, and she has no idea what we are. Make sure none of you slip. Pass the word. Cherry? Call Elle and warn them. I forgot to say anything. And if Darnell is still here when the wedding happens, we're going to have to have a talk with Meg and Zach, too."

As he walked back outside to meet Evan and Darnell, Trak heard Cain's soft comment to Brad. "It looks like things are going to get a lot more complicated at Feral Passions this week."

Chuckling, Trak held his arms out for a hug from Darnell. Cain was right, but one thing he'd learned about this resort. At Feral Passions, nothing was ever boring.

CHAPTER 3

They'd gotten word out to the entire pack just in time. Trak heard Tuck's big truck coming up the drive and glanced at the group up on the deck. It didn't take long for Trak's pack to come up with a reason for a party, especially since the women had joined. The end of a successful season in the resort business plus Darnell showing up were both good reasons to break out the margaritas and munchies. Christa and Steph, Cherry's sister and her girlfriend, had just arrived but already had drinks in hand. Cain had a towel around his waist, playing the proper bartender and pouring refills for Darnell and Cherry. Jules had walked down to Growl to get Drew, Manny, and Lawz.

And Evan? Well, Evan looked as if he'd finally found his slice of heaven in a cute little Hollywood makeup artist who seemed awfully comfortable—not only with Evan but also with the folks who'd shown up to greet her. She already knew most of them, and there wasn't a shy bone in her body, as far as he could tell. But the best part? Evan.

Evan had a blissed-out expression on his face, sitting beside Darnell, his beer untouched, his smile unwavering.

Trak envied him. He wasn't sure if he was looking forward to the next few hours or dreading it. A rogue female wolf. He'd never heard of such a thing, but he trusted Elle and Tuck. He'd decided to close the bar, since the party was obviously here at the lodge, and figured Growl would be the best place to have a talk with the woman. Consuela de los Lobos. He'd had Cherry do a quick search for her, but she hadn't had time to go very deep. There'd possibly been a flower shop in Washington State, but they'd find more out once she arrived.

He was definitely curious to hear her story, and a little apprehensive as well.

He couldn't let any of the guys pick up on that—alphas were never supposed to show any weakness, though his pack had certainly rallied round when he'd been recovering from that bullet wound. Still, the last time he'd brought a new member into the pack, it had been Cain Boudin. For many years, that had not gone well. He remembered it like it was yesterday, even though it happened back in 1948, shortly after Cain got out of the military. He'd served honorably with the U.S. Army in Europe during World War II, but Cain wasn't welcome back to his home pack where he'd challenged his alpha when he'd still been a cocky young man with more balls than brains.

The alpha had graciously spared Cain's life with the caveat that he get the hell out of Idaho and never come back. The army took Cain first and then Trak had taken him in, but he and Cain had never gotten along well, something that only Cain, and possibly Brad, understood.

Cain was an alpha. A much stronger alpha than Trak, who had feared for years that one day the younger wolf would challenge him and most likely win. Instead, Cain had saved his life this summer when Trak was shot by poachers. And finally, in that single selfless act, Cain had convinced

Trak that what he'd been saying all along was true—he might be a powerful alpha, but all he wanted was a home with Brad Martin, the man he loved, and the woman they both adored and shared as their mate.

Trak hoped this rogue wouldn't be as big a pain in the ass as Cain still managed to be, though at least he didn't drive Trak batshit crazy the way he had for so many years. In a way, it was nice to have the understanding they now had, though it was hard to break the habit of blaming Cain for everything.

Trak was going to have to think about that for a while, but right now he needed to walk out and meet a woman with the potential to become another new member of their pack.

Chelo sat in the truck as Tuck and Elle climbed out, but she waited. Waited and watched the man coming down the steps from the deck that surrounded a beautiful lodge, walking with the easy, sexy swagger of an alpha in his prime. He was absolutely beautiful. Even at this distance she felt his power, felt the alpha strength of him merely sitting here, inside the truck, so scared of what could happen that her knees were knocking.

She remembered a young man coming to their alpha, asking for sanctuary. It was a right that every rogue had, to go to a pack alpha, immune to injury while they asked for permission to stay as part of the pack. The rules were that you could not be harmed, that you had the freedom to leave should you not be welcome.

Jorge, her mate, his brother Rube, and their alpha had torn the poor kid limb from limb. She'd had to stand there,

her knuckles jammed in her mouth to keep from screaming as they killed without mercy, turning his death into
blood sport while the women and their young watched.

She was almost sure that wouldn't happen to her, but
she couldn't get that horrifying visual out of her head. Then
Elle reached for the door handle, opened the door, and Tuck
held out a hand to help her down. Trembling, Chelo took
his hand and stepped carefully out of the truck.

They were all such large men, these shifters. The men
of her pack were big, though not as tall. Broader in the
shoulder, thicker bodied—brutes, every single one. Even
Tuck, for all his size, was a handsome man. There was nothing brutish about him.

Neither was there anything brutish about the one who
was their alpha. He was absolutely gorgeous. Refined, almost regal looking. She'd never seen a man like him, standing there smiling at her, as if waiting to see what she would
say. Except she couldn't say anything. It was as if her jaws
were locked.

Thankfully, Elle seemed to realize something was wrong.
Smiling, she took Chelo's icy hand and rubbed it between
her warm palms. "Trak, I want you to meet Consuela de los
Lobos. She wants us to call her Chelo."

Trak held out his hand. He was smiling; his dark eyes
actually seemed to reflect his humor. Trembling, Chelo
slipped her fingers into his hand, and the oddest thing
happened.

Her trembling stopped. Immediately.

"Welcome, Chelo." He glanced at Elle. "Darnell arrived
just ahead of you folks, and the party is already rolling. I
thought maybe I'd introduce Chelo to the group and then
we can go down to Growl where it's quiet." Gently, he tugged

her around to his side. "Chelo, the young African-American woman at the left end of the table is human. She has no idea who or what we are, so please be circumspect whenever you interact with her."

Elle laughed. "From the look on Evan's face, I don't imagine Darnell's going to be human much longer."

"I have a feeling you're right." Trak grinned. He had a beautiful smile. "Lucky bastard."

Chelo wasn't sure what he meant by that, but Trak was still holding her hand. She couldn't take her eyes off their clasped fingers. His grasp was strong, but so gentle. She couldn't recall any gentleness. Not since she'd been kidnapped by the man who raped and then mated her back in 1930.

"Elle and I are going to head on down," Tuck said. "I could really use a cup of coffee."

"Sounds good. Get a pot going. Chelo and I will be there in a couple minutes."

Tuck waved and, taking Elle by the hand, walked back the way they'd driven in. Chelo watched them go, envious of the obvious bond they shared. She'd never seen that. At least not among any of the shifters she'd known.

"C'mon. They won't bite." Trak tugged gently, adding softly, "And neither will I."

Chelo followed him up the stairs. She was so relieved that he didn't let go of her hand, so afraid she'd start trembling all over again, and she didn't want to do that. She was tired of being afraid.

"Everyone. Heads up. I want you all to meet Chelo. She's a florist in Weaverville and we're hoping she'll do the flowers for Meg and Zach's wedding next week. Chelo, you'll get to know all these reprobates before too long. They're basically harmless." He named off everyone at the table, though Chelo knew she'd never remember all their names, but they were all smiling and so nice she wasn't sure how to behave.

She hoped she said all the right things, but she was really nervous. She didn't know how to act anymore around decent people. Would she ever have a normal life again? She glanced at the alpha. He smiled back at her and tugged her hand, said good-bye to the ones at the table.

Then, still holding her hand, he led her down the stairs and back down the road she, Tuck, and Elle had just driven in on.

She felt so relieved, she had to remember to breathe.

This was nothing like the Rainy Lake pack. Nothing at all.

Chelo wanted to stay. She wanted to stay so badly she was ready to beg for the privilege.

Evan watched Trak head down to Growl with the little shifter in tow. He'd been absolutely shocked when Trak introduced her as the florist. Obviously the man knew she was a shifter, but with Darnell sitting here sipping on her margarita it wasn't like he could announce it to them.

Evan wished he knew her story. She seemed like such a timid little thing, and she had to be rogue to be here in their territory without a pack. Trak would let them know when he could. That was one thing about this pack. They really were more of a democracy. Unusual among werewolf packs. Generally the alpha was the supreme commander of his pack. He wielded the power of life or death over each of the members.

Trak wasn't like that, thank goodness.

Darnell's fingers wrapped around Evan's wrist and she leaned close to whisper something. He tuned out the others at the table. "Cherry asked me if I wanted to stay in one of the cabins."

She glanced away, like she was checking to make sure no one was listening. Evan wasn't about to tell her that with their werewolf hearing she might as well have been using a megaphone. "I'm probably being pushy, but I was really hoping to stay with you."

He nuzzled the soft skin just under her ear and wished he'd kissed her earlier when he'd had the chance. Having her this close to him, breathing in her scent with every breath he took, was killing him. "Since I'm really hoping you'll stay with me, I figure we've got that covered. My cabin's not far from Growl. We'll take the truck down later tonight, so you don't have to unpack your stuff until we get settled. You okay with that?"

Darnell nodded, but her stomach actually clenched. She'd known from the first moment she saw him out by her car that she'd be in Evan's bed tonight. Wasn't that what she'd wanted all along?

Hell, yes! She'd wanted it badly enough to blow off a decent contract for an upcoming film, pack her suitcase, stop the mail, and leave town. She'd never done anything like this in her life, but she had to know. There was something about Evan, something that hadn't let her forget him. Something that, even now, merely sitting beside him, had her more aroused than she could recall. She'd fantasized about him every day, every night, since the first time she saw him.

The time to second-guess herself was over.

Trak tried to remember the last time he'd walked along a country road holding a girl's hand. Maybe he never had, but for whatever reason, Chelo's small hand in his much larger one was the most erotic experience he could recall. She'd been trembling—obviously terrified—when he first took her hand back by the lodge. Within seconds, the trembling had ceased.

He wasn't about to let go of her now. It appeared Brad knew what he was talking about. They'd all teased Brad when he said he knew that Cherry was going to be his the very first time he saw her, shortly after she and her sister and girlfriend had pulled into the parking lot in front of the lodge.

Trak hadn't believed, either, but now, walking to the bar with Chelo's hand in his, he had the most powerful sense of destiny he'd ever felt. Chelo was his. She didn't know it yet, but that only added to the challenge.

She was nothing like the women he was usually attracted to. Barely five three, with long, dark hair and skin a dark golden shade of honey, she was round and soft, with full breasts and hips. In a lot of ways she reminded him of Cherry with her full figure and nipped-in waist. She certainly did amazing things to a pair of black yoga pants and a dark green knit top.

They were almost to Growl when she paused and, still holding his hand, met his curious gaze. He was surprised at how easily she met his eyes. Most of the guys still subtly averted their eyes from his direct glance, but only a female who was a very strong alpha could look him eye to eye.

"You okay?" he asked. Obviously not. She looked nervous. Afraid even. But she didn't avert her eyes, didn't back down.

It was good to know there was a backbone in there!

"What are we going to do at Growl? That's the pack's bar where we're going, right? We drove past it."

He smiled. Tried his best to look reassuring, because if anyone ever looked as if they needed reassurance it was Chelo. "Yes. Actually, it's mine, but the guys think they own it." He laughed. "It's not worth the argument. Anyway, we're going there because Elle said I need to hear your story from you directly and there's no privacy at the lodge, not with everyone on the deck having drinks. I thought it would be more comfortable for you. She and Tuck will be there as your advocates. Witnesses to what you say, pack members who want you to feel safe. Are you okay with that? If you'd rather tell me in private, I'm fine with that. And no matter what you say, none of what we discuss will leave the room."

She closed her eyes and sighed. "Thank you. I feel so stupid, but one time when a young male rogue showed up in my old pack's territory they didn't give him a chance to ask for asylum. The alpha led a couple of other guys against him and they just tore the boy to pieces in front of all of us. It was a long time ago, but I still hear his screams, still have nightmares."

There were no words. Trak stood there, trying to figure out what kind of hell this poor woman had lived through. Finally, he cleared his throat, took a deep breath. Let it out. "I honestly don't know how to respond, except to say that would never, *never*," he emphasized, "happen here. I may be the alpha, but we're a team more than a pack. I'm captain of that team, but I'm not omnipotent and these guys always let me know if I've screwed up."

He winked and smiled at her, hoping to help her relax. "Of course, that never happens."

She nodded, and he felt it like a punch to the gut when she smiled and said, "Obviously."

He tugged and they started walking again. "Well, it sounds good in theory, don't you think?"

She was actually laughing when he shoved open the door to Growl and the two of them stepped into the dark little bar. This had been their gathering place for almost a hundred years, updated now with electricity and a decent refrigerator, though the wood-burning stove in the corner still provided heat in the winter.

It was home, as far as Trak was concerned. This was where they'd always handled pack business, a place where they could relax and forget who was the alpha, which one of them was the pack enforcer, a job Cain had held without any problem at all for almost seventy years. Trak's mind kept going back to Cain, to the guy he'd treated badly for so long, and he hated to admit that Cain had been the better man, not merely the stronger wolf.

Trak owed him. A lot of the nature of the Trinity Alps pack was due to Cain's even hand whenever things got dicey. Which they did, on occasion, though now, with most of the guys mated, Trak had noticed a definite sense of calm that hadn't been here before.

"Hey, Chelo." Elle was standing behind the bar with the blender on the counter and a bottle of tequila beside it. "You want coffee or a margarita? Tuck's the caffeine addict, but those drinks the girls were having sure looked good."

Chelo glanced at Trak. He squeezed her hand. "You don't need my permission. I'm guessing you're at least twenty-one."

She giggled and slapped a hand over her mouth. "I was born in 1903. Guess that makes me old enough." She turned to Elle. "I would love a margarita. I've never had one before."

Elle just shook her head. "Every time one of you old-timers mentions your birth date, it purely blows my mind, but not nearly as much as hearing you've never had a margarita."

The whir of the blender crunching up ice drowned out everything for a few seconds.

"Trak?" Tuck walked out of the tiny kitchen in back with a plate filled with sandwiches. "I've got a pot of coffee on, but I hear a beer calling your name."

"Good hearing. That sounds better than coffee. I don't know how you drink that stuff all day. I'd still be wide-awake at three in the morning." He pulled a chair out for Chelo and she sat at the round table, but he'd been fully aware of her watching them, the way they interacted. As if they were all some breed of exotic creatures. Feeling overly protective, he took the seat beside her. Tuck set the sandwiches on the table, grabbed the beer Elle handed across the bar to him, and gave it to Trak.

Elle brought over two margaritas and placed one in front of Chelo with a flourish and then grabbed the coffee she'd poured for Tuck.

"I know it's late for lunch," Tuck said, "but Brad left these here for us in case we went into the dinner hour. And you know me. I'm always hungry."

Elle patted his hand. "S'okay. You're a big boy." She kissed his cheek and Tuck blushed. Trak glanced at Chelo and wanted to take her hand again. She looked so terribly sad, he almost hated to ask her why she'd left her pack.

He honestly wasn't sure he was strong enough to ask her to relive what must have been a horrible experience.

She took a sip of the margarita, though, and her eyes lit up. "That's really good." She took another big swallow.

Smiling broadly, Elle put her hand on Chelo's wrist. "Take it slow. If you've never had one, they pack a punch."

"Yeah," Trak said. "Elle's sneaky. She puts a slice of lime in it and salt around the rim to make you think you're drinking something good for you, but we all know better."

This time Chelo sipped. "Thank you for the warning. Passing out in your bar probably isn't the way to make a good first impression."

Trak handed half a turkey sandwich to her. "Eat this. It'll soak up the alcohol."

Nodding sagely, she took a bite of the sandwich and a much smaller sip of her drink.

Darnell covered her mouth to hide the third yawn in the past ten minutes. They'd been sitting out here on the deck for a couple of hours, the sun was still high in the sky, but she'd had a long drive, a lot of exhausting emotions bubbling in her bod, and at least one too many margaritas. She definitely didn't want to pass out—again—on this, her first real night with Evan.

Leaning against his shoulder, she looked up at him, at the strong jaw shaded with a healthy five o'clock shadow and the dark tuft under his full lower lip. His dark blond hair was always tousled, his gray eyes surprisingly intense despite his laid-back mannerisms.

He hid a surprising intelligence and a wry sense of humor beneath that "aw shucks" persona he played to the hilt. She wondered why. Hoped she'd have enough time with him to find out. Wondered what he'd say if she told him she wanted a lifetime with him.

He glanced at her and smiled, leaned close, and kissed her very gently. "You look ready to fold. Want to go to the cabin, get settled?" He wiggled his eyebrows. "I can promise clean sheets on the bed."

She stared at him for a long moment. Pictured him naked and had to shut her eyes or moan out loud. "Sounds perfect, but I definitely need a shower. I probably stink."

He nuzzled her hair. "Actually, no. You don't stink at all. You smell like limes."

Laughing, she stood and pulled him to his feet. "That's the lime in my margarita, big guy. C'mon, before you have to carry me."

He let her tug him to his feet. "Been there, done that. You weren't much fun, but you sure sleep cute."

Smiling, she waved to the rest of the group but turned away, ignoring Evan, and stomped down the stairs. When he caught up to her, she turned and glared at him. It was hard not to laugh. "Would you consider never reminding me of that again? My most humiliating night ever?"

He scooped her up and slung her over his shoulder. She squeaked but managed not to scream. "Maybe. If you give me another visual to replace that one."

Darnell planted her hands on his back and raised her head. "Isn't anyone gonna rescue me?"

"You?" Cain stood at the railing, laughing. "And here I was worried about Evan."

CHAPTER 4

Chelo finished her sandwich and carefully wiped her lips. She took another small sip of the drink Elle had fixed for her. She'd been careful not to drink too much of it too fast, but she appreciated the calming effect of just a little alcohol.

She wasn't holding Trak's hand any longer, but her hands had stopped shaking. She glanced at him, tilting her head, catching his profile in her peripheral vision. He was talking to Elle, something about a wolf cub one of the men had raised when the mother was killed, how she was now a mother herself.

It was like Chelo had moved to another planet. One where people were good to one another, where no one was afraid.

She'd forgotten what it felt like, to live without fear.

"Chelo?"

She sucked in a quick breath. Trak was looking at her. Smiling, though. At least he was smiling. "What?"

"What's your story? Why is a lovely young woman like yourself a rogue? Can you tell us?"

She nodded. "I can. I told Elle earlier and she said I would need to tell you why I'm here. Why I'm never going back to the Rainy Lake pack."

"No one is going to make you go anywhere. I know it's not easy, but please. Trust us."

"I do, but it's a strange feeling. I haven't felt as if I could trust anyone since I was taken. I was born in 1903 in a little village on the Canadian side of the border. My father had emigrated from Spain; my mother was mostly Minnesota Chippewa. She was raised in a farming community and moved to Canada when she married my father. She didn't speak about her childhood much, but she and my father were good parents. I met a Frenchman when I was in my midtwenties; we fell in love and we were married in 1929. I had just turned twenty-six." She smiled at Elle. "I was already considered an old maid, but I was picky, and Henri Fournier was very handsome."

She glanced away when she felt her eyes prickling with tears. After a moment she took a deep breath and gathered what composure she could. This was so hard to tell. The telling brought it back, made it hurt as if it happened yesterday. "I was pregnant with our first child, not very far along, when the wolves came. There were two of them. They attacked Henri in the yard and he was dead before I knew we were even in danger. They broke into the house and I ran for the loft. I figured they couldn't come up the ladder, but they turned into men and caught me. I thought they were monsters. I was right. They were."

Trak handed her a clean handkerchief. She hadn't realized the tears were already flowing, but she wiped her eyes. Barely whispering now, so caught up in those horrific memories, she went on. She spoke in a monotone. That was the only way to get the words out. It was almost as painful as when Jorge was beating her—telling these nice people just how awful it had been.

"They took me away. The bigger one threw me over his shoulder and ran into the forest. They never seemed to grow tired, but the pain was horrible and I knew I was losing the baby. I screamed at them. I screamed at God. They laughed."

She paused, took a deep breath, and whispered, "I think God wept." Pausing again, she gathered her thoughts and moved forward. She had to tell her story. It was time. Maybe now she would finally find help.

"I must have passed out, because the next thing I remember was waking up in a cave. There was a fire burning and the men were arguing. They were drunk and I remember the stench of their unwashed bodies. There was so much blood. I knew then my baby had died. When the men realized I was awake, they took turns raping me. By then it didn't matter. I only wanted to die."

Elle's arms wrapped around her, pulled her close, and snuggled her against her big breasts as if she were nothing more than a babe. Chelo hadn't even been aware of Elle getting up and walking around the table, of taking the chair beside her. Trak had hold of her hand once again, and Tuck? Big, strong Tuck sat across from her, openly weeping.

For whatever reason, his tears made her strong. She sat up. "Thank you. I can do this," she said. Elle smiled and nodded encouragement when Chelo moved away from her embrace, but Chelo didn't let go of Trak's hand. "I passed out at some point, and the men must have fought again, because the one who became my brother-in-law was lying against a wall of the cave, his arm broken. His name is Rube. The one who mated me, Jorge, turned into a wolf again and I thought he was going to kill me. He bit me and the pain was excruciating. Once again I fell unconscious. When I awoke, I was like you. I could become a wolf. My injuries had healed, and I felt strong, healthier than I could remember.

"I ran away. Jorge caught me and beat me, but he didn't kill me. I ran away again, and again, but each time he was able to find me. Each time he beat me. He knew just how many bones he could break, how much he could hurt me without killing me. That went on until a little over ten years ago when he was killed in a bar fight in Minnesota. His brother was badly hurt, and that time when I ran no one came after me. I ended up in Washington State, where I opened a flower shop, but I was stupid and used my maiden name." She took a deep breath, let it out. "Rube found me. I barely got away."

"Rube? Your dead mate's brother?" Trak held her hands in both of his and his gaze was hypnotic. She wanted to fall into those dark eyes, into depths filled with compassion.

"He said that I was supposed to be his mate the night they took me, that Jorge changed his mind and beat him up when he was sleeping off the booze, but now that his brother was dead, Rube wanted me. He wants to breed me. I told him I don't think I can have babies anymore. After my baby died, I didn't get pregnant again." She shrugged. "Maybe I did, but if so, the constant beatings must have ended the pregnancies. Rube is even worse than Jorge. I will kill myself before I let him take me."

"If he comes for you, I will kill him myself." Trak stood, still holding on to Chelo's hand. "Tuck? Elle? Will you bear witness?"

"Damn right." Tuck was on his feet immediately.

"Of course."

Confused, Chelo watched as both of them stood beside her.

"Kentucky Jones, Elle Marcel? As members in good standing of the Trinity Alps pack, will you act as sponsors for one Consuela de los Lobos, rogue wolf, once a member of the Rainy Lake pack, now offered provisional entrance into the Trinity Alps pack?"

Elle and Tuck glanced at each other and together said, "We will."

Wide-eyed, Chelo stared at Trak.

"Do you, Consuela de los Lobos, accept provisional membership into the Trinity Alps pack? Full membership to come with the vote of all members in good standing?"

"I do."

"With the power vested in me by virtue of my status as alpha of the Trinity Alps pack, I offer you provisional membership into this pack, with a full vote to come as soon as the members have had a chance to get to know you."

He pulled her close and hugged her. "The vote is merely a formality, Chelo. Welcome. I think you're going to love it here."

Darnell walked out of the shower wrapped in a towel that was obviously designed with a man Evan's size in mind. She was practically lost in its soft, absorbent folds, one hand clasping the thick terry close above her breasts. She stood in the doorway to the small bathroom, watching Evan. Lying stretched out on the bed with his nose buried in a book, he wore a clean but ragged-looking pair of sweatpants and nothing else. His chest was bare, showing off the glorious tattoo, a full sleeve design on his left arm that spread across his upper back and shoulders and all the way around to his right side.

She'd first seen it when she stayed at Feral Passions as a guest. He'd been working in the garden beside the lodge wearing faded cutoffs and hiking boots, the muscles on his back rippling beneath all that color as he turned the damp earth. She'd thought then it was absolutely beautiful, a twisting, swirling design of leaves and vines with birds and lizards, even a tiny frog peeking out of the intricately worked ink. It was the perfect accent to Evan's powerful body; almost whimsical, it told her there was more to the man than most people knew. Now, after four months of fantasizing about Evan and his tattoo, her fingers practically itched to touch it. To touch him.

He carefully marked his place between the pages, set the book aside, and only then did he raise his head and look her way. "All clean?" he said, and winked. Then he rolled smoothly to his feet and walked across the room almost as if he were a predator and she was a tasty-looking rabbit. She loved the way he walked, all smooth sexual power hidden beneath a truly sweet and kind nature. There was nothing cocky about him, none of the arrogance she'd long associated with men his size. Men who looked as if they'd stepped off the cover of a magazine.

He locked his gray-eyed gaze to hers and focused on her until he stopped directly in front of her. Raising his big hands to her shoulders, he took a deep breath, glanced from her face to her toes and back again. Then he wrapped his powerful arms around her, nuzzled close against the sensitive dip where her throat and collarbones met, and inhaled deeply.

Shivers raced across her entire body, puckered her nipples, and left her a quivering, needy statue unable to move with Evan so close. He surrounded her, blanketed her in his warmth and strength, in the steady tempo of his heartbeat. His scent.

"I never realized how sexy this would be," he whispered, his breath teasing her jaw, his lips taking quick little nips along her throat. "I love smelling my favorite soap on your body."

She held her breath as he ran a fingertip along the side of her throat, across her shoulder, down her arm. "Do you really think you need the towel?" he asked. "It's such a warm night."

Darnell didn't answer. Couldn't. Her words had lodged somewhere in her chest, held captive by the pounding thunder of her heart. She was so not accustomed to this, to a sexy man watching her through half-lidded eyes, the way his simple touch left her heart racing and her entire body yearning for more.

"We hardly kissed when you were here before. Do you have any idea how many nights I lay awake in this room, imagining your kisses? The way your lips would feel, how you would taste?"

He swallowed, audibly, and the sound made her smile. He wasn't nearly as calm as his steady voice indicated. No, not at all. That sense of vulnerability, the fact that he wasn't totally in control of his feelings, gave her the strength to release her frantic grip on the towel.

Of course, it didn't fall in the sensual way she'd hoped, mainly because she'd been so freaked out about what Evan might be thinking that she'd wrapped it around herself really tight and, with Evan holding her close, it stuck there, in place. She raised her arms and held on to his broad shoulders, lifted herself against him.

She heard the quick intake of his breath, knew realization

had finally hit that she was no longer holding on to the towel. He slipped his hands beneath the soft terry, cupped his palms under her bare bottom, and lifted her even higher, pushing the towel out of the way, managing to stroke her hips and thighs with one hand while holding her entire weight with the other.

He was chuckling by the time he freed her of the towel, untangling it first from around her breasts, pausing to enjoy the view until she felt herself growing languid beneath his intense gaze. Then he tugged the towel down her legs, though it still hung off her left foot. "Next time," he said, "I'm giving you a smaller towel."

Laughing, she wrapped her legs around his waist and pressed herself close to his flat stomach. Evan actually groaned when she rubbed herself against the line of dark hair running from his navel to the waistband of his sweats. He turned, holding her close, still dragging the towel behind them, and stopped beside the bed. Gently, he leaned over and deposited her right in the middle of the sleek down comforter.

The towel was still tangled around her foot.

"This has got to go!" Laughing, he tugged the towel out from under her foot and dropped it unceremoniously on the floor. Then he straightened and slipped the sweats down over his hips. Kicked them off and to one side.

Darnell feasted her eyes on the body she'd not seen before. There was no denying the facts—he took her breath. Tall and strong, shoulders broad and muscular, the thickness of his thighs emphasizing the lean hips and the dark mat of hair at his groin. His cock was absolutely perfect, fully erect, curving out and up, larger than any she'd ever seen.

Not that she'd seen all that many. She almost laughed, thinking of where she was now after her nerves this morning about actually coming, uninvited, to chase this man down. She couldn't have imagined a better outcome to her day.

Raising her arms as Evan bent over her, Darnell stroked his broad shoulders. He studied her so intently, his expression one of need and something that made her feel warm and liquid and oh, so wanted by such a sexy, beautiful man.

He planted his knee on the bed beside her. "I want you, Darnell. You and only you. There were so many women who came through as guests this year, and none of them were you. I've been wanting to call, to beg you to come back, but I didn't think you felt the same way. I'm hoping this means you do. I'm so glad you're here."

Warmth blossomed inside. "I'm here, and you're going to have to physically remove me from the property if you don't want me around. I've never missed a man before, Evan. Never cared enough about any man to miss him the way I've missed you." She laughed, but it was a soggy laugh and she really didn't want to cry. Not now. She ran her fingers over his cheek, traced the line of his jaw.

He came fully onto the bed, kneeling between her legs and then sitting back on his heels.

She ran her fingers along his sides, touching the sharp jut of ribs. "All I kept thinking was that if I hadn't been so insistent that I had to have that stupid drink, we might have spent the night discovering what we felt, might have spent the whole summer together."

His soft smile warmed her. His words made her hot.

"I can tell you now, girl. I want more than just a summer. I think I'm going to want a whole lot of summers." He leaned forward, dipped his head, and tongued her left nipple, then the right.

She arched into him, pressed her pubes against the thick length of him, and shivered with need. "I want you. Now, Evan."

"No." He sat back on his heels again, grinning broadly. "Not yet."

Before she had a chance to complain, he was sliding back between her legs, leaning close and nibbling at her inner thighs. Her breath caught as he moved closer, his tongue trailing between her legs, carefully separating the petals of her sex and using his lips to pull and tug at the sensitive folds. He grasped her nipples, tugging them almost to the point of pain, sending jolts of pleasure directly to her clit.

Writhing against him, whimpering with the need he built with each flick of his tongue, each tug on her swollen nipples, she arched her back, lifting herself closer to his mouth. He took her thrusting hips as an open invitation, it appeared. With fingers and tongue, teeth and lips, he kept her hanging over a chasm promising untold pleasure.

Perspiration covered her body. She twisted, pressing against his mouth, pleading her frustration, laughing when he teased and took her just a bit closer. Then he ran his tongue around her clit and sucked that bundle of nerves between his lips, thrusting two large fingers deep into her moist channel. When he curled them forward, her body froze in mid-twist and a single low cry escaped her lips. For a moment she actually wondered where the sound had come from.

Planting her feet on the bed, Darnell lifted herself to his mouth, grasping the soft down comforter in her hands, twisting, gasping short, sharp sounds as he launched her into that chasm. She wasn't afraid—Evan was there when she landed, holding her in his arms, bringing her back, showing her with hands and lips and his beating heart just how very much she meant to him.

He laid her back against the tangled comforter, sheathed himself, and slowly, carefully, entered her. He was thick and long and bigger than any man she'd ever been with, but he filled her perfectly as her feminine muscles tightened around him, pulled him deeper.

She sighed when the coarse hair at his groin pressed against her pubes, when the thick head of his cock rolled over the mouth of her cervix, amazed that he actually fit so well.

Almost as if they'd been created for each other. She looked up at him, at the face she'd seen in her dreams for four long months, and realized that she hadn't been wrong. This man was hers, and she wasn't letting him go.

Darnell slept so soundly that when Evan picked her up to put her under the comforter she didn't even stir. He'd lost track of how many times they'd made love. He was going to have to stock up on condoms if they kept up like this, and he wondered how long he'd have to wait before asking her to be his.

She looked exactly the way he'd imagined she would, lying in his bed, her lips pursed in sleep. He wanted to kick his own ass for not going after her when she'd left so many months ago.

But maybe this was better. Maybe the separation helped chase away any questions that might have lingered in either of their minds, if they'd not had the chance to think about what almost might have been. But now it was, and it felt absolutely right.

Somehow, during the time they'd been making love, the sun had disappeared behind the mountains and night had fallen. He went into the bathroom and got a quick shower, dried himself off, and crawled into bed beside Darnell. He'd almost called her Nellie tonight.

That was probably something he'd have to spring on her when she was ready to hear exactly how much she meant to him. And how he truly hoped to make her his—quite literally—forever.

CHAPTER 5

Elle stood and grabbed Tuck's hand. They'd been sitting here at the bar since Chelo had been offered provisional status, but it was growing late. "Tuck and I had a long day, Chelo, so if you want to go back to town we can take you now, or you're welcome to stay here for the night. We've got plenty of empty cabins and I speak for all of us when I say we'd love for you to stay."

Trak shook his head. "You two get some rest. I can give Chelo a ride back if that's what she prefers."

Chelo stood and wrapped her arms around Elle. "Thank you. Elle, thank you so much for caring. All of you." She turned to include Trak. "You are showing me an entirely different way of life, and I will be forever grateful." Tuck wrapped his arm around Elle, but he leaned close and kissed Chelo on the cheek.

"I'm glad we found you," he said. "You've been without a healthy pack your entire life. I think you'll be a good fit for this crowd."

When they left, the bar felt terribly intimate. Chelo wasn't quite sure where to sit, what to say. Elle was so full of life, and Tuck was obviously head over heels in love with his mate. It was a beautiful thing to watch, but now Elle was gone and she was here alone with Trak. She wasn't afraid, but there was a different sort of tension in the air. An unfamiliar sense of . . . something.

Trak stood. "Why don't you help me close up the bar and then we can go back to the lodge, see if the party's still going on. I'd like to let the rest of the pack know that you're going to be joining us as soon as the formalities are over." He gathered his beer bottle and a couple of glasses off the table.

Chelo cleared the plates—they'd finished off all the sandwiches and she'd had a second margarita, but that had been hours ago. Now they cleared the table and she wiped it down while Trak loaded everything in the dishwasher behind the bar. He locked the cash box in a safe in the small office in back, checked to make sure everything was turned off, and then followed Chelo out the door and carefully locked it behind him.

The night was dark with just a quarter moon on the horizon. Trak took her hand and they followed the road back to the lodge. So much had happened tonight; so much was still happening. She never could have imagined walking hand in hand with the Trinity Alps pack alpha, knowing that he had welcomed her into his pack even though she'd told him she was a risk, that Rube was probably still hunting for her.

She was so tired of running. She thought of her parents. They would have found Henri's body, but they never would have known what happened to her. That was so many years ago, and yet their faces were still clear to her. Oddly, Henri's not so much. She'd loved him, but they were together such a short time. His death had, in many ways, been her death as well.

She was not the woman he'd married. Would never again be that simple girl on a small farm in the north country.

"You seem sad, Chelo." Trak stopped and turned, took both her hands in his. "Do you want me to take you back to town?"

She couldn't meet his eyes when she shook her head. "No. I don't want to leave here at all."

"Good."

His emphatic answer startled her. She raised her head and caught him looking at her with almost a sense of longing. But that couldn't be right. He hardly knew her and what he did know was all the ugly stuff. "But where . . . ?"

"I want you to stay, Chelo. You're safe here and no one will harm you. Ever. I'm concerned about Rube finding you if you're alone in town. We need to figure out where he is and essentially neutralize the problem at some point, but for now I want you to know you're welcome to stay. I want you to stay. There are rooms in the lodge or, if you prefer more privacy, we can give you one of the cabins for now, though they're all going to be filled midweek for the wedding."

She smiled. She'd totally forgotten about the wedding! "It's late. I'm not ready to sleep yet. I'm still pretty wound up."

He tugged her hand and they started walking toward the lodge again. "I've got the perfect solution. C'mon."

The lodge was dark when they were close enough to see it through the trees. Only a small lamp inside cast a soft golden glow across the large dining room. The party had obviously ended. Trak led her across the parking lot and up the stairs. The door was unlocked and they entered the empty lodge, but he obviously had a destination in mind. He went behind the bar at the back of the dining area and came out with a bottle of dark red wine, the cork shoved halfway in.

"I think you'll like this. Come back to my cabin. I've got an extra room where you can stay, and I promise you're safe from me. I'm not like those men you're accustomed to. You can sleep in the guest room—it has a lock on the door—when you're ready for bed, but until then we can sit in the main room or even out on the deck and have a glass of port. It will help you relax and I can guarantee you a good night's sleep."

She might be crazy to take him up on his offer, but he was the nicest man she'd met since becoming a shifter. "That works," she said, acting as nonchalant as she was able.

She couldn't imagine Trak forcing her to do anything she didn't want to do, and she wasn't ready to leave him. Not yet. He was absolutely fascinating—tall and handsome, and strong looking. He wasn't as physically big as Tuck, but the sense of power around Trak was intimidating all on its own.

"Good." Trak took her hand again and they walked back down the road toward the bar and then veered off to the right on a much narrower trail.

They followed it about a hundred yards before coming out into a small meadow with an absolutely lovely cabin set against the forest. Tall cedar and pine trees framed the structure and there was a full deck that appeared to circle the entire cabin, similar to the one at the lodge. A soft light glowed from within; pale moonlight threw shadows across the clearing in front.

The cabin was so perfect, the way it was nestled in front of the tall trees, as if it were part of the woods. "It's beautiful," she said, taking in the attractive deck, the heavy stone foundation, and the natural logs that made up the main structure. A fireplace and chimney of the same river-worn rocks as the foundation covered one corner, and she imagined a snowy winter's eve with a fire crackling inside, warming the cozy cabin.

Tonight, though, was much too warm for a fire. It was a perfect night to run, but no one had mentioned shifting and racing the moon, maybe because it was waning and barely more than a sliver. She'd had so few chances to actually enjoy her wolven nature.

Trak tugged her toward the cabin. "Come see the inside. It's really comfortable."

"It's perfect." She glanced at him, loving the pride in his voice, the fact that he was obviously enjoying showing her his home.

"I built it with help from Lawson, my older brother. You met him earlier this afternoon. He's an engineer—quite successful, actually—and real handy when trying to build a home that fits all the county regulations." He chuckled softly. "Not something we used to have to worry about, but my other place wasn't nearly as well-built and it was time for a new one. When we applied for permits for the cabins for Feral Passions, we added this and homes for the others in the pack to the proposal."

He shoved open the front door and followed her through. The light she'd seen earlier was over the gas range in the kitchen, a beautiful dark bronze stove that matched the other appliances. She'd never seen anything like it before. This was obviously a much wealthier pack than the one she'd left.

"Do you want to sit on the deck or inside?"

"The deck, I think. It's too beautiful out tonight to come inside yet. If that's okay with you."

"Definitely."

He let go of her hand and went into the kitchen, which was all part of one big room with a dining area and comfortable chairs around a big-screen television. Stairs led to rooms upstairs and what appeared to be an office or extra bedroom on the ground floor. The furnishings were all beautifully made from what looked like native woods. The same craftsmanship was visible wherever she looked. Beautiful original paintings of wolves and other wildlife covered the walls.

"Here we go." Trak handed two wineglasses to Chelo and grabbed the bottle. She followed him back to the deck and they took seats by a small table. Trak poured wine for each of them and handed a partially filled glass to her.

He held his glass up in a toast. Flustered, she wasn't sure what to do with hers, but then she copied him and laughed when he touched the two goblets together. The ringing sound they made was sweeter than any bell she'd ever heard.

"Welcome to the Trinity Alps pack, Chelo."

When he smiled, she loved how his eyes smiled, too. He was obviously a powerful alpha and his pack loved him, but there was nothing cruel about him, no sense that he was looking for a way to dominate her, to make her feel less than she really was.

"I am really glad you've come to us." He shook his head and actually looked confused for a moment. "I feel a connection to you, but I'm not sure what it is. Only that it's something I hope we can explore as you grow more comfortable with us. With me."

He took a sip of his wine. "Taste it. I'm curious to see what you think."

She took a sip and held the liquid in her mouth, savoring his unexpected words along with the unfamiliar taste of the wine. She'd never heard of port.

She'd never had a man speak to her the way Trak did. As if she had value. As if he cared about her feelings. "This is good," she said, thinking that everything about Traker Jakes was good. She was thankful for the glass in her hand. Something to focus on besides her swirling thoughts. "It's really good. I don't know anything about wine, but I really like this one."

Laughing softly, she set her glass down. "I'm not much of a drinker, and after two margaritas today and now this?"

Shaking her head, she stared at the wine. The glass wavered, blurred, and she realized she was crying. So embarrassing! Wiping her eyes with both hands, she turned away, but Trak was there in a heartbeat, kneeling beside her chair with his big hands holding her thighs.

"Chelo? What's wrong? Did I say . . . ?"

"No." She interrupted him before he could apologize. There was nothing for him to apologize for. She was the one who was losing it. "Nothing you've done." She hiccupped. "Well, actually, it's everything you've done, but it's all good."

She took the handkerchief he handed to her. It was still damp, the one he'd given her when she'd had her meltdown at the bar, telling her story. She never cried, but as she wiped her eyes suddenly she was laughing and crying at the same time while Trak knelt at her feet looking totally confused, studying her as if she were absolutely crazy.

Maybe she was. This entire day had been a dream and she was so afraid she'd wake up and find out none of it was real. But it had to be real. It just had to.

Trak tried to imagine what was going through Chelo's mind. She'd lived an absolutely brutal existence for almost ninety years. The amazing thing was that she'd survived. He wondered if he would have been as tough.

"I'm sorry." She held up the handkerchief. Her eyes still sparkled with tears, her thick, dark lashes were clumped together, but she was actually smiling. "I should probably consider buying you a case of these. I'm not usually prone to tears, though at this point I don't expect you to believe me."

He shook his head. "Not at all. I think you're one tough lady. I was just wondering if I would have had the guts to survive what you've been through."

He got up from his knees and sat in his chair again, but he never took his gaze off her.

She just stared right back at him. There was no response to a silly comment like that. He had so much power. Not even their alpha had power like Trak's. She often wondered if that's why the men of that pack were so cruel, because they knew they were losers, knew they could never compete against a truly strong alpha leader.

"What happened to me never would happen to a man like you, Trak. You're a strong male. I was physically incapable of protecting myself. The only thing I'm really proud of is that when Jorge died he didn't take me with him. I fought his pull and won. And then I ran."

"He tried to take you with him? Damn. Chelo, you won because you're a strong alpha in your own right. I imagine you were more powerful than your mate, which is probably why you were able to fight him for so many years. It's why he couldn't pull you into death with him. We choose not to practice that archaic tradition in our pack. The only way a mate will join their partner in death is by choice, a pact they make together. We've never had to test it. No one in this pack has died since I built it."

"It's all yours? You're the founder?"

He nodded. "In a way. My brother and I. My birth pack was originally east of the Mississippi before the Civil War, which is around the time Lawson and I were born. The pack was growing older, but the alpha was still strong. He was a good man, a good leader, and I wasn't willing to challenge him, so a few of us moved west. Lawz and I ended up in this area in 1900 and settled here. The older folks tended to stay together. A few mated couples followed us out west. They're not actually part of our pack, but they maintain occasional contact. They've settled over on the eastern side of the state, but most of them live in towns now and never shift anymore. A few others went into the mountains. They stay in their wolf form; a few chose to die that way."

"I've rarely shifted over the years." She gazed toward the dark forest. "I used to shift in order to escape, but the beatings were horrible. When Jorge died and I ran, I ran as a woman. Stole a car and learned how to drive it on the way out of our community. I've hardly shifted since."

"We could run tonight. Would you like to explore a little?"

She opened her mouth. Shut it. Shook her head. "We can do that here? Run as wolves without fear?"

He grinned. "It's a wolf preserve. The wild wolves accept us. They haven't quite figured us out, but they're okay with us. C'mon. I'll take you for a quick run. That will definitely ensure a good night's sleep."

He stood and kicked off his moccasins, pulled his shirt over his head, and slipped out of his jeans. Chelo realized she was staring. He was so gorgeous and she wanted to see, but then he raised his head and caught her looking. She was positive she turned at least ten shades of red.

Turning her back, she quickly stripped out of her clothes, folded them, and stacked them on the chair. When she turned around, Trak was the one staring, but he didn't get embarrassed at all when she caught him.

"You are absolutely beautiful." He stared at her a moment, appreciation evident in his dark eyes. Then he sort of shook himself and turned away. He grabbed his wineglass, tilted it to his lips, and emptied the glass. Chelo did the same.

Trak bent at the waist, changing from man to wolf faster than she'd ever seen anyone make the shift, so quickly that a wolf turned and stared at her by the time his palms—now paws—touched the deck. It took Chelo longer, though not by much.

She'd forgotten the joy of shifting, the change not only in her body but also in her mind, her senses. The night was suddenly redolent with scents she'd barely noticed in her human form. Deer frequented the area, and rabbits munched grass nearby. It had rained a few days earlier and the air still carried the scent of damp earth and new moss. And Trak!

The scent of his wolf was an aphrodisiac, calling her close with so much power it was hard to fight the desire to rub against him, to nip and chase. Hard, but not impossible. She wasn't ready for anything like that. Wondered if she ever would be again.

Trak trotted down the steps and Chelo followed. His wolf was larger than hers; his silvery coat with fur tipped in black rippled like liquid mercury in the pale moonlight. The upper edges of his ears were black, as was the top of his tail from his rump to the tip. He was absolutely magnificent. If she'd searched the world over, Chelo knew she could never have found a better man to protect her.

His Nellie stirred in his arms and Evan smiled into the darkness. He'd wondered if the wolves might wake her. He recognized Trak's powerful howl, the power of the alpha ringing true in his song, but the other wolf was unfamiliar.

He'd bet good money Trak ran with his little florist tonight.

"Wolves. I hear wolves!" Smiling, Darnell pushed herself to a sitting position beside Evan. She turned to him, blinking herself awake. "How long have you been awake?"

He kissed her. Just a quick one before he answered. "I haven't been asleep. I think I was afraid if I closed my eyes you'd disappear."

She smiled even wider. "I told you, big guy. I'm not going anywhere."

"That's good." He ran his fingertip over the edge of her ear. "I've imagined you in my bed ever since the first day you showed up at the resort."

She made a face. "You could have let me know. It's not like I was playing hard to get."

"I didn't want to scare you off. My feelings, even then, were pretty strong. I knew if I ever got you here I wouldn't want you to leave."

She leaned close and wrapped her arms around him. "That might have been negotiated. I like it here."

"I like having you here." The wolves howled again, a little closer this time. Trak must have taken her up the hill toward Blackbird Lake. There was a promontory on the way up, a perfect place for wolves to howl when you were really looking for an echo. Even the wild ones had figured it out. "After you left, I used to lie here in bed and imagine you beside me. Now don't laugh, but I always thought of you as my Nellie, just a name I could call you."

She laughed. "Nellie? I am so not a Nellie. Dar, maybe. I get that a lot."

"You've been Nellie—or Nell—to me since the very beginning. I'm not sure why, but I think it suits you." He laughed and kissed the smile off her face.

"I guess I can deal with it." She looped her arms over his shoulders, adding, "Since it suits you." She kissed him, a long, leisurely kiss that definitely got his attention. There was a twinkle in her eyes when she innocently said, "The wolves are quiet now, but I'm wide-awake. What we were doing before seemed to help me sleep really well. Are you at all . . . ?"

"Oh, yeah." He rolled over and trapped her with his body. She shrieked with laughter as he caged her in with elbows and knees, capturing her sexy mouth with his and trying really hard—and failing—to quiet his needy groan as he licked into her mouth, teasing an answering whimper from her.

He had a good four months' worth of deprivation to make up for. Tonight was as good a time as any to begin. Tomorrow was soon enough to start thinking about how he was going to tell her exactly what she was getting into, should she choose him as her mate.

―――――

It was close to two in the morning before Trak led Chelo up the steps to his cabin. He couldn't recall another run where he'd had this much fun. Tuck had mentioned how much more he enjoyed running now that he had Elle. Trak finally understood. Chelo was fast, and her wolf was absolutely stunning. A shimmering copper reflecting russet flashes in the moonlight, her coat was more like that of a red fox than a typical wolf.

They'd hunted without a kill, but that was by choice, stalking rabbits to watch them bound away to safety, coming up behind a large buck and growling to warn him off. There was no point in taking life when they weren't hungry and the herd didn't need culling. He liked the fact that Chelo seemed to understand this without his need to shift and explain. The wild wolves on the preserve managed to keep everything in balance and the werepack only took game on rare occasions.

Since the problems with poachers in the last few months, there'd been no reason to hunt. At least those bastards were in jail and Trak's bullet wound had entirely healed, but the deer herd would need time to rebuild to match its former numbers. Too many had been taken before the pack had realized what was going on. The preserve was huge, but they needed to do a better job of guarding the animals from the hunters who thought anything on four legs—even behind fences and "No Trespassing" signs—was fair game.

At the top step Trak shifted, grabbed their folded clothes off the chairs, and opened the door for Chelo. "C'mon in. It's getting chilly out here. You can shift inside where it's warm."

She entered the cabin and waited while Trak set her clothes on a chair in the main room. Naked and wanting, transfixed by her beauty, he watched her change. She paused by the chair, glanced his way, and then focused on the floor between her front paws. Her body rippled and shimmered beneath the overhead light, flowing like molten metal. Coppery gold and rust-red fur gave way to silky honey-toned skin. Her muzzle flattened, her ears lost their points, her bone structure changed, as she gracefully morphed from wolf to woman.

Her long, dark hair fell loosely over one shoulder, pooling on the hardwood floor.

Her shift wasn't as fast as his, but she was still faster than some of the guys in his pack, denoting her alpha status. Oddly, Chelo seemed totally unaware of her own power. He wondered how much she even knew about what she was. Had anyone told her anything at all?

Her shift complete, she stayed on her hands and knees for a moment, blinking into the light. He recognized that momentary disorientation when the body's senses shifted from the ultrasensitive wolf to their more mundane human abilities. He'd worked at overcoming that, and with a bit of training he imagined Chelo would learn to work through it as seamlessly as she'd shifted her body.

He was doing his best to ignore his erection when he walked over and held out his hand. She raised her head, blinking as if coming out of a sound sleep. Then she smiled, realized what she was looking at, and her pupils flared. She took his hand and he pulled her to her feet.

She was a truly remarkable woman, her body curved in all the right places, full breasts standing proud, broad hips flaring from a narrow waist, her bottom more than a handful but perfectly formed. With her thick, dark hair falling to her waist, she was the epitome of an ancient fertility goddess, an open invitation calling for his touch.

He released her hand, crossed his traitorous arms across his chest, locked his fingers around his elbows. Literally holding himself back from touching her. "Thank you for the run tonight, Chelo." He kept his voice level, the cadence smooth. At least his alpha strength was good for some things. Staying calm when everything told him to act was an alpha ability he'd rarely had to call on. "It's been a long time since I've had the chance to shift and run for the pure joy of it." He loosened his grip on himself, scooped up her clothes, and led her to the stairway. "The guest room is upstairs. It has its own bathroom; you should find everything you need. Do you have to go in to work tomorrow?"

Still bemused, probably from her shift, she shook her head. "No. I'm closed on Sundays."

"Good. It's late. I think I might just sleep in." He paused in front of the first room. "If you get hungry, there's stuff in the refrigerator and the coffee is on the counter. I should be up before you, but if I'm not, make yourself at home." He handed her folded clothing to her, leaned close, and lightly kissed her lips. "Sleep well. If you need me, I'll be in the room downstairs."

"Oh. Is that your room? The one off the great room?"

"No. Usually I sleep up here, the room at the other end of the loft. Good night."

"But . . . ?" She touched his arm. "Why are you sleeping downstairs?"

He ran his hand over her dark, shining hair. "I don't want you to be afraid." He shrugged, hoping she understood his intentions. "I think you've had enough men running your life. I want you to know there won't be any pressure on you here." He smiled. "Not unless you want it."

She stared at him for what felt like a very long time. Then she let out a breath and closed her eyes. "Thank you. I think that's the nicest thing any man has ever done for me."

"Good night, Chelo. Sleep well." He turned and walked back to the stairs and went down to the room he rarely used. It might have been the nicest thing a man had ever done for Chelo, but as far as Trak was concerned, walking away from her when he wanted her like he wanted his next breath was easily the hardest thing he'd ever done.

CHAPTER 6

On Monday morning, Trak gave Chelo a ride into town. Already he was growing used to her company and hated the thought of leaving her, of returning to the resort alone. Sunday had been one of the nicest days he'd had since they'd built Feral Passions.

Trak had taken Chelo to the lodge and introduced her to the members of the pack who'd decided to hang around. Elle and Tuck had gotten word out about her background, and everyone knew to be on the lookout for Rube. From Chelo's description of the man, it shouldn't be hard to recognize him. At six feet tall and around 280 pounds of muscle, he'd be easy to pick out. Besides, all of them would recognize the scent of an unfamiliar were.

Chelo said he was a mix of Chippewa and Russian with harsh features and a short temper. She wasn't sure if he'd be alone or with others—he was very unpopular, even among members of his own pack. There couldn't be many who'd want to help him take her back.

He didn't sound like anyone Trak wanted to make nice with. Rube was definitely on his mind when he pulled up in front of the florist shop, parked, and reached for his door.

Chelo put her hand on his arm. "You don't need to get

out. Thank you for a lovely weekend, Trak. This was honestly the nicest time I've had that I can recall."

He covered her hand with his. "I'm glad. I'm hoping it's the first of many. And I am most definitely getting out and walking you into the shop." He leaned close and kissed her. "Don't argue."

They'd progressed to easy kisses and lots of laughter since Saturday. She was still sleeping in his guest room and Trak remained downstairs. As much as he would love to explore what appeared to be growing between them, he planned to keep things that way until Chelo said differently. She'd had too little free choice in her life. If she chose Trak, it had to be because he was the man she wanted, not because he'd forced the issue.

With that in mind, he got out of the truck and walked around to the passenger door, reached for Chelo's hand, changed his mind, and grabbed her around the waist to lift her out. "Big truck, tiny woman," he said as he set her feet gently on the ground. "I keep forgetting how little you are."

"Well, it is a long way to the ground," she said, but at least she was laughing. "Besides, I'm not that small, at least not around. Now my mother was tiny, barely five feet tall and maybe ninety pounds."

"Chelo? You're pushing it when you say you're five three." He shrugged, biting back a grin when her eyes flashed. "You're more than a foot shorter than me."

Taking her keys out of her handbag, she gave him a sideways glance. "Want me to bring you down to size, big boy?"

Shaking his head, he took the keys from her hand. "Nope. I know when to shut up."

"Good." But she was smiling.

He opened the door and Chelo marched through. Everything looked fine, but . . . "Stop." Trak put his hand on her shoulder. "I'm scenting a strange wolf here."

"Not strange." She paused by the counter. The register was empty, but she'd put everything in the safe before she and Elle left on Saturday. She took a deep breath and wrapped her arms around her waist in a defensive position. "It's Rube. He's been here."

If he'd been a wolf, Trak's hackles would've risen. He squeezed Chelo's shoulder, punched in a number on his cell phone before handing it to her, and growled, "Take my phone. That's Tuck's number. He and Elle should be in town. Tell them to stop by. I want them to get the bastard's scent so they'll recognize it." He walked to the back of the shop and opened the door to the office. The scent of the other male was strong in there, though not fresh. He checked to see if it looked as if anything had been taken and, after a moment, walked back to the showroom. He shut the door behind him.

"Has he been in there as well?"

"Yeah." He bit back a curse. "Did you get Tuck?"

"He's at a ranch just outside of town. Said they'll be here in about fifteen minutes."

She handed his phone back to him. He tucked it into his pocket. "Good. You live upstairs, right?"

Nodding, she said, "Through the office."

Trak glanced at the closed door. "Is there another entrance?"

"Stairs in back, but we need to go through the office, or walk around the block to the driveway that leads to the parking lot back there. That's where I park my car."

He turned and raised an eyebrow. "The one you stole?"

She actually blushed. "No. I left that one in a parking lot in Spokane. I bought this one a couple years later. Even have the pink slip."

"Good girl." He was acting like such an ass. It wasn't her fault she was being stalked. He hugged her shoulders and tried to relax, but it was impossible, now that he'd seen actual proof of a threat to her safety. Proof that the threat knew where she lived, had trespassed in her space. "Let's go through the office and up the back stairs. Can you lock the door in the office that leads to the apartment?"

She led him into the small room and turned a dead bolt. "It's accessible from inside, but you have to know how it works. That will keep it shut. It's a solid wood door. C'mon."

They went out through the office. The back door opened into a parking area that appeared to serve several businesses. The scent of wolf was stronger out here, though not fresh, and not the same wolf. Trak wasn't willing to risk shifting here, even though his wolf could set the time the others had been here to within an hour or so. As he followed Chelo up the stairs, he was positive their visitors were long gone.

She stopped at the landing outside the door to the apartment. Trak tried the door. It was open, the lock destroyed. He didn't notice the same scent of the intruder downstairs, though the scent of the other wolves lingered. Trak pushed the door open. Chelo's little apartment had obviously had visitors.

"Oh, no. Damn it! Look at this mess." Chelo stepped into the main room of a small studio apartment ahead of Trak and they both surveyed the damage. Her clothes were ripped from the closet, the drawers on her small dresser open and tossed about the room. Food had been thrown around the kitchen and smeared on the walls, and from the smell, it had obviously been done either Saturday or Sunday.

A potted orchid lay broken in the middle of the floor. She walked over and picked it up, but the bloom-covered stem had been snapped and the roots torn to pieces. Trak watched her for a moment, unsure what was going through her mind, but then her legs just folded and she sat on the floor, cradling the broken plant.

Trak was kneeling beside her in a heartbeat. "Ah, sweetheart. We'll clean this up. I'll get a couple of the guys out here to take care of the mess for you, but you can't stay here." He sat on the floor and pulled her into his lap. Still clutching the broken orchid, she sobbed against his chest. "I want you to come back with me, but we should probably report this to the sheriff. The department should know to keep an eye on things here."

"How can we involve the authorities? They don't know about us, do they?"

"No, but they know we're good citizens. The wolf preserve is a draw for the community and brings in tourists, and we patrol a large area of land around here and keep an eye on things. They know we're quiet and fairly reclusive, that we've got a terrific vet the people here have come to count on, and they are always willing to help us."

The words spilled out of her. "I thought I was finally free of them. This wasn't just Rube. I recognize the stench of at least three others from the pack. They're all big and dangerous, Trak. I can't bring that danger to your pack. I won't do that to you."

He tightened his arms around her. "It's not just my pack,

Chelo. It's yours, too. You're one of us now. As a member of the Trinity Alps pack, you deserve the same protection as any member, and we'll give it willingly."

His phone chimed with a message, and he pulled it out of his pocket. "It's Tuck. He's downstairs, looking for us." He sent a message back. *Stay there. We'll be right down.* Standing, he helped Chelo to her feet.

She set the broken orchid on a table and went into the kitchen, grabbed a paper towel, got it wet, and scrubbed away the tears. "Okay. Do I look presentable?"

"You are always beautiful. C'mon." He tugged her hand and they went down the staircase that led to the shop. Chelo showed him how the lock worked and they stepped into the office. Elle and Tuck waited in the showroom.

Chelo stayed back to put a couple of arrangements together while Tuck, Elle, and Trak went out the back door and up the stairs to her studio. She'd been so excited about moving into the cute little apartment, excited about opening her new shop. Now she just wanted to go away. She didn't care where, but she was so afraid of that bastard Rube and furious that, once again, he'd found her.

She looked at the rose stem in her hand and threw the tattered flower back on the counter. She'd gone from stripping thorns to essentially mutilating the entire stem of the poor thing. She reached for another one when she heard voices, realized that Tuck, Elle, and Trak had come down the stairs into the office.

Tuck and Elle stepped into the showroom. "We've picked up four different wolves," Tuck said. "And you say the one that's after you, this Rube, it's his scent that's strongest in here? I didn't pick it up in the apartment, don't smell the others down here."

"I agree." Chelo leaned against the worktable. "His is the only scent in here. I imagine he left the others to trash my apartment and then came down here to snoop around. I checked and it doesn't look as if he tried to get into the safe, and the stuff in the cold room is fine, so this was done purely to intimidate me."

Elle knocked her hip against Chelo. "Did it work?" She was grinning like a fiend.

"Nope. But it sure has me pissed off."

"Good." Elle glanced at Trak as he stepped into the room. "Did you call the sheriff?"

Trak nodded. "I just got off the phone. He wants me to text him some pictures of the damage before we clean it up, said he'd have noticed four men in town this weekend, that it was pretty quiet. I imagine they're shifting and sleeping during the day as wolves, and probably hunting as well. I told the sheriff it was an old boyfriend who's been stalking you, that you thought you'd lost him."

Chelo nodded. "That works. Can you get the pictures? I need to open the shop."

"I'll do it," Elle said. She pulled her phone out of her pocket. "Just point me in the right direction."

Chelo led them up the stairs instead. While she was there, while Tuck was still cursing the mess, she found the broken orchid and carried it back down, along with the pot it had been in. She'd found that on the kitchen floor.

"That poor little plant is important to you, isn't it?"

Nodding, she pulled out some butcher paper to protect

the counter and set the plant in the middle. "It's the first thing I bought just for me after I left the pack. It's torn up, but it's tough. I think I can save it."

"I've heard orchids are a lot tougher than they look."

She glanced at him sideways. "So am I."

Trak hung around while Chelo brought out a few potted plants and took flowers out of the cold room to make a fresh display for the store window. He took the broom and swept the sidewalk out in front and helped her set up an outside display of small arrangements filled with fall colors. Tuck and Elle came back downstairs, loaded the photos onto Trak's phone, and then went off on their next call. A few customers stopped in to leave orders for arrangements.

The shop was surprisingly busy, and since Trak wasn't comfortable leaving Chelo on her own, he managed to find plenty of things to do. A broken latch on the cold room door needed repair, and there were baskets in cabinets out of Chelo's reach that he was able to move into a handier spot. Drew arrived to clean the apartment. Around noon Trak walked down the street to a deli he liked and brought back sandwiches for the three of them.

While Chelo was in the office eating, he went out in front and talked to a customer who was merely browsing, and ended up making a sale. The lady walked out with a beautiful fern. Feeling as if he'd just made a huge business transaction, Trak strutted back into the office, where Chelo high-fived him after the woman left.

"You're good. I might just have to hire you."

Trak sneaked a quick kiss. "You can't afford me."

"Oh?" She walked her fingers down his chest and then

latched her thumbs inside the leather belt riding just above his hips. "I'm willing to get creative."

This was the first time she'd instigated anything at all that could be called flirting. Trak wondered if she heard his heart pounding in his chest. In the short time he'd known her, the attraction had only grown stronger.

Until now, he'd felt as if it was a one-way street. Maybe there was hope for him yet. "How creative? Fancy flowers for the lodge? Maybe a bouquet for my cabin?"

"How about rose petals on the sheets, next time you have a lady friend over?"

He shrugged. "I don't have any lady friends to invite over. Only one lady who's staying at my house, but she's got her own room."

"I can see where that might be a problem." She stepped closer. Close enough that her full breasts rested against his chest. Close enough that she had to feel the hard length of him pressing against her stomach. "A very big problem."

He ran his hands over her shoulders, down the smooth line of her back. "It's a problem I'm sure you could deal with, if you're of a mind to help me out."

"Is that all it would be? Helping you? Wouldn't I get anything out of the deal?"

He leaned in and nuzzled the side of her throat below her ear. She shivered beneath his lips and he scented her arousal, a heady blend with the shop's aromas of roses and daffodils, the rich perfume of gardenias. Chelo's scent was a combination of all of that and more. Intrinsically, personally hers. He knew it, even though this was the first time he'd picked up the faintest scent that she might be aroused.

Proof that she'd lived a life of unmitigated hell for most

of her life. There was no way he was going to rush her, but he wasn't going to make her wonder, either. "Chelo, you've already got me, even without the sex, but I can promise you, that if . . ."

"When," she said. "Say when."

He kissed her quickly. "*When* we make love, you'll have all of me. All of me for as long as you want me." He bent to kiss her, a deeper, more meaningful kiss, when the bell on the front door tinkled.

"Don't expect to be saved by the bell every time, sweetheart."

She laughed and brushed by him to help the customer who'd just walked in.

While Chelo talked to a couple of women about providing flowers for their church this coming Sunday, Trak went up to check on Drew. He stepped into the apartment, surprised at how far his pack mate had gone toward putting things in order. "You're good," he said, channeling Chelo. "I might have to hire you."

Drew flipped him off, which had both of them laughing, considering the fact that he wore pink latex gloves. "Pink? That the only color you could find?"

"Jules bought them. Need I say more?"

"Guess not. Find anything suspicious?"

"Yeah. I have. There are little notes left all over the place, hidden in dresser drawers, stuck in the refrigerator, in the dishwasher."

"Where are they?"

"Here." He handed a plastic bowl to Trak. It was filled with pieces of paper obviously ripped off a tablet, notes written with a pen. The author had terrible handwriting but obviously a vivid imagination.

"Tear the place apart if you have to, but I want all of these."

"You're not going to show them to her, are you?" Drew pushed his hair out of his eyes. "I hate to think of anyone as nice as Chelo reading that filth."

Trak sighed. He really didn't have a choice. "Chelo has finally taken control of her life after what amounted to a lifetime of abuse. I'm not going to make any decisions about her without consulting her. I'll ask her if she wants to see them, but ultimately, it's her choice."

"You're right." Drew wiped down the kitchen counter as he talked. "But if you can talk her out of reading them, I hope you do."

"Thanks, Drew. I promise to try. I'm not even going to mention them until you're through in here. Just clock this time as double your hours at Growl."

He left Drew working and went back down the stairs. Chelo was on the phone, but she ended the call as he entered the room, turned, and leaned against her worktable. "Got it. Just ordered the flowers for delivery on Friday. Stock, delphinium, iris, calla lilies, and freesia."

"How'd you know what to order?" This whole business was entirely foreign to him.

"I talked with Meg yesterday. She called Cherry to let her know the schedule. She and Zach will be here Wednesday and they want to have bachelor and bachelorette parties Thursday night, separate, of course. Ladies get the lodge, guys can have Growl, but mainly I wanted to find out about flowers. She doesn't want a lot—just an arrangement wherever they're going to stand for the vows, her bouquet, a boutonniere for Zach, and bouquets for her bridesmaids, Elle, Jules, and Darian. I met Darian yesterday before she and Lawz went back to Eureka. She's really nice."

"That she is. You'll be able to do all of that before Sunday?"

"Not a problem. Are the guys dressing up for this? Like in suits and ties?"

"I think they are. I am. I'm officiating. Does it matter?"

"It does if you want a boutonniere."

"Is that really necessary?"

"Mmmmm." She cocked her head and stared at him.

"What does that mean?" He arched an eyebrow, pushed his alpha strength.

She never even blinked, but she practically purred. "Many women think a flower in a man's lapel is sexy. Very sexy."

He was close enough to stroke a long curl of her dark hair, close enough to curl it around his fingers. "What about you, Chelo? Do you think it's sexy?"

She turned away but still watched him from the corners of her eyes. Flirting. She was obviously flirting with him. "I do. If the right man is wearing it."

"I see. I'd hate to waste a perfectly good flower. I mean, if I'm not the right man."

Her smile lit up her face. When she licked her lips, she lit up more than her face. He had a very low threshold when it came to Chelo. "I think you might be. I'll order them, just in case."

Tuesday morning
Evan rolled over and ran his fingertip over the silky curve of Nellie's breast. Even though she was still half-asleep, she

arched her back to his touch. He'd never known a woman as responsive, never responded to another woman the way he did to his little Nell.

It was fun to think of her as Nellie, to call her that when they were together. Never in front of the other guys, though. It was for the two of them, and she actually seemed to like it.

Of course, whispering it in her ear when she was verging on orgasm might have something to do with it. He propped himself up on one elbow, leaned over, and tongued her left nipple. It immediately stood at attention, so he stroked the right one with his fingertips and sucked on the one he'd already tasted.

"I'm sleeping."

He turned and looked into the one eye she'd opened. Turned her wet nipple loose. "Not now you aren't."

"What time is it?" She closed her eye.

"Almost eight. We need to go into town and get your car. Remember? The one with the flat tire?"

"Damn. I forgot all about it." She pushed herself up against the headboard. "So this wasn't a seduction? You were merely waking me up?"

"Pretty much." He swung his legs around and got up. "C'mon, Nell. I'll buy you breakfast in town. You can check out the sights."

"Certainly, Ferdinand. Whatever you say."

"Ferdinand?" He cocked an eyebrow.

"Well, if you're going to call me Nellie, a name better suited for a farm animal, then you, my dearest, will be Ferdinand." She got out of bed and wrapped her arms around his waist. "He was a bull."

"Ah, that works." He flexed his muscular arms and the

tat on his left arm danced. "Me Ferdinand. Big fierce bull with big cojones." He leered at her and twisted an imaginary mustache.

She leaned back and grinned. "Actually, Ferdinand was a wussy bull. He preferred sitting under a tree, smelling the flowers." She ducked under his arm and headed into the shower.

He watched her go. Damn but he loved the way her mind worked. And he really liked the way she looked walking away from him. Her ass was a work of art. He followed.

An hour later, they drove by Chelo's flower shop on the way to pick up Nell's car. She was still calling him Ferdinand, and funny thing was, he seemed to get a kick out of it. She wondered if anything ever pissed him off. He was a truly gentle soul with a fun sense of humor that was every bit as addictive as the rest of him.

Evan pulled over and parked.

Darnell rolled the window down. "Hey, Chelo. I like the shop."

"Thanks. Want to come see?"

"Maybe later. We need to pick up my car. Had a flat."

"Okay." She went back to sweeping the walkway, and Trak stepped out of the shop with a couple of potted plants in his arms, waited for Chelo to point, and then set them down and walked over to the truck.

"What are you two doing in town?"

Darnell hung out the open window. "Ferdinand here promised me breakfast and we have to pick up my car."

Trak glanced over her shoulder at Evan and raised one expressive eyebrow. "Ferdinand?"

"Long story," he said. "One day I'll tell you, but it's going to be over more than one beer. You might have to get me loaded first."

"I'll remember that. Enjoy yourselves. I'll be here most of the morning, but I want to get together with you and the guys sometime this afternoon."

"Just let me know when."

They pulled up in front of a small café and went inside. It appeared the morning rush had slowed—an older lady was clearing the tables and a group of guys in the back looked like they were finishing up.

For some reason, they made Darnell think of the men after Chelo. They were rough looking, dressed like transients, and for whatever reason didn't look like they fit the area or this cute little café. Evan seemed to have the same sense about them that Darnell did, and she noticed his gaze slide over to their table before he led Darnell in the opposite direction. He pulled out a chair for her at a table the waitress had just cleared.

The woman left menus for both of them, asked if they wanted coffee, and went to fill two cups. Evan pulled out his cell phone. "Just a sec, babe."

He typed his message, sent it, and Darnell's phone chimed. She frowned, but before she could say anything he shook his head. She took out her cell phone and saw he'd copied her on a text to Trak. *The guys after Chelo are at the diner. Look left of the front door. Nell, don't say anything.*

She glanced at Evan, who was reading his menu as if nothing were going on. "What's good here?"

He grinned at her. "Everything. I always get the lumber-jack special."

She found it on the menu. "You could feed an entire city with that."

He shrugged. "I'm a growing boy."

She grabbed her cell phone and typed a message. *Is Trak coming down here?*

"That he is. Decide what you want yet?"

She glanced up as the waitress stopped by their table, set two cups of coffee down, and pulled out her pad.

"Thank you. Eggs Benedict for me."

"Cook does a great job on that one. You'll love it."

"Regular for you, big boy? Lumberjack special? Four eggs scrambled, fried potatoes, sausage, and bacon?"

"Yes, ma'am."

Darnell laughed. "You've been here before, I take it?"

"A time or two."

"I'm glad you're here." The waitress leaned over as if wip-ing the table and whispered, "That group in the corner is making me nervous. I think they were waiting for the place to clear out, but then you walked in."

Evan kept his voice just as low. "Don't worry, Maisy. We'll hang around as long as you need us. Trak's on his way down, too."

She patted his hand. "You're a good boy, Evan. Thank you."

Darnell grabbed his hand. "You are a very good boy, Fer-dinand. I think you made her day." She glanced up. "Trak's here."

Evan turned and waved. Trak walked over to their table and sat next to Darnell.

"I hope you appreciate the fact that Evan's brought you to the best place in town."

"Believe me, I do." She took a sip of coffee just as Maisy walked back to their table and set a cup in front of Trak.

"Did you want something to eat, Trak?"

"No thanks, Maisy. I'm good. I just needed a cup of your coffee. Best in town." He held his cup up in acknowledgment before taking a sip. "Definitely better than what I make."

Evan laughed. "Trak, I've had your coffee. Anything is better than what you make."

"There is that." He glanced toward the four men and then turned his back on them when he spoke. "Manny and Drew are at the shop. Not leaving her alone."

"You staying in town today?"

"For now. I'll call you when I get home. We need to talk." He took another swallow of coffee and set the cup down. Then, instead of going out the door, he walked toward the four men at the table, and Darnell held her breath. Trak walked past them without acknowledging them at all and went through a door leading to the restrooms. Darnell noticed how the men watched him. Did they know he was with Chelo? But how could they?

A minute later Trak came out, glanced at the men and nodded, and then left the restaurant. It was all very strange, and for some reason Darnell felt as if she was missing something important.

Maisy brought Darnell's and Evan's breakfast about the same time the four men got up from their table. An older man wearing a white apron and a chef's hat came out of the back to ring up the men's tab while Maisy cleared their table, pocketed what appeared to be a tip, and carried the plates into the back.

Again, that strange sense that she was missing something, which made no sense at all. Darnell concentrated on her food and the sexy guy across the table from her. No point at all in wasting time worrying about four butt-uglies she hoped never to see again.

CHAPTER 7

After breakfast, Darnell and Evan picked up her car and she followed him back to the resort. A while later, Evan took off for his meeting with Trak while she sat out on the deck in front of his cabin with a book in her lap. One she hadn't even opened yet.

There was just too much to think about. She'd never tried to imagine where Evan actually lived, but this place was unbelievable, and he said he'd built it himself. Well, with help from the other guys, but still . . .

It sat in a small clearing with forest all around. The deck wrapped across the front with a view of the most magnificent mountains ever, and while the cabin wasn't huge, it didn't feel at all small. There was a neat kitchen downstairs that opened into one big room with a stone fireplace against the wall at the opposite end. He had a bar with tall stools instead of a kitchen table, though there was room for one. Two rooms downstairs shared a bathroom between them.

"Kids' rooms," he'd said when he gave her a tour. Which, of course, had her thinking of what his kids would look like if they were hers, too. For some reason she imagined sons, not daughters. Strong sons with their father's beautiful body and quiet disposition. He was such an easy man to be around, and he'd make a wonderful father. She didn't doubt that at all. Yeah, she could imagine filling those kids' rooms with their sons. Upstairs was a big loft—the master bedroom with a nice bathroom and a shower that she'd discovered had plenty of room for two. It was open to the rest of the house, now, but he showed her how easy it would be to close it off and make it more private should she ever want to do that.

And that was how he'd said it—if *she* ever wanted to close it off. He still hadn't said he loved her or asked her to be his, but he talked about them as if that was a given. Obviously, it was too soon to make any commitments, but Evan was definitely talking long term.

She glanced toward the driveway. His truck was still parked next to the cabin and now her little red car was right there beside it, but Evan was still gone. She wished he'd come back. Trak had called some sort of meeting at the lodge, probably about those big guys after Chelo, and Evan left.

She'd have to ask him about the guys here. They weren't related except for Trak and his brother, but they all seemed as close as brothers. It was obvious that Trak was the one in charge. She could see why—he was smart and certainly had an air of authority about him. She'd been around actors like that, usually men who, when they walked into a room, owned it. Trak was like that without ever actually doing anything to reinforce the image. His charisma was part of him. He epitomized the concept of a natural leader, but leader of what? She could ask Evan, but there was always so much more to talk about when they were together.

And just what did Evan do? Did he have a job somewhere away from the resort, or was this it? When she thought about it, there really were a lot of questions about him. About everyone here. Except every time she and Evan started talking about stuff, they ended up making love. That beat just about anything they could possibly need to discuss.

She glanced up as a big gray wolf with reddish highlights glimmering under the sun trotted toward the cabin. She remembered this one! He'd spent a lot of time with her last time she was here. "Hey, big guy! Do you remember me?"

The wolf stopped and watched her.

She set her book aside, walked down the steps, and sat on the bottom one. She knew better than to approach a wild wolf, though this one should remember her. Shouldn't he? She waited while he stood there. "Ya know, fella, my feelings are really going to be hurt if you've forgotten who I am. I haven't forgotten you. Don't tell Evan, but I actually dreamed about you after I left, even more than I dreamed about him."

The wolf's ears pricked forward and he took a couple of steps closer. "The dreams about Evan were sexier, though." She laughed. "Oh, yeah. A whole lot sexier. You I just wanted to pet."

He yipped and trotted close enough for her to reach out her hand and almost touch his nose. He stepped closer and licked her fingers, wrapping that long tongue around her palm. Then he moved even closer. Close enough to butt her chest with his head before trotting up the steps. Darnell followed him, well aware she hadn't stopped grinning since the moment he'd arrived. A wolf had come to see her. This was just too cool for words. She sat down on the deck with her back against the cabin logs and the wolf lay beside her on the warm planks. After a moment, his head was in her lap and she sat there, stroking his ears, wishing Evan were here to share this.

Of course, it wouldn't be special to him. He saw wolves

all the time. Still, she wished he'd come back. It had only been a couple of hours, but she missed him.

Evan quietly climbed the steps to the deck. Darnell still slept. She'd dozed off while petting him, totally unaware he was the big wolf she thought was so beautiful. He still wasn't sure how to tell her. He'd talked to Trak about it this afternoon, almost certain Darnell loved him, and while he expected her to be shocked, he didn't think it would make her fear him, fear what she would become when they mated.

The men still weren't comfortable telling their women in advance. Cherry had figured them out and told her sister and Stephanie, but that had worked out okay because they'd loved their guys. Same with Darian and Lawz, and Jules and her two guys. She'd figured them out and no one knew how she'd done it, but it was similar to Darian. Somehow they just knew.

Elle and Tuck had been a unique situation—Elle had her own magic, the ability to heal, and she'd saved Trak's life when he'd been shot while in his wolf form. But Darnell? So far there was no sign at all that she'd figured them out, which meant he had to be sure. Completely sure, before he told her.

Then Trak had told him more about the mess with Chelo's brother-in-law, that he could show up here on the preserve with three other shifters, all of them determined to take Chelo. That wasn't going to happen, but it could get ugly. It was too risky to say anything to Darnell now, not until he could safely turn her. If she were in that deep sleep after he bit her, the one that women fell into while going through the change, there'd be no waking her until the change was complete. It would make her vulnerable should the rogue pack make it onto the preserve.

Should they somehow overpower the guys, maybe even kill him . . . If that happened, he wouldn't be here to protect her. No way could he let that happen. Trak had agreed.

Which meant they waited. Waited until the threat was neutralized. In other words, until they killed the rogues before the bastards managed to steal anyone away from the Trinity Alps pack. After seeing those four this morning, he was sure the pack could handle them, but it was never a good idea to take anything for granted.

He knelt beside Darnell, leaned close, and kissed her. She made a soft humming sound, stretched her arms overhead, and the moment her fingers touched the rough logs behind her her eyes flew open.

"Evan! When did you get here? Where's the . . . ?" She glanced at the spot where he'd been dozing beside her with his head in her lap. "Oh, damn. He's gone." She wrapped her arms around Evan's neck and he pulled her to her feet.

"Who's gone?" He nuzzled beneath her ear and ran the tip of his tongue over the ticklish spot he'd found.

She scrunched her shoulder against the side of her head and giggled. "Stop that. The wolf is gone. The same wolf I remember from my week here in May. He came to see me and I guess I fell asleep while I was petting him. He put his head in my lap. It was just so cool!"

"Hmmm. Hope you don't have fleas . . ."

"Evan!"

She gave him such a look of utter disgust that he bit the insides of his cheeks to keep from laughing. It was so much fun to get a rise out of his Nellie. She seemed to get a kick out of the nickname, though he was more often than not Ferdinand now.

"He wouldn't dare have fleas. He's much too beautiful, and he didn't scratch once."

"That's because he leaves them with the unsuspecting women he visits."

"Yeah. Right. Where've you been? I missed you."

"The meeting went longer than planned." He opened the door and they went inside. "He wanted to tell us more about Chelo's old boyfriend. I guess they totally trashed her apartment yesterday, which is why she's staying here at Trak's. He's afraid they might try and come out here after her if they find out where she's staying. If you see them anywhere close to the preserve, you need to call and raise the alarm."

"How? There's no cell service out here."

"There is, now. We added a tower after Cherry moved in with the guys. She's telecommuting to her job in San Francisco along with the work she's taken on here. I want your phone so I can add all our numbers. You see anything, send a text and it will go to . . ." He coughed, cleared his throat. "Everyone here."

Crap, he'd almost said "to the pack." This was going to be so damned confusing until he could make her his mate. Darnell got her phone and Evan created a group for her with all the pack names and numbers. "Okay. You're all set. Brad's cooking dinner at the lodge tonight, so we'll eat down there, if that's okay with you."

"What time?"

"About an hour."

She set the phone aside and slipped her hands under his shirt. "I have a really good idea how to fill some of that time."

"Oh, really?" He arched an eyebrow as she ran her hands along his ribs. "How much time?"

She tilted her chin and gave him a seductive grin. "How much time ya got?"

"Plenty." He reached for the hem of her shirt and tugged it over her head.

She shrieked and covered her naked breasts with her crossed arms. "Evan! We're outside. Anyone could see us."

"No one out there but critters." He went to his knees and tugged her shorts down her legs, pleased to note that her tiny scrap of bikini panties went with them.

She was still grumbling, but she lifted her feet out of the shorts, one at a time. When she tried to cover the dark triangle at the juncture of her thighs, he picked her up and set her on the railing with her back to the forest.

"Hang on," he said. Nellie wrapped both arms around the upright beam attaching the porch railing to the roof. Evan grabbed a footstool, positioned it between her dangling feet, and planted his butt on the cushion. He adjusted her position, pulled her forward on the broad railing, spread her legs, and then smiled at her from his spot between her legs.

"You look like my gynecologist, except he's about sixty."

"I'm not your gynecologist, though I am planning to check things out."

"Oh. Really?" She scooted her butt around a bit, obviously getting more comfortable. "What are you looking for?"

"Sensitivity." He grinned. "Comparing feminine erogenous zones to find the most sensitive."

"I see. Where do you plan to begin?"

"Here." He reached for her right breast and rubbed his thumb over her soft nipple. It tightened immediately into a taut peak. "Mmmmm. That one works." He repeated the same test on her left. "So does that one."

"That's good, right?"

Her voice sounded breathy. He bit back a grin. She was so responsive. Already his sensitive nose caught the scent of her arousal.

Running both hands down her sides, Evan noted the involuntary tremors as he passed over her ribs and then grasped her thighs. He spread her legs wider, leaned close, inhaled, and then used his tongue to gently separate her folds. The muscles in her thighs clenched and the moisture of her arousal dampened her dark curls.

He swept his tongue between buttery folds, drawing a soft whimper from her. Swirling the tip of his tongue even higher, he found the sensitive bud swelling out of its protective hood, circled it, and backed away. Not yet. He wasn't about to rush, even though Nellie obviously wanted to fly. Instead, he took his time, licking, nipping, and tasting, keeping her just this side of the edge. Her body jerked. He wrapped his arm around her hips, holding her safely on the railing, lifting and resting her legs on his shoulders. Then, certain she was safe in his arms, he continued his very thorough investigation of all her feminine charms.

She'd never felt so exposed in her life, stark naked with her bare ass planted firmly on a smooth pine railing, safely held by a wonderful man with his tongue between her legs—a tongue that should probably be outlawed. Her entire body throbbed to the beat of her pounding heart and she was certain she'd bitten into her lower lip, doing whatever she could to keep from screaming.

She was there, so frickin' close to coming that her entire body shivered and trembled, and his tongue . . . oh damn! His tongue was everywhere except where she wanted it!

She wasn't going to beg; she wasn't. "Evan!"

He glanced up when she screamed his name. His lips and tongue covered her clit, and he sucked, hard. Lights flashed behind her eyes, and maybe a screaming rocket or two. She vaguely remembered rolling into a ball as her body flew. She didn't remember moving, but the next lucid thought was that they'd somehow reached Evan's bed, so he must have carried her. He was sheathing himself and filling her, so long and hard and hot that she knew they'd go up in flames.

But she knew something else even more important. She loved this man.

Darnell was actually surprised she wasn't walking funny when they finally headed down to the lodge. She'd never had so much good sex in her life, and impossible as it seemed, it just kept getting better. Maybe that's what love did—made everything better.

She glanced at their clasped hands, hers so much smaller than his, her skin a honey shade to his ruddy tan. Evan was the most powerful man she'd ever known. He made her feel safe when life hadn't always been that way. No father, a mom into drugs, growing up biracial in a poor white neighborhood after her aunt took her in and raised her. She'd always felt like the odd one out, like everyone else was in a special club, but the doors were closed to her.

Evan didn't make her feel that way. He accepted all of her—her silly sense of humor, the fact that she'd chased him down and moved right in on him. She'd never tell him how much she loved him calling her Nellie. Stupid name, but it was special to Evan and that made it special to her. Of course, Ferdinand worked, too. Evan was a guy she could easily imagine sitting under a tree, smelling the flowers while bad stuff went on all around him.

He made her feel special, like the dress-up princess she'd loved to play when she was little, before the drugs took her mom. Darnell had loved the fancy makeup, the brushes and glitter, and intricate princess hairstyles.

Was that what she was doing here with this amazing man who seemed to love her enough to want her forever? Was she projecting him into the role of prince to her princess? She wanted to believe that forever part. That's what he kept saying, but she hoped she wasn't a fool for believing in the magic. Except Cherry had found it. So had every other woman here. It was obvious in the way they looked at their men, the way they seemed to feel about themselves.

Was it wrong to want that for herself?

No, she thought. No, it wasn't wrong at all.

Trak and Chelo were among the last to arrive at the lodge for dinner. Her nose practically twitched with the scents of rosemary and garlic and roasting meat. Whatever Brad was cooking was going to be wonderful.

This was the first time Chelo had seen the entire pack in one place. Counting herself, there were eighteen of them, two more than usual according to Trak because Darian and Lawz had come over to spend the week ahead of the wedding. It should have been overwhelming, but it wasn't. Instead, it felt how Chelo'd always thought a big family would feel. The guys teased one another the way siblings might, and the women all seemed to get along like sisters.

Even Darnell, the one human in the group—a human who had no idea she was surrounded by werewolves—fit right in. There was so much love in this room. Love and friendship and respect. Chelo had never experienced anything even remotely like it in her life.

Not even before her change.

"Hey, Trak. Can you give us a hand?"

Trak led her to a chair next to Elle and across from Tuck. "Sure," he said. "If it gets me out of dishes."

"Dream on." Cain's snarky retort had everyone laughing.

"A guy can try, right?" Trak leaned close and kissed her cheek before following Cain into the kitchen.

Chelo smiled at Elle. "They never stop trying, do they?"

"That's for sure." Elle rolled her eyes at Tuck.

"I think that's my cue." He kissed Elle and followed the guys in to help bring the trays of food out.

Elle leaned close to Chelo. "Trak installed a security system this afternoon so we'll know if anyone comes in through the gate. There's no practical way to monitor the entire property, but at least it's a start."

"I hate that I've brought this to your home. I'm sorry."

Elle shook her head. "Don't be. It sounds as if Rube and his band of idiots would need to be dealt with no matter where they decided to cause trouble, because you know that's what they're going to be doing. It's just as well they're coming here, because our guys can deal with them." She glanced about the room. "And so can our women."

"I hadn't thought of that. The women in the Rainy Lake pack are treated no better than chattel. Here you are better than equals."

Elle frowned. "Better than equals? How so?"

Chelo glanced around the room, so aware of the laughter and overall sense of contentment. "Because your men treat you like queens. They wait on you, they love you, and yet they still respect and treat you as equals. They expect you to carry your weight because they trust you to do a good job. They defer to you when there's something they don't understand, and appreciate your suggestions, trust your decisions. It really doesn't get any better."

"I never thought of that, but you're right. Oh . . . looks like dinner's on." Trak, Tuck, and Cain had set up a bucket brigade from the kitchen, moving platters of all types of food. Pork and beef roasts, a tray of baked chicken, and half a salmon. Salads and vegetables, a casserole of some sort. So many different foods that Chelo's head was spinning.

Finally Brad walked out and surveyed the way Cain had organized everything on the buffet table. "Looks like we're good to go. Thank you, gentlemen."

Everyone lined up, filled plates, and found their seats. Cherry and Cain made Brad sit while they waited on him before serving themselves. Brad, who was sitting across from Chelo, leaned across the table and said, "Don't be impressed, Chelo. They're just trying to make themselves look good."

"I think they're trying to get out of the dishes," Trak said. He took a bite and savored it. "Brad, even if it's all for appearances, you deserve the attention. This is delicious."

"Thank you. I'm trying out some of the recipes I'm planning to fix for the wedding. Have you got a head count from Meg yet?"

"Looks like they're just inviting Zach's employees. Neither of them has family—well, Meg does, but they're not invited and she's got good cause. Looks like about twenty extras will be here, counting spouses. No children. Not with the threat of wolves roaming the place."

Chelo touched his arm. "Because of Rube? Is Meg not able to have the wedding she wanted because of . . ."

His finger over her lips stopped her. She thought about biting it. How could he so easily dismiss the threat? The problems because of her?

"I'm talking about the wild wolves. They roam in and out of the area and we've never had a problem with them bothering guests at the lodge, but a small child running in the woods? It's too great a risk to take. Besides, Meg's fine with it, and so are the employees. It's an excuse to spend time with a significant other without the kids around. It's not because of you, okay?"

She nodded, but still she worried. Where was Rube? She didn't think he was stupid enough to come here, which meant she was in more danger at her shop. But maybe he was just that stupid. If so, everyone could be in danger.

Her life wasn't worth a single person here. She gazed around the room, at the people who had welcomed her into their world as if she belonged. They'd brought a viper into their nest. They were too good, too welcoming. They were everything she'd always yearned for and she wanted to stay more than she'd ever wanted anything in her life.

"I need to make a couple of announcements." Trak leaned close, kissed her lips, and pulled her out of her dark thoughts. While she was still savoring the taste of his kiss, he stood and walked to the front of the room, which happened to be in front of the dessert table.

"I figure this will get you to look my way, even if it's only because you're checking out the amazing desserts Brad's

putting on the table behind me." He smiled and Chelo's
heart melted.

"Okay, we're going to have a busy week. Meg and Zach
will be here tomorrow afternoon, and we're planning the
bachelor and bachelorette parties Thursday night. That
way, if Zach . . . or Meg . . . gets shit-faced, they'll have time
to recover before the wedding Sunday morning. Guests will
begin arriving Saturday and we have all six cabins rented
for both Saturday and Sunday nights, though I'm not sure
how many, if any, will stay over Sunday. Meg wasn't sure,
either. It's going to be a morning ceremony and they're planning to leave Sunday after the reception. Meg and Zach
will have one cabin, and five couples will take the others.
The rest of the guests will be staying in town, which earns
points with the local businesses."

Cain raised his arm. "What do you think of my setting
up a security checkpoint at the front gate? I'll need a guest
list and maybe the kinds of vehicles they're arriving in. That
way we can lock it once all the guests are here and make it
a little more difficult for any unwanted visitors to drive in."

"I think it's an excellent idea, Cain. Thank you. Make
sure you get some help so you're not stuck out there for the
entire party."

"Will do."

"That's about it. Evan? Can you grab someone to help
you check the cabins, make sure they're freshly made up
and well stocked?"

"Not a problem." He glanced at Darnell and she said
something that made him laugh. Even with all the worry
about the wedding and guests, they worked together. They
laughed.

Chelo glanced up as Trak walked back to their table. He

was smiling at her. Smiling at the ones who stopped him to ask a question, make a suggestion. They loved Trak, their alpha, without fear. Without reservation. It was everywhere in this room, that love.

They loved. She hardly knew Trak, but the way he watched her, the way his eyes lit up when he looked her way . . .

She sighed. She could so easily love him, but not with Rube out there. Not with the threat that he could come after her at any time. He knew where she was, and if anything happened to these good people because of her she'd never forgive herself.

She had to leave. Not yet, though. Not until after the wedding. She'd promised to do the flowers for Meg, a woman she'd never met but one she already felt she owed so much. Please, she thought. Please just let us have this celebration.

And then I'll go.

CHAPTER 8

After all his teasing, Trak stayed to do dishes after the meal. The party moved out to the deck, but Trak, Drew, and Manny took over the kitchen and ran everyone else out. Somehow, Chelo ended up sitting with Darnell and Evan. She wasn't really sure how to talk to them, what to talk about.

She and Darnell had both arrived at Feral Passions on the same day, but their circumstances couldn't have been more different. Evan was obviously courting Darnell, and the human had no idea she was surrounded by werewolves. It was actually sort of sweet, the fact that everyone was so careful not to let anything slip, while still making certain that Darnell didn't feel as if she was at all different or excluded from anything.

Chelo understood the need for secrecy, the unspoken law that said you couldn't divulge your shape-shifting abilities to any nonshifter. It was interesting, though, the way Cherry and some of the others had figured it out before they were turned. None of the women here had been bitten without full knowledge of what their men were and how their own lives were going to change.

So different from what had happened to her. They'd talked earlier, before Evan and Darnell had joined the group. A couple of the older men here had admitted that, while it had still been considered acceptable when they were first old enough to hunt for a mate—to kidnap a woman and turn her without her permission—none of the men here had ever considered it.

Hence the resort. She'd laughed when Trak explained the reason they'd built Feral Passions, that it was essentially a hunting ground for the men of the pack who were desperate for mates. Only Evan and Trak were unmated after what sounded like a very successful summer.

Maybe they were waiting for that one perfect woman. She'd always heard it was a myth, but some of the newly mated guys here had been really open about their feelings, that the women they'd found were fated to be their mates—and the women agreed.

It made her wonder.

Was that actually something that the packs had neglected to search for over the years, a woman for each male, destined to be mated? Was it merely ignorance that had led Jorge and Rube to the small farm she shared with her husband?

She'd never know. Just as she'd never know whether she and Trak were meant to be together. She wasn't staying long enough to find out.

Darnell glanced up from her drink—something frothy and pink that actually looked more like a dessert than a cocktail—and smiled at Chelo.

"I'm not sure if anyone's said anything to you," she said, running her fingertip through the pink froth and licking it clean, "but I'm supposed to do hair and makeup for Meg and the bridesmaids. Can you describe the flowers so I'll know how to work with them?"

And, just as easy as that, Chelo found common ground with Darnell. Before long, they had a sketch pad and ideas for the flowers that would work in hair and as bouquets and Chelo shoved Rube and his disgusting friends totally out of her head.

Trak stood in the shadows below the deck and listened to Chelo and Darnell laughing about different fiascos in their line of work. It appeared that flower-fails and makeup-fails were equally disastrous, no matter the situation. The other women had gathered around and were laughing right along with them.

So was Trak. He'd never had the chance to observe Chelo around other people, not like this, where she was relaxed and enjoying herself and apparently not thinking about that bastard who was somewhere out there, stalking her. At least she was safe, here. With her surrounded by pack, there was no way Rube could get to her.

There'd been no sign of Rube and his guys tonight. After finishing up in the kitchen, Manny and Drew had taken off for an evening run with Jules with plans to check the perimeter areas that had road access. Brad, Cain, and Cherry had gone off in the opposite direction, and all of them had worn pouches for their phones.

Trak had gone down to close up the bar and while he was at Growl had received calls from both teams that all was quiet and there were no scents of rogue wolves. It was late and he knew Chelo had to be tired. He certainly was, but then stress had a way of doing that to a man. He walked up the steps and took an empty seat at their table.

"We could hear you laughing all the way down at Growl."

"Growl?" Darnell gave him the stink eye. "Last time I saw you, you were elbows deep in dishwater. In there." She pointed toward the kitchen in the lodge and flashed him a cheeky grin. "It's a really good look on you. I was impressed."

"Thank you." He glanced at Chelo, loving the big smile on her face. "I think." He looked over Darnell's head at Evan, Lawz, and Darian sitting at the next table. "Your woman is picking on me. Have you no control, man?"

Evan got up and stood behind Darnell. "I thought she was sounding a little cheeky." He leaned over and kissed her. Then he grabbed her around the waist, lifted her out of her chair, and slung her over his shoulder. "Sorry about that, boss. I'll deal with it."

"See that you do!" Trak shouted as Evan trotted down the steps with Darnell squirming against his shoulder, laughing and pounding on his back.

After they were gone, Trak leaned over and kissed Chelo. "I'm exhausted. I'm sure Lawz and Darnell will walk you back if you're not ready to go. Their cabin's not far from mine, or are you ready to leave?"

She huffed out a breath, but her eyes were definitely twinkling. "Well, since you ran off the woman I was talking to, guess I might as well go with you." She got up and grabbed the glasses off the table. Trak held the door for her and she carried them inside and set them on the kitchen counter. "Should I rinse them out?"

"I'll stick them in the dishwasher. Brad can run it in the morning." It only took Trak a minute and the mess was cleared. By the time he and Chelo walked back out to the deck, the others were cleaning up their things as well.

It was a beautiful night. A bat squeaked overhead and the grass rustled as some small critter scurried away, but the wind had died down and it was calm and quiet. Hopefully not the calm before the storm. Trak held tightly to Chelo's hand, but knowing that Rube and his guys were out and about—and aware of where Chelo was staying—meant he couldn't relax. Not until they'd been dealt with.

"Did you have a good time tonight? I hope you didn't feel abandoned, but it sounded like you and Darnell hit it off really well."

She laughed. "We did. I was wondering how easy it would be to talk with her and not give anything away about what we are, but she's just so funny and easy to talk to. And Trak, she is so in love with Evan. Why hasn't he told her?"

Trak couldn't meet her eyes. Instead, he shrugged as if it were no big deal. "Timing isn't quite right," he said. "Not with the wedding and all. We're still not comfortable talking about who and what we are until it's time to turn our mate. It was different with the other women—they'd all pretty much had us figured out, but Darnell doesn't seem to have a clue. I think Evan's worried that she'll be disgusted by the idea of him shifting. He wants to tell her first, but then he wants to turn her as soon as he can after that." He laughed. "I don't think he wants to give her too much time to think about it, but with the wedding coming up and the time frame between the bite and waking as a wolf, it's just cutting it too close."

He couldn't tell her the whole truth, that the threat of Rube and his guys made it dangerous for Darnell to be in that deep sleep in case they were attacked, which meant Evan would have to wait until after they'd figured out how to stop Rube. It was a waiting game that the Trinity Alps wolves fully intended to win, but none of them were willing to take the chance that if something went wrong and Darnell was in that deep sleep she'd be helpless.

Chelo, however, wasn't stupid. She stopped when they reached the meadow in front of Trak's cabin and took both his hands. "You're worried that Rube might somehow get in here, that he could hurt her while she's changing, unable to awaken. It's all on me, Trak. I've brought this on your pack. I am so sorry. Look, as soon as I do the flowers, I'm going to leave. I can't stay, knowing that he'll be haunting your people until—"

"Stop." He hadn't meant to pull on his alpha strength, but when Chelo's eyes went wide he knew he'd screwed up. "I'm sorry. I don't want to coerce you, and I didn't mean to do that."

"Do what? You're the alpha, Trak. You're doing what you're supposed to do. You're protecting your pack. I'm the source of the danger facing you right now. You have every right to pull rank on me. Every right to want me gone."

He barked out a harsh laugh. "You think that's what the little power play was all about? That I want you to leave? You're wrong, Chelo. So fucking wrong." He planted his hands on her shoulders. She had to tilt her head to look up at him, and he didn't want to use his height to intimidate her. Though looking at the fire in her eyes, Trak knew she wasn't the least bit afraid of him. She'd been through hell. He was nothing.

"About what?" she said, meeting his eyes without hesitation. She was just so damned perfect for him. "About the threat? About the fact that since I showed up you've had nothing but trouble, all of it related to me? Tell me how I'm wrong."

The quiver in her voice told him the truth, that she wasn't as strong as she wanted him to think, that she might not be afraid of him, but she was scared to death of what was going on, and that she had absolutely no idea how he felt about her.

He knew all too well what he felt, that she was his. Chelo just didn't know it yet because he hadn't told her. Maybe it was time to man up and be honest with the woman who already owned his heart. He sucked in a deep breath, let it out slowly, concentrated on stilling his thundering heart. "Chelo, I want Rube and his crew of jerks gone. Dead, preferably, but gone in any manner we can find that works, but I want him gone so you won't have that threat hanging over your head. I want time with you without worry, time when we can get to know each other, when hopefully you'll one day see me as someone you can trust."

She frowned. He tightened his fingers on her shoulders. "I'm a guy who wants you in his life. Forever, Chelo. I don't want you to leave." He took another breath, wondered if she had any idea what was in his mind. In his heart. He leaned close, pressed his forehead to hers. "Chelo, my heart will fucking break if you leave. Please. Don't go."

Not even Henri, on the day he proposed, had affected her so deeply. Trak was everything she could ever want in a male. He was strong and kind, loving and powerful. He cared for his pack and they cared for him. He'd created a utopia here in the mountains of Northern California, a place where people like her had become members of the local community while still maintaining their secret, their strength, their autonomy as a pack.

She knew he liked her, but she'd had no idea how much he really felt. Here, now, she was seeing a strong man with so much sensitivity, so willing to bare his emotions without any promise of her response that it made her heart ache. She so wanted to be free to go to him, but until Rube was gone, until . . .

She cupped his cheek with her palm. "You are everything I want in a man, Trak. But until I can deal with Rube, we can never relax. He is a threat to your entire pack. He's vicious and crazy and the men with him aren't much better."

Trak wrapped his arms around her and she pressed her face against his chest. He was so much bigger than she was. So much stronger. He made her feel safe, though she knew it was a fantasy more than reality. She would never be safe while Rube lived.

"Let's go in. It's late. We'll be able to think better, plan better, after a good night's sleep."

She nodded against his chest and they went into the cabin. Chelo walked slowly up the stairs, thinking of Trak, of his patience and his concern. She knew he wanted her, figured it was more than just sex for him, but she'd never made love with another shifter. Jorge and Rube were the only two male shifters she'd had sex with, and it was never by choice, never anything more than rape.

The women here were so happy with their men. Sex with Henri had merely been fast and messy, and then she'd been pregnant and throwing up. There had to be something more. She wished she'd asked Darnell. She was so open and funny, she probably would have had Chelo laughing about an act that terrified her.

But Trak? There was nothing mean or hateful about him

at all. She paused at the top of the stairs and glanced over the railing. He stood below her in the center of the room, and there was such a look of need in his eyes. She licked her lips, tried to moisten the inside of her mouth.

"Trak? Would you sleep up here tonight? In your room?"

"Are you sure? I don't want you to be afraid."

That she could smile about. "I don't think I can be afraid of you. Even when you pull your alpha stuff." She shrugged. "I want to be with you. I guess . . ." She let out a long sigh. "I guess I want to know what it is that makes the women here so happy with their men. I don't know what that's like, and you . . ." This was so awkward, she almost laughed. "You know a lot more about pleasing a woman than I do about being pleased, if that makes sense."

"Perfectly." He walked over to the front door, checked to make sure it was locked, and turned off the lights downstairs. Then he walked up the stairs and met her at the top. "My room's right down there. Why don't you let me show you what it's like?"

"The room?" She opened her eyes wide and figured that if she pretended this was fun it just might be. "I'm guessing it's like a regular bedroom."

"Not really. It will be totally different once you step through the door. You see, there's never been a woman inside. Not ever. I think you're exactly what it's been missing."

He sensed her fear, like a third party in the room, hovering now beside her but not coming between them. Not yet. He hadn't expected this tonight, had hoped to have a more romantic setting, but he didn't want to miss this unexpected chance to, he hoped, break down a few barriers.

She'd never known love, at least not since her very brief marriage a lifetime ago. Was he the man who could teach her, show her that not every male was a beast? She'd called Rube and Jorge monsters. From her description of them, she'd been right. Worse than monsters, because they'd treated her unmercifully with the full knowledge of what they were doing, how they were hurting her.

She and Trak walked together down the hallway to his room. He'd hardly been in here since she'd arrived, beyond grabbing a change of clothes when needed. He opened the door, flipped on the light, and stepped back. Chelo walked into the room and stopped. She stood there with her hands clasped at her waist, slowly turning from one side of the room to the other.

The sense of fear seemed to dissipate, the longer she stood here. It really was a beautiful room and he was proud of the way it had turned out. The cedar logs glowed like warm honey beneath the dim lighting. Bits of dried pitch in the wood caught the light and sparkled—golden diamonds decorating the peeled logs. He'd built every piece of furniture himself, all handcrafted from local hardwoods, except for the headboard. He'd made it of pine, carved to look like the mountains that he saw out his front window every morning. There was a thick down comforter covered in dark forest green, and a hand-crocheted afghan folded over the foot of the bed. The afghan was the oldest item in the house, something his grandmother had made back in the 1700s. He'd carried it out west when he and Lawz first made their move.

A long time ago.

He had one of Tuck's wolf paintings over the bed, a scene of each of the male wolves in the pack running through the winter meadow behind the lodge when snow covered the ground and bent the branches of trees in the background. The sky overhead was tinged with the colors of dawn and the rising sun. Tuck's art really held a magic all its own.

He realized Chelo's gaze had stopped at the bed. He stood behind her and rested his hands on her shoulders. "Nothing has to happen until you're ready. Why don't you just come to bed with me and we'll sleep. I won't touch you unless you want me to."

She turned and he dropped his hands. "You would do that? I know you've been aroused a lot of the time, but you've never acted on it. Is it fair to you, for me to sleep beside you and not allow you to touch me?"

He laughed, even if the sound was a bit strained. "Probably not in the man's book of rules, but I only want to do what you're ready for. There's no need to push."

She nodded. "Then yes. I would like very much to sleep with you tonight."

He leaned close and kissed her. "I need to get a shower. How about I meet you in here after you've had time to get ready for bed?"

She nodded. And then she quietly slipped out of his room and headed down the hall to hers.

CHAPTER 9

Trak was still in the shower when he heard Chelo come back into his room. He'd taken time to put fresh sheets on the bed first, but when he heard her in the room he quickly finished rinsing shampoo out of his hair and dried off. Then he slipped on a pair of knit boxers and walked out of the bathroom, still towel drying his hair. Chelo was already in his bed, her back to him, though he knew she wasn't sleeping.

He turned out the lights and slipped in beside her. Her body was damp from her shower. He snuggled close behind her and ran his fingers over her arm. "Chelo? May I ask you a personal question?"

She didn't speak, but after a moment she rolled onto her back and nodded her head.

"Chelo . . . sweetheart? Have you ever experienced an orgasm?"

He waited for her answer. Finally, very softly, she said, "I don't know. What's it like?"

He'd suspected as much, knowing her history. "Will you let me show you what it's like? We don't actually need to have sex, but I can show you pleasure with my hands and my mouth. I think you'll like it. I can guarantee you'll sleep really well."

A hell of a lot better than he would. He almost laughed out loud, thinking of how well acquainted he'd become with his right hand.

"You would do that? For me?"

"I would love to do that for you." He leaned over and kissed her. "Tell you what. Sometimes fantasy helps. You're going to use your alpha powers on me, and command me to give you pleasure. That way, you're totally in control."

She laughed out loud this time. "What alpha powers? You said that about me before, that it was how I kept from following Jorge into death, but that's not true. I'm not an alpha."

She really didn't know. "Actually, you are. Many women are alphas, though very few alpha leaders want that info to get out. I think it's stupid not showing women how to use their strength, because it adds to the overall strength of the pack, but there's no doubt in my mind that you're an alpha. Do you feel as if you have to look away when I make eye contact?"

When she just watched him, her gaze unwavering in the darkened room, he nodded. "I thought so. Chelo, I believe you're at least my equal, if not a little bit stronger, and it's probably part of the reason I'm so damned attracted to you. Your mind amazes me, your strength. Your sense of humor." He ran his hand through her dark hair and over her bare shoulder. He hadn't realized until now that she'd come to his bed naked. His body responded. Immediately.

"Of course, that lush body of yours works for me, too. One of these days, when you're finally comfortable with me, I'm going to bury myself inside you and give you pleasure unlike anything you've ever experienced. But right now we're going to have a lesson in orgasm one-oh-one. Tonight, I'm your prisoner and you're going to have me serve you."

"Really?" She stuck a couple of pillows against the head-board and scooted back against them with the blanket barely covering her full breasts. "I'm not sure where to begin."

He sat up beside her with the blanket just covering his hips. There was a night-light in the bathroom throwing just enough light. He could see her, see the sparkle in her eyes, but all was still in shadow. "You might command me to give you an orgasm with just my mouth or my fingers."

"You can do that?"

He nodded, doing his best to ignore the ache in his balls. If his erection got any harder he could probably pound nails with the damned thing. "I can. If that's what you want."

"How about with your mouth and your hands? At the same time. Can you do that?"

"Even better."

"What do I need to do?"

"Just lie back and remember that you're in charge and I have to do exactly what you want."

"I like that." She snuggled back against the pillows. After a moment she gave an imperial wave of her fingers. "Be-gin," she said. "I'm waiting." Then she put a finger to her lips. "Wait. Take off those pants. If I'm naked, you have to be, too." She waved her fingers at his boxers.

His cock twitched. "Of course. Whatever you wish." He slipped out of his boxers and tossed them aside, trying un-successfully to ignore an erection that had to be consum-ing most of his blood supply. "I'll need to pull the blankets back so I can see you."

She paused, just long enough for him to picture the

thoughts going through her head. Finally, she nodded, flipped her fingers at him. "If you must."

Still in character. That was good. Slowly, he dragged the fluffy down blanket off her breasts, uncovered her torso, paused at the dark edge of pubic hair at the juncture of her thighs, and then carefully exposed her all the way to her toes.

He'd seen her unclothed when they'd shifted, but here in his bed with her full breasts overflowing the width of her chest, the dip of her smaller waist to full hips and the soft curve of her belly, the thick, dark hair covering her pubes and her shapely, muscular thighs, he felt as if he was in the presence of a being far beyond a mere shifter. She was so much more, and if he could possibly convince her, she was going to be his.

This was the best of all possible ways to begin.

He gently spread her legs apart and knelt between them, but he leaned forward and began with her breasts, sucking one turgid nipple between his lips and then moving to the other, back and forth, drawing each in its turn into his mouth, using his tongue to press the taut flesh against the roof of his mouth.

Back and forth, one after the other until she was moaning softly. He gathered her breasts up in his hands, holding them close together, managing to draw both nipples into his mouth, squeezing her breasts with a gentle kneading motion that she seemed to love. Then he kissed his way down her body, nipping and teasing, his fingers still tugging and lightly pinching, keeping the stimulation going on both her nipples.

Already her body was covered in a fine sheen of perspiration and the scent of her arousal filled his senses. He'd noticed it earlier, Monday at the shop when she'd let him tease her, but it was nothing like this, rich and addictive, luring him closer, making him want.

She was so much smaller than he was, it wasn't awkward at all to continue tugging and twisting her nipples and still use his mouth on her. He nuzzled the tender flesh of her inner thighs, licking and kissing his way from one leg to the other, much as he'd done with her breasts. She had her hands wound tightly in the sheets beside her, and her hips had begun to roll with his mouth, almost as if she followed him.

He wondered if she had any idea where this was heading, then figured that yes, she had to at least have some idea. He used his tongue to separate her feminine folds, used his lips to tug and taste. He stayed away from her clit—as much as he wanted her to want him there, she didn't appear to know what was the source of her agitation. Trak couldn't remember a time he'd more enjoyed going down on a woman. He wanted this to be perfect. He wanted Chelo. There had never been, nor could he imagine ever wanting, another woman. There was no other. Only Chelo.

The moisture between her legs was flowing now, the taste salty and sweet at the same time. He swept his tongue deep inside her. She sobbed short, panting breaths as he took her closer to her peak, arched her back, forcing herself against his mouth.

Voice hoarse, breath ragged, she cried out, "More! More, Trak, please. More . . ."

He raised his head to watch her, a woman on the edge of ecstasy. Her lips were parted, nostrils flaring, eyes closed. He dipped his head once again and placed his mouth over her, using his tongue to sweep inside once again before abandoning her breasts. He grabbed her hands, put her fingers to her breasts, and watched to make certain she knew to tug at her own nipples while he found other things to do.

She figured it out immediately and he wanted to cheer. This was a woman who had never known how to pleasure herself, had never felt the thrill of sharing a climax with either her husband or the bastard who'd raped and mated her. What idiots those men had been. Trak was glad they were dead, or he'd have to kill them both for this alone.

He lifted her, slipping his palms beneath her bottom, bringing her to his mouth as he sat back on his heels. Her feminine flesh was ripe and swollen for him, her clit glistening with her fluids. Gently at first, barely touching her, he swirled his tongue around the tiny bud. Her body jerked and he did it again, lighter this time until she began to thrust against him, following the rhythm he led. Wrapping his lips around the most sensitive part of her, he thrust two fingers deep inside her pulsing channel, increased the pressure on her clitoris, and felt the first tremors of her climax.

She arched her back and cried out, a long, low moan of release as he took her higher, felt the tight muscles grasping his fingers, and wished it could be his damned cock inside her.

Not now, but soon. He knew it would be soon.

Slowly, he brought her down with gentle licks and kisses. As her soft whimpers subsided, he laid her back against the rumpled sheets and crawled up her body to plant a kiss on those full lips.

She licked into his mouth and had to be tasting herself.

He tasted salt. Tears. She kissed him again and then again and still the tears flowed, so he scooted up against the headboard and lifted her into his lap, held her against his chest. "You okay, sweetie? It wasn't too much, was it?"

He felt her head move against his chest. "No? That's good. You're absolutely beautiful when you come. Your skin flushes a deep burnt umber, your nipples tighten up into little buds, and the muscles inside fluttered against my fingers and then held on like you'd never let me go. Imagine how that would be with my cock inside you. One of these days, we're going to do that. When you're ready."

She nodded her head against his chest and sniffled. More tears flowed. He grabbed a tissue from a box on the table beside the bed and wiped her cheeks. She took it from him, sat up, and blew her nose, looked around like she didn't know what to do with the soggy thing, so he took the tissue from her, wadded it up, and set it on the bedside table.

"Are you okay?"

She stared at him and he had no idea what she was thinking. "Actually, I'm furious."

"What?"

This time she laughed. "Not at you. Not at all. I'm absolutely furious with Jorge and Rube, and even Henri, for that matter. They're the only three men who have touched me in my entire long life, and not once did any of them stop to think of my pleasure. I had no idea I could even have an orgasm. None. And then you come along and change my entire life. Do you know what that means, when you save someone's life?"

He wasn't really sure where this was going, so he shook his head.

"It means you're responsible for me now. You saved me, you got me." She closed her eyes and leaned back against the headboard. "Thank you, Trak. I had no idea what it was all about." She turned and smiled at him. "I have a feeling there's so much more you can teach me."

So caught up in her body's response, it took her a few moments to realize that Trak hadn't had an orgasm when she had. In fact, he hadn't had one for as long as she had known him, unless he did them all by himself. She knew she hadn't scented another female on him. He seemed to welcome questions, so . . . "What about you?" She gestured toward the tented covers. "Do you want to try with me?"

He smiled and shook his head. "I'll be okay. I've been making do with my right hand for a long time."

Frowning, she glanced at his hand and then at the tent. "How do you mean?"

He actually blushed. The big, tough alpha's face had turned a dark ruddy shade all the way to his hairline and down across his chest. He had a beautiful chest. She leaned close and stroked it and he practically purred. "Are you going to tell me?"

"It's a thing guys do when we don't have a willing woman to make love to. We take care of it ourselves. Women do the same thing."

"We do? I never have."

"I know, and I'm sorry. You should have known about that, though I don't think young women when you were young were taught things about their bodies. Now most girls learn all about how to pleasure themselves. It's part of their sex education. Your pack must have been very primitive in their treatment of their women."

She rolled her eyes. "Ya think? I'm getting a whole new

perspective here, but forget about me. I want to know about you." She pulled the covers back, exposing him the way he'd exposed her. His cock stood high and proud, blatantly begging for attention. She was positive he wanted her to touch him. Wondered how he would react if she asked him.

"You're bigger than Jorge. Rube, too, for that matter, and Henri. Is that because you're an alpha?"

He shrugged. "I'm about average for the guys in my pack."

He looked embarrassed and she wondered if it felt weird for him to be sitting here, both of them staring at his cock, one of them the woman he'd just brought to climax. "Of course, I'm really erect right now because I haven't come since yesterday."

She hadn't even thought about him coming by himself. She was almost positive there couldn't be another woman he had sex with. "How did you do it yesterday? Were you alone?"

He nodded and smiled at her. She really wondered what he was thinking. "I was. I was out in the woods."

"How? What did you do?"

He shrugged and then grinned at her. "Grabbed it and jerked off."

Jerked off? That didn't make sense. "Show me."

He stared at her for a moment and she was afraid he'd turn her down, but he surprised her. "I could," he said. "Or you could do it for me."

That worked. "Okay." She rose to her knees. "What do I do?"

He wrapped his fist around his cock and squeezed and then slid his fist up and down, slowly pulling the loose cowl of skin over the tip and then back down again. He did it a couple of times and suddenly quit. "If I'm not careful, I'll come too fast."

She scooted around between his legs so that she was facing him. Her breasts felt fuller than usual, and they were already big. Her nipples had pebbled into hard little points, and that usually only happened when she was cold. She picked up a scent that was hers but not, and a different scent about Trak, too. One she really liked. It made her want to rub against him and she wondered if that was the same kind of scent she was putting off.

It had to be arousal. She knew about that but didn't know what it smelled like. The scent of her arousal seemed to somehow blend with his, and she started getting that anxious feeling she'd had when he was giving her an orgasm.

She wrapped her hands around him—both hands because he was a large guy and she was a relatively small woman. He groaned, and she figured that was a good sign. She loved the feel of him—hard as a branch but soft to the touch, the skin covering him almost silky smooth. Except for the veins. There were thick veins running the length, but she loved stroking him.

"You can do it harder," he said. "Faster, too. And play with my balls if you want. It all feels really good."

She'd wanted to but was afraid she'd hurt him. She'd kicked Jorge there one time and he'd almost killed her when he caught her. Carefully she cupped Trak's sac and rolled his testicles around, separating them, then rolling them between her fingers. There was a tiny drop of fluid at the tip of his penis. Without even thinking, she leaned over and licked it off.

He groaned, so she did that again. She remembered one time when Jorge forced his thing into her mouth and she bit him. He never tried it again, though he used to threaten her, say she'd swallow his cock and like it.

She hadn't liked anything about him, but she loved everything about Trak. With both her hands around his shaft, she leaned close and wrapped her lips around the tip.

His hips jerked. "God damn it, Chelo. Holy shit! That feels so fucking good."

She slipped him free of her mouth and laughed. "It must. You don't usually cuss like that." Then she sucked him back between her lips while Trak lay back against the pillows, moaning and laughing at the same time. She must be doing something right. She used her tongue and her lips, sucked him deep enough to hit her gag reflex, and decided that was a little too far for the first time.

After a minute Trak stopped her. "I'm close to coming and you're going to get a mouthful if you don't stop."

She thought about that. She'd liked the taste of those first few drops. "It's okay," she said. "I want to learn to do this right. I've never done it before."

"Crap." He groaned. "Don't say I didn't warn you."

She felt the first pulse in the base of his shaft and tightened her lips around him. He thrust forward, though she could tell he was trying not to, but she sucked and licked and her mouth was suddenly filled with his release. She swallowed as fast as she could, but there was a lot and she almost didn't get it all. When he was done, she kept sucking gently, the way he had for her, and after a couple of minutes his thick erection was half its previous size and not at all hard.

She got up and went into the bathroom to rinse her

mouth and get a drink of water, and then she crawled into bed with Trak. She wasn't at all nervous, now. She'd been practically frozen with fear when he'd first gotten into bed with her, but now? Now she had proof he would never hurt her. No man as patient and gentle as Trak would ever threaten her.

They fell asleep as if they'd always shared a bed. She'd never slept with Jorge. He'd used her for sex at least once every night and then kicked her out of the bed. She didn't even have a bed, just a pile of blankets on the floor where she'd slept like a dog. If he would have let her shift she'd have been perfectly comfortable, but he knew she could get away if she was a wolf. So she'd slept on the hard floor while Jorge had the bed to himself.

Sometime during the night, she awoke to the feel of Trak's shaft, engorged again and resting against her bottom. She shifted around a bit until it was between her legs, and then she moved a bit more and felt him slip gently inside her channel. This wasn't really having sex. It couldn't be, because it felt much too good. Sex always hurt, though she hoped that when she and Trak had sex he'd be as gentle as he'd been earlier.

Maybe then she'd get used to it and actually enjoy the penetration. If he was really careful. She drifted back into sleep, fully aware of the connection holding her to a man she was afraid she'd never be willing to leave.

He hadn't had a wet dream this good since he was just a kid. The woman was warm and more voluptuous than any he could recall. The warm globes of her ass were pressed against his pubes and his cock was buried deep inside the tightest pussy he'd ever felt in his life. He carefully wrapped his right arm around her waist and found her breasts. Perfect. Full and warm, the nipples rising to his fingers, just waiting for him to tug and tease.

He tugged and she moaned. He thrust his hips and she pressed back against him until they found the ideal rhythm of thrust and retreat, thrust and retreat. It was all the way he loved it most—her scent, her full hips and rounded ass, the soft swell of her belly and breasts beneath his palms. He spread his hand over her belly, tangled his fingers in the thick hair between her legs, and then slipped his fingertip over her swollen nub.

It only took a couple of strokes and she was flying! Her inner muscles clamped down on his cock, squeezing him like a living vise. She grabbed his wrist in both her hands and held him against her as her whole body went stiff. Her climax brought his, a shock of sensation from the small of his back to his balls and cock, until he filled her with spurt after spurt of his seed.

He buried his face in her long, dark hair, suddenly awakening as realization hit him. This wasn't a wet dream. This was Chelo. After he'd promised he would never make love to her without her permission, he'd just done exactly that.

"Chelo? I'm sorry. I didn't mean to do that. I thought I was dreaming, sweetheart. Will you forgive me?"

Slowly, she rolled over. He slipped out of her warm sheath, and even as guilty as he felt, he wanted to be back inside her. Instead of showing anger, she kissed him. "S'okay. In fact, that was amazing. I think we can assume I'm not going to freak out when we have sex now, okay?"

"You're sure? Because I'm going to want to do that again. As soon as I can recover."

"Good. And I'm the one who needs to apologize. I set you up."

"What?"

"Last night I woke up during the night and you were hard again and it was between my legs, so I just sort of moved my butt a little and spread my legs, and voila!"

"Voila?" He rolled to his back and laughed. "Chelo? I hope you realize I am never letting you go. And for a werewolf that's a long, long time."

"I know." She rolled over and kissed him.

And Trak didn't take long to recover at all.

Much later, they were having breakfast when Trak set his fork down and stared at her. "Chelo? I know how he keeps finding you. Didn't you say that both Rube and Jorge raped you before you were mated?"

Frowning, she stared at him. Not your usual morning-after conversation, but, "Yes. It was horrible."

"He marked you. Rube didn't actually mate you, because Jorge bit you—he's the one who changed you—but during that night he marked you. There was probably saliva and there was definitely blood. In essence, it's like a mating in that he's linked to you through your blood. He always knows where you are."

No. She would never be free of him, never know a moment's peace, never . . .

Trak's hand covered hers. "Don't you see? If I mate you, in our case merely mark you because you're already wolf, I think the newer marking will be stronger than what happened almost ninety years ago. I need to know, though, if you could bear to be my mate for oh, the next century or so. Are you okay with that?"

"Are you asking me?"

He took both of her hands. "Of course I am. It's not the most romantic proposal, but I can't imagine life without you. You're the only woman I've met who can truly be my partner as alpha of this pack. You're strong and you're beautiful. You complete me, Consuela de los Lobos. And besides, I already told you that I'm never letting you go."

He had, hadn't he? "Trak, when I was lying in bed with you this morning, when we had just made love for the second or maybe the third time, I realized that I was falling in love with you. I'm never letting you go, either."

"I need to shift. It's the wolf's bite that creates the mating link. Be sure and show me where you want it. I'll try not to hurt you." He leaned close and kissed her. "I'm sorry if I do."

He carried his plate to the sink and left it there before stripping out of his clothes. His body thrilled her—tall and lean with well-defined muscles partially disguised by the dark pelt across his muscular chest. He kept his hair fairly short and his beard was barely more than a shadow. She'd never actually seen him clean-shaven, but the dark hair on his cheeks and chin merely accentuated his good looks.

Again, his shift was almost instantaneous, his wolf every bit as beautiful as the man. He trotted across the room and sat at her feet, waiting, she knew, for her to show him where she wanted her bite. There was no doubt in her mind. She untied the robe she'd put on after her shower and dropped it behind her. Then she leaned close and held her left breast. Touching the top curve, she said, "Here. Over my heart.

I want a scar, just a small one. Something that will always remind me of today."

He looked at her for the longest time. He probably wondered if she was just flat-out crazy, but then he licked her breast, swirled his tongue around her nipple as if for emphasis, and nipped her quickly, his teeth sharp and the bite deep enough to draw blood. She held perfectly still while he licked the blood away, leaving his saliva in the small wound.

She reached for a paper napkin to staunch the drips, and then Trak was human again, covering her hand with his, kissing her mouth, her breast, the place where he'd bitten her.

"Does it hurt? I tried to make it fast. I really didn't want to hurt you."

She leaned close and kissed him. "I think that tongue/nipple thing took my mind off the biting part. Can I say it now? I love you, Trak. You are more than I ever dreamed and I will love you forever." She kissed him again. "But we're going to be late. I have to open the shop."

CHAPTER 10

Wednesday morning, Chelo's flower shop

Chelo wondered if she'd ever be able to wipe the silly smile off her face. She loved Trak. That was the only explanation, but the most wonderful thing was that he loved her back. He didn't see her as damaged, didn't even seem too concerned about Rube, though he was here with her, protecting her until, as he phrased it, the pack could "deal with the bastard."

And he was now, physically at least, her mate, though he said they'd still need to go through the official mating ceremony for the pack to recognize her as the alpha's mate. She couldn't wait to tell the others, though that would have to wait for a time when Darnell either knew what they were or was gone, though Chelo doubted that would happen. Darnell loved Evan and Evan loved Darnell. They'd figure it out.

She stood at the worktable with the front door open for customers on this beautiful autumn day, putting together an arrangement for one of the B and Bs in town. She had almost finished—a colorful mix of chrysanthemums and dahlias with graceful columbine and sweet-smelling stock in a beautiful antique basket the owner had dropped off—when she felt the tiny hairs on the back of her neck start to rise. Glancing up, she didn't see anything unusual, and with the door open her view of the front was unimpeded. But just in case, she left her work area and stepped into her office. Trak had brought his laptop and was checking over some paperwork that Cherry had sent to him this morning. He raised his head, smiling, but he quickly shut the laptop and was on his feet, reaching for her hand.

"What's wrong?" He kept his voice low and soothing, but his grip on her hand was tight.

"I don't know, but something isn't right."

He nodded and followed her back into the showroom. "Nothing in here. Wasn't the door open?"

It was closed now. She nodded. "Yes. Definitely open."

"Stay here." He walked to the front door and pulled it open.

Rube's scent was thick in the air. Opening the door had pulled the stench inside. "Ya know," she said, proud of herself for maintaining at least a semblance of calm. "If the idiot bathed once in a while it wouldn't be nearly as easy to know where he was."

"Good point." Trak propped the door open. Then he checked the floor and the walls, even inside the potted plants in the front window.

"What are you looking for?"

"I dunno. Listening devices, cameras, anything to spy on you or just to make you nervous." He went outside and paused in front of the display.

Chelo watched from her spot by the worktable, continuing to work on the arrangement while Trak checked the entire display out in front. A few minutes later he was back inside, where he went through the items in the front window again.

When he walked back to Chelo, he held a finger to his lips, opened his left hand, and showed her three small listening devices. She knew her eyes had to be as big as saucers, but she was really curious when Trak walked back to the window and returned one of them to the potted plant where he'd found it.

"Yeah," he said, standing close to the one in the front window. "I think that's it. Two of them in the display out in front. I don't see anything in here."

So that's how he wanted to play it. "Are you sure there aren't any in the shop? Did you look everywhere?"

"Yeah. Nothing inside. I don't think he had time. You were only out of the room for a few seconds."

"What are you going to do with those? I can't believe he'd try something like that. What's the point?"

"No idea. He's an idiot. This is what I'm doing with these." He took the two he'd kept and pulled out the batteries, then set the devices on the workbench. Grabbing a small hammer Chelo used for building some of her displays, he gave the little gadgets a couple of solid hits and turned them into nothing more than bits of cheap metal and broken plastic. Sweeping the parts into his palm, he tossed the rubble into the wastebasket. "Took care of that," he said. "Shouldn't be any harder to deal with Rube. Wonder where he is now?"

"I don't know, but I really want him gone."

Trak tugged her into the office. "Come with me a moment. I want you to take a look at this . . ." Then he closed the door. "Speak softly. I doubt the mic is strong enough to pick up our voices in here." He hugged her close and then planted a big kiss on her, but he made it a fast one. "You were great! When you're near the bug, I want him to think he's hearing stuff that we're not aware of, so just carry on the way you normally would. I'll be in the office with the door open. Don't leave the shop for anything unless I'm with you. He's probably close by, as those were really cheap devices and their range is limited."

"What do I do if he comes to the shop?"

"Scream bloody murder."

"What?" She covered her mouth to keep from laughing. "Do I look like a screamer to you?"

"Absolutely not, and I will venture to say that Rube never once made you scream."

"You're right. He didn't. Not once."

"Exactly. If you scream it's going to startle the hell out of him. With luck it'll give me time to come after him. One more thing. You're an alpha. There's no doubt in my mind, and I've watched the reactions some of our guys have when you say something and, without planning, put your alpha bitch into it."

She actually smiled. She'd sort of noticed that a few times. Some guys more than others.

"Have you ever ordered Rube to do anything? He might fight it, but if he doesn't expect it from you his instincts might take over, force him to act in a way he doesn't expect. That might give you an edge. Plus, I'm going to talk about the fact we're mated, that he'd better think twice before coming after the pack alpha's woman."

"I think that will just piss him off. He thinks he's invincible."

"Possibly." Trak hugged her close. "But I want that asshole to know that if he messes with you he's going to have the entire pack after him. I love you, Chelo. I can't stop thinking about this morning, how wonderful it felt to slide inside you, how beautifully our bodies fit together. I love the way your mind works; I love the way you look, the way you feel. You're even more than I ever dreamed of for a mate. I want you and all that you are for a long, long time, and I want that bastard gone."

Darnell walked up the front steps of the lodge and flopped down on the porch swing next to Cherry. "Evan's gone. You have to entertain me. So tell me about Meg and Zach. What's their story?"

Cherry laughed. "I keep forgetting you haven't been here all summer like I have. Of course, if you and Evan keep on doing whatever you're doing maybe you won't have to leave ever again."

"I wish. Do you think Evan's happy with me here, or is he just being polite? I mean, he's such a flat-out nice guy. Would he tell me if he wasn't happy?"

Cherry grabbed Darnell's hand and squeezed. "Evan's no pushover, but I've never seen the guy as besotted as he is with you. Women were after him all season long and he'd spend time with them and was always pleasant, took groups on hikes and that sort of thing, but he never paired up with anyone. I think he was missing you."

"Besotted, eh?" Now that was a word she hadn't heard in a while. "Well, I hope he is, because the one thing I've learned since coming back here is that I don't want to leave. I really don't want to spend another four miserable months wondering what Evan was doing or if he ever thought about me since I was obviously obsessing over him." She glanced around the area and realized she and Cherry were the only ones there. "Where is everyone? Evan went into town to help Trak with something, but this place is quiet!"

"Well . . ." Cherry held up her hand and started ticking off fingers. "Brad's working on menus and checking to see if he has to make another trip to the store; Cain's checking the perimeter and cleaning up the entrance so it looks nice when guests arrive; Steph and Christa are working. They both telecommute to their old jobs in San Francisco and only have to go down there about once a month, if that often. Mostly they hold their office meetings on Skype. Wils and Ronan are checking the fence line on the north side of the property. We've had some poachers and one of them actually shot Trak not too long ago. He's completely recovered, but it was a scary reminder that there are bad people out there."

"Wow. That is scary. I'm glad he's okay. Did they catch the one who shot him?"

"Yeah. Got him and some other poachers. They're still locked up."

"Good." She breathed a sigh of relief. Trak was always such a gentleman. She hated to think of someone like him being hurt. "Okay. I know Elle and Tuck have a couple of calls in town this afternoon. That leaves Lawz and Darian, Jules and her guys, and Trak and Chelo."

"Lawz and Darian are probably doing the nasty at their cabin." Cherry laughed. "When I first met Lawz, I thought he was such a pompous jerk. He's actually really nice and he adores Darian. I saw him hauling her off in that direction about an hour ago. I mean that literally. He'd slung her over his shoulder, but she wasn't trying to fight him off. They'll show up for dinner, probably looking a bit rumpled.

Jules, Drew, and Armando—that's Manny—are giving Growl a good cleaning. The bar will probably be busy after the wedding and reception, and the guys are having their bachelor party there tomorrow night. And last but not least, Trak and Chelo are at her flower shop. She's been closing it around four, so they'll be back before long. Trak's not comfortable letting her go into town without him, at least until they get rid of the ex-boyfriend, so he's taking work with him and doing it in her office."

"That's something that's really unusual but special about these guys. They're all very protective of their women. It's sort of old-fashioned, but it's sweet, too."

Cherry just smiled. Darnell had a feeling she was remembering something special.

"You're right. Brad and Cain are unlike any other men I've ever known. I've only been with them a few months, but I can't imagine life without the two of them."

Darnell choked off a giggle. "Sorry. You were such a sweet young thing, Cherry. I just never pictured you for a woman with two hunky men in her bed."

Cherry didn't even try not to laugh. "Darnell, I never pictured me with *any* man in my bed. And yet here I am with two of the sweetest, most gorgeous men I've ever seen, much less known, and they're making love to me every night, reminding me that yes, there really are miracles and they can come true. What's really special is that they've loved each other for years and they both told me they always felt they were missing something, that I'm that something. You can't imagine how special it makes me feel, being loved this much."

Darnell thought about the different couples that made up this very special group of friends. They watched out for one another and protected those they loved. They teased one another, but they were all equals, though she'd noticed that even though he never acted like he was boss, Trak was definitely their leader. The one they all deferred to.

She'd actually wondered if it was some kind of cult, but there was nothing weird about them beyond the fact that they were all really wet-panty, drop-dead gorgeous. As if that were strange . . .

And Evan? He was the nicest of the bunch and definitely one of the sexiest. She wondered what he was doing in town for Trak. He seemed to be Trak's assistant, the one Trak called on for things. She really needed to ask him, but the minute she was with him all she wanted to do was drag him into the sack. So she asked Cherry, instead.

"What does Evan do here, exactly? I don't think he's ever said."

"A lot, actually." Cherry gave the deck a kick and set the swing to slowly swaying. "The resort and the wolf preserve are two separate businesses, and the guys are all partners in the business. The resort generates income for profit, and the preserve, which is a nonprofit, generates enough income to keep the habitat safe and the wolves that need care, cared for. Point being, there's a lot of work behind the scenes to keep everything running and Evan is key to a lot of that getting done. There's nothing he can't do. He's an amazing carpenter and helped build all the cabins. During the season he handled a lot of the housekeeping and laundry, any repairs on things—plumbing and electrical, mostly. We get some wild storms here that can mess with the power. He keeps the vehicles tuned up, helps patrol the preserve— Manny's in charge of that, but Evan's part of the crew— and whenever there's a pup in trouble or an animal that's left orphaned or is injured, after Tuck checks them over Evan raises them and then turns them free. He's truly a gentle soul."

"He is. And everything you've told me makes me realize he's even more special than I imagined. Thank you."

"You're welcome." She laughed. "Always love to be of service. Well, are you ready for the wedding?"

Darnell rolled her eyes. "This conversation began with me asking about Meg and Zach. Who are they? What are they like?"

"They're wonderful. We met when Meg planned her bachelorette party here at the resort mainly because she figured it would give her time to talk herself out of marrying Zach."

"What? Doesn't she love him?"

"That's the thing. She loves him to pieces but didn't think she was worthy of his love. Zach's really handsome and a successful businessman. He owns a company that builds luxury yachts and Meg went to work for him right out of college as his administrative secretary. They started dating and he proposed; she moved in with him but still didn't think he really loved her."

"But why?"

Cherry shrugged. "You're tiny. Meg's like me—generously proportioned, to put it kindly." Smiling, she added, "Or if you want to be politically correct. She's spent her life feeling imperfect because of her size and some other issues. You know, the kind of stuff that can ruin your life and yet means absolutely nothing to anyone else?"

"Oh, yeah. Got some of my own."

"Don't we all. Zach missed her so badly after a couple of days apart that he drove down from Portland to see her, but he swerved to miss a bear not far from Weaverville and it ended up being a pretty bad wreck. It put him in the hospital with amnesia. Tuck and Elle are the ones who found him there, but it was Trak who helped Meg and Zach start really talking to each other about how they felt. Turns out, they both had issues, but they appear to have gotten past them. I can't wait to see Meg. You'll love her. She's got the world's greatest laugh and a wicked sense of humor. She really fits in with this crowd. So does Zach. They're both terrific."

"We've talked." Darnell had really gotten a kick out of her. "She's bringing her own makeup and some pictures of how she wants her hair. I might need rollers and stuff like that. I have no idea what she wants."

"I've got a curling iron with lots of different-sized rollers. Will that work?"

"It should." She raised her head. "I think I hear a car."

Cherry checked her watch. "Bet that's them. They're due about now. Time to break out the margaritas!"

Evan held Darnell's hand as they walked back to his cabin. "You sure you don't want me to carry you?"

She giggled. "I need to prove that I'm still sober enough to walk."

"You're walking just fine." He chuckled as she tripped and he caught her. "It's the staying upright and maintaining a straight line you're having trouble with."

"I'm really sorry, Evan." She hiccupped.

"What for?"

"I had too much to drink. I promised I wasn't going to do that, but everyone was having such a good time, and I sort of lost track."

"Blame Brad. He's the one who kept filling your glass. He knows you're not driving anywhere."

"Okay. I can do that. As long as he doesn't mind." She wrapped her hands around Evan's arm and hung on.

"He better not. Though at least he didn't bring you a Long Island Iced Tea."

She shook her head. "I'm never having one of those again. Ever."

He caught her when she stumbled, finally just went ahead and did what he'd been wanting to do and lifted her against his chest. He loved her, and as soon as they got rid of the rogue who was after Chelo he was damned well going to make her his.

There'd been no sign of Rube and his cronies this afternoon when Trak had asked Evan to come into town. They'd decided to leave the bug at the store to give the bastard something to listen to. They hoped it would keep him busy, but Trak was worried Rube and his partners in crime might crash the wedding. That could get ugly. A bunch of dangerous werewolves at a human gathering? At least Trak had taken Zach and Meg aside and let them know about the risk, but they'd been angry for Chelo's sake, had discussed it privately and decided there was no question of postponing the wedding or doing it anywhere else.

Evan noticed, though, that Zach stayed stone-cold sober tonight. So did every male wolf in their pack, himself included. He wasn't about to drink or do anything that would make him less capable of protecting his Nellie.

He tilted so she could reach the door and open it, then carried her into the cabin. Since Nell had been here, the place felt more like a home than ever. She'd picked a bouquet of late wildflowers that graced the mantel over the fireplace, resplendent in a large canning jar. There was a bucket filled with branches, their fall leaves dark red and brilliant yellow and every shade in between, sitting beneath the kitchen window. Blazing splashes of color, those feminine touches made him smile whenever he crossed the threshold.

The same way Nellie made him smile.

"You gonna put me down, big guy?" Nell tightened her grip around his neck, pulled herself close for a kiss, and somehow shifted in his embrace until she straddled his waist, arms around his neck, slowly kissing him, running her tongue across his, over his teeth, tickling the roof of his mouth. Essentially driving him insane.

"Never." He cupped her bottom with one hand, her back with the other, and pulled her closer, stealing greedy kisses from her lips, her throat, her shoulders. She moaned and stretched in his arms, locking her legs around his waist, arching her back, and thrusting her breasts forward.

He turned and leaned his butt against the kitchen counter, carefully working her sweater up and over her head, tugging it off her arms and dropping it on the floor. Her bra came next, a lacy little thing that cupped her beautifully shaped breasts and effectively kept him from tasting what he wanted so badly. The closure was in the front, one suitable for undoing with merely two fingers and his thumb.

It popped open and her breasts spilled free. She had absolutely gorgeous breasts with beautiful nipples—large and very dark, a deep chocolaty raspberry that tasted as delicious as they looked. He tasted. With tongue and lips and teeth, he tasted, until Nell was writhing in his arms, rubbing against him like a cat in heat. He turned and rested her bottom on the kitchen counter, undid the snap on her jeans, pried her ankles loose from around his waist, and pulled her pants down her long legs. Her panties came with the denim and he tugged her sandals off as he dragged the pants over her feet.

They were both panting, both aroused, and he reached into his pocket for his wallet, found it, and spread it open on the countertop. There. The last condom. He hadn't been carrying them because he and Nellie had spent their time together in a comfortable bed, but there was no way in hell he was breaking out of this moment to go up the stairs.

He unsnapped his jeans, tugged the zipper down, and cautiously drew his erection out of his pants, paying careful attention to the metal teeth on the zipper. He was so damned hard he ached, so close to coming that his tip glistened with cream. Hands shaking, he rolled the condom on, smoothing it down along his shaft.

Nell panted, watching every move he made, her eyes slightly glazed, her lips parted and shining from their kisses. Tugging her forward on the counter, he slid inside her wet heat, slowly, carefully, filling her until he bottomed out against the hard mouth of her cervix. They both sighed and he lifted her, holding her against him, turning to rest his ass once more against the counter. He loved her slight size, the fact that he could make love to her like this, lifting her up and away, pulling her close, knowing the angle of penetration was absolutely perfect, that he rubbed against her clit on the upstroke and down.

He knew this wasn't going to last. It was so hard the first time with Nell. Even the second and the third, but he knew that by the fourth he'd be able to spend a respectable amount of time before he finally came. And it was really sexy in a truly decadent way, standing here fully clothed with his pants unzipped and shoved down, his balls still caught behind the opened fly, his cock buried deep inside Nellie. A totally naked, moaning Nellie.

He loved her. He had to fight the urge to shift and bite her, to make her his for all time. Her safety came first. Her safety and her pleasure. He would wait, but he didn't have to like it.

Her soft moans and sexy whimpers escalated, frantic, needy sounds growing with each breath. Her body writhed in his arms and she clutched at his shoulders with surprising strength. He thrust deep and hard, so close to coming, but he had to hold out, had to watch his favorite part of sex with Darnell Deya. That moment when her body tightened, when he heard her thundering heart, felt the rush of blood in her veins, and knew it was time, knew he'd managed to give her the ultimate pleasure any man could share with a woman.

She arched her back and screamed. Her inner muscles clamped down on his cock as if she wasn't going to let the damned thing get away. He wasn't going anywhere. Far from it, as his own climax quite literally exploded out of him, a surge of power from his balls to his dick and into the condom. His shout as he thrust against her, drove deep inside her, probably rattled the dishes in the cupboards.

Times like this, he was really glad the pack's cabins weren't close together.

After a moment Nell slumped against him. Her ragged breaths and sweat-slick body told him everything. Told him there was no going back. She was his. Forever his, but damn it all, he couldn't tell her that. Not yet.

There was something he could tell her, though. Holding

her tightly against his chest, he kissed her forehead, her cheeks, her lips. "I love you, Nellie. I love you more than life itself. I don't want you to leave. Stay here with me, please? I really want you to stay."

CHAPTER 11

Brad was the only one in the lodge dining room when Darnell and Evan finally made it down for breakfast. He was adding fresh bacon to the buffet, keeping food available at the lodge while Meg and Zach were here. The pack wasn't about to ignore Brad's cooking, either.

Evan reached over Brad for a plate and handed it to Darnell before grabbing one for himself. "You must have known we were coming. Thanks, Bradley."

Brad just shook his head. "I swear you guys can all smell bacon from a mile away. G'morning, Darnell. Has he driven you batshit crazy yet?"

Darnell kissed Brad's cheek. "No, but he's trying his best. You've got to give the guy credit." She glanced around the empty space. Where is everyone? I'm not used to seeing this place without a crowd."

"Most of them came through early. Let's see. Trak and Chelo went into town to open up the shop, and Manny went with them. I think Trak wants the extra insurance until the ex-boyfriend is out of the picture. Cherry's in the office; Cain's still working on the entry, making sure it looks good for Sunday; everyone's essentially doing what they do. It's just that you and Evan are about two hours later than usual."

Darnell rolled her eyes. "Don't ever keep auto-filling my glass when you're making margaritas."

"You looked like you were stone-cold sober. I would never keep pouring for someone who's had too much to drink." He glanced at Evan. "She hides it well."

"That she does. Until she doesn't. I think we'll need to ration her from now on."

Darnell filled her plate and walked away while the guys were still talking about her as if she weren't in the room, but she had to bite her lip to keep from grinning. Brad was every bit as gorgeous as Evan, and so frickin' nice. What was it with this place? She found a small table off in a corner and parked her butt with a view of the room. Evan was right behind her. He took the chair next to her so they both could look across the big dining hall.

About that time, Zach and Meg came wandering in, looking half-asleep and very much in love. Darnell wondered if she had that same look on her face—it was pretty obvious how Evan felt when he looked at her. Darnell's heart felt like it was going to burst when she turned and caught him smiling at her. Just staring and smiling. She wondered what he was thinking, if he was on the same wavelength as she was, if his mind was also filled with thoughts of last night.

She hadn't expected his declaration of love. She'd hoped he felt that way but never imagined what it would be like to actually hear the words. Hear them and know she felt exactly the same way.

Which had made it so much easier to tell Evan she loved him, too.

Meg and Zach greeted them, then left their jackets at another of the small tables. They filled their plates at the buffet and then pulled their chairs close together and held hands. Meg leaned against Zach with a soft smile that spoke volumes.

There was obviously something special about Feral Passions.

About three cups of coffee later, Meg and Zach finished their breakfast and walked over to join Evan and Darnell.

"Mind if we join you?"

Evan stood and pulled a chair out for Meg. "I was wondering when you'd finally get enough caffeine in your systems," he said. "We're moving pretty slow, too."

Darnell laughed and saluted Meg with her coffee cup. "I'm having a margarita morning. It's going to take more than coffee. I probably need a major cleansing. Tell me, what do you want to do for your party tonight? Do you have any plans?"

Meg shrugged. "Not really. I just want to spend time with my besties. Jules, Darian, Elle, and me—we go back to grade school. And Cherry, Steph, and Christa are amazing. I already feel like they're family, too. And it's weird because I hardly know you, but you're like one of the group already." She leaned against Zach. "I mean, I love my man, but there are times when girls just wanna be girls, ya know?"

"Exactly." She glanced at Evan and winked. "But it also gives the guys time to get together where they can drink and cuss and scratch their balls without anyone complaining."

Meg turned to Zach, wide-eyed. "I know you occasionally utter an expletive and you do enjoy a good cognac come evening, but you don't really scratch your balls, do you, Zachary?"

Looking every bit the executive, he turned to Meg and said, "No, sweetheart. Of course not. I have people who do that for me."

Things sort of went downhill from there. By the time they cleared their plates and headed their separate ways, Darnell actually hurt from laughing and Evan wasn't in much better shape. Tonight was going to be an absolute hoot.

Evan was going through his collection of old movies. Somewhere in this stack he had some really old, classic black-and-white porn, so bad it was hysterical. There! He knew he'd find them. He grabbed the three DVDs and set them aside.

Trak had seen some of it, but not all the guys had been so blessed. Evan figured it would make for some good laughs, especially when all of them had such gorgeous women of their own. He glanced at Nellie. She looked utterly beautiful in a pair of red leggings and a soft, cream-colored top that was all gauzy and soft and hung off one shoulder. She was so serious, packing a small overnight bag with all sorts of bottles and tubes, brushes and lotions. Pulling stuff out of two large suitcases, choosing and checking before moving things into the smaller bag.

He sat back on his heels. "So. What are you ladies planning to do tonight?"

"I'm going to try makeup on the bride and bridesmaids so I can get an idea of what they want for Sunday. Their coloring is all so different, so I'll get to play with all my paint."

"Sounds like work, considering what you do for a living."

She turned a bright grin his way. "I love what I do for a

living. I can't wait to get back into playtime with my war paint." Then she went back to packing.

He thought about that for a moment, watching her, the way she concentrated on every item she took from one large bag and moved into the smaller one. This was what Darnell did. She was a makeup artist in Hollywood. What was she going to do here? Would she expect to go back to her job once they mated? He didn't think he could live in LA, that far from the pack, and if she was his he wanted to be with her. What if she couldn't live here? They hadn't discussed any of the practicalities, and he couldn't change her without telling her everything.

He'd been living in a goddamned fantasy world all week long.

Trak was just going to have to understand. Their alpha really didn't want them to tell anyone what they were, but Evan had to agree with Cain, who'd insisted that the women had a right to know before their lives, not to mention their bodies, were forever changed.

Evan loved her so fucking much, and Nellie'd said she loved him, too, but would she be able to move up here to the middle of nowhere? Damn. Why did he have to think about this shit now? He really needed to get down to Growl and hang out with the guys. Maybe then he'd get his head on straight, figure out how to broach the subject with Nell.

"Okay. I'm ready. What time are you guys getting together?"

"I'm just waiting on you. C'mon. I'll walk you down."

She grabbed her little suitcase, the kind you normally hauled through an airport with tiny little wheels, but it rolled along the hard-packed trail through the forest as if it were designed for this territory. Evan held her hand as they walked to the main road that wound through the preserve.

"Oh! Look how pretty that is." Nell tugged him to a stop.

They'd stepped out onto the edge of the road and Evan stood there holding her hand, enjoying the view. Of course, he was looking at Nell. When she caught him, she poked him in the ribs. "The lodge, Evan. Look at the lodge."

He glanced up. The lodge was all lit up with blue and white strings of LED lights across the deck and more lights blazing inside. It really did look beautiful, especially with all the little twinkling lights glowing in the forest. That had been Manny's idea, to light the trails to the individual guest cabins with tiny white Christmas lights. The road to Growl was down a dark stretch and Evan didn't have a flashlight, but he had excellent night vision. He turned toward the lodge, but Nell stopped him

"You go ahead," she said. "I can see just fine and you're going to be stumbling along in the dark."

"Are you sure?"

"It's right there, Evan. Go. Have fun. Watch your dirty movies and then come back to the cabin and teach me everything you learn."

"I like that idea." He wrapped his arm around her waist, leaned over, and kissed her. He loved the way she melted against him, the way her lips went all soft and sexy beneath his. He really hoped this party didn't go too late. He was already counting time until he could get her alone.

"Have fun, Evan."

She kissed him again, and then she turned and headed toward the lodge. He watched her until she reached the deck and started up the steps. Then he turned and jogged along the road. He could already hear laughter down at Growl. He couldn't wait to pull out his old movies. The guys were gonna love them.

Darnell walked into the lodge and bowed to applause. Everyone was already here; there was a table filled with food and a big bowl of what looked and smelled like a rum punch. There were bottles lined up along the counter and she went over and took a look. "Yum. Smells really good. What's in the punch?"

Meg laughed. "This one's in your honor, Darnell. It's Long Island Iced Tea. Cherry says you're fond of it."

"You, Ms. DuBois, are going to die."

"Aw, c'mon. You don't have to drink a gallon of it, and it's just so good! I told your story to Meg and it was her idea. Blame the bride-to-be."

Sighing dramatically, Darnell walked over and stared into the depths of the huge bowl. "There's enough in here to kill us all."

"Not quite, but it's why I wanted the party tonight and not the night before the wedding." Meg took a sip and sighed. "Time to recover."

"Good point." Christa and Steph raised their glasses. "To the bride!"

"Hear, hear!" Jules, Darian, and Elle surrounded Meg. "It took you two long enough."

"I know. I'm picky."

While the old friends were laughing and drinking, Darnell took her case over to a table in the corner and set up her wares. She reached for the large bottle of makeup remover, and there was nothing in the pouch. She went through every pocket and pouch in the case. Nothing. There was no way she was putting industrial-strength makeup on any of these women without a way to get it off.

"Anyone got a flashlight? I left some stuff at the cabin. It'll just take me a minute to get it."

Jules walked over to a cabinet near the door to the kitchen and pulled out a small halogen light. "I just used this last night. Manny put fresh batteries in it."

"Thanks."

She went down the stairs and cut off into the woods. It was so pretty here during the day, a little spooky when she was all alone at night, but Evan's cabin wasn't all that far and she was there in a couple of minutes. Once inside, she went straight to the mess she'd left in the corner by the fireplace. The bottle was sitting right where she'd left it.

She grabbed it and headed back to the lodge. There was no moon, but enough light filtered through the trees from the lights on the deck that she turned off the flashlight, just to experience the forest alone. It was absolutely beautiful, and so peaceful. She paused at the edge of the trees, mere steps from the parking lot, and watched her new friends inside the lodge.

Living here would be an amazing experience. She thought about leaving her work and the people she knew in the business, but none of them were what she could call close friends. They were fellow employees in what was essentially a transient business. Each job meant a new crew. Sometimes she knew everyone on the set; other times she didn't know a soul.

Some jobs were fun and filled with laughter, but not all. Not even that many. It was stressful work and there were no guarantees. She could make a fortune one year yet have to live off her savings the next. Thank goodness she had savings. She didn't imagine that Evan made all that much money, not after she'd heard what kinds of jobs he did, but it was good, honest work.

And she loved him. They'd make do.

Something caught her attention. Voices? More like whispers. Were the guys coming down to tease the girls? She wouldn't put it past them. Even big boys could be pretty juvenile at times, especially when booze and women were involved. Moving quietly, she kept to the woods and worked her way toward the lodge, following the shadows. Voices again, but they weren't familiar. They were definitely whispering. Luckily, the sound carried on the still night air.

Shivering from nerves, not the warm air of this balmy night, Darnell crouched down behind a couple of large rocks bordering the parking lot. That's when she saw them. Four men, moving through the shadows on the far side of the lot, crouched low and definitely trying to hide.

It had to be Rube and his cronies. Chelo was in danger, but the guys were at Growl and she hadn't even thought to bring her damned phone. The four were too close to the lodge for Darnell to slip in the back way to warn the women. She needed to tell the guys. She tucked the jar she'd carried against the base of the rock.

Moving quickly but quietly, she went back into the woods and headed toward the bar. As soon as she was out of sight of the lodge, she put it in gear and booked it down the road. The bar was just around the first bend and she got to the front door faster than she'd ever run in her life.

Grabbing the door, she ran inside and flipped on the light. The guys turned as one, and Evan was there, holding her. "Nell! What's going on? What's wrong?"

"Four guys sneaking through the woods. They were almost to the lodge when I saw them. Hurry! The girls don't know. I went back to the cabin to get some stuff and saw them when I was going back to the lodge." But she was talking to an empty cabin. Evan was already running outside. Trak yelled, "Zach! Stay with Darnell. We'll take care of this. If it gets bad, there's a cellar behind the bar. Lift the mat."

But why was he tearing his clothes off? Stunned, Darnell stood in the doorway and watched as all of them—Manny and Drew, Brad, Wils, Ronan, Lawz, Tuck, Cain, and Brad, all of them—stripped out of their clothing. Trak went first and by the time his hands hit the ground he'd . . . "Holy shit." She turned and Zach was behind her, holding her arms, watching them as if he'd seen this before.

"What are they?"

"This isn't how Evan wanted you to find out."

No shit. She couldn't take her eyes off of them. Trak had already raced ahead, and now Manny and Tuck followed; at least she thought that's who they were. And where Evan had been, a huge dark wolf paused only a moment and turned to look at her.

It was him. The wolf she'd petted. The one who'd fallen asleep with his head in her lap. "Evan?" He turned away and raced into the darkness. And that's when she heard the screams. "Ohmygod!" She twisted out of Zach's grasp. "We have to go. They're after the women. They're going to take Chelo."

"I promised Trak I'd let them handle it, if those men showed up."

"That's not an old boyfriend stalking Chelo, is it?"

"No."

Zach held her arms tightly. He wasn't hurting her, but he wasn't letting go, either. Holding her here?

Another scream cut the night air. Zach tensed behind her. "Meg! Shit. That was Meg."

"We might be able to help."

Zach grabbed her hand. "I can't stay here, either. But we're only human."

"And they are?"

"Werewolves, Darnell. They're a pack of fucking were-wolves, and some of the best friends I've ever had in my life. C'mon."

"Wait a minute." She went behind the counter and reached under the bar. It took just a little bit of a search before she came up with a handgun, a small but deadly .38 Special. "I've never seen a bar without a handgun somewhere under the counter." She checked to see if it was loaded—it was, and it was a small enough revolver to fit in her hand.

"Do you know how to shoot that thing?" Zach was already in motion. "Because I've never fired a gun in my life."

"I grew up in a really poor part of LA, so yes." And her childhood had been a rather eclectic experience. She might want to discuss that with Evan, too. Once he explained the werewolf thing.

She really couldn't let herself go there. Not until every-one was safe.

They'd reached the lodge in record time. Evan circled around the entire building but didn't see any sign of the rogue wolves on the deck. The women were all inside, sit-ting on the floor against the north wall of the dining room, and he saw at least three men inside with them. They hadn't shifted, and Nellie had seen four men. Where the hell was the fourth?

If he were a wolf, Evan was certain he would have picked up the scent, but there were so many scents here that he was having trouble separating all of them out.

Chelo was inside with the rest of the women, and he was so damned glad Nellie hadn't been caught. Thank goodness she was safe with Zach. He felt horrible. He'd really wanted to have a chance to tell her what he—what they all—were. The look on Nellie's face had been utter shock, but what else should he expect? He should have told her. He'd had every opportunity to tell her, but he hadn't done it and now it was too late.

But these women needed help. He'd have to worry about Nell and what this meant to them later. Right now, he needed to find that fourth wolf.

Trak shifted, turned, and tapped Cain's shoulder. "Shift," he said, pushing when he gave the order. Combined with Cain's natural strength, it gave the wolf an extra boost, and he stood as a man beside Trak in mere seconds. The others backed off a bit, a subconscious act with so much power in the air, but now wasn't the time to explain.

For the first time ever, Trak was damned thankful for Cain's alpha nature and innate power—a power that could help save lives tonight.

"What's the plan?"

"You go in from the back; I'm walking in the front door. When I step into the lodge, I want you coming through the back door at the same time. We're both going to command them to drop, and the combined strength behind the directive should at least throw them off stride, if not have them belly down on the floor."

Cain nodded. "I can do that. It might drop the women, too."

Trak merely shrugged. "If it does, it might piss them off, but it'll save their lives."

Cain touched Trak's shoulder. "I'll know when you go inside. I'll do my best to match your timing."

Trak nodded. He'd wondered sometimes if Cain could do that, something only the strongest alphas had—the ability to sense other wolves, to know exactly where they were at all times. Trak occasionally had a flash of such power, but it was not a natural part of him. It explained Cain's success as an enforcer. After this was over, he really needed to spend some time with the guy. They still had issues, or at least Trak did.

Issues heavily colored by admiration.

Trak mentally drew the attention of the rest of the pack. He rarely used his alpha power, and their response was immediate. "I want the rest of you surrounding the lodge. Be ready to catch anyone who might try to escape. Manny? You and Drew stay behind me and out of sight, in case I need help. Tuck? Follow Cain as backup. The rest of you, spread out and be ready. Once Cain and I are inside, I want you right behind. Hopefully we'll get them when they're still confused by the strength behind the order."

He watched as his pack mates shifted into position. Then he stepped out onto the front drive, in full view of the lodge. Cain headed into the forest, running silently on bare feet. Trak walked across the parking area and up the stairs. As he reached the deck, he had a clear view inside, the women sitting against the north wall, the fourth wolf, a big gray beast, standing in front of the women. Guarding them.

Not a single woman looked frightened. Meg, the only

human in the room, looked flat-out pissed. He liked that. Darnell was safe at Growl with Zach. That was good. Chelo looked absolutely regal. She was the only one standing, and she glared with unfiltered hatred at the big man across the room. Even better. Damn, she was absolutely perfect. A true alpha bitch.

Trak shoved the door open. It hit the wall hard enough to rattle the building. Everyone turned his way. Rube stepped forward, pushing the other two men back. The wolf turned and snarled.

Chelo hated the fact that she was stuck here with the women, unable to fight. She knew the men must know by now that something had happened, hoped Darnell had seen something and warned them, but where were they?

The front door suddenly flew open so fast it slammed against the wall hard enough to shake the room. Trak stepped into the lodge. He was utterly magnificent, standing tall and muscular, his nude body a study in masculine beauty. At the same moment, a door behind the men opened and Cain was there, equally beautiful, his power filling the room.

Rube's men spun around to see this second threat when both Cain and Trak shouted as one.

"Drop!"

The word was infused with power, two strong alphas working in tandem, but that never happened! Chelo felt the power wash over her, but she fought it, fought to stay free of it. The wolf in front of her had gone down and two of the men were on the floor, but Rube somehow fought it off. He turned and raced toward Chelo, grabbed her around the waist, and threw her over his shoulder. She screamed as both Trak and Cain converged on Rube, but the bastard tightened his hold on her and went straight for the big plate-glass window.

He leapt into the air and hit the window midway, shattering it. Chelo cursed as shards of glass flew all around. Rube went to his knees on the deck, but he was up and over the railing in a heartbeat.

There was nothing to stop him. The dark forest was mere steps ahead. He held her tightly, locked against his foul body as he raced toward freedom.

CHAPTER 12

"He's got Chelo."

Zach gripped Darnell and jerked her back and down behind the rock as glass exploded outward and shards flew through the air. Rube leapt over the railing with Chelo over his shoulder, but she was struggling, throwing him off balance.

Darnell pulled free of Zach's grip, stepped into Rube's path, raised the gun, and shouted, "Stop!"

Rube stopped, but he threw Chelo roughly to the ground and reached for Darnell. She spun out of his grasp, raised the pistol in both hands again, and fired.

The blast deafened her. Rube stopped and shook his head at the noise. How the hell could she miss this close?

Lunging forward, he grabbed the gun out of her hands as Chelo scrambled out of his way. Cursing, Darnell slipped beneath Rube's hands just as Zach launched himself from behind the rock. He tackled Rube around the knees at the same moment Evan flew off the deck and grabbed Rube around the shoulders. The three men tumbled to the ground.

Darnell ran to Chelo. She was still on the ground, holding her head, obviously stunned by the fall. "Are you okay?

I can't believe I don't see any blood." She reached up and picked a large splinter of glass out of Chelo's hair. "That's got to be good, right?"

Chelo cursed and tried to sit. Darnell helped her sit upright while Evan and Zach wrestled with Rube. The fight rolled closer and Darnell practically lifted Chelo to her feet. They backed out of the way. Rube was thickly muscled and fighting like a crazed berserker, with both Evan and Zach struggling to hang onto him.

His face began to change, his canines growing.

Darnell shouted, "He's shifting! Evan, he's turning into a wolf!"

Evan didn't hesitate. He wrapped his forearm around Rube's head and jerked. The loud crack turned Darnell's stomach. She'd never heard that sound before, but there was no doubt what Evan had done. Rube went limp. Evan lowered his body to the ground, Rube's head lolling at an unnatural angle.

Zach was on his knees, head down, gasping for breath. Evan straightened slowly, but he didn't even look in Darnell's direction. Instead, he held his hand out to the other man. Zach glanced at Evan's hand and took hold. Evan pulled him to his feet. They both stared at Rube's body for a long moment, and then Zach shook his head, a short, sharp jerk as if shaking off the fight. "Thank you." He raised his head and looked at Evan. "That guy's the strongest sonofabitch I've ever disagreed with. If you hadn't shown up, I think he would have had me way too easily."

"We'll never know." Evan stared at the body. "I should feel badly." He looked at Zach again. "I've never killed before. Came close, but . . ." His words sort of faded out and he turned as Trak leapt over the railing and went straight to Chelo. Unlike Evan, who was still gloriously naked, Trak had found a pair of sweatpants. He didn't say a word, just gathered Chelo up in his arms and held her close. She didn't cry, but Darnell noticed she was still trembling.

For that matter, so was Darnell. She wasn't sure what to do. She wished Evan was holding her the way Trak held Chelo, but he still hadn't even looked at her. She wanted to go to him, but she didn't know what to say. Instead, she picked up the handgun that Rube had taken away from her, opened the chamber, and removed the bullets. She stared at them a moment and would have laughed, but they'd all think she was crazy.

Carefully she replaced the shells.

Meg came running down the stairs and straight into Zach's arms. "I didn't even know you were here. The guys said you were keeping Darnell safe at the bar. Are you okay?"

"I am." He glanced at Rube lying on the ground. "He's not." Pulling Meg into his arms and turning her away from the body, he kissed her. "Do you mind calling off the party? I want to take you back to the cabin and just hold you all night long. This was a little more excitement than I ever want to be in the middle of again."

Meg laughed, but it was a pretty watery laugh from what Darnell could tell. She tried to smile at Meg but couldn't manage more than a grimace. "Let's try some makeup and hair ideas tomorrow. Is that okay with you, Meg?"

Meg sniffed and raised her head from Zach's chest. There was a soggy spot with smeared mascara on his shirt. She used the hem of his shirt to wipe the tears from her eyes— and further smeared the mascara. "Yeah. I don't think makeup would work right now."

Zach kissed the top of her head, but he kept his arm around her. "If you folks don't mind, I'm taking my woman to bed. Trak, do you need anything from me?"

Trak slowly stood and Zach held out his hand. Trak took it in his. "I need to thank you. You and Evan and Darnell. He had to die. We couldn't let him live, knowing he'd never give up trying to take Chelo. I owe you. All of you." He smiled at Darnell and then focused on Zach again. "Yes. Take your woman home to bed. We can figure out the details tomorrow."

Cherry walked down the steps and over to the small group standing around Rube's body. She handed a pair of sweatpants to Evan. "You look cold," she said. "Cover the dangly bits, Evan. We don't want anything to get hurt."

He smiled at her. He still hadn't even looked at Darnell. "Thanks, Cherry. What's with the three inside?"

"The wolf shifted and apologized. The other two are sitting at the table having coffee and spilling their guts. It appears that Rube, here, is . . . was the pack bully. He's got something over each one of them, enough to force them into this trip. I promised them that Rube won't be going back. Obviously I was right." She kissed Evan on the cheek. "As I usually am. I think we should just let them go."

Trak nodded. Then he turned to Darnell, who sat by herself, though closer to Chelo than to Evan. He held out his hand. "Gun, please?"

She nodded and handed it to him, but she wouldn't look at him.

"That was a good move on your part, Darnell. How'd you find this thing?"

Shrugging, she stared at her toes. "Like I told Zach, I've never once been in a bar that didn't have a handgun under the counter. I looked and found it, saw it was loaded." She finally raised her head and glared at him. "I did not, however, expect blanks."

Smiling, Trak merely shrugged. "A good loud noise is usually pretty effective with werewolves. We've got really sensitive ears." He glanced at Evan. So did Darnell, and he looked so miserable it made her feel even worse. "For what it's worth, Darnell, Evan had orders not to tell you about us. If you want to blame anyone, blame me. In a werewolf pack, there's only one leader, and that's me. I'm the pack's alpha and it was my decision that he not tell you anything, but there are good reasons for not saying who and what we are. In this case, because this jackass was after Chelo and we had an idea he'd be trying something at some point we weren't willing to take the risk with your safety. Evan can explain it to you since it appears this particular cat's out of the bag." He turned to Evan. "Or wolf, as the case might be."

Darnell stared at the body lying on the ground. She'd been so angry at Rube when he was carrying Chelo and coming at her and Zach. Angry and frustrated, and sad that Evan had kept such a huge secret. And now Trak was telling her not to blame Evan, that he was only following orders. "Then it's okay now? He can tell me about you guys? About himself?"

She chanced a quick look at Evan. He was staring at her as if she held his life in her hands, like maybe she hated him, but that wasn't it at all. She'd been shocked when they all stripped out of their clothes and shifted, though it explained a lot of things she'd wondered about.

"He can tell you whatever he wants, and that's whether you choose to stay or go. We don't usually tell anyone about us. It's frightening to think about what would happen to our simple lives should our secret get out, but you've proved that you have what it takes to join the pack if you choose, and I think we can trust you should you choose not to. It's all up to you, Darnell. Talk to Evan. Let him tell you our story and we'll see you in the morning. Find out what you've decided."

She actually smiled at Trak. "I'm amazed you can call your lives simple and actually say that with a straight face, Mr. Jakes." Then she focused on Evan.

He held out his hand. She placed hers in his, thinking just how right it felt.

"What do you want to do, Nellie?"

"I think I want to go into the lodge and pour a pitcher full of that punch Meg put together and maybe carry it back to your cabin. And then I want to crawl into bed with you and hear all about what you've been hiding from me."

"You do, eh?" He nodded. "I think we can manage that." He tugged and she turned to follow just as the three men who'd come with Rube walked down the stairs. They had an old blanket and some rope. Darnell had a feeling she knew what they planned to do with it, but she wanted to see what they had to say.

The largest of the three stepped up to Trak and bowed his head. "We've come to apologize for defiling your land and scaring your women." He glanced at the men on either side. "What we did was wrong and we hope you'll forgive us for something none of us wanted any part of. We also ask for permission to take our fallen one home. Our alpha will want to be assured he's finally gone."

"Granted." Trak had folded his arms over his chest and he kept his eyes focused on the three men. None of them appeared able to meet his steady gaze.

"We want to thank you, too." The spokesman glanced at

the body between them. "He was an evil man. We'd hoped that when his brother died someone would finally take it into their head to kill Rube as well. None of us had the balls to try, but we all wanted him dead. Chelo? We owe you even more of an apology. None of us wanted any part of this, but we were afraid to cross him. Or his brother. Please forgive us."

Chelo merely nodded. Darnell tugged Evan's hand. She'd heard enough from them. She really wanted to hear what Evan had to say. It still hadn't sunk in, not entirely. All these people she'd grown so fond of, every single one of them except for Meg and Zach, were werewolves.

Never in her wildest dreams. And then another thought struck. Cherry and Elle? Darian, Jules, Christa, and Steph? All of them . . . were they wolves, too? She and Evan stepped into the lodge and Darnell headed straight for the punch bowl. She spotted Brad in the kitchen. "Have you got a large pitcher I can borrow?"

She heard laughter, and Cain stepped out of the kitchen with a big half-gallon Mason jar with a screw-top lid, filled to the brim with punch. He handed it to Evan and then leaned over and kissed Darnell. "Don't say we never think of your well-being, Darnell. Have a good evening."

She glanced at the jar in Evan's hands. "I fully intend to. Trust me on that."

They were all laughing when Darnell spotted Trak and Chelo coming up the steps to the lodge.

Trak really wanted to take Chelo home, but he needed to speak with the members of his pack, all of whom were still hanging around the dining hall. Tonight's event had been unsettling, but he had a feeling they were more concerned with Cain's role in what happened than the danger they'd faced.

A few of them knew that Cain was an alpha, though the man did his best to hide his nature, but Trak didn't think any of them had any idea just how powerful Cain was. Trak had needed Cain's help tonight or he never would have asked him to reveal himself so publicly.

There would be questions.

First, there was Chelo. He stopped outside of the door into the dining room and dropped a light kiss on her forehead. "I need to speak with them. They're going to be concerned about Cain's part in tonight's attack. Even more important, I want to tell them about us."

She nodded. "Good. Because I am very proud of the fact that we are an 'us.' I love you, Traker Jakes. I love you so much, it fills me up."

This time his kiss found her mouth. It was much more satisfying.

Chelo blinked away a nicely dazed expression on her lovely face. "Okay. Now, please stop interrupting me. I would like to speak with the pack as well. Your people have been so welcoming. They've all done whatever they could to protect me. I was not one of them, merely a stranger who disrupted their lives and brought danger to their homes. I'm not proud of my role in this, but I am so proud of your pack. There aren't enough words to thank them all, but I need to try."

He took her hand and they walked into the lodge together. He paused long enough to set the revolver on the mantel over the fireplace, then glanced around the room. Everyone was still here. Even Darnell and Evan, who were holding hands and laughing about something. He imagined it had something to do with the big jar Evan was holding, filled with what looked like punch from Meg's punch bowl. He'd heard Brad laughing about the quantity of Long Island Iced Teas he was mixing up for the ladies' evening, and they all knew Darnell's history with that particular drink.

Tonight he wouldn't mind one of those for himself.

Their gender-separate celebrations certainly hadn't turned out the way any of them had planned, but thank goodness the danger was over, Rube was no longer a threat, and—most important—Chelo and his pack were safe.

The laughter and chatter died down the moment everyone realized he and Chelo had entered, so Trak led her to the spot near the buffet table where he generally held court. He grabbed a chair for Chelo from the closest table and seated her next to him, but he stood beside her, holding her hand. "Chelo's sitting because, while she hasn't said anything, I know that she's a little the worse for wear after getting shoved through a plate-glass window and then tossed on the ground. I wanted to announce to all of you that Chelo and I mated last night. She is a strong alpha in her own right, and I am proud to call her mine."

The applause was loud, the whistles and cheers—and a few lewd comments—louder, much as he'd expected. But he was proud of his pack, too. They welcomed Chelo as if she were already one of them. When Trak looked down and saw the tears in her eyes, he squeezed her hand. "I'm going to give Chelo a chance to speak to you, but first I have a few things to say that are probably even more important than me and the fact I have finally found the perfect mate." Gazing at her, he chuckled softly. "You have to realize, they'd all essentially given up on me. Now they can rest assured that I'm not an entirely hopeless case."

He raised his head and focused on them, the ones who'd been his family for so many years. His voice was thick with emotions he had no need to hide. These people knew him, in some ways, probably better than he knew himself. They had likely already sensed the depth of his feelings. He took time to think about this moment, the feelings filling him, spilling over, and making his eyes burn and his throat ache.

Taking a deep breath, he slowly let it out and said, "I am so fucking proud of this pack. This is the first time we've faced a serious threat to the safety of any one of us, much less a threat against our women from an outside force." He looked at each of them in turn, men he'd thought of as brothers over the years, and realized that yes, he really was choking up.

He cleared his throat before continuing, well aware of the strength in this room. The love. "You can't possibly imagine how much you guys mean to me, how much I love every single one of you and the women you've brought into our pack. We are a powerhouse, by virtue of our connection, each to the other. There was never any doubt in my mind that we would win tonight, but that's because I've always known that, if we faced adversity, you were going to be there, every damned one of you, ready and willing to help."

He shook his head and focused on Cain. "I was right. You always come through. But there's one in here, and you know who I'm talking about, who deserves a very special thanks from me, and a public apology that's long overdue. I owe Cain a lot more than any of you might realize, and not just because he saved my life this summer, but also because my guilt for acting like a horse's ass for the past, oh, almost seventy years is something I will always regret."

He waited for the soft laughter to stop. Took another deep breath and realized he was holding onto Chelo's hand for dear life. Why was this so fucking hard to do? But he knew. It was never easy for an alpha to apologize. It really wasn't part of their nature, but it should be. Especially now. "When Cain first came to me in 1948, he was a soldier fresh out of the army, back in the States after a long and distinguished tour of duty in Europe during World War II. Cain never told me this, but I did some research and learned that he was a recipient of a Distinguished Service Cross for gallantry in the face of enemy fire. All of us know we have never had cause to doubt his bravery or his loyalty to this pack, but at the time he was looking for a pack to call home. He was young and cocky, a trained soldier with attitude and brains, but the thing that scared me the most was that I knew immediately he was an alpha."

Trak glanced at Chelo, another alpha, and possibly stronger than he was as well. "The thing is, he wasn't just any alpha. You might have noticed tonight that Cain's a lot stronger than I am. I took him on as a member of the pack with his sworn promise not to challenge me for control. He didn't have to make that promise, in fact, he could have challenged me then, but he didn't. He promised and then offered to take on the position of pack enforcer, a role that needs a strong alpha."

Manny glanced at Cain and grinned. "Why the secrecy? I think all of us figured out that Cain was alpha years ago, but it never seemed important."

"Good question, and all my fault. I didn't trust him, because I didn't trust myself. When I broke away from my original pack to move west, I honestly didn't know if I had it in me to manage a pack of shifters. Remember, I never challenged my alpha, so I didn't know if I would have been strong enough to win in a traditional challenge fight. I still don't, and that's probably not something I should admit. But then? I was still learning my way when Cain first came to me. I knew if he challenged me the odds were he would win. He was smart, strong, and battle-hardened by war, and I didn't trust him because I was afraid."

He shrugged when he looked at Cain. "I'm sorry for that, Cain. You've always been trustworthy, but it was my own lack of confidence, the fact I built this pack when I was very young and not entirely sure of my strength. It's a huge responsibility and I was scared shitless a lot of the time. I handle the pack's money, our investments, and all that keeps us solvent. I'm making decisions that have long-range implications for the health and strength of the pack, and I'm doing it without a guidebook. Along comes a sharp, powerful young alpha, one obviously stronger than me who wants to join and, 'oh, by the way, I won't challenge you.' Yeah. Right."

He bit back his own laughter when everyone else was chuckling. "Cain's rarely had to do any enforcing with this pack. In fact, I can't recall a single instance where any of you have created a problem, but he's been called on by the alphas of other packs and he's handled some pretty dangerous situations. By doing so, he's built a strong reputation for both himself and this pack. And for me."

This time he did laugh. "The other alphas see how strong Cain is and figure I've got to be like the *Mad Max* alpha on steroids. I don't do anything to dissuade them. And please,

I'd prefer that you not pass that information out beyond these walls."

Cain stepped forward. "What Trak didn't say is that the reason I joined the army was due to the fact I was a rogue. We all know what it's like to be a wolf without a pack, and I didn't handle it well, but after I'd challenged my pack leader back in Idaho and had my ass handed to me on a platter, the army was the closest thing I could think of to fill the place of a pack. When I got out, I hung around a couple of packs in Colorado and Utah, just watching them, but the vibe wasn't right. I finally caught wind of a pack in Northern California that was still fairly new. This was my last hope. I knew as an alpha I was probably going to have to fight for a spot no matter where I went, but I have never wanted the responsibility of a pack of my own. Trak offered me exactly what I wanted—a home without bloodshed."

He pulled Cherry close, wrapped his arm around Brad's neck, and hugged him. "These two. Wow . . . yeah, these two give me what I need. It really doesn't get any better. So, Trak? No need to apologize. It's all good, and I'm happy for you. Chelo, welcome to the pack. Now if you folks don't mind, I'm going to take my mates upstairs. It's been a pretty wild night."

"Not yet you don't." Chelo stood and she was looking at Cain. "Not before I thank you for keeping Trak safe. I want to thank everyone here for accepting me and for dealing with all the trouble I've brought, for protecting me at great risk to yourselves. I promise to do my best to keep your alpha happy. I know all of you will keep him safe. Good night, Cain. Good night, everyone. Please, Trak? I'm exhausted."

Trak tugged Chelo to her feet. "Drew? Can you or Manny make sure Growl is locked up?" He grabbed the revolver off the mantel. "You know where this goes."

Manny took it. "We'll take care of this. Get some sleep. Chelo? You said the flowers for the wedding are coming in tomorrow. Do you want us to pick them up for you?"

"Thank you, but no. I need to go in and go over the order, make sure everything's right. And then I have a wedding to prepare for, and arrangements to make for Sunday services."

Evan watched while the group broke up, everyone going their separate ways. Darnell had been quiet during all the talk, and he wondered how much she really understood about Cain's situation. She had no idea about their long life spans, but she had to be wondering. He leaned close and whispered, "Let's lock this place up, okay? Cain and his crew went straight up to their rooms, but I want to check everything first."

He took her hand and they checked to make sure the stove was off, the doors closed. No point in locking them with the front window blown out. That had to be repaired before the wedding.

So did his relationship with Nellie.

"Let's go," he said. Then he grabbed her Mason jar of punch and, still holding on to Nell, walked out of the lodge and down the trail to his cabin.

CHAPTER 13

Silently, Trak and Chelo walked hand in hand to his cabin. He had no idea what she was thinking, wasn't even certain what was tumbling around in his own brain. He hadn't thought beyond the threat of Rube. Hadn't really considered how his life would change, now that he had a mate. He glanced her way, caught her watching him, and almost laughed.

He still couldn't believe she was his. His *and* safe. Finally.

Instead, she smiled and so did he, feeling unexplainably shy for some reason. They'd made love most of the night last night, exploring each other with the utmost abandon, almost as if it might be the only chance they'd ever have for that amazing intimacy. In the back of his mind he'd worried about Rube somehow taking Chelo away, and losing her, if not to her psychotic brother-in-law, then to death. His or hers, it didn't matter. Their chance at love would have ended before anything had really begun.

Now, though? Now they were beginning, the two of them on the threshold of an entirely new life. Chelo had survived a lifetime of pain and abuse with her spirit intact. He was amazed the cruelty she'd suffered hadn't broken her. Instead, she was so powerful, so strong, he was awed by her strength. Without even thinking it through, he stopped in the middle of the dark wood and held both her hands in his.

"You are an amazing woman, Consuela de los Lobos. You are better than me, stronger than me . . . definitely a lot prettier than me." He kissed her quickly when she laughed. "But no one will ever love you more than me. I promise to love you until the day we die, and if there is a life beyond, I will love you into that one. You make me a better man, and I hope like hell I'm a good mate to you. We will have amazing sons, you and I. And a long life together, the two of us. I promise you a lifetime of love, and I will always honor you."

Her trembling hands tightened their grasp on his, and he realized her entire body shook. Her eyes sparkled with emotion—tears ready to spill—and she bit her lips as if searching for control. When she spoke, her voice was raspy with those unshed tears. "I have never truly known love, and yet I recognized it immediately the first time I saw you. I think my wolf knew her mate long before the human side understood, but I promise I will always love you, that I will stand by your side as you lead this pack, and I will forever be your lover, your helpmate, your confidante. And if we are blessed with children and our sons are anything like their father, I will be forever grateful. There is no finer man."

Trak pulled her into his arms and kissed her. And then, as if they hadn't just opened their hearts and made vows more important than anything they might share before the pack, they took the final steps to the front door of Trak's cabin and went inside.

He closed the door and then just stood there and watched her. With her long, glossy black hair falling almost to her waist, her head turned a bit to one side so that he saw her in profile, she looked like some ethereal goddess come to bless his home.

But wasn't that exactly what she'd done? He'd given up hope of finding a mate, and yet the woman who was now his was more than anything he'd imagined.

Chelo had stopped in the main room, her hands clasped in front of her, and looked about as if this were her first time inside. When she turned to Trak, her smile split her face. "Why does it feel new tonight? Almost as if I've never been here before."

He stepped up behind her and wrapped his arms around her waist. "When you were last here, you were still afraid. Rube was a threat we knew we'd have to deal with; there was always the chance that he'd get lucky, that one of us could die. That someone in the pack would be hurt or worse. That woman, that Chelo, had lived her entire life in fear and knew no other way to be."

He swept her into his arms, holding her close against his chest. Laughing, she wrapped her arms around his neck. "I'm not afraid. Not anymore. You're right. That's why it feels new."

"It's because you're new." He planted a heartfelt kiss on her mouth and then turned and walked up the stairs with Chelo in his arms. "You are new and fresh, and while there is no way to forget the years you were with that other pack, it's molded you into a woman more powerful than any I've ever known. I can't believe you're mine, Chelo. Thank you for coming to me, for letting me love you."

"Well, I'm certainly hoping that you plan to do it again. And again. And then, after we rest a bit, again."

By the time he hit the top step he was running, and in

mere seconds he had her in his bedroom, tumbled onto the middle of the bed while he stripped off his clothes. She crouched there on her hands and knees, laughing as he kicked off his jeans and ripped his shirt when he pulled it over his head. But when he stood before her, stripped of his clothes, chest blowing in and out with a combination of adrenaline and lust, his body and mind equally aroused, Chelo stopped laughing.

It was terribly gratifying, the way she watched him. Eyes wide and pupils dilated, she reminded him of a fawn staring into the eyes of a wolf, though this woman was no timid fawn. He flattened his palms on the bed and raised one knee, moving closer. She watched him, the hint of a smile barely tilting her lips, the scent of her arousal coming off her in waves of heat that had him harder than he could recall.

But something was off. Was it arousal or had something else invaded? An acrid scent he'd not noticed before. Faint, but still part of the scents his sensitive nose detected.

He crept closer until they almost touched. Then he leaned close and realized she was trembling, that her smile was gone and her face seemed almost frozen with fear. He thought of all the years she'd been afraid for good reason, the beatings and the rapes, the horrible life of never knowing when her psychotic mate would want to fuck her or beat her or both.

Trak never, ever wanted to frighten her, but he didn't want her embarrassed that he'd recognized her fear, as she would be when she realized that no, he wasn't going to hurt her.

That knowledge would come, but she didn't truly believe it yet. Not at a level that went deep enough to cancel out fear born of a lifetime of abuse. He crept a bit closer, and then he leaned close and kissed her nose and sat back on his heels. "You're still much too covered in clothing, my love. May I help you remove it?"

She shook herself, and he wondered where her mind had been. "No." She sat back on her heels. "I'll remove it myself. I saw what you did to your shirt. I don't have a lot of clothes."

He glanced over his shoulder at the torn shirt lying on the floor and shrugged. "I promise to be careful."

"How do I know I can trust you?"

She was teasing, but the undertone was definitely serious. She had every right to fear men. "You can always trust me, Chelo." He flipped around until his back was against the stack of pillows covering the headboard, giving her distance he'd rather close than open. "I never have and never will hit any woman, and that includes you. No matter how angry I get, and believe me, in any longtime relationship we're bound to have anger at times, I will never hit you or hurt you in any way. And if I do go out into the forest and sulk, I will always come back to you."

She crawled up his length until she was lying against him. Still fully clothed, but at least she didn't seem as afraid anymore. He wondered where her thoughts had gone. There was that brief moment where . . .

"Do you really sulk?"

"Sometimes." He sucked in one side of his cheek to keep from laughing. "I've been known to sulk on occasion. I've been around for over a hundred and fifty years, Chelo, and yes, I've been thwarted a time or two, which resulted in a bit of a sulk. But only when I had a really good reason."

"I see."

He wrapped his arms around her and she snuggled

against his chest. A scent hit him then, one he'd not noticed earlier. *Rube.* The bastard had carried her out of the lodge, held her against his sweaty shirt. He wondered if that stench was still in her nostrils, fouling her senses. He slipped away from her and got out of bed. "Come with me."

Frowning, she followed him into the bathroom. He leaned into the large shower and turned on the water, adjusting the valves until the temperature was right. Then he turned to her and slowly helped her out of her clothes. When she was naked, he wrapped everything into a bundle, tossed the clothing into the hamper, and shut the lid. Tight.

"I don't want to start our life together with the scent of another man on your clothing." He rested his forehead against hers. "I didn't notice it until we were on the bed and you crawled up next to me, Rube's scent on your clothing and your hair. I'm sorry, Chelo. I love the way you smell, and his scent is just wrong."

She covered her face with her hands. "I can't smell it anymore. I think my senses are so filled with his stench that I can't smell it."

"It's not your fault. C'mon." He stepped into the shower and tugged her along with him. She immediately stood under the water and tilted her head back to wet her hair. Trak squirted citrus-scented shampoo into his hand and then washed her hair, cleaning every bit of Rube's stench away from her. She leaned against him as he bathed her. Thank goodness she hadn't been insulted, but there was no way in hell he was bringing that bastard into their bed.

The moment Trak mentioned Rube's scent, Chelo realized that was the reason she'd felt so unsettled. Trak wanted to make love, but she couldn't let herself go with him. Crazy, after the way they'd been last night, but it must have been Rube's disgusting stench. She wasn't consciously aware of it, not with it covering her, but her subconscience knew. That explained the way she'd frozen when Trak wanted to take her clothes off.

Now, though, with his hands gently working the conditioner into her hair, she wanted him to touch her everywhere. The source of her fear was gone—Rube's stench, washed down the drain with the suds.

She turned and rested her forehead against Trak's chest so he could rinse her hair. It felt so good, his hands a gentle caress, the warm water beating against her sore muscles. She couldn't believe she hadn't been cut. When Rube jumped through that window, her body had caught the brunt of the blow. She felt it now, her muscles bruised, her body battered and tired.

But Trak? He'd been erect since they'd gotten inside the cabin. There was one thing she could do for him, and she wanted to try everything with Trak. She knew what it was like to take him in her mouth, already knew she loved the taste of the man she would love for all time.

But in the shower? With water streaming over the two of them? She shivered, merely thinking about it. Sinking slowly to her knees, she wrapped her arms around his thighs and laid her cheek against his groin.

"Chelo?"

The question in his voice had her raising her head, looking at him. "Hmmm?"

"Are you okay? What are . . . ?"

"I'm sleepy but very curious. We've never done this in the shower. And just think, if I miss any, I won't make a mess."

"Ah . . . I see. You're a very practical woman. I like that."

She heard the laughter in his voice. This man found humor in just about everything and he always seemed to understand her subtle attempts. She liked that. Wrapping her fingers around the thick base of his penis, she tilted him to her mouth. He was so much taller than her. So much larger . . .

"Uhmmm . . ." Her mouth fit around the silky tip perfectly and she slipped her lips over the tightly drawn cowl of his foreskin, caught in place behind the broad crown. He was hotter even than the hot shower, hot against her tongue, but the taste of him was nothing more than the taste of the flowing water that washed his scent away.

"I want to get out of the shower. I can't taste you and I want that. If there's a mess, you'll just have to help me clean it up."

"I dunno about that," he said, but she heard the laughter behind the fierce declaration, and within minutes they were both dry and back on the bed.

"Here," she said, pushing him back until he sat on the edge of the bed with his feet on the floor. "This is a good height." Grabbing a pillow off the bed, she tucked it under her knees and knelt between his legs. Tugging him forward, she finally had him where she wanted him.

There was so much she wanted to do with Trak that she suddenly had all kinds of energy. She studied all those fascinating parts. His erection hadn't subsided a bit and there was definitely more than a mouthful, so she started by merely licking the length of his shaft, teasing him with her tongue, then lifting his erection out of the way and running her open mouth over his testicles. She pulled first one and then the other into her mouth, stroking him with her tongue, tasting him, growing more aroused by his wonderful scent.

Fluid gathered at the slit on his crown, and she licked that off. He tasted wonderful, so she did it again, but she wanted more. Wrapping her fingers around his shaft, she ran her lips over the smooth tip until he was slick; then she took him into her mouth, using her tongue and lips until she sucked him as deep as she could.

She held on to the thick base of his cock and worked him with her mouth, taking in almost all of him. He'd grown quiet. She opened her eyes and glanced along his body. He lay back on the bed, hands grasping the bedspread, his mouth twisted in a grimace that possibly could have been interpreted as pain but pleased her no end.

He was close to coming. Because of her. She sucked him deep again, used her tongue and lips, and sped up the whole process. His body jerked. "Chelo? You're gonna make me . . ."

She slipped free of him and said, "Good." If he thought she was going to stop now, the man was absolutely clueless. She increased her efforts, lightly grasped his balls in one hand, and rolled them between her fingers.

She felt his muscles go stiff, heard his curse, and caught the first spurts of his seed as his body bucked beneath her hands. She swallowed as his cock seemed to flex within her mouth and she took everything he had to give. Swallowed every drop and licked her lips when he was finally finished.

Then she licked the length of his cock and around his sac, well aware that she was marking him in the only way she knew how. Marking him with her scent. Telling Trak and any other woman who might find him interesting that he was well and truly taken.

She crawled into bed beside him and turned out the

light. He pulled her close against his chest and slipped his fingers between her legs. They were exhausted, but he gently brought her to climax before they both drifted off.

It was a quiet walk back to his cabin, but Evan was afraid to say anything. He had no idea what Darnell was thinking. Would she ever be his Nellie again? Did she still love him? Did she think he was a freak? Was she afraid of him?

She held his hand, but she hadn't said a word.

He was terrified he was going to lose her. She'd seen the worst of him tonight. He'd changed before her eyes; he'd lied by omission, no matter that Trak took the blame. Nellie didn't strike him as a woman who forgave easily. The worst thing of all? She'd watched him kill a man.

Granted, the bastard needed to die, but she would never be able to look at him again without realizing he had the power to hurt her badly if he wanted to. How did a powerful werewolf convince a human woman that the only way he'd use his strength around her was to protect her from harm?

They climbed the steps to his cabin and Nellie opened the door, but only because he held the big jar of Meg's punch in his other hand. Nellie hadn't turned him free, yet. That was a good thing, wasn't it? He went ahead of her into the cabin and she closed the door behind him, but she turned loose of his hand when she turned to the door. When she turned around, her hands were behind her and she leaned against the door.

He set the jar of punch on the counter and walked back across the room, but before he could say anything she stepped away from the door and into his arms. He held her close and didn't even try to hide his sigh of relief.

She hugged him just as tightly with her head pressed against his chest. "Are you okay?" she asked.

He chuckled softly. "Shouldn't that be my question? I'm sorry, Nell . . ."

She leaned back and pressed her finger to his lips. "No. Don't be sorry. Trak said you weren't allowed to tell me anything, and I actually do understand that. Plus, it means I'm not crazy. Remember when you jumped from the road all the way up the hillside to me the first day I got here? And you had to jump *over my car* to reach me?" She shook her head. "It's good to know I'm not crazy. What I'm worried about is how you feel about killing that man tonight. I could tell it really upset you, but I'm glad you did it. I'm just sorry that you had to be the one to do it, but someone had to. Zach certainly couldn't have, and I was using a gun loaded with blanks, so you saved both of us, not to mention Chelo. There was no other way, not when he started to change."

Damn, he loved her so fucking much. "Thank you. I accept the fact that Rube had to die. He was psychotic, to say the least. Even the men with him were afraid of him, and there wasn't a bit of regret from them over his death. The thing that made it difficult to accept is that I've never done that before. Never taken a life. I've always wondered if, when the time came and I had no other choice, I would be able to do exactly what I did, but I realized it wasn't as difficult a decision to make as I'd expected."

"Why do you think that was?"

He shook his head. "Because I didn't kill him just to make a bad person go away. I killed him to protect you and Chelo, and Zach as well. I knew that if he fought us and won, Zach and I would both be dead, or too badly injured to protect you from his rage. I sensed his change, but I was caught up in my own fight, in worrying what you thought of me, if you were going to hate me for not telling you. For being something a lot of people would call a monster."

He ran a finger over her silky cheek. "When you called out a warning that he was beginning to shift, I knew you weren't afraid of me, that you didn't hate me. You were warning me. I'm hoping that warning was because you might still love me. C'mon." He took her hand and led her into the kitchen. Then he set the jar filled with punch on the counter, wrapped his hands around Nellie's waist, and set her on the counter beside the jar. "Give me a minute."

He walked to the cupboard, pulled out a couple of glasses and filled them with ice, then poured some of Meg's punch into the two of them. Handing one to Nellie, he took the other for himself. "Will you toast to new beginnings, Nell? There is so much I need to tell you, but honestly, I don't know where to start. I have to know, first. Can you still love me after what you know now? Or is this whole shape-shifting wolf thing a game changer?"

She took a sip of her drink and then studied him a moment, but her eyes were almost as bright as her smile. "Well, it's definitely a game changer, but maybe not the way you think. I knew you were special from the beginning, but I fell in love with your wolf long before I knew how I felt about you, so knowing you two are a package deal is a plus. As far as loving you? Evan, that ship sailed before I left here last summer, but I never had the chance or the courage to say anything." She slipped off the counter and headed into the front room, drink in hand.

Evan followed her. When she sat on the couch, he sat

beside her, though not too close. She turned to him and rolled her eyes. Shrugging, he moved closer.

"Will you answer my questions?"

"I will."

"Good. Okay, just how old are you guys, anyway? Cain's a World War Two vet? That means he's at least ninety, right?"

He shrugged. "More like a hundred and six or seven." Her eyes got bigger. "He was born a little after the turn of the last century. I'm a little older, almost a hundred and fifteen. Trak's brother Lawz is the oldest in the pack. He was born right around the start of the Civil War, in 1861. Trak's three years younger."

"Holy shit." She slapped her hand over her mouth. "Sorry." She took a bigger swallow of her drink. "This flips that whole 'but how old are you in dog years?' thing on its butt! But you all look about the same age. How?"

He was still chuckling over the dog years comment. This was sounding better all the time. "Werewolves only father male children. Our sons are like normal human kids until their late twenties, early thirties, when they go through their first shift. However old they are when that happens, that's how old they stay. We think the shifting is the reason—it replicates our cells so the cells don't age whenever we shift. There are some weres alive who came across with the Pilgrims. The truly older weres have shifted regularly all their lives, so it appears that the shifting is what helps keep us young. We all appear to have started out in Europe, though I'm not certain if anyone's ever figured out exactly where or when."

"Then what about the women? Are Cherry and the others old, too?"

"No, they just met their guys this summer. That's sort of

why we built Feral Passions, to get to meet women, but it was really weird because all of the women had pretty much figured out what we were before they actually agreed to be mated. Mating means the guy bites his woman."

When Nellie grimaced, he leaned close and kissed her. "Not a bad bite, just a little nip to infect you with your mate's saliva, but then you'll go through a change and come out of it able to shift. The thing is, the change will put you into a deep sleep for at least twenty-four hours, and with all the uncertainty over Rube and his guys, Trak and I were afraid you'd be too vulnerable, sleeping like that. What if Rube prevailed and killed me or Trak? You'd be entirely helpless, and we couldn't risk that.

"Another thing is that there's always been a law among our kind, that we couldn't tell anyone what we were, even a woman we loved and wanted to mate. We had to bite her first so she wouldn't be able to go back to her people, but the rest of the guys and I are totally against that. It's an old custom that goes back to ancient times when women weren't nearly as sophisticated as they are now. None of us were, but their lives were really hard, so life as a shifter actually gave women freedom they couldn't have otherwise.

"Times have changed and women have more options. Now it feels wrong not to tell you. If a woman chose not to change after finding out about us, she was in a position to give us away, and you can only imagine what would happen if the media got wind of our existence. Essentially, we felt the risk was worth it, because it's a pretty big deal to spring on a woman." He stared at his moccasins. "I was planning to tell you as soon as we got through the wedding. Trak doesn't know that."

"So all the women here are shape-shifters now? Even Meg?"

"Meg and Zach are completely human. They found out about us purely by accident, but they accept what we are and have promised to keep our secret. They love each other, love their work, and want to continue living perfectly normal human lives. Not aging makes it tough to do that. We have to avoid contact with people sometimes for years on end; then we can come back and tell people who used to know us that we're actually our own children. That's why some of us rarely go into town."

"How's that going to work for Darian? I mean, she's on the news every night. How's she going to carry that off?"

"Good makeup? I have no idea. That's a problem we haven't faced before. The same goes for Lawz. He's been working for the state as an engineer for a long time now. At some point, he'll have to change jobs, manufacture a new identity. Or he might just retire and take consulting jobs. That way he'd not always be working with the same people who might notice he doesn't age."

"It sounds like a lot of work." She took another sip of her drink and then set the glass aside. "Why don't you take me to bed?" She winked. "Where we can discuss this in more depth."

Evan felt as if someone had just lifted a ton of bricks off his chest. Smiling, he stood and offered his hand to Nell. She put her hand in his and he pulled her to her feet. Laughing, she grabbed her drink and took it with her as he tugged her toward the stairs.

CHAPTER 14

Friday morning

Chelo couldn't remember a more beautiful morning, though she imagined the man sitting beside her driving the big SUV had a lot to do with it. This was what happiness felt like, this sense of freedom, of well-being. Excitement. She had never looked forward to her days before.

There'd been nothing to look forward to.

They opened the shop and she set out her displays. The truck arrived with the flowers for the wedding as well as for the displays ordered by local churches. One restaurant had left a phone order for a last-minute dinner that she'd have to do for tonight.

Trak took his laptop into her office and went to work on a list of things Cherry had asked him to handle, while Chelo got busy in the shop.

By the end of the day, she was absolutely exhausted and still smiling. The orders were done; she had quite a few of the wedding items completed and boxed—they'd go in the extra refrigerator at the lodge. It was all good.

Trak wandered out to the showroom. "Well? How's it feel to work your tail off and know it's just the beginning of a busy weekend?"

"Wonderful." She stood on her toes and kissed him. "I'm ready to load everything in the back of the car. I've got a sign up saying that the shop is closed for the weekend due to a Feral Passions wedding, and I've got my tools all packed. I'll spend tomorrow putting the displays together. Boutonnieres are done and so is the crown of flowers for Meg, along with an extra box of flowers for the bridesmaids' hair. Darnell wanted those.

"I'll put the bouquets for the bridesmaids together tomorrow along with the big flower arrangement for the wedding site. Brad told me I can use the laundry room behind the kitchen for my work. There's a big table for folding clothes that will double as a worktable, and a really nice big country sink. It's close to the walk-in refrigerator—Brad said there's room in it to store the flowers. It should work perfectly."

"Good." He kissed her again, taking the lead this time and doing a thorough job of it.

She felt almost giddy driving back to the resort. This wasn't just a wedding for Meg. It was the beginning of Chelo's new life.

Evan and Nell went through each of the cabins. It was Nellie's idea to put bouquets of wildflowers in each one. "Don't they look wonderful?" Nell set the final one in the fifth cabin. Meg and Zach had the sixth, and they were having a quiet day together, before all the guests began arriving tomorrow.

Evan finished a final check in the bathroom and walked out to admire Nellie's handiwork. She'd gotten the idea from Chelo, and the bouquets really did make a beautiful addition, each a burst of yellow lupine, pink checkerbloom, blue delphinium, and white valerian in a Mason jar wrapped in brown burlap and tied with a bright blue bow.

Evan knew he'd never forget picking flowers with Nellie. She'd tied her hair back and put on an old pair of jeans and hiking boots with one of his flannel shirts so they could pick the flowers in the early morning when they were fresh and covered in dew.

The shirt was huge on her, but she'd tied the tails at her waist and he'd spent the morning waiting for glimpses of her smooth belly. They'd even managed a little bit of down and dirty in the meadow. Spreading his flannel shirt on a patch of green near the creek, he'd made love to her as if it were their first time, though, in so many ways, every time with Nell was like their first, and always unbelievably good. She never failed to surprise him. He loved her. It was as simple as that.

He couldn't wait to make her his. They'd already decided to do it Sunday night after the reception ended and everyone headed out. Meg and Zach were planning a morning wedding, a luncheon reception, and then a honeymoon on one of Zach's yachts, tooling along the northern coast and up to the San Juan Islands.

Someday, that was a trip he'd like to take with Nellie. So many things he wanted to do, places he wanted to go. So many dreams, and Nellie was featured in every single one.

Dinner was over, the kitchen cleaned up with everyone helping out, and the entire pack—except for Trak, who always seemed to have more to do—had gathered on the deck. Chelo had parked her butt near Darnell, and Meg joined them a few minutes later. All the other women were in the vicinity, tossing barbs back and forth at one another. Laughter really was infectious, and Chelo couldn't ever remember laughing as much or as hard—or at such silly things.

Zach was busy pontificating on something of utmost importance, over in the corner with the guys, where the humor tended more to the raunchy side. Trak had just rounded the curve in the long drive, walking back up the road from Growl, where he'd gone to check the liquor supplies. Preparation was important, he'd said, for a party that would most likely begin tomorrow afternoon once guests began to arrive and then last through the wedding and possibly well into Sunday night.

There was a wonderful, relaxed sense of celebration tonight, a last blast before the human guests began arriving tomorrow. Darnell laughed at something Evan shouted to her across what they were calling the great divide, between the group of men and the growing group of women, and Meg merely flipped them all off. That nonexistent space between men and women who loved to laugh and tease had never seemed so wonderfully infinitesimal. Chelo had never laughed so much, nor loved so freely.

Meg followed up her timeless hand gesture with more laughter. "That was meant for all the males of the species, Evan. Not merely you, so don't think you're special." The women applauded; the men laughed and offered sympathy and suggestions. Evan merely whimpered, but the smile on his face was obviously meant for Darnell. Chelo was so relieved that Darnell finally knew the truth about them, and all was as it should be. Evan had promised to turn her Sunday night, after the wedding.

They all figured they'd be so tired after Meg and Zach's

big party that no one would even notice if Darnell slept a few days away. Chelo took another sip of her wine—she was finally figuring out which ones she loved and those she didn't care for. She was fascinated by the scents of the various kinds of grapes, the mixture of fruits that seemed to come from every glass.

She held her glass of sauvignon blanc to her nose and tried to pick out the various scents. A hint of melon, a bit of peach, the slightest touch of apple. All from something as simple as a grape.

Closing her eyes, she drew in another breath and jerked away in disgust. A new scent on the evening air fouled the fruity wine. She set her glass down and closed her eyes, turned, and inhaled into the evening breeze coming out of the east. She stood, continuing to sniff the air. Still concentrating on the unexpected scent, she walked over to the railing. Down the stairs, moving quickly now toward Trak. Suddenly the stench hit with familiar nauseating force.

She knew that smell. It could only be the alpha from the Rainy Lake pack.

A glimpse of movement at the edge of the woods, much too close to her man. "Trak! Look out. To your right!"

A large, burly, naked man stepped out of the dark trees, faced Trak, and shouted, "I challenge you, you bastard!" And then, without giving Trak a chance to respond, he shifted. A huge black wolf charged Trak.

Chelo screamed. Cain flew by her, stripping his clothes off as he ran. Trak was fully dressed with jeans and boots and a heavy shirt and vest against the night's chill. There was no way he could get out of his clothes and shift. Spinning away from the wolf, he nimbly sidestepped the animal's leap for his throat, throwing up an arm to ward off the attack.

He shoved, using the weight of his human body to throw the wolf off course. The beast landed hard, rolled to his side, and came up snarling. Cain ripped off his jeans and shifted, launching himself from human feet and catching the alpha with wolven jaws. Trak was out of his clothes and on all fours by the time Cain brought the interloper to the ground.

As soon as Trak reached them Cain backed away. The alpha twisted and leapt to his feet, but Trak grabbed him by the throat and brought him down once more. Cain shifted, essentially ignoring the action behind him as he walked over, recovered his pants, and slipped them on. Then, tugging his sweatshirt over his head, he walked back to the alpha, now flat on his back. Trak held him down by the throat.

Cain squatted down beside the two wolves. "Ya know, Trak, I've got a simple and relatively painless solution to this irritating situation. It certainly wouldn't hurt you or me any."

Trak snarled around his mouthful of hair and wolf.

"We've got a really good vet. He does a lot of spaying and neutering. I imagine Tuck could take care of this guy pretty easily. Might make him think twice before challenging a pack leader for no apparent reason. Hard to get it up over a fight when you're missing your gonads."

Frantic now, the wolf struggled, twisting and turning in Trak's grip, but he couldn't break free.

The rest of the pack, along with Tuck, had meandered down during the conversation. "I could do it easy enough," Tuck said matter-of-factly, "but I don't know if he can shift back without his balls. Of course, I'm just guessing. I've never neutered a werewolf before."

"One way to find out," Cain said. He glanced at Tuck and winked. "How long does the surgery take?"

Tuck just grinned. "Ten minutes, tops, maybe less. Depends on how long it takes to knock him out. Unless you want me to do it without anesthetic. Might make a better impression on him, make him rethink his stupid challenge."

"We'll have to discuss that one," Cain said. "After Trak shifts and he can be part of the discussion."

"Sounds good. I'm going to give him a shot now so Trak doesn't have to hang on to him all night. As far as cutting the bastard's balls off, it will definitely take care of the aggression, and if he can't shift we can just turn him loose here on the preserve."

Cain shook his head. "That won't work. He strikes me as the kind who'd hold a grudge." He stood back while Tuck pulled a syringe out of his bag and injected the wolf. Once he finished giving the wolf the shot, he grinned at Cain. "That conversation's going to give the bastard some nightmares."

Chelo waited until the wolf's body went lax. "I figured you didn't mean it. Cutting his balls off. Personally I think it sounds like a great idea." She glared at the wolf.

Trak stood, shifting so quickly that he was fully human by the time he was upright. Grabbing his pants off the ground, he slipped them on. Bare-chested and barefoot, he stepped over the wolf and held out his hand to Cain.

"Once again, it appears I owe you my life. You're one hell of a fighter, Cain. I don't think I've ever seen you in action before. I'm definitely glad I've never seriously crossed you. Just let me know when you want to take over so I have time to get the hell out of town."

Cain chuckled as they shook hands. "It's all yours,

Mr. Jakes. I am not pack leader material. This came under my job description as enforcer." He glanced down at the wolf. "I'm sorry I didn't kill him. At least he heard the discussion about removing his balls." Cain laughed. "I think I saw his pickup down by the road. I noticed one earlier, just figured someone was hiking, but I think it might have had Minnesota plates. Didn't get close enough to pick up any scent. The idea of the alpha coming all the way here to attack never even crossed my mind."

"Why should it?" Trak stared at the unconscious wolf. "I'm sorry he's still alive, too. I'd prefer he went the way of Rube, but I think just putting the fear of losing his balls into him should make him think twice. Anything you can inject him with, Tuck, that could make him think he's had the surgery?"

"Yeah. I've got some hormones I use when we're trying to get a mare to ovulate. Doubt he'll be pumping out eggs, but he'll know something's different. Might develop breasts after a while, but they won't stay once the drug wears off. I'm going to keep him sedated until the wedding is over. I don't want to have to worry about him trying another attack, though if there is a next time I say we get rid of him permanently. Any pack alpha that would allow a woman to be mistreated by members of his pack deserves whatever happens to him. His life has very little value in my book."

He squatted down and grabbed the wolf by his front and back legs, picked the huge beast up, and slung him over his shoulders. Chelo watched as Tuck walked back down the road toward his cabin carrying almost two hundred pounds of deadweight wolf as if he were nothing at all. Elle went with him, his black satchel in her hand. Tuck had a small surgery in the back of their place and there were cages for wolves being treated. Closest thing they had to a jail cell.

Chelo was actually sorry they weren't really going to do it. She thought it was only fair. But Tuck was right. He was going to think they'd castrated him when he woke up in the clinic. She was mostly hoping the wolf would leave and be afraid to come back.

Trak and Cain cleaned up and joined the women and the rest of the guys on the deck. Meg was snuggled up with Zach, looking very content and not at all nervous about the wedding on Sunday. Trak took the chair next to Chelo, but he easily lifted her and set her in his lap. Cain did the same with Cherry, and that was when Chelo noticed that all of the couples were paired up.

She leaned close to Darnell and whispered, "Are you ready, Darnell?"

"I am, though I was a bit disappointed when Evan told me I wouldn't be able to shift as fast as Trak. Guess that's something I'll need to work on, right?"

"It is. But just think how much fun you'll have, learning about your new life."

Darnell laughed and snuggled close to Evan. She looked about as satisfied as any woman possibly could.

CHAPTER 15

Sunday, late afternoon, after the wedding . . .

Meg had her bags in the car and a wad of tissues in her hand. She and Zach had said good-bye to the last of their guests, the mess from the wedding and reception was all cleaned up and put away, and it was time for them to head back to Portland and their honeymoon aboard the yacht Zach had built especially for Meg as a wedding gift.

He'd named the sixty-five-foot boat *Wolfsong,* and it was all loaded and ready for them to head out. In a flurry of hugs and tears, they were on their way. Once the car pulled out and headed down the driveway, Trak thought the resort seemed unnaturally quiet.

All the guests had left—Monday was a regular workday for a lot of the spouses, though not for Zach's employees. He'd closed the business down for the entire month of October.

For the Trinity Alps pack, this was the end of a very busy, very productive summer. Trak should feel better about everything, but he was still worried about that damned alpha in Tuck's wolf cage. Sighing, he got up and walked into the lodge.

Tuck followed him, so Trak led him into what was now

Cherry's office. She was most likely taking a nap about now with her guys. They'd all worked hard to make Meg and Zach's wedding a success. It had gone off perfectly.

Tuck closed the door behind him. "I've still got the alpha in the clinic. I'm planning to take him out to a rest stop east of town in the morning and leave him. Elle found his clothes in the woods, along with the keys to his truck. She checked and the one Cain saw is definitely his, so she'll follow me out; we'll give him his keys and tell him to get the hell out of here, not to come back. We photocopied all the stuff in his wallet so we can sort of keep track of him."

"Is that safe? Traveling with him?"

"I'll sedate him for the trip, try to time it so he's coming out of it when we get him where we want to leave him. I've got a hundred pounds on him, easy, and close to a foot in height. I don't expect much trouble. He's still in a locked cage in the clinic right now, but the guy is definitely scary. I'm almost sorry we didn't just get rid of him when we had the chance. Trak? Honestly, I don't know if Chelo will ever be safe. For some reason, he's fixated on her, blames her for all sorts of bad things that have happened to the pack."

Trak thought about that for a moment. "Do you think I should take care of him?" Trak wasn't a killer. His only thought when fighting the alpha on Friday night was to keep his pack safe. Killing the other man hadn't even been on his radar. He hadn't been able to quit thinking of Evan, of the look on his face after he'd killed Rube. None of them were killers, but there were some animals that really needed to be put down. As pack alpha, administering justice was Trak's job. Dealing with the alpha was his responsibility. But cold-blooded killing?

He wasn't sure he could go there.

"No." Tuck was shaking his head. "No need. I gave him some hormone shots while he was out and added an estrogen implant in his sac. He's got stitches and there's enough swelling that he thinks I actually removed his nuts. He's pretty pissed off at me right now. The female hormones in his system are going to cause some feminization for a while before the implant wears off. It's actually good for a couple of years. He should be losing a lot of the aggressiveness that had him going after you."

"So, he's shifted?" Trak hadn't even asked.

"Yep. I let the sedative wear off after the wedding this morning to see how he was doing. He's pissed and was still woozy, but he did manage to shift."

"Thanks, Tuck. It's not the ideal solution, but at least he'll be gone for now."

Evan and Nellie finally made it back to the cabin. Nellie flopped on the couch and threw her arms over her head.

"What a day!" She glanced at Evan and thought he was absolutely gorgeous in the dark suit he'd worn today. The wedding had been perfect; Meg and Zach's guests were really nice people and loved the fact that there were wolves wandering around the reception. The guys had all taken turns shifting so that no one would notice any particular person gone for very long. It had turned into a game for them and gave the guests plenty to talk about, along with lots of photo ops.

Evan slipped out of his black suit coat and hung it over a chair. Then he removed the tie he'd worn since this morning, unbuttoned the white shirt that still looked damned hot on him, and toed off his black leather loafers.

"Did I mention that you clean up really well, Mr. Dark?"

He nodded. "That you did. But no one was as beautiful as you, Ms. Deya."

"Oh . . . this old thing?"

She'd worn a designer gown, one that Darian had loaned to her. They were fairly close in size around, though Darian had a good five inches on her height. Darian said the dress hit her above the ankles—on Darnell it swept the floor—but she'd felt so beautiful today.

"That old thing makes you look like a goddess. Come upstairs with me. I want to make love to you, and then I want to make you mine. You'll sleep all through tomorrow, but when you awaken you'll be able to run with me in the woods. I can't wait to see what your wolf looks like. I bet you'll be gorgeous."

He carried her up the stairs, and when he made love to her Darnell had absolutely no doubt that Evan was hers and this huge step they were taking was right. She came apart in his arms, her body pulsing around his, her heart pounding in her chest, and her mind spinning. He kissed his way down her throat, across her breasts, and then along her ribs to the flare of her hip. Then she watched, awestruck, as he shifted and the wolf nipped her there, a tiny bite that felt more like a pinch than an actual bite into her skin. She was aware of the hot flow of blood and the warmth of his tongue as he licked the wound he'd left.

Then he shifted again and the mystery and the beauty of the change that was going to be hers brought tears to her eyes. Evan made love to her again, slowly, sweetly, his big body over hers, his thick cock filling her, owning her. She remembered her climax, a world of shooting stars and soft mountain breezes, and then she drifted away on the night with the sound of Evan's heart thundering in her ears.

Trak's climax was so powerful he could have sworn he saw stars. Chelo arched beneath him and her fingernails left long red streaks across his shoulders. He held his chest off her, blowing as if he'd just run a mile, head down, resting his weight on his elbows and forearms, but then he leaned close and kissed her, and just like that, he wanted her again.

"Chelo, you are magnificent." He kissed her again. "But I swear you're going to wear me out. Will we ever grow tired of this?"

"I hope not." She nipped his chin and ran her fingers along his ribs. "Because I will never let you go. 'Never' isn't just a euphemism with us. You realize that, right?"

"Oh, yeah."

He was hard again and so ready when his phone rang. Glancing at the clock, he groaned. "It's after eleven. What could they want me for now?"

"You'd better get it. Your phone doesn't ring this late."

She certainly thought like a pack alpha's mate, always putting the pack first. He could not have found a more perfect woman. "I know. Doesn't mean I have to like it." Regretfully, he crawled off his woman and walked over to the dresser where he'd left the phone. Tuck's name flashed on the screen. "Tuck? What's up?"

"Lock your doors, Trak. The bastard got loose. I was in the shower and he somehow got out of the locked cage. Elle heard some noise and went down to check and he cold-cocked her."

"Is she okay?"

"She'll be fine, but she's got a badly bruised jaw. We've got ice on it. I'm calling the pack, but I'm sure the bastard's headed your way. We'll get there as soon as we can."

"Stay with Elle. Call Cain and the others, tell them what's going on, but you keep her safe."

He hung up the phone and turned to Chelo, but she was already pulling on her robe. "Is he human or wolf?"

"I'm guessing he'll come as a wolf. I locked the doors before we came up here, but I need to meet him. This has to end now."

Chelo grabbed his arm. "Trak, the man is crazy. He's strong and he has no sense of conscience. He'll do his best to kill you."

"Well, I intend to kill him and I've got you to come home to, so I think that gives me a lot more incentive to beat that bastard. Stay in here. You're too important a target, and if I'm worried about you I might end up getting hurt." He kissed her. "I really, really don't want to get hurt."

"I don't want you to get hurt, either. Be careful. I love you. I promise to stay inside. I'm guessing you're right. He'll come as a wolf. He's stronger then."

"Figured as much. I'm going to shift inside, so follow me so you can get the door, okay? I'm going out the back. Stay safe. I'll come home as soon as I can." He pulled her into his arms and held her close. "I want to finish what we were just starting. Keep the lights off in here. I don't want him to see you."

He shifted. Chelo followed him down the steps and opened the back door. Trak slipped out into the darkness. He glanced over his shoulder and watched her close the door. He didn't move forward until he heard the dead bolt click into place.

Trak picked up Cain's scent not far from the cabin, but there was no sign of the crazy alpha. Slipping quietly through the trees, Trak went straight to Cain. They both shifted. "Any sign of him?"

"I picked up his scent near Tuck's place and he was heading this way, but I lost him near the swampy area in the meadow. He might have rolled in mud to throw us off."

"I'll keep that in mind. Is Brad with Cherry?"

"He is. We've got all the women at the lodge. Wils and Ronan are patrolling together, Manny's over by the lodge in case he heads that way, and Drew's with Brad and the women. Lawz and Darian left for Eureka about an hour ago. They were both out of vacation."

"I've always told Lawz he's got great timing." He heard a snap, just the sound of a single twig, but it was way too close. Trak and Cain shifted and slipped away in opposite directions.

He didn't smell wolf, but he did pick up the foul miasma of old mud and algae. Cain had been right. The sound had come from the direction of the boggy meadow. Trak moved quietly to a point where he could see the meadow. He quickly spotted Cain slinking through the grass toward a spot of darkness that was most likely their wolf.

Watching Cain Boudin in action was actually pretty exhilarating—he moved so quietly, so carefully, that the grass didn't even wave with his passing.

Trak slipped closer, keeping to the opposite side of the meadow, crouching low in the thick grass. Cain was still drawing closer to the dark shadow when it suddenly rose up to full height and charged Trak in an aggressive flash of sharp teeth and powerful jaws.

Trak dove low, feinting as if going for the wolf's throat but snapping his jaws on the upper half of the beast's front leg and taking him down. A loud yelp and the sharp crack of breaking bone was proof his attack had been successful.

There would be no mercy tonight.

Chelo sat alone in the dark cabin, waiting. Trak wouldn't face the bastard alone. His pack loved him and would do anything for him, but she couldn't help but fear for him. A lifetime of abuse at the hands of monsters had conditioned her to expect the worst.

It wasn't easy to be an optimist.

She had to hope, though. It was all about hope. Hope had kept her alive and helped her escape. It had led her to Trak, a man she loved with all her heart.

He would be safe. He had to be.

A sharp knock at the back door startled her. She walked across the room. "Who is it?"

"Chelo, it's Armando. Manny. Sorry, you've probably only heard my nickname. Are you okay?"

She quickly unlocked the door and let him in. "Have you heard from Trak? Is he okay?"

Manny stepped inside and locked the door behind him. "He's going to be fine. Cain's with him and nothing can stop that guy. Trak's pretty tough on his own. I was worried about you here by yourself. Thought I'd stay and keep you company. Are you okay with that?"

"Thank you." She drew her robe more tightly about herself. She'd not spent much time with him—his work as a forest ranger took him out on the trails a lot—but she knew his mates, Drew and Jules, and liked both of them. Armando was definitely welcome. "I appreciate it. I hate waiting. I'm so sorry all of these bad things are happening because of me."

"Don't be. None of this is your fault. If you want to blame anyone, blame the two who kidnapped you so many years ago. I've heard your story, Chelo. It's terrifying and amazing."

He walked over to the counter and went about making a pot of coffee as if he'd done it many times before, so comfortable in Trak's kitchen that Chelo realized she was actually beginning to relax.

"You're a strong woman, and an alpha besides. This pack needs you as much as we've always needed Trak." He poured two cups. "You take anything in this?"

"Black, please. Thank you.

"How does the pack need me? Trak has said that, too, but this is the most stable group of people I've ever met, and your lives were safer before I showed up. You can't deny that."

Manny laughed and took a sip of his coffee. "I won't even try to deny that, though we're not bored, either. Chelo, Trak has been lonely for too many years. All of us were, but this summer each of us found mates, and that's made a huge difference in all our lives. We've been worried about Trak because he hadn't found anyone, because not a single woman who's come through here over the past few months would have been right for him. You are. Hold on to that and know that we all accept you as the one who will make this pack stronger because you're making our alpha stronger. We're pack animals, Chelo. Not meant to live alone. With you and Darnell joining us, we are finally complete. We're all excited to see what the future holds."

Trak stood over the dead wolf, head down, sides heaving as he struggled for air. A bloody gash along his rib cage was his only injury, but the alpha had not been an easy kill. Tearing out the wolf's throat had finally stopped him, though he'd fought a brutal fight on three legs until he'd finally gone down from loss of blood. Cain had sat back and watched, ready to help should Trak need him, but he'd stayed out of the fight.

As it should be. This was Trak's battle and he'd prevailed. Standing here over his vanquished rival, he realized he'd always wondered if he could handle himself in a fight to the death. He'd feared that he didn't have what he needed to lead this pack when it got down to the feral side of fighting for control.

Tonight's battle had settled that argument. His heart had finally stopped trying to beat its way out of his chest, his ears were no longer ringing with the sound of growls and yips, and the damned wolf had finally stopped breathing.

From the amount of blood at the scene, it appeared he'd finally just bled out.

Trak shifted. Cain joined him, the two men standing over the dead animal. "I'll get the guys to help me bury the body," Cain said. "Tuck's got a graveyard for wolves that have died over the years. This one won't be shifting back, so that's where he belongs."

Nodding, Trak turned away. "I need to get back to Chelo. She's there alone and probably worried sick."

"I think Manny's with her. When I left to meet you, he

was talking to Jules about going over to sit with her until you got back."

"Thank you. Thank you for worrying about us. Cain, inviting you into this pack has got to be the smartest move I ever made as an alpha. Sorry it's taken me so long to figure that out."

Cain slapped him on the shoulder. "S'okay. I wasn't worried about it." He looked at the dead wolf for a moment and then raised his head. "I say we leave him here, take care of the body in the morning. It's been a long day."

Nodding, Trak agreed. "Hell of a good wedding, though. And we handled it all without a wedding planner."

"Only because Chelo and Darnell showed up when they did. Of course, that makes the whole idea of doing weddings a more workable concept, the fact we can do stuff in-house."

"Good point. I think I need to go and let Chelo know that." Trak turned to go but thought of something else. "Can you stop and tell Evan that all is okay? He was going to turn Darnell tonight, so I imagine he's afraid to leave her at all, thinking that guy's still running loose."

"Will do. See you in the morning."

Trak watched as Cain shifted and trotted off through the woods. Then, without a backward glance at the dead wolf lying in the weeds, he went back to Chelo.

Tuesday morning

There was a sense of heightened expectation on the deck at the lodge this morning. Evan was officially introducing his mate to the pack. Darnell had awakened the night before and made her first shift with Evan standing by. He'd called Trak to tell him that she was fine, that he'd taken her on a short run because she'd been too excited to wait for her official acceptance into the pack.

Trak sat with the rest of the pack, telling them about Evan's phone call and laughing. He couldn't imagine Darnell waiting for much of anything. She'd certainly given up waiting on Evan, and it hadn't taken her long to wrest control of that situation. "Anyway," he said, "they should be here any minute."

A moment later Evan stepped out of the forest and into the sunlight. Beside him was a beautiful wolf, average sized with a creamy belly and silver, gray, and tan coloring around her head and body. A dark bar made a striking pattern across her chest and over her shoulders.

Trak turned to Cain and, behind his hand, said, "She even walks cocky."

"Evan's going to have his hands full with this one." Cain didn't even try to lower his voice, and when Darnell's ears pricked forward it was obvious she'd heard.

The women were already spilling off the deck and running out to meet her. Trak hung back a bit, watching, listening.

Laughter. There was so much laughter with his pack. He remembered not that long ago when it had been only a pack of men, all of them knowing what they lacked and willing to do what it took to find their mates.

They'd had more success than any of them could have imagined, and the women now part of this pack had only made it stronger. One of these days, there'd be babies, too. Sooner rather than later, he hoped. It had been a long time since there'd been any young, and never any with his pack.

He realized Chelo hadn't gone down with the others. She

stood behind him, waiting patiently. No point in making her wait any longer.

"What were you thinking about, Trak? You looked sort of pensive."

"Thinking about how much healthier this pack is, and all because of the women who've become a part of us."

"And that makes you sad?" She took his hand and led him down the steps to greet Darnell.

"Not sad at all. Just thinking of what the future might hold. Imagining children. Are you okay with trying? I know your past is . . ."

"My past is over, Trak. I'm only looking at beginnings. And yes." She grabbed his arm and hugged him close as they walked. "I want to try. I realized I've lived my life on hope for things to get better. They are definitely better. Now I can start looking at my future. At our future. We'll never know if babies are part of ours unless we try."

He leaned close and kissed her. And there in the parking lot in front of the Feral Passions Resort lodge, Traker Jakes stripped off his clothes and shifted. With his lovely mate beside him, they turned with the pack and raced into the woods.

Chelo was right. They truly were racing into a brand-new future.

BOUND TO THE WOLF

A. C. Arthur

PROLOGUE

"I'm. Not. Interested," Marena said pointedly for the third time.

He wasn't going to listen. She could tell by the way his eyes narrowed, his mouth opened slightly, and his chest heaved. He was going to come closer and touch her and that was the last thing she wanted.

She took a step back, and then another, the high heels of the black pumps she'd worn to the firm's anniversary celebration sinking into the plush hotel carpet. Getting a room at the same hotel where the party was being held had been a mistake. Marena should have gotten into her car and driven the twelve miles back to her house, even if it was almost one in the morning. She hadn't been drinking, so she was fine to drive. But she'd wanted to treat herself. This hotel had a spa with a great reputation, not to mention the pool and five-star restaurant. She'd planned to make a weekend of it, to take some time for herself to relax and unwind after back-to-back cases at work. After all these years Marena had finally decided to follow the advice of every girlfriend she'd ever had. She was doing something just for her pleasure.

Only tonight, she feared that wasn't going to happen.

"I'm simply trying to help you celebrate the win on that Vale case. You've just made millions for the firm and all but solidified your partnership in a six-hour settlement conference. You deserve a grand celebration," he said, with a smile spreading slowly across his wide face.

Davis Sumpter was already a partner at The Arrington Law Group, one of San Francisco's largest law firms. He wasn't a very tall man by her standards considering her own height. He was maybe six feet tops, with a medium build, his love of fashion apparent in the custom-fit designer suit and Italian leather tie-ups he'd worn to the party. And on a good day, Marena would even go as far as to say that he was an attractive man with his strong jaw, almond skin tone, and dark, exotic-looking brown eyes. Of course every female at the firm would swear Marena was blind or too overworked to see straight if she didn't admit to Davis's good looks, because they all loved Davis Sumpter. They all wanted to sleep with him, hoped he would marry them, and all that fantasyland crap that tended to take place in a firm with over one hundred attorneys and two hundred and fifty staff, and that was just in the San Francisco office.

Still, to Marena, he was just a man. A man she had no intention of celebrating with tonight, or any other night for that matter.

"I've done as much celebrating as I plan to, Davis," she told him. "I have twenty other cases on my desk waiting for my return on Monday morning."

"Just twenty?" he asked with a coy smile as he moved closer.

They were in the sitting area of her suite. She hadn't known, but Davis had apparently left the party and come upstairs behind her, so that when she opened the door to her room he was right there, slipping inside just as she let herself in. Davis was like that, she thought, slippery as a snake and as charismatic as a practiced Hollywood actor. That's how he won most of his cases.

"It's late, Davis. You should go," she continued, being sure to keep her voice level and serious, just as she did when she was in the courtroom, cross-examining a witness.

He shook his head, loosening the navy blue-and-white tie at his neck.

"I don't think so," he told her. "You've been strutting your thick ass around that office for years now. Turning down one guy after another, holding your head up high like nobody was good enough for you." He pulled the tie from his neck and undid the top two buttons of his shirt. "But I never asked," he finished just before he removed his jacket, tossing it on one of the ivory-colored couches.

Marena took another step back until her butt met the edge of the sofa table where she'd placed her purse when she came in.

"I never asked if I could have a taste of you," Davis continued, licking his tongue along his bottom lip, his eyes glazing with lust.

A huge fan of crime-procedural shows, Marena could see exactly where this was leading. This was the first few minutes of the show where the brutal rape and murder that it will take the remaining fifty minutes to solve would occur. Unless the unwitting, but not defenseless by a long shot, female quickly got her act together.

"No need in asking," Marena told him while reaching a hand behind her back, attempting to unzip her purse. "I'll go ahead and give you an answer. No."

Davis laughed. "You're funny," he told her. "Never figured you for having a sense of humor, but that was really funny."

His hands had moved to the belt that he quickly undid. He unbuttoned his pants, and then there was that undeniable sound of unzipping. Her arms and legs shook as she struggled to hold back that piercing scream that would alert someone to his presence. Davis Sumpter in her hotel suite after midnight was not going to go over well. Rumors would spread like wildfire throughout the firm and her dream of making partner would be shot to hell. Marena wasn't about to let that happen.

"I'm serious, Davis. I know it may seem strange to have someone tell you they're not interested, but I'm really not," she told him. "And it has nothing to do with you as a person. I'm just not interested in dating anyone right now. I'm really focused on my work." Marena talked as her hand worked.

But she hadn't worked fast enough.

Davis seemed to close the space between them in the blink of an eye. He locked one hand at the back of her neck and pulled her flush against him. Marena gasped and he pounced, sticking his tongue through her slightly parted lips. It was wet and messy and had her stomach roiling in disgust, but Marena tried like hell to keep it together. Even when his other hand gripped her ass painfully.

"I'm gonna fuck that sweet ass tonight and you can get back to work in the morning," he told her, his teeth scraping along her bottom lip.

There was a pinprick of pain at that action and her heart raced, all but exploding in her chest. Her mind screamed now, even as she tried to reach back for her purse again. When Davis had grabbed her he'd pulled her away from the table, so it wasn't within her reach as it had been before.

"This is not a good idea, Davis. I promise you . . . it's n-n-not," she stuttered.

"No," he insisted. "I promise you this will be the best night of your life."

His words ended with a slight chuckle and then what she might have thought was a growl, if her heartbeat hadn't been thumping so loudly in her ears. She was shaking her head, his hand still holding her neck tightly. His other hand was working her dress up until he managed to touch the bare skin of her upper thigh.

"Please don't do this," she said in a voice that sounded nothing like her own, tears stinging her eyes.

"I knew I'd get you to beg," was his response as his tongue traced a line down her neck.

Her body trembled, mind racing with what might happen, what could go down in just a few more minutes. Everything she'd ever worked for would be gone, down the drain because she hadn't been paying attention to her surroundings. He was going to rape her and laugh about it in the morning. She would have to press charges against him, solidifying the end of her career at the firm, because she knew for a fact there were other partners who wouldn't believe her. She reached back, trying to move her feet and to get closer to that table once more. She'd gotten her purse unzipped; if she could just get her hand inside, all she needed was to get—

Pain seared through her shoulder, like a billion fire-hot needles sticking into her, ripping her skin and possibly part of her soul. The tears that had been burning her eyes poured down her cheeks and that scream she hadn't wanted to break free sounded throughout that room like a siren.

Davis was laughing. That's what Marena heard next,

348 A. C. Arthur

laughing, and she felt him rip her panties, his fingers touching the bare skin of her crotch. Adrenaline soared through her veins and she reached back far enough to get her hand into her purse. The eighteen-hundred-dollar designer bag probably fell to the floor, she'd put her hand inside and pulled it out so fast, but Marena didn't give a damn; all she knew was that she had to stop this madness, before it went too far.

With her other arm she pushed against Davis with all her might, sending him stumbling back a few steps. He looked startled, then smirked, his lips . . . bloody. Shaking her head so her mind would clear, Marena lifted her arm, the gun she'd taken from her bag clenched tightly in her hand.

"Get out of my room," she said in a surprisingly steady voice.

He had the audacity to free his erection at that point, gripping it in his hand as he said, "Not until I'm done with you."

She released the safety on the gun and aimed at his dick. "Now!"

It happened so fast Marena didn't have a moment to do anything other than react. Davis lunged for her and she squeezed the trigger, catching him in the stomach. He paused for only a second, smiled, and came at her again. Marena fired off another round and another and then another, until the gun was empty, clicking loudly in her hand as she continued to pull the trigger.

Her entire body trembled now. She felt like she was on fire, her heart racing so fast any second she was certain it would explode out of her chest. She dropped the gun taking a step back to try to catch her breath. Her next thought was that she needed to call the police, but when she turned to look for her purse again the room spun around her. Marena clenched her stomach that churned and bubbled as nausea swept through her body. She was cold and she was hot and in the next instant she was falling to the floor.

"Ma'am. Ma'am, just calm down. I'm Detective Silverman from the SFPD."

Marena could hear his voice, gravelly, with a sort of Southern drawl that didn't seem to fit here. The throbbing headache and sick feeling in the pit of her stomach didn't fit, either. She'd just left the party, had planned to get a quick shower and climb into the bed. It was a king size, just like the one she had in her bedroom. Only this one she wouldn't have to make up when she woke in the morning, because she was in a hotel. She would order room service and have breakfast-in-bed in the morning and lounge around for a while until it was time for her spa appointment.

But wait . . . she wasn't in here alone. He was here and he . . . oh, no!

Marena sat up, or at least she tried. Pain soared through her right shoulder with such intensity her head spun.

"Just take it easy," that Southern voice said again. "Take your time. You've had quite a busy night."

Had she?

Yes, Marena thought with an inward sigh. She had.

Opening her eyes, she found herself staring into an unfamiliar face. A fortysomething-year-old face with a scraggly beard and a pudgy nose.

"I'm Detective Ron Silverman," he told her with a slight nod of his head. "Are you Marena Panos?"

Marena began to nod but stopped abruptly when pain from the motion almost blinded her. "I am."

"And you work for The Arrington Firm, the company that had a big party downstairs earlier tonight?"

She knew better than to attempt a nod this time. Instead, she spoke in a soft voice, "Yes."

"Then you came up here to the room you reserved," Detective Southern Drawl continued.

"I did," she admitted.

His gaze grew just a little more intense on her as he said slowly, "And then what did you do?"

Nauseous and with her head throbbing like a boulder might have fallen on it, Marena was still a lawyer. She knew exactly what an interrogation was, as well as her rights regarding same. She also knew the look the detective was giving her—the "she's a slut, so she must have asked for it" one—and she wasn't offended. She was pissed off.

Coming to a stand wasn't easy—the room tilted and her stomach wheezed its displeasure—still she kept moving, until the detective was taking a step back to give her space.

"I'll call my lawyer . . . now," she said, swallowing hard to keep everything she'd eaten earlier down where it belonged.

Before the detective could reply Marena tried to take a step, but her legs rejected that notion and she felt herself going down quickly. There were two cops there now, the detective and a female wearing a uniform.

"She needs a doctor," the woman spoke.

The detective frowned.

And Marena passed out. Again.

Twenty-four hours had passed and Marena still felt like crap. The doctor in the emergency room had ruled out a concussion, calling what Marena was suffering some sort of trauma. Although the female cop who had accompanied her to the ER had repeatedly told Marena that there was no one else in the room when they arrived.

She'd been lying on the floor, her gun beside her, with the door wide open. Another guest in the hotel had heard the shots and came over to find her. The police wanted to know what happened.

And so the hell did she.

"Hello?" Marena said, groggily answering her cell phone.

She had no idea what time it was, just that it was daylight again. When she'd returned to her apartment from the ER she'd taken a shower and sat on the side of her bed preparing to call Gail McGovern, a woman she'd met in law school and the closest friend Marena had ever claimed. But she'd never made that call, or at least she didn't think she had. Exhaustion had overtaken her and Marena had fallen asleep. For an entire day.

"Marena? Hi. It's Tammi, from the office," the female voice spoke loudly through the phone.

Frowning, Marena tried to sit up in bed. She was still a little dizzy, but at least her stomach wasn't feeling as if it were ready to revolt at any minute.

"Hey, Tammi," she replied. "What's going on?"

"That's what I was calling you to find out," Tammi said. "What the hell happened on Friday night?"

Marena was sitting straight up now, staring across her

bedroom, confirming that she was still in a familiar place. The last time she'd awakened it had been in a hotel room with a strange cop staring in her face. "What do you mean?" she asked her secretary.

"The partners are here in the conference room. They called me about an hour ago and asked me to come to the office and to log on to your computer," Tammi told her.

"What? What for? Wait, it's Sat—no, Sunday?" She shook her head, trying to clear the fog that insisted on hanging around. They'd given her pain medication in the ER, but that was hours, no, a day ago, she thought, but she was having a hell of a time keeping hold of the time in her mind.

"There's a cop here, too," Tammi continued. "I mean, he said his name was Detective Silverman."

Detective Southern Drawl. Marena did remember his name at least.

"What are they saying, Tammi?" she asked, her hand tightening on the phone as she stood slowly from the bed.

"Davis is missing," Tammi had said, her voice low.

Had she been whispering this entire time? Marena wasn't sure. Her head still hurt. But she was walking across the room, going to pull the blinds closed at her window. She didn't know why she did it, but she went to the second window and did the same thing.

"What do you mean he's missing? I sh— I mean, I just saw him at the party on Friday," Marena said.

"I know. That's what they're saying. I mean, they said that you and Davis were at the party and that the two of you left to go up to your room. He told Stan he'd call him in the morning, you know, after," Tammi reported, not an ounce of judgment or disgust in her tone.

Because Tammi was another one of the females at the

firm who thought they were in love with the fabulous Davis Sumpter.

"That's not—" Marena replied immediately, then snapped her lips shut. She knew better than to admit anything, to anybody. Even her secretary. "I'm coming in. Tell them I'll be there in an hour."

"No!" Tammi immediately exclaimed. Then her voice lowered once more. "That's why I'm calling you, Marena. I heard them talking about getting a warrant for your arrest. They think you did something to Davis."

Marena remained silent because she *had* done something to that asshole. She'd shot him.

But if that was true, then where the hell was his body?

Marena closed her eyes. She'd shot a man. Twice, or was it three times? She couldn't remember. What she did know was that he'd intended to sleep with her that night, regardless of whether she agreed or not. And she had definitely *not* agreed. So she'd defended herself. Now Tammi was telling her something different. Davis was missing.

And she was a suspect in his disappearance.

"I'll call you back," Marena said quickly, disconnecting the call with Tammi before the woman could say anything else.

Her hands shook now. She looked down at them, at the fingers that had squeezed the trigger of that gun. Her ring was still there, the one her father had given her for her sixteenth birthday. She wore it on her left ring finger because Matthew Panos would forever be the love of her life. The only man she had ever allowed in her heart.

With that thought she willed herself to stop shaking. She was not weak. The youngest of five children and the only one to move away from the small coastal town in Florida, to go to college and to make something of herself, was definitely not a weakling. She pressed another button on her phone and had to leave a message for Gail.

Then Marena did something she never thought she'd do.

She went to her closet and pulled out a duffel bag. In the next moments she was throwing clothes inside, grabbing her makeup bag, her bottles of Ambien and multivitamins, tossing them all into the bag as well. As she pulled on her jeans, Marena jumped when her cell phone rang. Checking the caller I.D., she frowned when she saw the office number.

Slipping her feet into her flats, she was moving again, heading to her closet. She retrieved a T-shirt, quickly pulling it over her head, but taking another second or so to get it properly adjusted. Marena wasn't a small girl by a long shot. She was curvy or plump, voluptuous or luscious, as men had called her in the past. Chubby or round, as her siblings used to tease. Cute-as-a-cherub, Darlene Panos used to tell her when she tucked her in at night. A beautiful, independent woman who needed to purge her closet of these shirts that might be a size too small, Marena thought as she closed the closet door and decided the snug fit of the T-shirt over her triple D–sized breasts would simply have to suffice.

She ignored the phone call, grabbing her phone off the bed and her Kate Spade clutch. In the next ten minutes Marena was out the door, down the elevator to the underground garage in her apartment building. Climbing behind the wheel of her Mercedes SUV, she started the engine and pulled out of the garage. She drove for almost an hour before realizing she had no idea where she was going, or what she planned to do when she got there.

All Marena knew for certain was that something strange had happened in that hotel room Friday night. Something a lot stranger than a man she'd known for the last five years coming on way too strong and getting his ass shot in the process. Definitely more bizarre than the fact that Davis had simply gotten up after those shots she'd put into him and walked out of the hotel.

No, the most inexplicable part of that evening was the searing pain still shooting from her shoulder down her arm, spreading to every part of her body. She'd remembered the start of the pain in that area, how it had pierced clean through to her soul, causing not only physical discomfort but also an opening or awakening that she could not readily explain. Then she remembered seeing the blood around Davis's mouth. He had really bitten her. As weird as that sounded—and as that realization bounced around in her mind—Marena knew it was true. And then he'd disappeared. So now she not only felt like crap, but she also was wanted by the police.

Yes, everything she'd recalled seemed outlandish and served as motive enough for her to try to find someplace safe to stay until she could figure all this out.

Until she could discover who the hell—or, rather, *what* the hell—Davis Sumpter really was.

CHAPTER 1

He was in.

His dick throbbing with each step he took. Down the long winding, underground hallway and up two sets of stairs, Phelan moved steadily, his mind and body focused on one thing only. Sex.

The urges had driven him for the past two hours as he'd pressed every bit of speed out of his Ducati 1098 Superbike on the highway leading him from Blackbriar to Bozeman. He'd made this ride weekly in the past two months, needing more than he'd ever had before.

Phelan was a lycan who possessed every lycan trait, including the insatiable sexual appetite. At thirty-one years old, six feet and three inches tall, 184 pounds, he was almost as powerful as an alpha and better trained than any of the human's military soldiers. He'd lost count of the number of people he'd killed in his lifetime—human and others. There was no family for Phelan, just his pack. No fun and games, just the mission at hand. Life wasn't a gift, it was a job, and Phelan knew how to do his job.

He also knew how to slake the burning need that for the last eight weeks had been raging through his veins like adrenaline. In the morning when he woke, until the second he was finally able to close his eyes for a night's rest, he thought of sinking into a perfectly warm and wet pussy, drowning in its goodness until he could think of nothing else.

Not the threat on Blaez's life.

Not the house full of lycans and their mates where he lived.

And certainly not the curse that Eureka had called herself, putting on him.

Eureka, the beautiful vixen who had taken a part of him one summer's night long ago and turned him into the cold, hard bastard he was now. It was amazing that one woman could do so much damage in such a short time span. But Eureka was no ordinary woman. In fact, she was a fury.

Phelan yanked the door open, stepping inside the room where he knew they would be. They were always here in the hours before the club opened. Always naked and aroused and doing whatever they could to calm the sexual storm brewing inside of them.

It was as if every being that was not human on this earth was fueled by its sexual desire and inside these walls, in the club that was owned and run by furies, there were no holds barred. They could all find complete ecstasy before they had to return to the real world.

Phelan's booted feet were silent as they moved over the plush bloodred carpet. He heard the sounds before he saw any of them, moans of pleasure, sighs of bliss. His blood warmed. Turning the last corner to where the furniture would be positioned just right, studio lighting would be in each corner, casting everyone in a bright golden light. Huge black pillows would be thrown on the floor, matching the black drapes at the two windows along that back wall.

He came to a stop at a chair, the one he liked to sit in. It was ready and waiting for him, just as he knew it would be.

She knew exactly what he liked. Always had.

Sitting down slowly, Phelan looked across the room to where a woman with red hair lay naked on the floor. Her legs were spread wide so that Phelan could see the slick folds of her pussy, seconds before another man's tongue stroked them. Small, palm-sized breasts were being grabbed from each side by two different women, while a fourth woman straddled the redhead's face, allowing her to lick along the folds of her juicy pussy.

A few feet away a busty brunette stood with one leg up on a man's shoulder. He thrust deep into her pussy while another man stood behind, pumping wildly into her bottom. The moaning grew louder, mixing with the sound of sweaty bodies slapping against one another, tongues slipping and slurping. It was a smorgasbord of pleasure, one that Phelan knew men and women alike, all over the world, would pay to witness in person.

As for Phelan, he only glanced at them momentarily. They weren't what had drawn him here. He was waiting for something . . . or someone else.

She knew he had arrived, just as she always did. The scar beneath his left eye twitched only seconds before she came through a side door wearing all black leather. Boots that came to her thighs, a bra that barely covered the light pink of her nipples, and a thong that displayed the perfect globes of her ass. She walked slowly, being certain not to look at him directly. Her body was slim and compact, breasts just enough to fit into his palms, ass just slightly bigger. Long, bone-straight, dark brown hair hung down the center of her back, barely covering the two dimples above the curve of her ass.

Her nipples were already hard and Phelan was willing to bet every dollar in his pocket, and his bank account, that her pussy was wet. Eureka was always wet, especially for him.

When she'd come completely into the room, she turned her back to him, and gyrated so that her ass bounced for his viewing pleasure. He despised everything about her. From her husky voice to her penchant for revenge and spitefulness. The latter he could attribute to her DNA. She was a fury; her main purpose in life was to punish people by literally driving them insane. Well, Phelan could attest to the fact that she was damned good at her job.

The scar on his face tingled and he lifted a finger to rub along the gashes in his skin that had healed as much as they ever would. Lycans normally healed from all their wounds in record time. But this one, the one that was inflicted by another otherworldly being, was there to stay. Just as the curse she'd said she put on him. Phelan would have tried to argue that curse, but the fact that he was sitting here, for the ninth week in a row, his legs gaped open, dick hard and waiting, was proof to the contrary.

Another lycan came in at that moment. Taller and much slimmer than Phelan, his skin darker than Phelan's olive complexion, long fingers gripping the black paddle in one hand as he walked. Phelan flexed his fingers, remembering all too well how good it felt to hold that handle in his hand, to wield that dominant power over Eureka.

Without a word Eureka leaned over a high-backed leather chair, so that she was facing the action of the others

in the room, her upturned ass on display for Phelan to enjoy. Or to hate, whichever was his passion tonight. It was
that way with her now. He hated her for what she'd done to
him all those years ago, a searing dislike that went well beyond the physical scar she'd put on him, to the white-hot
pain she'd inflicted on his soul. And then there were the moments when he craved her like his next meal. He needed to
be near her, to scent her pussy, to watch her climax, to hear
her moan in ecstasy, although none of that had come at his
hand in the years since she'd scarred and cursed him.

The lycan stepped closer to her, extending his palm and
laying it over one bared ass cheek. She remained perfectly
still, without him having to instruct her. That was part of
the act—she appeared to be submissive when in reality that
was the very last thing that Eureka Trisk would ever be.

The lycan squeezed her cheek, gripping it tightly in his
hand. and Phelan's mouth watered. His hand moved down
slowly to unzip his jeans and release his thick length. Grabbing the root of his cock, Phelan jerked upward, hard as he
watched the lycan rub along Eureka's other cheek. Without warning the lycan reared back his other arm, bringing
the paddle down over her ass with a loud whack.

She didn't move.

Her cheek instantly turned red.

He paddled her again and again, rotating from one cheek
to the next. With each strike Phelan jerked his cock harder
and harder, pre-cum already beading and dripping from his
slit. When the lycan ripped the black thong from Eureka's
waist, Phelan's teeth clenched together tightly. The lycan
paddled her ass again and again, stopping only to slide his
fingers down her slit. When he pulled his finger out, it was
dripping with her desire and he immediately put it to his

mouth and licked. Phelan pumped viciously into his hand. Another round of paddling and her ass cheeks were so red he could almost feel the heat emanating from them, while rivulets of her essence dripped down the inside of her thighs.

Phelan came at that moment. Like a storm that had been brewing, his release burst free, dripping down onto his hand and the front of his jeans. He cursed with the pressure that had built along the base of his spine and the tension that remained stretched across the breadth of his shoulders. He'd come, but he wasn't relieved. Not by a long shot. He never was.

Reaching down beside him, he opened the black case that was always left there for him. Using the wipes and hand sanitizer, he cleaned himself, and stood from the chair, not caring to see the lycan finally thrusting his rigid length into Eureka's pussy, or the others who were still there, very near to finding their final release.

Phelan didn't give a damn about any of it. He wanted to leave. Just as he always did. Hating the fact that he'd driven all the way out here in the first place, but unable to stop the monotonous routine.

Phelan's boots thumped loudly on the stairs as he made his way out of the building, thoughts and recriminations roaring through his mind while he moved.

"Leaving so soon," her voice carried through the air, echoing off the cinder-block walls.

"Got what I came for," was Phelan's terse reply.

"And that's all you ever wanted," Eureka countered.

Phelan turned quickly, staring up the last flight of stairs to see her standing there, a sheer knee-length robe covering what remained of her leather outfit.

Once upon a time there was so much he'd wanted to say

to her, so many things he'd thought about sharing, about admitting, but then he'd found out her true purpose.

Shaking his head, he responded. "Don't do that," he warned. "There's nothing for us down that road."

"This time?" She arched a brow, crossing her arms over her chest, looking like a goddess—a goddess of temptation and rage.

"Any time," he said, turning again to leave.

Her screech was loud and long and pierced straight through to his gut, but Phelan didn't stop moving. So what she was angry. He'd given up on caring about the way Eureka felt about anything he did or said a long time ago.

"It won't go away!" she yelled after him. "I will never leave you, no matter how far you try to run!"

Phelan kept moving, kicking through the door and stepping out into the night air. He had no idea what time it was now, just that the sky was black, overcast, with no stars in sight. Typical, he thought as his feet crunched on gravel before he stood near his bike once again. Grabbing the helmet, he slipped it on, throwing a leg over and lifting his bike beneath him. He sat for a moment before starting the engine, inhaling deeply, exhaling slowly.

She was right.

She had never left him. Not in the ten years they'd been separated, the years since he'd found out she'd been sent to kill him. Her excuse for betraying him had been that she'd fallen in love with him, but that was a lie. Just like everything else she'd said and done. She hadn't loved him, only the thought of bringing him and the leader of the Trekas pack to Zeus had intrigued her. Aroused her, yes, that's one thing Phelan could lay claim to. But Eureka was easily aroused. She was fuckable and she was an evil bitch with vengeance flowing in her veins.

And she had been with him every day since then in his mind and, infuriatingly, his soul. Every fucking day. The scar was the physical reminder, but the hardening of his heart, the firm set of his jaw, everything down to the strict rules he put on his sex life, were a direct result of his experience with Eureka.

Starting his bike, Phelan drove away from Club Entice. He left the thoughts of his past behind to instead focus on more pertinent matters. The human world had been aware of the existence of shape-shifters living among them for a year now, but the residents of Blackbriar—the small Montana mountain town where Blaez, the alpha of his pack, had moved them more than a year ago—were now up in arms about them being there.

After Malec had killed the Solo—a lycan with no pack and no affiliation to the Hunters or the Devoteds—who had been threatening Malec's mate, Caroline, in her apartment, the town had let loose on the pack that had renovated the log cabin in the woods. So far, however, the security measures that Phelan had instituted had kept them away from the lodge, but tempers were brewing. The humans were planning and Zeus was still hunting Blaez. A bounty had been set for the capture or killing of the half demigod, half lycan, and Phelan and the other betas in the pack were charged with keeping him safe.

To say Phelan had other shit on his mind besides the claw marks on his face and the still-raging hard-on pressed uncomfortably against his thigh was an understatement. And as he rode along the highway in the dark of night, nobody would ever guess the weight lying heavily on the lycan's shoulders.

Nobody, but . . .

The night air had been growing cooler as it was now in the midst of the fall season. It had rained earlier in the day drenching the area in scents of wet leaves, damp mud-packed grounds, and, for a Devoted lycan, the scent of their archenemies, the Hunters. The pack had picked up the aroma earlier in the week, even though they'd all been expecting more of the lycans who had vowed to destroy all Devoteds and especially the one true-blood relation to their creator, Nyktimos. But the full moon was weeks away, so an attack wasn't expected until then.

Yet as Phelan inhaled deeply once more, his shoulders hunched, his fingers tightening on the handles of his bike. He leaned in closer, his gaze trained forward, to the car driving a short distance in front of him. The scent was coming from there. He sped up without another thought, leaning into a lane change until he came along the side of the SUV. The windows were tinted so that he could not see inside, but the stench had grown stronger, more potent than it had been just seconds before.

It wasn't simply a Hunter's scent, either.

No, Phelan thought with a shake of his head. It was too strong, too feral, unrestrained, desperate, and possibly afraid.

It was a new blood.

She was going to be sick.

Marena had never gone through a registration so quickly in her life. But she'd barely managed to get out of her car and run up the steps to the quaint little B and B nestled just off the road, surrounded by a copse of trees. Once in-side she murmured something about needing a room for the night and slapped her credit card on the desk. Deep breaths while the desk clerk spoke what Marena knew was prob-ably important information but somehow sounded like gib-berish had kept her from keeling over right there in the lobby, on the lovely and most definitely expensive Aubus-son rug.

By the time the clerk, a woman wearing a thick beige sweater and wire-rimmed glasses, handed her the credit card and room key, Marena could feel the bile burning at the base of her throat. She snatched the items from the woman's hand and raced up the stairs, barely reading the room numbers but somehow getting the key into the right lock and flying into the room, heading straight to the bath-room. She made it just in time and ten minutes later felt like collapsing on the pretty black-and-white-tiled bathroom floor.

She'd just managed to pull herself up to use the facili-ties in another way and then went into the outer room to retrieve her toothbrush from her bag when she heard some-thing. Footsteps, she thought, but then shook her head when she also heard some ringing and the definite rum-bling of her stomach reiterating the fact that she hadn't bothered to eat during her fifteen-hour ride from San Fran-cisco to Montana. Of course, she'd stopped for gas and to use the restroom, but somehow food just hadn't appealed to her tumultuous stomach. Now she was thinking maybe she should at least try something light.

Marena was in the bathroom, toothpaste foaming at her mouth, when she heard the footsteps again. This time they echoed in her head as if someone were walking right beside her. Inside, her heart thumped wildly, sensations moving just beneath her skin like a live entity, and she shivered. Leaning forward, she rinsed and spit, grabbing one of the soft light blue towels from the pearl-white rack and wiping her mouth. After she shut off the water, Marena stood, listening.

The footsteps had stopped, but whoever had been walking wasn't gone. No, that person was near. Very near, and Marena wondered what that meant.

Without even knowing why, she walked into the bedroom and stared at the door. Not only was her heart pounding, but her temples throbbed now, too. The sickness in her stomach rolling around as if it were ready for an encore. She was standing there, holding her stomach with one hand, her head with the other, when the first knock sounded.

She didn't want to answer. A voice yelled loudly in her head for her to ignore the intrusion, while something deeper inside told her not to. It didn't make sense. None of this did. Why couldn't she open the door? She had no idea who was on the other side. And why the hell was she feeling all these strange sensations? She wanted to sit down, or lie down and get some sleep. Surely that would make her feel better.

But then it didn't matter what she did or didn't do because he was there. He came up behind her, pushing her hand away from her head and wrapping something over her eyes. Instinct told her to turn and fight, to swing and kick and get to her purse, to her gun . . . again. But something else, that same something that had insisted she let him in, calmed her and Marena stood still. The thumping in her heart and the pain in her temples ceased immediately. Her stomach stopped churning and warmth ensconced her.

"You don't need to see right now," the male voice said from behind her. "You need to feel. To experience and to learn. It is just the beginning."

Marena jerked against the covering over her eyes, but he was stronger and he pulled it tighter, and, when he was done, let his hands slide slowly down her arms to grasp her wrists. She moved again, a weak attempt at getting away because there was something overriding all the fight-or-flight instincts she'd developed over the years of being a single woman. Something that she craved much more than her own safety. It was peace.

Her head no longer throbbed with incessant pain and her stomach was no longer revolting against her. In fact, Marena felt calmer now than she could remember ever feeling in her entire life. Why was that?

His hands moved back up her arms after her seconds of contemplation. Tender touches that she wasn't sure were meant to be intimate but had her thinking of warm winter nights, cuddled in front of a fire with a man who loved her as much as she loved him. It was a foolish thought to have at a time like this. Foolish and out of place. Weird and un-explainable. Just like most of the things that had been happening to her in the last forty-eight hours.

When those fingers touched her shoulder, heat soared through her body and still she shivered. She wanted to open her eyes, to turn and look to see who this was who had come into her room this time. Her luck with hotel rooms and guys walking in on her sucked!

Marena took a step forward, until his hands were no longer on her. She turned slowly in the direction in which she'd thought she'd heard his voice. Then, as if just realizing it, she reached up and yanked the blindfold from her eyes.

"Who the hell are you?" she asked immediately upon seeing the tall man dressed in black leather standing in the middle of the room. "And how did you get in here?"

For a few seconds—which actually seemed like an eternity—he simply stared back at her. The intensity in his piercing green eyes warming her in places they definitely should not be able to touch. She had no idea who this guy was or what he wanted. And she wasn't anywhere near her purse this time.

"You left the door ajar. I knocked, but you didn't respond," he told her.

"So you just came inside," she countered. "You came inside and tried to blindfold me. Who does that? Never mind, don't answer. Just leave. Now! Before I call the cops."

She'd made the threat, but she knew she wouldn't do that. For all she knew there was now a warrant out for her arrest due to Davis's disappearance. Well, at the very least the cops in San Francisco were actively looking for her to question her again. She hadn't checked her phone in the last few hours, but at the last rest stop she had noticed that Gail hadn't returned her urgent call. That troubled her, just as this guy who was still staring at her did.

"They cannot help you," he told her simply, hooking his thumbs in the belt hoops of his pants.

It was a cocky sort of stance, one that said "you need me and you don't even know it." Marena didn't like it, but she couldn't help staring back at him with what she felt might be intrigue.

"And you can? You don't even know me," she quipped. "Are you high? Did you get lost and need to find your own room?"

She attempted to walk around him then, to go to the door and hold it open wide for his departure. But he grabbed her arm. The touch was electrifying, sending jolts of what felt like fire-tinged tendrils up her arm and exploding throughout her body.

"Let me go," she started to say, attempting to pull away from him but stumbling back instead.

He reached out both arms then, catching her by the waist before she could fall flat on the floor. And that was no easy feat. Marena was a big girl, always had been. She was proud of her size 18 on a good day—20 on a viciously horrific one—curves and went the extra mile to select the most stylish in plus-sized clothing to ensure she looked her very best at every moment. Even now, after hours of traveling, her jeans were still crisp, the long-sleeved charcoal-colored T-shirt was only marginally wrinkled, and her Stuart Weitzman Rialto flats still managed to look cute on her unusually small feet. Still, all of her weight was relying on his hold on her and Marena knew that was no slight matter. Yet he was staring down at her as calmly as if they were sitting on a park bench sharing a hot dog.

"I'm not leaving you," he said without blinking. "You don't know why yet, but you need me here. I'm guessing that's why our paths crossed in the first place."

She shook her head, noting the electrifying green eyes and the ugly scar beneath one of them. "What the hell are you talking about? I don't even know you."

"But you know what you feel," he told her.

His hands were still wrapped securely around her waist as they now stood face-to-face, so that she was a lot closer to this man she didn't know than she figured she should be.

"You know that you feel better in my arms," he continued.

"Can you say 'conceited'?" she asked with an arched brow.

He shook his head. "No. But I can say 'relief.' That's what I see in your eyes. You were sick before I came in. I could hear you all the way downstairs. I picked up your scent a couple miles back on the road. You're still sick. It will last a few more weeks and then you'll be all right. Different," he said solemnly. "But all right."

"You're nuts," she replied, but not with as much agitation as she should be feeling at this moment.

She did flatten her palms against his chest and attempt to push away. He held her firmly without any effort at all.

"If I let you go and walk out of here, you'll likely be sick again. You need the closeness of a ly . . ."

His words trailed off and for the first time since he'd come into this room Marena thought he looked indecisive. Contemplative maybe. He was a good-looking—no, correct that, because Marena prided herself on being right the majority of the time—he was a damned fine-looking guy. Broad shoulders and what felt like biceps more commonly referred to as "cannons" beneath the leather jacket he wore. She'd glimpsed his slightly bowed legs in the leather pants and steel-toed boots. The light beard and medium-length spiky haircut he was sporting gave him a definite biker look—a dangerous biker from the looks of that scar. But there was more, she suspected, so much more to this stranger holding her so tightly in his arms.

"I don't need you because I don't know you," she told him evenly. "Now, if you came in here because you were concerned that I was sick, I thank you very much. But really, I'm fine now."

He looked down at her for another second or so. This meant he was tall, because Marena was five feet nine and a half inches. Yet this guy was looking down at her, almost as if she were no bigger than a nymph. And for all that she'd been declaring she didn't need him and asking him to go, the second he released his hold on her she couldn't help but stumble back a step.

His eyes stayed glued on her even as he backed away, heading toward the door, she thought. Good, he'd taken her advice. She was going to lock that door and try her best to push the dresser up against it the second he left. No way was she going to lie down in this bed with thoughts of another man making his way, unwantedly, into her room. No way was she—

The nausea came back so fast and so potent, her knees buckled and Marena went to the floor, leaning forward as her arm clutched her abdomen. As she heaved, pressure built at her temples once more, so intense this time that she felt like she might actually faint. She trembled with the effects, wondering what the hell was going on with her.

And then he touched her.

His hands to her arms again, then down her back and beneath her legs as he easily picked her up from the floor and carried her to the bed. He laid her down, one hand brushing away the strands of hair that had escaped her ponytail, while he watched her closely.

"I told you," he said in a flat, deep voice. "You need me to stay close. It's just the way it is in the beginning. In a few weeks it will pass."

"In a few weeks? What the hell is wrong with me? And why you? I don't even know your name. I don't know what's going on," she whimpered at the thought that her stomach had calmed once again, her head feeling much better at his touch.

Marena hated not being in control of herself, her thoughts, her emotions. She'd worked too damned hard to get where she was to have some guy barge in here thinking she needed him to what? To live pain-free? This was crap and she was getting angry. But she'd never been a fool and she couldn't deny that he'd spoken a bit of truth—she did feel much better with him standing so close and touching her.

"I will tell you everything you need to know, if you tell me one thing first," he replied.

"What?" she asked. "What can I possibly tell you about the strangeness that has been going on in my life since that bastard barged into my room last night?"

His brow furrowed. "What bastard? And what did he do to you while he was in your room? Did he bite you?"

Bite?

Her shoulder ached at the sound of that word.

How did he know?

"Oh, my . . . no . . . no." She was shaking her head, sound bites and news flashes sifting through her mind in seconds. Shape-shifters—cats, wolves, beasts. They were real. People had seen them, had worked with them. The stories were true, she knew this, and yet—

Marena opened her mouth with the intent to scream; instead, only one word broke free to be followed quickly by a pitiful moan, "No."

CHAPTER 2

"You're where? With whom?" Channing asked through the phone.

Phelan frowned, turning his back on the woman lying asleep in the center of the queen-size bed.

"Just run the tag I gave you, Channing. Text me with the name and address ASAP," was his testy response.

"If she's been bitten you need to get her back here right away. She's too dangerous right now to be left alone," Channing warned.

The beta's words were unnecessary, as Phelan had already taken that into consideration. He knew everything Channing did about new bloods, which was part of the reason he'd pulled his bike off the road behind her and followed her into this B and B.

Squeezing the bridge of his nose, Phelan let out a breath and said, "I know what I need to do. You just get the information I asked for and text me back right away!"

"I'm on it," Channing said before disconnecting.

Phelan was pushing his phone back into his pocket thinking that Blaez and the others would know about this in another 2.4 seconds, because Channing wasn't the best at keeping secrets. Not that this was something that should be kept from the others in any case.

With that thought in mind, Phelan turned to her again, wondering who she was and what had happened to put her in this place, in this condition, at this time. She was fast asleep, thanks to him, resting quietly for what he guessed was the first time since she'd been bitten. He was glad at least, that he had been able to give her that.

As unbelievable as it might seem considering their current circumstances, there was an advantage to being a lycan who could not only walk in the human world but could also cross over to the Olympic realm.

That was Phelan's gift as it were. Some lycans had extraordinary powers—for instance, Kira, Blaez's mate, was a Selected. In addition to being specially chosen by Selene, the Moon Goddess, to marry a powerful alpha such as Blaez, Kira also had the power of sight. Using her sight, Kira could see snatches of things about to come, as well as things from the past. Phelan had learned of his gift early on in his life, when he'd inadvertently crossed the realms after a particularly angry episode with one of his teachers.

Since that time it had been a place of solace for Phelan, leaving the world where he was forced to conceal his true nature and living in hiding because one angry god wanted to kill the closest friend Phelan had ever had. In the past weeks, Phelan had gone to the Olympic realm more than he had in previous years because he wanted to find answers. There was a bounty out on Blaez's head. Just a couple of months ago, a harpy had found them as they'd hunted the Solo on a cliff near the Blackfoot Mountains. Fortunately, Blaez was quick enough to shift into his full wolf form before the harpy saw him. Only the pack mates knew of Blaez's half-lycan, half-demigod gift—and he was the only one of his kind. Phelan had recognized the harpy and knew that she also had connections to Eureka, which reinforced for him again that the fury who had come to be the bane of his existence was quite possibly a threat to his alpha and their pack. That was also the other reason Phelan continued to travel to Entice to see Eureka. What was that old saying? "Keep your enemies close"?

Enter another woman. A new blood-lycan female. The second Marena looked at him with knowledge and fear in her eyes, Phelan had offered her a glass of water. She'd accepted his offering not knowing that he'd used some of the sleep-opium he'd received from Hypnos, the god of sleep. Phelan carried the small packet of powder with him as humans might carry their drug of choice. It was a crutch that Phelan wasn't proud to have, but one that had saved him from lashing out and hurting others when the pain and disgust of his own past threatened to choke him. The glittering silver powder gave him rest in his personal world of turmoil; without it, he had no idea where he would be.

Now he watched her sleeping soundlessly, lying on her back, one arm draped over a pillow arching near her head. Her skin looked so soft, a color very similar to that of heavily creamed coffee. Her hair was like black silk, fanned out straight behind her. And her body . . . Phelan wasn't going to even go there. He kept his gaze trained on her from the neck up, ignoring anything else he may have felt when he'd first walked into this room.

It had been like being led by a leash, he'd thought as he'd parked his bike behind the B and B and come inside. He had no idea who this woman was or what type of situation he may have been walking into, but he could not stop moving toward her, had not been able to talk himself out of approaching and offering his help. That was the first thing that was out of character for him. Phelan was not the sociable type. He wasn't a Good Samaritan by any stretch of the imagination. He was a lycan with an attitude, a loner who just so happened to belong to a pack, a trained killer who had no problem doing what he was taught to do without recriminations.

Despite his lycan genetics, Phelan was not a man easily aroused by a woman, and especially not a human, no matter what time of the month it was for him. He had strict control over his sexual hungers; that's why he was able to sit at Club Entice night after night, not touching a single soul there but only watching, taking what he needed with his own hand. That happened by Phelan's choice only. He was always in complete control.

That's why his hand was reaching out now, cupping Marena's large breast, watching as the mass spilled through his fingers. He groaned then, his breaths quick and shallow. She was arousing him. This woman who did not look anything like the women at the club or those Phelan had ever shown interest in was making his dick jump and harden by a simple touch. He squeezed her breast again. She did not move, but her lips did part slightly. Phelan stared at her face for endless seconds, her breast in his hand, as he watched and waited. He wanted to see her tongue, to watch it slip through her teeth to rub slowly over her lips. When it did he would suck it, which was a decision quickly made. He would suck her so hard into his mouth that she would have no choice but to moan. That sound would echo in his ears, spurring him on until he finally thrust his hard dick into her waiting pussy.

But her tongue never appeared.

With disappointment spearing through him, Phelan touched her other breast, looking down at his large hands. She was soft, overflowing his palms in pliant delight. He wondered if she awakened right at this moment what she would do. Would she readily accept his touch, moan with pleasure, spread her thick thighs, and welcome him inside? His body reacted one way, while his mind drifted in another. Phelan gritted his teeth in consternation.

Pulling his hands away from her begrudgingly, Phelan tried to get his mind right and focus on the matters at hand— the fact that this human had been bitten, by a lycan, to be exact. The look in Marena's eyes just before Phelan had put her to sleep said she knew and she feared. Now what the hell was he supposed to do about that? And why was it his responsibility to deal with it in the first place?

He wasn't the one who had first let the world know there were shifters on earth. That was the Shadow Shifters. And he wasn't the one creating more lycans. That was Channing and Malec, and a good number of Hunter lycans with the notion of ruling the world, or on some other stupid power trip like that. But he was the one who had found her; he had listened to her through that partially opened door, attempting to rid her body of the animal toxins that were at this very moment infiltrating every cell in her body. How could he leave her here to figure this out on her own? The answer was, he couldn't.

Just as he couldn't keep his hands off her.

Reaching out once more, Phelan touched her inner thighs, feeling even through the denim material how soft and pliable her skin would be here. The feeling, along with the thought, had him shaking. He inhaled deeply, his nostrils flaring as the soft musk and floral scent that was uniquely hers wafted up and into his senses. It was intoxicating and had his mouth watering, so much so he couldn't resist running his fingers over the crotch of her jeans. Any other man would not have picked up this aroma, would not have known it meant how sweet she was beneath those jeans and her underwear. But Phelan was no other man. He was a lycan. A lycan who was horny as hell and wanted to fuck this new blood he'd just met more than he wanted to take his next breath.

He was just about to inhale that blissful aroma once more when the pain striking his right jaw sent him sprawling back on the bed with surprise.

Not this time!

Marena's mind had screamed the moment she felt his hands between her legs. Davis wasn't going to force her to have sex with him, not if she had anything to say about it!

He'd been right there, in her room again, walking toward her with that smirk on his face, blood seeping through the white dress shirt he'd worn. The blood wasn't the only thing different this time, Davis's eyes were glowing a fierce shade of blue and his teeth were elongated, sharp, and deadly looking. He'd continued to come closer to her, no matter how many times Marena had warned him to stay away.

She had the gun in her hand again, just like the first time, and she lifted her arm, aiming at him once more, only this time there had been no bullets. He'd laughed as he reached for her, long, dark nails scraping against her arms. Even as she screamed he'd slid his hands over, cupping her breasts so tightly she felt those nails breaking into her skin.

When those same hands moved to rub between her legs, it was enough! All the flailing and slapping at him she'd been doing up to this point hadn't done a damned thing. Resorting to last measures, Marena had balled her fist and smashed it into his face. He'd been so intent on feeling her up he hadn't even seen it coming. And when he'd howled in pain, falling back from her, she'd pounced.

Straddling him, she punched and swung repeatedly. "Bastard!" she screamed. "Fucking arrogant, disgusting bastard!"

He'd caught her by the wrists at some point, moving so fast and switching places so easily she hadn't time to spew any other insults.

"Stop it!" he was yelling at her. "Wake up, dammit!"

Marena screamed again, kicking and bucking her body up off the bed in an attempt to break his hold on her.

"Get off of me!"

"Wake up!" he yelled, his face extremely close to hers.

She didn't stop screaming, couldn't find the OFF switch in her mind. He was strong and there was no way she could break free, but that didn't mean she had to let him take her. She wouldn't give in; she never had in her life and she wasn't about to start now.

Until his face contorted, his forehead enlarging, hair growing quickly down the sides of his face, teeth elongating as he opened his mouth and roared at her. Her mouth snapped shut so fast she almost bit her tongue, heart thumped so wild and loud Marena thought for sure it was close to ripping right through her chest.

Suddenly she realized something was off here. Something other than the animal-like face staring angrily down at her.

She wasn't wearing a dress that displayed her ample cleavage and thick, shapely calves. And he wasn't bleeding; at least she didn't think he was through the black long-sleeved shirt he wore like a second skin. This wasn't Davis and she wasn't being attacked. Or was she?

"Get off of me," she said slowly, sternly.

And he did, moving with deliberate motions.

She watched him move, his body as lithe as if he weighed no more than a hundred pounds even though she could tell from the size of his biceps and his chest that he was quite possibly double that weight. His waist narrowed, his shirt tucked into those leather pants neatly. At his sides his hands were large, with long, sharp nails, just as she'd thought Davis's had been in her dream.

But that had been just a dream; she was certain of that now as she sat up on the bed. Davis hadn't stood in front of her bleeding, continuing to attack her. The last time she'd seen him he'd been lying on the floor in the hotel room, bloodstains blossoming on his shirt from the gunshot wounds. She felt more in control this way and looked at the new guy directly.

Now she slid off the edge of the bed until she could stand.

"Who are you?" she asked. Not "What are you?" as she'd really been thinking.

He shook his head then, hard, as if he were—for lack of a better word—some type of animal, and in seconds the vicious face had settled into the very handsome one of the guy with the intense green eyes and black hair who had come into her room unannounced.

"My name is Phelan and I'm a lycan," he said as calmly as if he were stating his name and Social Security number for a job interview.

"A lycan?" she echoed.

"Yes," he replied. "A man cursed by a Greek god to have wolf traits."

Now Marena wanted to shake her head the way he had moments before, to make sure she'd heard him correctly. The reports were true; there were other beings walking the earth. She'd watched the news reports, seen a glimpse of what looked like normal big cats but were reported to actually look like humans. She frowned then because she'd never heard mention of any lycans.

"What are you doing here? Why haven't you gone by now? I'm not going to have sex with you," she told him, feeling a bit of déjà vu from the night she'd told Davis the same thing.

His nostrils flared, his eyes going cold, hard, flinty. Marena swallowed hard and squared her shoulders. "Answer my questions," she prodded.

"I picked up your scent back a few miles on the highway. I knew what you were and I followed you. I haven't left because I can't. So I suggest you grab your things and come with me."

He spoke sternly, as if he expected no argument to his pronouncements. Unfortunately, he had no idea whom he was dealing with.

Shaking her head, Marena took a slow step toward him. Because to her in equal parts dismay and intrigue, she felt an inexplicable need to get closer. "Why on earth would I come with you when I don't even know you? And you don't know me."

There was another pause and then he frowned, thrusting a hand into his pocket, and pulled out his phone. He looked down and began reading directly from the device.

"You're Marena Kay Panos. Born in Summer's Cay, Florida, now leasing a condo at Millennium Tower in San Francisco. Attended Penn State for undergrad, graduated tops in her class from Columbia Law. Holds an associate's position at The Arrington Law Group in the complex litigation department. Owns a polar-white Mercedes GLE SUV and possesses an excellent credit rating, which is commendable considering she's only twenty-eight years old and has already managed to pay down more than half her student loan debt." The frown deepened after those last words and when he looked up she noted his thick eyebrows almost touching as he continued to frown.

"You should come with me now," he added, as if she hadn't heard him say that before.

"Who— Someone sent you all that information about me. Why? Who sent it?" she asked, very uncomfortable with him knowing so much about her when she knew so little about him.

To be fair, Marena figured, she now knew the most important part about this Phelan person. He was a shape-shifter, or a lycan as he'd called it. She wasn't certain how she felt about that as she waited for him to respond to her questions.

Instead of answering, he—Phelan—moved to close the space between them quickly and touched her shoulders.

"We do not have time for all these questions. Whoever bit you may be looking for you. We have to move now," he said rather forcefully, even though he didn't make any move to drag her out of the room.

Marena was very aware of the fact that he could have probably succeeded at doing just that. She was glad he hadn't tried and still very much alarmed at all that he'd said.

She opened her mouth to say no, to deny it, but her shoulder throbbed, as if in stark reminder. Marena didn't know Phelan enough to trust him. She had no idea if he was in cahoots with Davis or had some other nefarious intention toward her. What she did know, however, was that whoever he was, she felt better around him than she did without him. That ought to count for something.

"Davis," she murmured.

"Who is Davis?" Phelan asked, the name spoken in more of a growl than any form of the English language Marena had ever heard.

"Davis Sumpter, a partner at the firm. He . . . he . . ." Marena cleared her throat and looked Phelan directly in the eye. This would be the first time she verbalized this admission, the first time someone heard her side of what had happened that night. It amazed her that it would be this total stranger.

"He attacked me and I shot him, and then I must have fainted. And when I woke up the police were there, but Davis wasn't. He was gone," she stated quietly, recalling the conversation she'd had with Tammi just before she'd left her condo. "They think I did something to him. They're going to arrest me for kidnapping or whatever charge they can come up with. I've already left a message for my lawyer."

Now Phelan did move her toward the door, his face growing darker as he spoke roughly. "Your lawyer won't call you back," he said tightly. "Davis Sumpter is a Hunter lycan. I've got to get you back to the lodge and then we'll figure the rest out."

"What is a Hunter lycan?" she asked, once again ignoring his order to come with him.

Phelan sighed. "I don't have time to go into all that now. Just know that—"

Marena shook her head and pulled away from him. "Just know that I'm extremely stubborn and full of questions. So if you want to get on with whatever it is you need to do, I suggest you answer me quickly."

There was no mistaking his irritation, but Marena didn't care. At least she didn't while he was in his human form. Besides, she needed to know more about these lycans, especially if Davis was one.

"There are two groups of lycans," Phelan began. "The Hunters and the Devoteds. The Hunters crave total dominance, but to gain that they have to be rid of the Devoteds, whose only goal is to coexist with the humans. Same old power struggle, different species," he ended flippantly. "Can we go now?"

"I'm not going with you," she replied. "I don't know what the hell is going on. Davis is not— I mean, he's . . . I thought he was just an obnoxious guy. But now you're telling me he's some type of hunter wolf, who bit me so that now I'm going to change into a wolf." Even to her own ears the words sounded unbelievable.

Davis was in a man's body, but last night he'd definitely had an animalistic look about him, a primitive air that gave him permission to do whatever he'd planned to do to her. And she thought about that pain in her shoulder again, the sickness she'd been experiencing since last night, and how, unexplainably, the moment Phelan had come in here and gotten close to her that sickness had ceased.

"What happens if I don't go with you?" she asked him.

He ran a hand through his hair, causing the short wisps at the top to stick straight up. "I only know that it won't be good. A Hunter wants to own its creation. He'll want to find you and keep you."

"Nobody 'keeps' me," she immediately replied.

Phelan's brows arched, his lips thinning. "He bit you, Marena. In just three weeks, on the night of the next full moon, you will become one of us. In the barest sense of our kind, you will be *his* lycan."

"The hell I will!" she snapped.

CHAPTER 3

"Who the hell is Davis Sumpter?" Malec asked a half hour after Phelan and Marena arrived at the lodge.

The pack had converged on them as if they'd been lying in wait as soon as Phelan and Marena had walked through the door. He had scowled at Channing, as he knew that's who he had to thank for the welcome party. The women, Caroline and Kira, had immediately come to Marena's side, introducing themselves and welcoming her, while Marena had looked skeptically at each of them.

She hadn't wanted to come with him; an innate need to stand on her own had held her still. Phelan knew that feeling all too well, hence the reason he'd been able to immediately relate to it. He also knew the second she'd changed her mind, opting to go with the obvious—he, for some reason, eased the pain of going through the change for her. Grateful that she was no longer trying to heave up her insides and wasn't looking as if she might faint at any second, Phelan opted not to think too long or hard about the why. If he made her feel better, so be it; for the next three weeks he would make her feel better. Then she would have her shift and they could all move on.

But he didn't want the pack to know about that part of

the plan in bringing her here. He had a feeling they wouldn't take it as nonchalantly as he did.

"Have a little rum in your tea, Marena," Kira had said while pouring the dark liquid into Marena's cup without waiting for a reply.

With a polite nod of thanks, Marena looked across the table to where Malec and Channing were sitting. Blaez, as the alpha of the pack, was seated at the head of the dining room table—the place where all their important meetings took place.

"He's a partner in the firm where I work," she replied.

It was Malec's turn to nod. "And you had no idea he was a lycan?"

Caroline had smacked Malec's shoulder, chastising him as she tended to do for being so blunt all the time. Phelan looked away from them at that point. He still wasn't totally on board with the mating of Malec, Caroline, and Channing. Not that Phelan had anything against a ménage relationship; the lycans were a very sexual species, which meant they tended to have all types of relationships with one another whether it be threesomes, larger groups, male and male, female and female, or a mixture of both. You name it, their kind did it, without questions or explanations. But they did it with their kind.

Caroline had been a human. A veterinarian who had gotten swept into the lycans' war and eventually ended up in bed with Malec and Channing. Two full moons ago, the betas had bitten her, turning her into a lycan and mating with her. In essence, they'd done exactly what Nyktimos had done in his rage against Zeus and what the god had done to Nyktimos's father, Lykaon. That was how their species had been created, when Zeus had turned Lykaon into a wolf and killed all of Lykaon's sons, except for Nyktimos, who had been safely hidden by Selene. When an angry and despairing Lykaon in his new wolf form came across his son he'd bitten him, turning Nyktimos into a werewolf—a human who could only shift into wolf form on the night of the full moon. It was Nyktimos who had fallen in love with a human. He'd bitten that human and they'd had children, and the lycan species was born.

A species derived from jealousy and anger and destined to fight a war they'd never wanted or perhaps even understood.

No, Phelan wasn't for continuing the long line of mistakes that had been made by his species; that's why he'd stuck with other beings when it came to sex. Only Eureka had still turned out to be a backstabbing bitch who had scarred him in more than just a physical way.

So, to put it plainly, Phelan wasn't happy with the threesome sitting across from him. But as that went, he hadn't been thrilled about Blaez taking Kira as his mate, either. All in all, Phelan was just against these unions because he felt like they had no right to join and attempt happiness, not when the world around them was going to hell at the hands of a vengeful god.

"How would she know he was a lycan? We're not supposed to wear the word tattooed on our forehead!" Phelan snapped, unwilling—as usual—to hide his irritation.

"No," Blaez interjected. "We're not. Why did he bite you?"

Marena shrugged. "I don't know. He was trying to attack me and I was defending myself. I told him to back off, to get out, and he kept coming forward. I didn't notice the bite except for the excruciating pain and then I shot him." She paused and swallowed deeply. "I thought I killed him."

"You should have," Kira quipped, her hand going immediately to Marena's shoulder.

"Are you all lycans?" she asked then, looking around to each of them. "Do you live all the way out here together? Where did you come from?"

"Ah, there's the attorney I read about on the Internet," Channing said with a smile. "She's ready to interrogate us now."

Marena shook her head. "More like cross-examine," she told him. "You've been interrogating me since I came through that door."

"She's right," Caroline said, and came to a stand. "We should be doing more to welcome Marena. How about I show you to your room and you can freshen up, or get some rest?"

"That's a great idea," Kira added. "And bring your cup with you."

The women were busily moving, not waiting for either of the men to interject. They'd helped Marena up from her seat and just taken a couple of steps to lead her to the only empty room in the house, the one right off the living room. But then Marena moaned. Phelan's gaze went to her immediately. She'd been standing between Kira and Caroline, a slight contrast between Kira's tall, curvy stature and very light complexion and Caroline's equally voluptuous figure but with her darker skin tone. Marena's skin was more of a golden hue, she was taller than both Kira and Caroline, and her body was definitely fuller, shapelier, more alluring than the other lycan females', at least to Phelan's eyes.

He was out of his seat immediately, crossing the short space to get to her. The moment he put his hands on her arms and she looked up at him, he knew.

"Why?" she asked.

He shook his head slowly. "I don't know."

Kira looked to Caroline as Phelan and Marena walked away.

"Did you just see what I saw?" she asked.

Caroline nodded. "I did, but I'm not sure I understand it completely."

"That makes two of us then," Malec quipped. "Is she injured?"

Channing was already shaking his head as Blaez spoke. "It's the pain of the change. The Hunter's DNA is working its way through her bloodstream, preparing her body for all the changes it will have to endure before the next full moon."

"Her temperature will likely rise and fall; her bones and muscles will ache. She'll probably be nauseous and feel generally out of sync for the weeks leading up to her first change. The extent of the suffering will depend on the individual. A stronger, more stubborn human will fight against the changes, causing more pain and discomfort. A more amenable human that accepts the new life, both mentally and physically, might experience less of these symptoms."

"I didn't experience any of this," Caroline said as Malec rubbed her back.

He'd instantly moved closer to her when Blaez spoke of the change, most likely because she'd just gone through it. But as Channing had gone into deeper detail about what they suspected Marena was experiencing, she couldn't help but notice the differences. In fact, she'd felt just fine up until the night of the full moon when the only thing that made the change even more special was the lovemaking she'd shared with Channing and Malec throughout the day.

"Because we claimed you," Channing replied.

He'd come to stand at her other side, flanking her with his strength and protection on one side while Malec covered the other. They did this frequently and she'd come to relish the feeling of being so important to both of them.

"And I accepted you," she answered when Channing lifted a hand to tuck a curl of hair behind her ear. "I accepted both of you and this change in my life, so I didn't experience the pain and suffering that Marena's apparently going through. Somehow that doesn't seem fair. That Hunter attacked her and she defended herself; now she has to face the fact that her life is going to be irrevocably changed. And because she hasn't done that yet, she gets to suffer."

Blaez spoke up next. "Marena did not want the bite from that Hunter and it was inflicted in anger and spite. He wasn't her mate and his intention wasn't to claim her, but to take and harm her," he said seriously. "And now she's paying for that. No, it's not fair. It's simply what is."

Kira hissed in a breath and her alpha immediately went to her, cupping her face in his hands as her eyes closed. She was having a vision and they all waited to hear what she saw.

"It's going to be harder for her than any of us can even imagine. He's not dead and he's not ready to let her go," Kira whispered.

"So he does want to claim her?" Blaez asked.

Kira shook her head, her large gold hoop earrings slapping against Blaez's hands. "I don't know what he wants. It's too dark, totally black, like a void. Only I can feel the evil, right here," she said, bringing her fisted hand to the center of her chest. "I can feel his hatred like a hot ball right here."

Blaez covered her hand with his own then, leaning down

392 A. C. Arthur

until his forehead rested on hers. "I won't let it stay there," he vowed. "I won't."

Caroline leaned into Malec and Channing's embrace, hearing Kira's words and knowing that the worst of this situation had yet to come. She worried about the future of the lycans and now about how Marena would handle all that was before her. Because unlike Caroline, she wasn't in love with the one who had bitten her. Marena apparently didn't welcome the change from a human to a lycan. And from the sounds of her explanation of things that had happened, she was now on the run not only from the police but also from the Hunter who wasn't ready to let her be.

Yes, Caroline thought dismally, the worst was still yet to come.

Phelan closed the door behind them as Marena walked deeper into the room. He'd switched on a light from somewhere behind her and she looked around. There was a large picture window on one wall, a warm burnt orange–colored valance draped across the top. The floors were a light hardwood, the same color as the walls. The headboard to the bed was a darker wood with a thick beige comforter on top. It was a great-looking room, but it wasn't hers, and Marena suddenly felt out of place. She turned, a little too fast, and felt everything swaying around her.

Phelan was there before she could reach out to grab hold of something to keep her upright and before she could open her mouth to call for help. Almost as if he'd known she would need him, just like when he'd shown up in her room at the B and B.

"I don't know why this is happening to me," she said, lowering her head and closing her eyes.

She didn't want to look at him as his strong hands held her at the waist. The dizziness immediately subsided, as she'd known it would. Even the relief of that knowledge was shrouded in dread. "Why does the pain and weirdness stop when you are near, when you touch me?"

He inhaled deeply and exhaled very slowly. As if he were measuring the breath himself, because he had that type of control.

"I don't know that answer," he told her. "But as long as it will make you feel better, I will stay by your side."

That was said matter-of-factly, as if he'd come up with and answer and that was the way it would be. Marena did not like that. She wasn't used to that. And yet the common-sense part of her kept her tongue still. Denying that his proximity and touch were helping would be idiotic and un-productive, two things Marena definitely was not. If she was going to clear her name and get back to her job, she definitely needed to combat the physical issues that damned bite on her shoulder was causing.

"How long will this last?" she asked after taking her own deep breath.

"About three more weeks," he replied.

She looked up at him then, her gaze resting on eyes as green and as deep as the ocean. "And you've got nothing better to do than to stay by my side for the next three weeks? Day and night? What about your job? Your life?"

"I'm military," he said sternly. "Special contract work only. I don't have any assignments lined up at the moment."

"And your personal life? Your girlfriend?" Because he

was beyond fine; her body's secondary reaction to his proximity could attest to that.

While it seemed that his touch stopped the agonizing pain and sickness that racked her body, Marena also had to admit how sexual his closeness made her feel. It wasn't something that she thought about often, not even something that was regularly penciled in on her agenda. But in the hours she'd been with Phelan she'd thought about sex, specifically about sex with him, more often than she had in years. Even now, with his hands still firmly on her waist, her nipples were already hardening, her pussy throbbing with a long-ignored need. It was no wonder the word "girlfriend" had popped so easily into her mind.

"I don't do girlfriends," was his clipped reply. "I'll start the shower. Channing and Kira will fix you something to eat, I'm sure. I can send them a text to let them know to knock when it's ready; that way I don't have to leave you to go out and get it."

He didn't do girlfriends.

And she didn't do boyfriends.

Marena almost smiled.

"I think I can run my own shower," she told him.

"You know the pain will start again the moment we part. I don't like to see you that way, so I'd rather not go through that again if we don't have to. I can run the shower."

"And then what?" she asked, immediately stepping behind him because he'd begun to move and she knew that he was right.

Whenever he was apart from her, the pain began anew, sometimes coming even stronger. The last bout in the living room had felt like something was crushing her bones. The intensity of that pain had caused the nausea to hit like a tidal wave and that's why she'd gone down. She'd been embarrassed and thankful all at the same time for Phelan's quick action in coming to her and putting his hands on her.

They were in the bathroom now, a bright and airy space with slate-tiled walls and marble floors.

"I'll stand right here," he told her after opening the glass shower stall door and leaning in to turn on the water.

"While I shower?" she asked. "I think I can manage this part by myself."

Sure, Marena had admitted that his proximity was good for her physical condition, but taking a shower in front of him was still a bit much for her to swallow.

He looked at her then, one brow arched in question. Then with a shrug he began to move, passing her as he went to the door. Marena was determined to get through at least this one task on her own. She didn't know this man and she didn't know these people. All she knew for certain was that she'd needed to get away from San Francisco before she was arrested and she needed to figure out where the hell Davis had disappeared to. He was obviously alive since he hadn't been in the hotel room when the police arrived, which meant that he could clear her name. If she could figure out where he was.

She had no idea how she was going to do that but figured she'd be in a much better frame of mind to think about it once she had a hot shower and some food in her stomach. After hearing the door click closed behind her she reached for the hem of her shirt and pulled it up over her head.

That action alone had spasms of pain racing up and down her back. She gritted her teeth, holding back the scream that threatened to erupt. Unhooking her bra was another painful task, but she toughed that out as well. She toed her shoes off and pushed the jeans and her panties down her legs. It was at that moment she realized she hadn't brought her bag into the bathroom with her, which meant she was going to have to go out there with a towel wrapped around her to get her clothes.

The quivering of her legs and dizziness hit her then and she forgot about the clothes, reaching out to hold on to the shower door handle. A part of her feared this was only going to get worse, while the fighter in her—the part that had worked three jobs to get through college and stayed up all night studying for the bar exam—demanded that she push forward. She stepped into the stall, letting the hot water pelt against her naked body. For an instant she thought there was relief, but then everything went dark and she felt herself sliding down until she was sitting on the shower floor.

Laughter, loud and clear, erupted in her mind.

I'm not through with you yet.

It was Davis's voice and Marena trembled when she heard it. She almost expected to see him standing right there in front of her, but her eyes wouldn't open and the darkness beneath her lids remained.

"Davis," she whispered just before pain seized every part of her body.

Her eyes watered and she felt the tears slipping past her closed lids as she bit down on her lower lip in an attempt to keep from crying out. She grew hot all over, until she felt like she was on fire. That coupled with the hot water splashing down on her was too much and Marena finally yelled out.

He was there in seconds, touching the side of her face. His touch immediately sent flashes of light behind her closed lids and what seemed like a cool breeze against the white-hot pain that had infiltrated her body. Her eyes opened immediately then and she saw him kneeling down next to her, the water drenching his clothed body. Gasping, she whispered, "Phelan."

She didn't know him. Yet a part of her recognized him. This new part that she hadn't quite accepted knew exactly who he was and welcomed his presence with an unexplainable emotion. The "why" to all of this was an equal mystery, but at this moment Marena knew one thing for sure: she wanted him right here with her.

And when he lifted her into his arms, cradling her in his lap as he sat on the bench in the shower, Marena sighed. She gave in and she wept because she needed him. Even if it was temporary, she knew now, without a doubt, that she needed him to stay near, to keep her from buckling in pain and, she hoped, from the voice that had sounded so close in her head.

"Let's get you washed up," he said after it seemed like he'd held her forever.

Her heart rate had slowed, the sweltering heat that had engulfed her cooled, and she'd just begun to notice that his hands were touching her naked body.

Without waiting for her reply, Phelan was standing, letting her move slowly until she was on her own feet. He grabbed the sponge and soap and lathered it in his hands. In seconds he had that soapy sponge on her body, moving methodically, as if he did this every day.

He circled the sponge at her neck, moving around, being extremely careful of the bite mark that was still sensitive on her shoulder. Returning to the front again, he soaped her right breast. Lifting it with one hand, he moved the sponge beneath and around, circling her nipple.

Marena sucked in a breath at the touch. It wasn't intimate in its intent; she could tell because Phelan hadn't slowed his motions at all. He simply continued as if he wanted to get the job done as thoroughly and quickly as he could. Still, her clit began a slow, delicious throb.

As he lifted her arms, rubbing down her torso and over her abdomen, that soapy sponge moved, her body warming with each swipe. Another woman might have been modest and quite possibly would have shirked at being naked in front of a man she'd only met hours earlier, but not Marena. She'd grown up in a two-bedroom house with three brothers and one sister. Privacy was a luxury Marena had never been afforded and so she'd never managed to feel any shame or embarrassment when it came to her body, not then and especially not now that she was an adult. Still, she couldn't deny that no other man had ever made her body warm and respond the way Phelan was doing.

Showering was a simple task, a necessity, and something a lot of people would consider humdrum at best. But not this shower, not this time. Marena's mind was moving a mile a minute as with each stroke of that sponge on her she imagined it was Phelan's fingers instead.

When he circled over her hips, going down to midway on her thighs, she imagined his thick hands sliding over her skin. At her sides her fingers tingled as she found herself wanting to palm her own breasts, to tweak her nipples until little spikes of pleasure were shooting straight down to her clit. That would, at least, give some semblance of relief. But she did not move.

That wasn't correct. She lifted her leg, placing her foot on the bench as he'd directed by touching the back of her thigh. He hadn't spoken a word, but she'd known he was ready to wash between her legs. Marena wasn't surprised that she was ready for that as well.

The first touch was lighter than she expected, a quick swipe that barely had the sponge touching her now-swollen vulva lips. She looked down to see if Phelan were looking at her, in search of those green eyes she was beginning to find solace in. He wasn't looking at her but down at his hand as he moved the sponge between her legs and back out again. This movement was slower than any of the others and Marena found herself watching it now as well. He held the sponge in the palm of his hand, his fingers on the sides. So each time he dragged the sponge over her, his fingers touched her lips as well. It was a featherlight touch that sent pleasurable tendrils soaring throughout her body. So many that by the third touch her thighs had begun to tremble. His free hand moved then, reaching up to cup her plentiful ass. Marena gasped at the quick and possessive squeeze, her hands immediately going to his shoulders in an effort to steady herself.

He did look at her then, questions clear in his eyes, but no words coming forth. Seconds later he was pulling back, letting the water splash against her body as he dropped the sponge to the shower floor, his hands sliding from her ass. Soap washed over and off her body in steady streams.

In the next moments, without his hands on her, Marena began to move somewhat robotically at this point, the sting of his apparent rejection ringing loud and clear. This was beginning to be too much, the up and down of emotions, the questions without answers, and now this persistent sexual need burning inside her that had so quickly and succinctly been denied. Marena wanted to scream as the inability to control herself, much less her surroundings, threatened to overwhelm her. Instead, she found herself gasping at what Phelan did next.

He touched her again, this time his fingers going between her legs, parting her tender lips just seconds before he knelt down, leaning in closer to twirl his tongue slowly over her clit. With his other hand he pushed against her inner thigh, spreading her wider. With an inward and grateful sigh, Marena gripped the back of his head, holding him in place while thrusting her pussy farther into his face. He was licking her, long and slow, the pad of his tongue moving sinuously over her plump folds and beneath the sensitive hood of her clit. Her body quivered, her mind turning into a passionate mush that had her biting her lower lip. When he speared his tongue, touching the entrance of her core, she bucked, her eyes closing tightly as her head fell back. It was ecstasy, plain and simple. And here, in this moment, there was no question of whether she wanted it or should allow it. There was only the gentle rocking of her hips, the flat of her palms against the back of his head, and the glorious continuation of his tongue licking her pussy.

Marena couldn't have stopped the waves of pleasure rippling through her with the ferocity of a tidal wave if she'd wanted to. Which she definitely did not. No, she wanted more, and so she thrust into him, loving the moment when his tongue thrust deep into her opening, soliciting even more of her nectar to be released. The slurping sounds were just as loud as the patter of water against the tile floor, his mouth working just as hungrily as her hips were moving over him.

His hands gripped her tighter, one cupping her ass again, the other still pressing against her thigh spreading her even wider still. Marena's eyes opened and fluttered closed with the myriad of sensations—the warm sprinkle of water on her sensitive skin, the spikes of heat as his tongue flicked over her clit, then sank inside her opening once more. The tremors began slowly, signaling she was ready to explode. It felt so good, she thought with a guttural moan, better than she'd ever been able to make herself feel with any of the toys she'd acquired over the years. As for another man making her feel this way, there had been no one she could even begin to compare him to. At twenty-eight years old, she had to admit that was a very sobering thought. Luckily for her, Phelan's deft fingers and very talented tongue pulled her thoughts right back to the here and now. As he thrust two fingers inside her while his tongue worked up a glorious frenzy over her clit, she finally surrendered with a long, deep moan as her release overtook her.

What the hell had he done?

Phelan chastised himself as he rubbed the towel over his head.

Fuck! he mouthed into the thick terry-cloth material before pulling it off his face. He still stood with his back to her, hoping like hell that she would be completely dressed before he had to turn toward her again.

He should never have gone back into that bathroom with her. In the other room had been a safe distance away, or so he'd thought. But even before she'd yelled out, Phelan had known he was too far away. He'd felt the distance weighing on him like a heavy blanket, stifling his breath and blurring his senses. With each step he'd taken farther from the bathroom door his legs had felt like lead, slowing down until the sound of her whimpering had him immediately turning back. Standing perfectly still, he'd waited, hoping all these strange feelings would quickly subside and that he could get back to his normal life. Then she'd screamed and Phelan knew that all bets were off.

Still, seeing her naked had been too much. Touching her with wet and soapy hands, like the sweetest torture ever. There was no excuse; he should have known better. He should have known he wouldn't be able to resist. Not for one damned minute.

It was just that she'd looked so good. Every curve and mound, his palms had itched to touch her skin to skin. His eyes had glazed seeing her dark nipples covered in the bright white soapy bubbles. Her breasts had been heavy in his hands, delectably so. He'd wanted his mouth on each nipple, wanted to feel the full breast lying against his face as he sucked her.

Hell!

He was hard enough to hammer nails and pissed off enough to punch a hole through the wall!

"Why does the pain go away when you're around? Are you some type of healer?" she asked the question that Phelan wished like hell he had an answer for, once again.

No, he didn't want to know why he could help her. He definitely did not want her to keep asking about it. He just wanted to do whatever was necessary at this moment to get them all through whatever was going to happen next. Nothing more and nothing less. He wasn't a dreamer; he didn't wish for any type of happy ever after, just a contentment for the here and now.

Phelan gritted his teeth.

Even her voice was sexy as hell, scraping along the raw

edges of his mind, stroking the length of his cock the way he wanted her lips to do.

"I don't know," he answered honestly. "I'm gonna need a change of clothes."

When she didn't respond Phelan walked toward the door, then cursed at the quick intake of breath he heard from behind. He dropped the towel to the floor and was tugging the hem of his soaked T-shirt from his pants and pulling it over his head when he turned in her direction.

"This can't be normal," she told him as she sat on the edge of the bed, using her fingers to massage her temples.

"Being a lycan isn't normal," he quipped, yanking the buckle of his pants free, then leaning forward to undo the ties of his boots.

"Well, no, not for me it isn't," she continued. "But you were born this way, weren't you?"

"Yeah, luck of the draw!" he snapped with a frown, and then decided it was being extra-bitchy because he was still ashamed about what he'd done to her in the shower.

"Look," Phelan continued, forcing himself to look at her and feeling another wave of arousal slap against him in response. "I'll apologize for what happened in there. I don't normally just take . . . I mean, I don't ordinarily give a woman pleasure unless . . . and never a—I mean, dammit!"

The words just wouldn't come and that pissed Phelan off even more.

"You don't normally give a woman you've just met oral pleasure. Is that what you're trying to tell me?" she asked, lifting one elegantly arched brow.

She sat on the bed wearing a white T-shirt that had pink letters scribbled across its front. It looked short from where he was standing, not nearly enough material to cover all of her ass and a good portion of her thighs, which was what he was going to need to keep from wanting to touch her again.

"No," he said, holding tightly to his composure. "I don't. And it won't happen again, so you don't have to worry."

He'd continued taking off his clothes until he was naked. They were only a queen-size bed's length apart and her gaze had fallen lower, her tongue slipping slowly over her bottom lip. His cock twitched at the sight and Phelan realized it wasn't simply seeing her tongue that had him thoroughly aroused but the way she was staring so hungrily at him.

"Stop," he said more for himself and the thoughts of taking a couple of steps closer feeding her his throbbing length than to her specifically.

She looked up immediately, her eyes blinking as if she'd just been awakened from a trance.

"I don't know what's happening," she admitted, shaking her head. "I mean, I'm not trying to sound coy or like I've really never seen a gorgeous guy naked. But this is just so out of character for me. It's just not what I do or how I feel."

"It's the change," he told her quickly, this time resisting the urge to grab his cock at the base and stroke.

She'd licked her lips again as she talked and she'd moved on the bed, that damned shirt riding higher up her thighs until he could see the curve of her ass.

"Lycans are very sexual creatures," he said before pausing and swallowing hard. He wanted her mouth on him. He wanted to look down and see her pert lips wrapped around his length as he slipped in and out of her mouth. "It doesn't go away," he continued. "We're like that all day, every day, and it gets worse as the full moon approaches."

"But I'm—" she had begun to say, but quickly paused.

"You know what happened," he told her seriously. "He was a lycan and he bit you. The pain you're feeling is your body accepting the traits of his DNA and preparing itself to change accordingly. On the night of the full moon you will become a full-fledged lycan."

She did not speak again and Phelan knew she was digesting his words.

"Like I said before, if you want to eat, I can get them to bring you something," he said, realizing once again that he would have to stay in this room with her tonight. He would sleep in this bed beside her without even the protection of his clothes to hold his obvious arousal at bay.

"I'm not hungry," was her quiet reply.

"Then we should get some rest."

In the morning Blaez wanted to begin looking for Davis Sumpter. As Phelan lay on top of the comforter being sure to keep his naked back to her, he thought they wouldn't have to look far. Davis was a Hunter, Phelan could tell by the scent the lycan had left on Marena; that meant he was definitely coming back for her. No way was he going to leave her for someone else to claim.

Not that the thought had even crossed Phelan's mind.

CHAPTER 4

The voice was in her head again and Marena wanted to scream. Instead, she rolled over in the bed until she was flat on her back, her eyes open wide and staring at the ceiling. He continued calling to her.

I'm coming for you.

The voice repeated that over and over again until she was convinced he was getting closer. Recognizing Davis's voice and feeling the sting of the bite each time was driving her insane. It was one thing to recall that slimy bastard had planned to rape her, another entirely to know that now—even though he hadn't achieved that horrific feat—he'd certainly imposed another. He'd bitten her and now she was going to turn into a wolf, or a lycan. And there wasn't a damned thing she could do about it.

All her life Marena had worked hard. She'd had no other choice. Her parents were regular working-class people; her father had been employed as the manager in the men's section of a local department store and her mother was a cafeteria aid in the elementary school Marena and her siblings had attended. Darlene had loved that position because, she said, it allowed her to be home with the children more, especially throughout the summer. Her income, combined with

Matthew's, had kept a roof over Marena and her siblings' heads and food on their table. But there wasn't much left for anything else, like vacations and the Barbie Dreamhouse that Marena had wanted more than anything else for three Christmases in a row.

Matthew and Darlene loved their children and had built a steady family, teaching Marena how to do the same. Only her aspirations had been much higher, and grander than she probably had a right to. The latter had come from her older brother Lorenzo. He'd taken a job at an auto body shop during his junior year in high school and almost twenty years later was still working there. He had, however, married his high school sweetheart and they now had three beautiful daughters. Similarly, Marena's other two brothers were now married with kids and her sister had finally gotten hitched last year. Marena was certain that baby news would be coming from that household very soon.

As for Marena, there would be no such news.

She wouldn't get married and have children. Not now anyway, because that added commitment and responsibility would surely disrupt the fast track she was on to career success.

On the surface that was cool with her, as Marena had never seen herself as a mother, or the homebody type for that matter. She loved working a case, spending hours into the night going over discovery motions and responses, strategizing and winning. Power lunches and networking events occupied any free time she ever had. Her condo was decorated with only the most stylish pieces, her closet full of designer clothes, shoes, and purses. It was a fulfilling and exhilarating lifestyle, one she was convinced she was made for. That's why she'd worked so hard in school to graduate at the top of her class in undergrad and law school. She'd clerked with one of the top judges in the state for two years and then had only sent her résumé to the largest and most prestigious firms in the area. To call her an overachiever wouldn't have begun to cover it. She had to be the best, buy the best, and own the best; there was no other road in life for her.

Now, however, through no fault of her own, she was on a different path entirely and she wasn't certain how she felt about that just yet.

What she was certain of was that hearing Davis's voice in her head was getting old pretty damned fast. She didn't want to hear him. She wanted to see the bastard so she could make him go back to the firm and prove that he wasn't dead. That would clear her name, even if it wouldn't explain all the bullets she'd known she'd pumped into his trifling ass.

That was her priority. Dealing with this supposed change into a lycan, well, that was just going to have to wait.

Marena flipped back the sheets and let her feet fall to the floor. A quick glance out the window showed a sky just barely changing colors from night to day and she frowned. She couldn't call Gail this early in the morning, but she could send her an e-mail. Reaching over to the nightstand, she grabbed her phone, dislodging it from the charger she'd plugged into the side wall. Her work e-mail box was programmed to come up instantly on her phone, so she went to her Internet application and logged in to her personal inbox, thankful that the Wi-Fi in this lodge wasn't password protected. That would have required her to wake Phelan, and she did not want to do that.

Hell, she hadn't been able to sleep good all night knowing he was lying so beautifully naked beside her. By everything in this world that was holy, that man had the body of a god and a dick with size and perfection that would put a porn star's to shame. No, she would let him sleep for as long as she possibly could. And that, to Marena's chagrin, might not be much longer, since as she'd been scrolling down her e-mail list she'd stood and attempted to walk to stand at the window. Even that little distance, no more than ten to fifteen feet away from where he lay on the bed, had her already beginning to ache.

This "changing" crap was going to be difficult, not to mention battling the lycan's sexual appetite. Yeah, she'd heard Phelan loud and clear when he'd said that—while his dick had been rock hard and her pussy had been throbbing with need. Shaking her head to those thoughts, she opened a new e-mail and started to type to Gail: *Need you to call me on my cell right away. Thimgs are not what they seem. I'm innocent.*

Just typing those words had Marena's heart beating wildly. She'd never thought there would come a time when she'd have to convince someone of that fact. All her life she'd made sure to do the right thing. How she'd ended up here and why she was the one selected to be here at this moment she had no clue, but she was going to fix it. She was going to make everything better because that's what she did. It's what she'd always done in her life.

"If the police are looking for you, your phone should be turned off."

His voice startled her and her fingers froze over the keys as she gasped. When she looked up it was to see that he was not only awake but also standing at the foot of the bed, the sheet—thankfully—wrapped haphazardly around his waist.

"I told you the lawyer wasn't going to call you back," he continued when she figured she was standing there gaping at him like some kind of lunatic.

Clearing her throat and squaring her shoulders, Marena reached for her calm. It was growing harder and harder to remain aloof around this guy. Especially when her body was constantly reacting to his, with or without his permission.

"I sent her an e-mail this time. From my personal account, not the business one, so she'll be able to respond," Marena said. But now that she'd spoken the words aloud she realized what he was really trying to tell her.

A guilty party, or even an innocent-until-proven-guilty person, was allowed to contact their attorney. And said attorney was allowed to call their client or potential client back, without any of them breaking any laws. Besides that fact, Gail was her friend. They'd gone to law school together and kept in close contact even though they worked at competing law firms. So there was no reason that Gail would not have returned Marena's messages, whether she called, e-mailed, or wrote a message in the sky.

Unless she couldn't.

"He wouldn't go to her," Marena said, taking a step toward where Phelan still stood. "Davis knows her, but there would be no need for him to approach her, right?"

He frowned. And damn, even that was sexy. It was something about his eyes and that beard and the wild way the top of his hair spiked that called to her. That in itself was strange since Marena was normally attracted to the well-dressed and -groomed intellectual type. She'd also never been attracted to a white man before. Seems she was breaking all kinds of rules now.

"He's looking for you," Phelan replied. "He'll stop at nothing to get you back."

"But he's already bitten me. What else could he possibly want?"

"To own you."

She harrumphed and attempted to run her fingers through her tangled hair. "Nobody's ever going to own me. It's illegal, you know."

Phelan nodded. "A person can still be owned," he told her, taking a slow step toward her. "Your body and your mind can both be owned, by the right person, that is."

Marena tilted her head, ready to ignore the throbbing between her legs and the fullness of her breasts as he came even closer to her, in lieu of becoming pissed off by what she thought he might be presuming.

"No, I'm not talking about someone paying for it, or even taking it by force. I'm not that guy," he said, making her feel as if he were reading her mind.

When she opened her mouth to speak—not sure what she was going to say—her words were stalled by him touching a finger to her bottom lip. Marena snapped her mouth shut. She must look a hot mess, after retching her guts out only moments before she first met him, then riding through the night on the back of his motorcycle. After her shower, she'd even gone to bed without running a comb through her hair and had yet to even rub toothpaste over her teeth this morning. Still, in his eyes all she could see was desire.

It was thick and potent and circled between them like a brewing storm.

"I want to taste you again," were his next words, and Marena felt like she would either faint, or spread her lips wide open at this very moment.

Just who the hell was this guy and why was she responding to him like this? She knew the answers, but damn, she still couldn't believe it.

Swallowing quickly, she still tried to hold on to her calm. "Just because I enjoyed that doesn't mean you or anyone else can own me that way."

The left corner of his mouth lifted in a half smile as he pushed his finger past her lips to touch the tip of her tongue.

"Your pleasure would be my purpose," he whispered, his voice deep and raspy. "Whatever I did would be to make you feel good, so that I could see over and over again how beautiful you are when you come."

Her tongue circled around the tip of his finger and his eyes grew darker, stormier. She wasn't even going to ask herself why she was doing it. What made more sense was to focus on how damned good it felt to see he enjoyed what she was doing.

"Ahhh," he sighed, his lips staying partially open until she felt herself craving the sight of his tongue. The same tongue that had lapped expertly at her clit last night.

"You would make me come so easily. I can see it in your eyes. The hunger, the desperate urge to submit to this—"

His words halted abruptly and so did her tongue moving along the length of his finger. The face that had been full of desire and need was quickly masked with tight consternation. His lips had snapped shut, his eyes going cold as he pulled his finger slowly from between her lips. Marena hadn't caught on to what he was doing until it was done and the popping sound her astonished mouth made echoed throughout the room.

There was an immediate knock at the door.

"We're meeting in the library in ten minutes."

It was one of the other men who lived in this house. She couldn't tell which one, as she hadn't memorized the sound of any voice but Phelan's and Davis's, of course.

"Turn off your phone and get dressed," Phelan said before moving away from her. "You'll need to go with me to my rooms so I can change and then we'll go to the meeting."

Marena was already shaking her head. "I need to get in touch with my lawyer. Finding Davis and clearing my name is all I'm worried about."

When Phelan turned this time, her breath caught. He'd only moved his head giving her a searing look over her shoulder, those thick brows of his arched.

"Davis is one of ours, so we'll find him and we'll take care of him. As for you, laying low here is the best plan. If I come up with something else I'll let you know."

He'd spoken so matter-of-factly, as if he expected no argument and no resistance. Marena was the queen of arguing, or at least that's what her sister and then a few of the other attorneys at the firm had said about her. She could argue the wrong point for hours and hours, until the person who was right had begun to doubt themselves. While there were so many things she thought of saying to this man at this moment, something deep inside warned her to remain silent. To bide her time and do what he said for now. It wasn't an easy feat, as evidenced by her fists clenching at her sides.

"Fine. If you want to be the one to find him, I'm okay with that. Just so long as his reappearance can clear my name," she told Phelan before grabbing her bag and heading toward the bathroom to change into her clothes.

The pain began a lot slower this time, like a growing ball

of heat in the pit of her stomach, and by the time she stood at the entrance to the bathroom Phelan was behind her.

"I'll stand outside the door while you change. The proximity should be close enough to make you feel better."

His proximity was close enough to make her want to turn around and jump on him, she thought, still trying to get control of the quick shifts of pain and pleasure between the two of them. Not sure what to say and hating the helplessness that came with this situation, she simply nodded and headed into the bathroom to get dressed. She didn't begin to understand the logic or the rules of the lycan world and insisted that now was not the time to find out. Now was the time to get things back in order. Later, after her job was secured, she would consider how her actually turning into a lycan was going to fit into the career and life she'd planned for herself.

"The supermoon is coming," Channing said, sitting on the arm of the leather couch in the center of the massive library.

"That's when he'll come for me," Blaez said in his serious tone.

He was standing beside the wing-backed chair that Kira was sitting in, his hand on her shoulder and her hand covering his. The alphas of this pack united.

"I haven't heard any more about the bounty," Phelan spoke up.

Since the appearance of the harpy a couple of months back, Phelan had kept an ear to both realms for news of what beings had accepted Zeus's challenge to bring Blaez to him, dead or alive. At the same time, Phelan had been keeping an extra-close watch on his own enemy who he knew could turn on him at any moment. Neither had given him any reason to believe that Zeus was aware of where Blaez was or that he'd even planned a special day and time to come for him.

"Excuse me, did you say 'Zeus'?" Marena asked.

She had opted to stand while the other females in the room sat, believing still that she had no part in what was going on here. Phelan had thought about reminding her of the bite on her shoulder and that once it healed completely she would be one of them for the rest of her life. He'd declined, figuring it was best if she came to terms with what her future held on her own, just as he had done so long ago.

"Yes," Kira replied. "Zeus is the one responsible for setting the ball that created the lycans in motion. He's the father of this big mess and he's attempting to exercise his parental control by killing Blaez."

Marena tensed.

Phelan couldn't see her because she'd opted to stand behind him as they came into the library. While he'd immediately joined the others, she'd still considered herself an outsider and stood as far back as her physical discomfort would allow her. He didn't agree with her not dealing with her new status in the world head-on, but he wasn't going to make that his concern. He didn't want to make her his concern any more than was necessary. Still, he couldn't ignore every sound she made, every time she winced in pain; even the scent of her arousal had seemingly been etched in his mind. That thought alone had him frowning.

"We're never going to let that happen," he said tightly.

Those words didn't calm Marena.

"Okay, so there's a god after you. Isn't there some type of otherworldly legal system at play here? Surely hunting and killing someone or some . . . *being* . . . is not simply allowed in your world?" she asked.

"The rules are a bit different in our world than in the human one," Blaez said to her calmly.

He would have noticed her distance as well; everyone in the pack would have. However, none of them spoke of it.

"We'll deal with this situation ourselves," Malec continued.

Channing nodded. "Other Devoteds have been in contact; they want to help."

"An army equates to the possibility of more deaths," Phelan spoke up. "We're all trained soldiers here. We can take Zeus."

"A soldier is no match for a Greek god, Phelan. You know that," Kira countered.

Phelan immediately shook his head. "Don't underestimate me."

"So wait, you're really talking about a battle with a Greek god?" Marena asked. "Here? On earth? Is that where this will take place? What about us? What happens to the human world while this little fight is going on?"

"The humans are hunting the Shadow Shifters," Blaez stated evenly. "They've brought together NATO to begin a combined effort to flush out all shape-shifters on this planet. Their goal is to kill them out of fear, because they do not understand them. I'd say they have their own wars to worry about right now."

Phelan could only stare and frown. He'd known about the military's attempts to round up all those they suspected of being shape-shifters. A few months back when Jace Maybon, a Shadow Shifter leader, had shown up on their doorstep looking for one of his fellow shifters, Phelan had been irritated beyond words. The Shadow Shifters had allowed themselves to be unveiled on national television. In one live news broadcast they managed to tap into all of the humans' fears of beings who were not like them. In the year since then there had been reports of caught and confined shifters; killings and robberies and all other types of crimes were being blamed on the illusive shifters. Now the lycan packs had to be very careful of everything they did, else the human world would learn that they had so much more to fear than the feline shape-shifters they were currently fixated with.

"I'm surprised you haven't received a call for us to come in," Malec commented.

"I did," Blaez told him. "I turned them down."

"You received a call for who to come in to what?" Marena asked. "I mean, if that's something I can ask."

"This situation involves you, too, Marena," Kira said, looking beyond Phelan. "Especially since you are staying here with us now. So I believe that full disclosure is warranted."

Those words were aimed at the alpha, who looked to Phelan. Marena was going to change into a lycan. There was nothing any of them could do to stop that from happening. Everything else—including which side she would select, the Hunters or the Devoteds, and what type of lycan she would become—was totally up to her.

So why was each member of this pack looking at him as if he somehow had some say in this?

"We're not just lycans," he began after Blaez arched a brow in his direction. The alpha apparently thought Phelan should be the one to tell her who and what they really were.

Phelan took a deep breath and then turned to face her. He'd been content telling himself that she was just a human who had been unfortunate enough to get bitten by a lycan and that the sweet taste of her honey still lingering on the back of his tongue was simply because it had been too long since he'd partaken of that delectable part of a female. Looking into her soft brown eyes at this moment, however, gave him momentary pause.

Her hair was bone straight, hanging past her shoulders, parts pulling to the front to lounge in a completely plain yet terribly sexy way. Her eyebrows were thick and arched perfectly, while her pert lips were only barely glossed. When she'd stepped into the bathroom to dress just a short while ago, he'd stood with his back to the bathroom door, his head hung low, trying like hell not to envision the clothes slipping over her naked body. Now he couldn't help but stare in what felt like a trance at the black jumpsuit that cinched at her waist and flared into cargo-type pants to the ties at her ankles. The outfit was strapless, hugging her full breasts in a way that made Phelan extremely jealous. Even the flat black shoes with the tiniest white bows at the tops had his dick twitching.

"Blaez is the alpha of our pack and Kira is his mate. The rest of us are betas in the lycan world. To the humans we— the guys and I—are members of a covert operations team that sometimes does contractual work for the U.S. military. We're all trained Marines," he told her, and was supremely grateful for the serious words he could speak, versus the sexual monologue that was currently running through his mind.

Phelan wanted to taste her again. This time he wanted her flat on her back, his face buried between her legs. He wanted her open and available to him for the taking, ready and waiting to submit to his will. The way she reached a hand up to tuck strands of hair behind her ear before meeting his gaze told him she was thinking along those same lines.

"So you're saying that the government has contacted you about hunting the shape-shifters that they already know exist," she said. "But you turned them down because you're keeping your own secret."

"We're trying to protect the human world," Channing added.

Marena shook her head. "Secrets do not equate to protection. They breed deceit, which ultimately unfolds in devastation. I suspect the feline Shadow Shifters thought they were doing the same thing you're attempting and look how that turned out."

"But you weren't surprised by the revelation of the Shadow Shifters, were you?" Caroline interjected. "When I first saw what Malec was I was shocked and intrigued, and a little bit afraid. I'd seen the news reports and watched the ones that the authorities had managed to capture. They called them shape-shifters and yet they looked just like you and me. They looked totally human. Until I saw the Solo in his lycan form reeking of revenge and evil. That was what made him different, not just the sharp teeth and wolf features. It was his purpose here on earth, the intent to do harm in his eyes. That's what frightened me. But you," she continued. "You don't seem daunted by all that you've endured in the past couple of days at all. Why is that?"

Phelan hadn't liked Caroline's line of questioning. He hadn't cared for the suspicious tone of her voice or the way the others remained quiet as if Caroline had spoken what they'd been thinking all along.

"We should go," he said. "The effects of the bite will drain your energy for a while yet."

Marena shook her head slightly as she let her arms fall to her sides. "I feel fine," she said coolly.

"To answer your question, Caroline, no, I'm not afraid," Marena added. "I learned a long time ago that fear was the result of ignorance, especially where man was concerned. I cannot summon any apprehension against a species that I know nothing about. You are right in the sense that this may be because before this weekend I've had no encounter with the feline shifters or lycans. Even the one I eventually found myself face-to-face with didn't scare me until the very end. Now, however, all I can think about is finding that bastard and making him face the destruction he's caused in my life. The fact that he is another type of being is of no consequence to me."

"Even though he bit you?" Kira asked her.

Marena's shoulders stiffened then. It was a barely perceptible motion that Phelan doubted anyone but him had seen as Marena shifted her attention from where Caroline sat on the couch to where Kira and Blaez were now standing a couple feet away. Phelan moved closer to Marena in that moment, standing so that the bare skin of his arm brushed over hers. The jolt of heat that fired through him was only the first bit of shock he would receive.

"That," Marena told Kira, "is something I will deal with at a later time. For now, my only concern is salvaging my career."

"And our concern is protecting Blaez and saving this world from unwanted turmoil," Malec stated firmly.

"That's a pretty ambitious goal, but I wish you the best of luck," Marena told them, before turning to leave the room.

Phelan didn't hesitate and he didn't look to the others to see how they'd taken her blatant brush-off. He moved with her as if they'd been thinking along the same lines the whole time, following her out of the library and toward the back doors of the house. She wanted to go out, needed air to breathe into lungs that felt congested and a mind that was all of a sudden weary of the changes going on within as well as around her.

It only took an extra step from him to cross in front of her in time to reach for the control panel to disengage the motion sensors and locks that were on all the windows and doors of the lodge. Pulling the sliding door open, he stood to the side and watched as she quietly stepped through. She walked to the very edge of the planked deck without looking back at him, almost as if she'd been there before. Phelan knew that wasn't possible, and he focused more on the lithe movements of her feet, the slight lift of her hair on the breeze, instead of tapping into all the strange déjà vu–like emotions he was having where she was concerned.

"I don't belong here," Marena said suddenly, her back still facing him.

She's right. She doesn't belong here. She should leave, the other voice sounded in Phelan's ears, instantly soliciting a growl.

CHAPTER 5

When Phelan didn't respond, Marena turned around to face him. She knew he was there, not only because she wasn't feeling sick but also because she was feeling something else. Something she only felt when he was near. She'd wanted to simply call it attraction, but she was smart enough to know that there was more to it than that. It was more because she'd never felt this way before for any other guy and no other man had ever elicited the quick and intense feelings Phelan did from her.

Right now her heart was thumping quickly as she'd wanted to run out of that room with all those eyes staring at her. Marena had never been the shy or introverted type. She came from a big family of boisterous and opinionated people. If she hadn't been able to speak up for herself, she would have been eaten alive. So being in front of others and saying whatever she had to say was not a problem, hence her success in the courtroom.

Standing in front of five lycans who were all looking to her for some specific answer or response had been a bit more than she'd ever imagined she would have to endure. Just the thought that in the blink of an eye each of them could look like Phelan had last night in the hotel room, and could be vicious killers, was enough for her to swallow. The thought that she would soon be one of them was by far the worst. She was determined not to think about that bite on her shoulder and to focus on what she knew she could control, but she'd been losing her grip in there. And so, for the first time in her life, she'd run. Well, she'd walked, really fast. Phelan had followed, but he wasn't speaking; she wanted to know why.

"Are you all right?" she asked when he was still standing a distance away from her looking around as if he thought maybe someone else was out here with them.

Considering she was standing on the porch of a log cabin in who-knew-where Montana, after a conversation about a pissed-off Greek god and the inevitability of him coming to earth to seek his revenge, Marena found herself looking around, too, because hell, there could be someone or something else out here.

"Why did you come out here?" he asked, ignoring her question completely.

Marena wasn't bothered by that because she was used to dealing with men who didn't think she was smart enough or a good-enough lawyer to challenge them in any way. She never let that stop her from moving forward with her cases zealously and she wasn't about to let it cause her pause now.

"Look, I don't know what you and your friends expect from me. But like I said, I don't belong here. I need to get back to San Francisco to clear my name and save my legal reputation. I have to find Davis," she said adamantly.

"He's the one that put you in this predicament," Phelan added, taking a step closer to her.

It was a measured step. Not the self-assured movements she had become accustomed to seeing from him.

"He's a partner at my firm, and if the police continue to suspect me of doing something to Davis I'll never achieve my career goals because those chauvinistic older partners are going to crucify me."

Phelan arched a brow. "And because you'll likely be put in jail."

Marena huffed because, unfortunately, she wasn't as concerned about that part of the situation as she suspected she should be.

"You don't understand," she told him. "I've come too far and worked too damned hard for this stupid incident to stop me."

"You mean the stupid incident where a man attacked you and you shot him in self-defense?" he asked when he was standing directly in front of her.

The day had passed without her even knowing, so that now it looked as if the sun were just settling in the sky, waiting for its descent into evening. The golden glow framed Phelan and his well-sculpted body in a romantic haze that for a moment or two had her wishing their circumstances were different.

What if he'd been a businessman living in San Francisco? Maybe he'd just moved there and she'd met him at a meeting. Would she have been so intrigued by his intense green eyes to ask if he'd like her to show him around? Or would she have immediately recognized the way her body warmed when he was close?

"It was stupid; I admit that. And it was self-defense. But now, finding him is about self-preservation. I have to make partner. It's what I've always worked for. What will my family think if I don't?" she asked, catching the admission and turning away to keep from saying more.

Her personal life was her own. Her goals and ambitions and the reasons, therefore, belonged to her. She'd never felt the need to explain them to anyone. Yet all she'd ever wanted was for her parents and her siblings to be proud of her. To say they always believed in her. It was probably a long shot, Marena admitted to herself, because the Panos family were not good with expressing their emotions. Unless it was to complain or to disperse some great conspiracy theory as her father and her brothers were known to do. But they were her family and they were all that had ever mattered to her.

"What will they think when you tell them you're a lycan?" he asked.

His question was stated so simply, so basic and yet producing more anxiety and hesitation than she'd ever experienced before.

"If you find Davis and he's completely healed, which I have no doubt he is because we can heal from most wounds, what will you do? Drag him in front of the partners and insist he tell them what he tried to do to you? He's never going to do that, Marena. You need to accept that now. He's a Hunter lycan; the only person he's going to look out for is himself and members of the pack he belongs to, because he's certainly not an alpha. Whether you like it or not, your life has been irrevocably changed."

Marena shivered at his words, even though it was warm outside. She did not like what he'd said or the fact that it was true. And she didn't like that he'd said them in the same tone Davis spoke whenever he decided to appear in her mind. She could hear him laughing now, telling her the same thing he'd been saying for hours on end: *I'm coming for you. I'm coming for you. I'm coming for you.*

"Stop it!" she yelled, slapping her hands to her ears and

shaking her head. "Just stop it, both of you. Please." The last word was a whimper and so foreign to her ears she barely registered it.

"Stop what?" Phelan asked her, his hands tightening on her shoulders. "Tell me what's happening?"

"He's talking to me," she said without thinking. "He's been talking to me, like he's standing right beside me. How can he do that? If you can take away the pain why can't you tell him to stop?"

Her heart was pounding, her hands shaking as they stayed clapped over her ears. She'd closed her eyes believing that maybe, just maybe, she could shut all of this out of her mind. The voice. The bite. The gun. Everything.

Phelan's hands on her didn't stop any of that, only added to it a powerful pull that Marena hated she couldn't resist. He was turning her to him then, his face drawing closer to hers as he pulled her hands away from her ears and asked her calmly, "What is he saying?"

He believed her was the first thing Marena thought. He believed that she was hearing Davis's voice even though they both knew full well that he wasn't there with them.

"'I'm coming for you,'" she said. "Over and over again he tells me that and then he laughs. What does that mean? What does he want with me now?"

Phelan frowned. His eyes growing darker and his jaw tightening.

"He wants you for himself, to claim you and make you his," he said disgustedly.

Marena pulled away from him then, his words circling in her mind. "What? I'll never be with him. I told him that and that's when he— I don't want him," she said. "All I want is for him to clear my name."

"Are you certain about that?" Phelan asked, looking at her with what Marena thought might actually be contempt.

His look, coupled with his question and this whole damned situation, pissed her off royally.

"What the hell does that mean?" she asked, then shook her head quickly, holding up a hand. "No. You listen to me. I don't know who or what you think I am, or was, before all this happened. But I can assure you that I've never been interested in Davis and that was before I knew he was a dirty, disgusting wolf! And as for you, I don't know you, either. I don't know why you have to remain close to me for me to even breathe normally and I don't care. All I want is my life back. That's all I need."

"Are you sure about that?" he asked, closing the space between them quickly and grabbing her by the neck.

His fingers were tight as they slipped through her hair to cup the nape of her neck. He applied pressure, only a little more gently than his first contact, until she tilted her face up to his. And then he kissed her.

His lips were like molten lava as they touched hers, beckoning her to open and let all that fiery heat inside whether she wanted to or not. When his tongue touched hers that heat traveled quickly throughout every inch of her body, until Marena felt like she needed to strip away every piece of clothing simply to find any solace. With bold and intoxicating strokes his tongue dueled with hers, his one hand at her neck, the other planted firmly at the base of her back, just before the curve of her ass.

He held her firmly as he deepened the kiss, forcing her to open her mouth wider and to tilt her head back farther. He hadn't asked nicely and there was nothing pleasant about this kiss. Only its urgency, its heat, its undeniable existence that kept her standing still, accepting, needing.

Cheater! You dare to betray me with her!

Eureka's voice sounded loudly in Phelan's head, just as it had when Marena had first come out here. She was in his head the way she'd been since that fateful night when she'd put that gruesome mark upon his face. Just as Davis was in Marena's head.

It was the blood curse.

The mixing of two otherworldly beings' blood could sometimes prove fatal, but in most cases it simply created a link between the two beings that was only breakable when one of the beings was claimed. The bond of a true mate would cancel any other bonds the beings had previously formed.

Eureka's nails had gone deep into Phelan's skin, scarring him on a deeper than physical level and cursing him with her presence in his life forevermore. In addition, Eureka had cast her own brand of sorcery on him, by declaring he would never find a mate, would never be content with anyone but her. It was both childish and foolhardy and he'd discarded it the moment the words were spoken from her lips, and then his own stubborn pride had ultimately proved her right. He had not sought out a mate or anyone he planned to be serious about. Instead, he'd retreated even further into himself than he had when he'd lived at the orphanage. He was meant to be alone. That thought had been drilled into him from the very beginning of his life; there was no use in thinking differently now.

Considering all that, Phelan still hated hearing her voice. He despised the intrusion and wanted her gone once and for all. Knowing there was really no way he could do that only speared the kick of desire for Marena on further.

His dick was already hard, seconds before he'd even thought to take her into his arms for that kiss. The one that was still scorching his lips and tongue as he delved deeper, attempted to let the taste of her drown out the voice and the anger.

Marena had grabbed his biceps, holding on to him as she tilted her head and kept the kiss going with her own eager tongue thrusts and small glorious moans. Phelan tugged on her hair and heard her gasp. He sucked her tongue deep into his mouth, keeping his eyes and his mind closed to anything but Marena. She was sexy and delectable and he'd been attracted to her from the moment he rode up beside her SUV. Sure, the new blood Hunter scent he'd picked up had been a draw, but if he had to be totally honest with himself, he'd admit that the aroma that had really pulled him toward her was of her arousal.

Heady and thick, it had called to him like a siren's song, and he'd come running. He hadn't been able to ignore it. The first time he'd touched her, initially to still the pain racking through her body, had sent spikes of desire shooting straight to the tip of his cock. And when he'd thrown caution out the damned window and put his mouth on her hardened clit last night in the shower, he'd sworn he'd died and gone to whichever heaven was made for lycans.

Now they were outside, a warm breeze blowing around them, and Phelan still couldn't take his hands off her. When he let his hands cup her face, then move down to the soft skin of her neck, to the bare softness of her chest, and finally to push down the elastic band of the jumpsuit that held it up over her breasts, all he could do was sigh. He looked down to see the heavy globes in all their fantastic glory.

The color of heavily creamed coffee until the areola formed a perfectly dark circle, her puckered nipple at its center. Phelan growled as he bent down, taking one into his mouth, gorging greedily, trying to suck as hard and as much of her breast as possible, while palming the other simultaneously. She grabbed the back of his head, similar to the way she had done when they were in the shower, rubbing her blunt nails along his scalp, feeding him her breast as if he were her child. He buried his face between the soft flesh, loving the feel of them along his cheeks and as his tongue stretched out to lick small paths over the mounds.

He wanted his dick right here, cupped between her breasts as he fucked her until he came, his essence shooting in thick rivulets over her silky smooth skin. That thought had him pushing the jumpsuit down even farther, until his hand cupped the pouting mound of her pussy. She bucked beneath him, trying to keep her balance and give him all the access he wanted. With a growl of frustration, Phelan stood, taking her by the shoulders and plunging his tongue deep into her mouth again as he backed her up until she was flush against the log siding of the house.

He cupped her breasts again, licking all around her taut nipples, and was just about to pull that jumpsuit down farther so that he could lick the sweet honey between her legs one more time, when she shocked him.

With a quick motion Marena's hands were on the zipper of his pants, pulling it down and reaching inside to wrap her fingers around his thick cock. Phelan gasped at the quick capture, his length resting in her palm as she completely freed him. He was just catching his breath when she slid down, her tongue licking the drop of pre-cum from his slit as he watched her through half-closed eyes.

Before he could stop himself, Phelan ran his fingers through her hair, pushing it back from her face so he had a clear view of her mouth on his thick length. She licked around the tip until it was glossy with her ministrations. He throbbed in her hand as she closed her mouth over him and slid down slowly. Phelan groaned while watching his dick disappear in her mouth. His fingers twisted in her hair as he began to guide her head to match the slow and measured thrusts of his hips. He wanted to go faster, deeper, to pound into the warm recess of her mouth until his cum came spurting out hot and long. But he resisted, enjoying the moment when she cupped her hands on his ass and moved him just a bit faster, her mouth taking him easily.

Closing his eyes, Phelan let his head fall back, swearing he'd never felt this damned good before. Her mouth was hot and wet and he wanted to stay right there forever, until she slipped a hand around to reach farther into his pants, tickling his scrotum as she continued to suck him.

"Dammit!" he moaned and yelled and then moaned again, about two seconds before he came in thick jets that she swallowed without hesitation.

All thoughts of Eureka, the threat against Blaez's life, hell, the air around him, vanished from Phelan's mind as he held her head tightly, watching as her throat constricted with each swallow, her lips still wet and swollen.

It was when she looked up at him, when their gazes locked, that Phelan knew without a doubt that he was in trouble. Big fucking trouble.

CHAPTER 6

What had she done?

And why the hell had she done it?

Marena had no clue what had come over her and made her give this guy oral sex—a man who she barely even knew, at that. All she knew for certain was the heat that had shot through her veins as he'd sucked her breasts had been intoxicating. She'd immediately wanted more. She'd wanted her mouth on him in almost the same way.

It was strange and then again it wasn't; it simply was.

She blinked as she realized that, licking her lips and coming to a complete stand. There was a deep attraction here; even if she'd just met him, the connection was undeniable. He wanted her and she wanted him, even though they both seemed to think there was a better option to their acting on this unexplainable magnetism. Marena could see it in his eyes. The doubt and the questions, the same ones that were most likely going through her head.

They didn't know each other and had been thrust together by circumstances beyond either of their control. Still, it was as if something much stronger were at play here, something that was carefully orchestrating every touch and moan between them.

With shaking hands she brushed her hair back from her face, searching for the appropriate words to say but unable to find them since she'd never sucked a guy and swallowed his cum before.

In the next seconds she realized words weren't necessary at all.

Phelan grabbed her by the waist then, pulling her against his chest as his lips slammed down over hers once more. His kisses were explosive, like a live detonation the moment his lips touched hers. Their tongues dueled, still as hungry for each other as they had been minutes ago. When he pulled away this time his eyes were closed and he was mumbling something under his breath, but Marena couldn't decipher what.

All she knew for certain was that he was pushing her jumpsuit down, lifting one of her legs, and removing her shoe so that she could step out of the material. When her leg was finally free, Phelan looped it over his arm, his fingers going quickly between her legs pushing the thin swatch of silk covering her juncture aside to part her throbbing folds and sink hungrily into her moistened center. She gasped, her head falling back until it slapped softly against the wall. He quickly replaced his fingers with his dick, slamming into her with such heated force Marena almost bit right through her bottom lip.

Like his kiss, this was no romantic taking. There were no candles, no chocolate-covered strawberries or champagne. Simply the raw edge of need bursting free as he pumped wildly into her and she grabbed hold of his biceps, squeezing tightly as the sound of their joined sex slapping together echoed into the air. He held her leg higher than Marena even knew it could go, his thick, long length filling her completely before pulling out and ramming back inside again. Her bare ass hit the wall as she opened her mouth wide, the moan that ripped free an almost primal sound.

When she turned so that she could look into his face, she was shocked to see he was staring directly at her. His eyes were glazed as if he possibly wasn't really seeing her at all and they were no longer green but a bristling cool blue that pierced straight through to her chest. His teeth were clenched, lips parted as he heaved with each thrust. He was seriously aroused and intent on making sure she received every inch of his dick, hitting her sweet spot over and over again until her legs began to tremble.

He growled then. Low at first and then louder, even though his facial expression hadn't changed at all. The sound was so raw and guttural, just like his strokes inside her, and Marena felt as if he was making the sound specifically for her. She continued to stare at him, while loving the feel of his cock sliding effortlessly in and out of her very wet pussy.

When she knew she was about to come, Marena licked her lip and acting on pure instinct leaned in to lick Phelan's bottom lip the same way. Their gazes remained locked, her nails digging into the skin of his arms as she used her teeth this time to bite down on his lip the second her body erupted in a blindingly delicious orgasm.

He pumped harder and faster, even when her essence dripped over his dick, onto her thighs and the wood-planked porch. He'd opened his mouth and she'd immediately released her hold on his lips to thrust her tongue deep inside. Phelan took her tongue, sucking it hard as he continued to pump inside of her, until finally he came with a shudder of his entire body. He held her against that wall, his dick still embedded deep inside her for endless seconds as he began to slowly stroke her tongue with his own. It was the sweetest kiss Marena had ever experienced.

In the seconds that followed, realization hit Marena once more and she noticed the swaying of the trees in the distance, the wind that had picked up, and the fact that they were standing on an open porch where anyone could have seen them at any moment.

As surprising as all those things seemed to her, none of them compared to the fact that she'd just had unprotected sex.

Her palms against his chest, Marena pushed at Phelan until he backed away from her. When there was enough space between them she hurriedly began reassembling her clothes. She assumed he was doing the same when she took a couple steps to the side to retrieve her other shoe, not chancing a look toward Phelan at all.

"I don't do this," she said, twisting her foot until it was in the shoe and then standing up straight. "I don't have sex with men I don't . . . and I definitely never have unprotected sex." Her breath came out in a rush as she verbalized the fear swarming through her stomach at the moment. "I'm not ready to have a baby and then there's the possibility of diseases and, well, it's just immature and irresponsible and I—"

"Lycans don't contract human diseases," Phelan replied from behind. "And conception can only occur on the night of the full moon. So you're safe and sound."

He was moving past her then, heading for the patio doors they'd come through earlier.

"I need to go to my room to research a few things. You can freshen up in there."

His words were curt and frosty, and if Marena hadn't known to take their little tryst for exactly what it was she may have been hurt by them. Luckily for her, she wasn't the romantic type; she didn't have hearts in her eyes and warmth in her chest at the possibility of having the big, strong, and sexy lycan fall for her. That's not why she was here.

So she followed Phelan back into the house, through the long hallway that passed the library and a few other rooms with closed doors, so she couldn't see what was in them. She and Phelan moved through the large living room area where Channing and Caroline sat on a plush blanket in front of the huge fireplace, magazines strewn all around them as they talked.

Phelan was moving quickly, his long legs giving him a wide stride. Marena could keep up because she was tall herself, but she did lose a few steps when she looked over to see Caroline giving her a sympathetic gaze. That irritated her because Marena did not like pity. She hadn't needed it when the scholarships at her small high school had all gone to the mayor's twin daughters who hadn't needed the money at all, nor did she need it when her first car—a ten-year-old Toyota Corolla—had coughed its last breath on the campus parking lot in the middle of a torrential rainstorm. No, she'd put her mind to it and found a solution to her problems and, dammit, that's what she was going to do this time.

She continued to walk behind Phelan as he passed the kitchen and down another winding hallway that curved around the sprawling staircase. As she noticed earlier, this was a very large house with painstaking attention to detail from the rugs that matched the furniture and the room-darkening blinds perfectly to the paintings of what looked like another world on the walls. Even the log-planked walls were glossed until their color was an exact shade, like golden honey.

Phelan turned right and immediately opened a door. Marena had seen him, but then she'd looked to the side and studied the painting on the wall. The one she'd been just as mesmerized by this morning. It was of a dark, stormy night with only the glow of the moon to add color. It immediately pulled her in, like a lullaby, and she couldn't help but stare at it. So much so that she continued walking without looking and bumped right into Phelan's broad chest.

"It's just a picture," he said stonily.

Marena disagreed. "I like it," she replied, squaring her shoulders, prepared for a debate.

Phelan only shrugged. "That's your prerogative. I'm going to go to my office. The bathroom is down those two steps toward the back. There's a television and a radio."

When he'd come in here to get his clothes earlier, she'd been enamored by that painting and so he'd gone in alone, quickly returning before any pain or discomfort could assail her. She walked in behind him this time looking around as he turned on one lamp and then another. The light was a soft golden hue that illuminated the space, which told so much about the man. There were two connecting rooms both decorated in a deep purple color. The furniture was large and made entirely of wood from what she could see—a king-size four-poster bed, two long dressers, and the entertainment center. Each piece was dark wood, burnished to a gleam as was the rest of the lumber in this house. There was a purple comforter on the bed and four pillows covered in purple cases. The previous room held a couch and two guest chairs, a coffee table, and end tables, all made of the same rich wood with thick purple cushions. There were no rugs on the planked floors and no curtains at the windows, only more room-darkening blinds.

Phelan was a powerful lycan, strong, steady, and respected. And yet his life was as solitary as he could make it while still remaining a part of the intricate group of lycans that lived in this house. Marena thought that was both strange and familiar.

"The distance shouldn't be too far if you sit in here to watch television, but if you become uncomfortable—"

The deep boom of his voice jolted her from her thoughts. "I'll run right and find you," Marena quipped as she stopped her perusal of the room and turned to face him.

His jaw was set, eyes cool, hands clasped in front of him. He looked like a sexy tour guide, quoting from memory all the amenities of the place, preparing to leave her alone full of information. He did not look like the hungry lover who had just brought her to a spine-tingling orgasm not even fifteen minutes ago.

For a moment she thought he was going to say something, maybe offer an apology for being so curt or possibly invite her into the office with him. She didn't know why, but she wanted to see that space, too, as she thought it might be where Phelan spent most of his time when he was back here. Something about the precise location of everything she'd seen in the bedroom and this sitting area said it went untouched more often than not. He didn't really live here, probably only slept in the bed, washed in the bathroom, and worked in that office.

"I'll be right in here," he told her before turning and walking away.

He was out of sight in seconds. Marena wasn't sure of

the exact amount of space they were parted, but she could no longer see him. She suspected they would both have to raise their voices slightly to hear each other, which meant . . . she waited.

And waited.

The pain would start at any moment. She even wrapped an arm around her stomach in anticipation and moved closer to the couch so it would be easier for her to sit when the waves of nausea hit. But they did not come. Maybe the sex cured it, she thought as she blinked. It was some good sex. No, it was some damned hot, good, and satisfying sex. Which she'd never experienced before and, she thought, with a frown, she may never have again.

Those thoughts reminded her that she needed a shower. She looked over her shoulder to see the bathroom door about nine feet away from where she was standing. Marena didn't move but stood there looking from the bathroom through the open archway in the other direction to where Phelan had disappeared a few minutes ago. It was a good distance and she wondered if it might be too far.

"Screw it," she mumbled, and then turned to walk toward the bathroom.

With each step—while in her mind she waited for the pain to stop her in her tracks—Marena was determined to keep going. When her shoes touched on the tiled floor, a contrast from the wood floors in the bedroom, she looked back once more as if she thought the pain might be lurking just behind her, waiting to finally strike. But it didn't.

Just as it hadn't this morning when she'd stood right outside Phelan's room.

Marena sighed and cleared the doorway, closing the bathroom door behind her. Switching on the light, she looked around, noting that the slate-gray tile on the floor and in smaller tile pieces around the interior of the shower was the only modern touch in the room. The sink was a large slab of what looked to be a chunk out of the side of a huge tree, smoothed and glossed to perfection, a pewter faucet atop the ceramic sink. The mirror behind the sink was even surrounded by pieces of rock that were strategically placed. adding an artistic edge to what she was already considering a rustic bathroom. When she turned from the sink it was to the shock of seeing what could only be classified as a mound of rocks, which actually served as the base of the deep soaker tub. Marena almost sighed at how comfortable—if different from anything she'd ever seen—the tub looked.

Of course the tub was different. It wasn't her bathroom after all. And she wasn't staying in this lodge as part of some sort of long-awaited vacation. There were serious issues at play here, ones that she needed to get on top of before they totally ruined all that she'd worked for. On that note, Marena undressed quickly and opened the glass shower stall door to step inside.

The shower was hot and invigorating, even with the memories of someone else washing her the night before still fresh in her memory. When she stepped out of the shower and dried off, she decided she didn't want to put on the clothes she'd just taken off. With a frown, because her clean clothes were in another room on the other side of the house, Marena looked around until she saw a robe hanging on the back of the bathroom door. Taking it down and slipping her arms into the long, wide sleeves, she wrapped the terry-cloth material around her body and belted it at the waist before leaving the bathroom.

Marena walked through that bedroom and sitting area as if she'd been there many times before, making a right turn around another wall. There was a step down and her bare feet, still slightly damp, slapped down onto the hardwood floor. This area was smaller than the other two, only big enough, it seemed, to accommodate the huge oak desk Phelan sat behind and the even larger high-backed leather executive chair. There were two tall lamps in opposite corners and another smaller table, which matched the wood of the desk, that held a printer and boxes of paper.

Phelan looked up at her and, like a moth to a flame, her gaze found his and held.

She wanted to walk to him, to move until she was standing on the other side of that desk, just inches away from him. While she'd been in the bathroom she'd felt perfectly fine, no pain at all. And now she felt something totally different. There was a tugging in the center of her stomach as if something very strong was pulling her—against her will, or perhaps not—toward him. The sensation was so powerful that it took every ounce of strength Marena possessed to keep her standing still in that spot.

"How was your shower?" he asked, his voice as smooth and deep as the strokes he'd made in and out of her pussy.

She inhaled deeply, exhaled slowly.

"It was fine," she replied curtly. "What are you doing?"

When he didn't immediately respond she stepped around the desk to see what he was doing on the computer. Not because she felt like she would somehow be able to breathe much better if she was closer to him. She stopped the moment she saw Davis's face on the computer screen.

"You're researching Davis? Why?"

"Because I like to know everything about my enemy

before I take his ass down," was his immediate and un-apologetic reply.

"Davis isn't your enemy," Marena replied just as seriously. "He's mine. And I need to find him so that I can take him back to San Francisco and show the partners that this was all a mistake."

"You're not that naïve," Phelan said without even bothering to look up at her. He simply clicked to the next screen, his gaze now trained on the computer.

"This is my fight," she stated sternly. "Davis is mine."

"He's a Hunter lycan that needs to be stopped. That makes him mine," Phelan countered.

"And what am I? A casualty in this war you keep talking about?"

If he gave another smart and curt answer, Marena thought she might smack him across the back of his head. Still raw from the rebuff after their tryst, she wasn't about to let him simply dismiss her from the search for Davis as well.

He seemed to pause as if he was actually thinking about his response. Marena felt a wave of triumph at that thought. It quickly dissipated.

"You're about to become a lycan, which may or may not turn out to be the biggest curse of your life. I wouldn't wish that on anyone and I'd feel sorry for you if I thought that was what you wanted," he said simply.

Yes *simply*, as if he'd just recited the items on tonight's menu. Not like he'd just told her she was nothing and she needed to step aside and let him do what was her right to handle. If she were ten years old Marena was sure this would be the point where she balled her fists at her sides and stomped her feet until her brothers or sister really listened to her. But she was an adult and she was more serious than she'd ever been before. This was her life—as a human or a lycan—and she'd be damned if she was going to sit back and let Phelan ride in like a knight in shining armor and save the day. She was no damsel in distress, so that theory had never appealed to her.

"He has a big case coming up in two weeks," she started. "He's not going to just blow that off."

Phelan's fingers stilled on the keyboard. "You think he's worried about some court case? He's a Hunter, Marena. All he's worried about is ruling. Channing's trying to find out if he's part of a pack or acting solo. Once we get an origin on him we'll be ready to go out."

"Go out?" she asked, taking another step closer to him. She leaned in, extending her arm until it blocked the computer screen in an attempt to force him to look up at her.

He did.

And her breath caught.

His eyes were fierce and glittering with flecks of hazel inside the deep green, his dark brows raised, lips parted so that she glimpsed just the white of his teeth. She swallowed deeply against the burning that began immediately in the pit of her stomach. It wasn't a sick feeling, but one of instant arousal. All he was doing was looking at her, but she was leaning over his shoulder, her breasts touching him, nipples hardening in response.

"You mean you're going to go after him?" she asked, licking her now-dry lips immediately.

"I am."

"And you're going to— What are you going to do when you find him?"

She could hear the words and knew the answer before he responded.

"Why?"

"Because he's dangerous."

"Only to me."

He shook his head. "To you and whoever else he decides to bite or, worse, kill."

"He wasn't going to kill me," she said quietly, swallowing again. "He could have, but he didn't."

"And he won't get another chance," Phelan replied vehemently. "I won't let him near you again, I don't care if he did bite you. I won't let him claim you."

"What does that mean?" she asked, her gaze slipping from his eyes down to his mouth. It was a nice mouth and it instantly sparked the memory of his scorching-hot kisses.

He frowned then but did not move. To be exact, his body had gone as still as stone from the moment she'd leaned into him.

"It means—" he began, then clamped his lips shut tightly.

"Tell me, Phelan," she persisted.

He moved quickly, as always, wrapping his arm around her waist and pulling her down on his lap.

"His bite automatically made you his beta," he told her, a hand reaching up to cup her chin. "He created you. But you're not his mate, not until he claims you. He can't do that until the night of the full moon. But I plan to kill him long before that."

Marena listened to him speak. She inhaled the insanely erotic scent of him, snuggling her ass into the already-rigid length of his cock. No man had ever held her like this before and a few days ago she would have sworn it wasn't something she'd missed. But now, especially with his hand tightly holding her head still, her gaze intent on his, she felt really good sitting here. Really good and damned aroused.

"I'm not anybody's mate," she said, because it just wasn't in her nature to be owned or "claimed" by anyone. She didn't give a damn about their lycan laws; that just wasn't happening.

He surprised her immensely by saying, "Neither am I," before taking her mouth in another one of those heated and hungry kisses that had her struggling to breathe.

"Take this off," he growled between placing nipping bites along the line of her jaw where his hand had just held.

Marena didn't have a chance to consider if she was going to acquiesce or argue; his hands had already pushed the material from her shoulders. The movement was so rough the loose knot at her waist slipped free and before she knew it she was bare from the waist down.

His mouth was instantly on a nipple, his large hand lifting her breast to accommodate the action. Her hands went to his broad shoulders where she could do nothing but hold on as his tongue circled around her nipple until she was bucking beneath him, her back arching as she moaned. When Marena thought she would surely come from the sinful acts of his tongue alone, Phelan switched to the other breast, paying the same homage until she screamed his name.

That seemed to flip another switch in him, because in the next seconds he had his hands on her waist as he lifted her onto the desk. The keyboard and the monitor moved farther behind her, until Marena was afraid they might be knocked totally from the desk. But Phelan reached around, moving them off to the side, then giving her an ominous look that warned her to "hold on."

Going on instinct alone, she let her palms fall flat to the desk, only seconds before Phelan grabbed the backs of her legs, lifting them until they were spread into a wide V. He dipped his head next and licked her from the tight bud of her anus to the hardened hood of her clit.

The silent warning hadn't been enough, and by the time Phelan was finished licking and sucking her Marena had felt her nails scraping along the top of the desk. His name fell from her lips like a CD stuck on loop and when she came the volume went so high she thought it was quite possible that everyone in that house had heard her.

CHAPTER 7

"You're fucking her and she hasn't even had her first shift yet," Malec said. His words tight and accusatory as they stood in the living room, near the fireplace that Channing had lit before dinner.

"None. Of. Your. Business," Phelan stated tightly, stepping closer so that he and Malec were now toe-to-toe. Their voices were lowered because Marena, Kira, and Caroline weren't that far away.

They'd all moved into the living room after dinner, glasses of wine or coffee or nothing in hand. The women—Caroline, Kira, and Marena—were standing close to the window because that's where Marena had walked to. She'd been looking out to the dark stretch of land that surrounded the back of the house. The forest wasn't visible on nights when there were no stars or moonlight in sight.

"Channing couldn't trace that Hunter back to any pack," Malec replied, not backing down.

Phelan gritted his teeth. "So we have another Solo." He didn't like the thought of there being another lycan with no ties to anyone as their next target.

Malec shook his head. "You know a Solo has a different scent than pack lycans. But you were adamant that this

Davis character was a Hunter. How did you come to that conclusion?"

His frown deepened as Phelan looked over Malec's shoulder to Marena. Caroline had brought Marena's bag and purse from the room she'd been assigned to last night down to Malec's rooms about an hour before dinner. Phelan had dismissed the blatant act, deciding not to give it a second thought. It was only moments after he'd brought Marena to yet another climax. His dick had remained rock hard as he'd stood behind the door, reaching his hand out to accept the bags from Caroline. There was no doubt the lycan had known what he and Marena were doing and had apparently wasted no time running back to tell Malec. These mated unions in this house were frustrating Phelan more and more.

Marena wore a gray dress tonight, belted at the waist and just a few inches above her knees. Her long, straight hair was pulled over one shoulder, and while the look on her face was that of someone just a little bit stressed, the confidence in her stance and tone was in direct contrast. Of course, all of that was the physical. It was what any other lycan in this room would have seen when they looked at her.

Marena's unique scent, however, was all his.

Even now in this room full of other lycans he could pick her out with his eyes closed. He could inhale deeply and let the soft, erotic aroma that reminded him of honey and pine trees filter through his mind, his body, and—

That was the scent he'd picked up that night on the highway. The deep earthy smell that reminded him of the wild, the uninhibited, the Hunters. Only it hadn't been that scent alone.

"I was wrong," Phelan said through clenched teeth. "Dammit, I was all wrong."

Malec nodded slightly. "She's more than just someone that got bitten by a lycan, isn't she?"

"No," Phelan replied immediately. "No. She has nothing to do with us, or them. Davis bit her; he pulled her in. She's—"

She doesn't belong here. She doesn't belong with you, Eureka's voice interrupted. *I told you it would always be me.*

"She's what?" Malec asked, continuing to stare at Phelan with his silent accusations.

Phelan shook his head. He closed his eyes in an attempt to get his thoughts, words, and feelings straight.

She has to go. Now! Or there'll be trouble, Eureka declared. *Trouble unlike anything you've ever imagined.*

"Phelan?" Malec asked, cupping a hand on his shoulder. "You all right?"

Phelan lowered his head, flexing his fingers at his sides as his claws extended, a growl rumbling low in his chest.

"Phelan?" Malec called to him again.

You know what you must do, Phelan, Eureka taunted. *She. Must. Go!*

"Phelan?" Channing was there now, calling his name as well.

Phelan felt himself swaying. He felt the room around him shifting. No, not the room, the world. And when he opened his eyes finally, his gaze went directly to her.

"Marena," he whispered.

His mate.

Phelan was staring at her. Marena could feel the intensity of his gaze bearing down like a heat lamp on the back of her neck, but she refused to turn around or acknowledge him. This was also how she'd decided to dismiss the fact that weird things had already begun to happen to her. She figured it was as a result of that bite on her shoulder that didn't look like it was healing at all.

That was the reason she was so drawn to Phelan. It was why all he had to do was look at her with those sexy as hell eyes, or kiss her with those dangerous and desirable lips, or touch her with skillful hands and she was like putty in his hands. She was ready and eager to do any- and everything she could to receive the pleasure from being with him. Whether it was simply his oral pleasure or the feel of his thick length buried to the hilt inside of her, she craved it and found herself wondering when her next opportunity to experience it would come.

It was ridiculous and demeaning and so she'd purposely spent the entire dinner looking in the opposite direction of him to where Channing and Caroline were sitting. She chatted with the two of them almost exclusively. That wasn't because she didn't care for Blaez or Kira, but they were sitting in Phelan's direction and she was trying to ignore him. Or rather, she was trying to ignore the crazy and intense desire she'd so quickly developed for him.

"So you didn't leave a boyfriend back in San Francisco, did you, Marena?" Kira asked as the three of them stood together.

The alpha female hadn't even tried to be subtle. Marena didn't think it was possible for her anyway, which she kind of respected. The last thing she wanted was to have to deal with catty women in the midst of everything else that was going on. Then again, she thought with an inner chuckle, how could they be catty if they were actually wolves?

"No boyfriend," Marena replied, taking a sip from her wineglass.

It was an excellent cabernet sauvignon, full bodied and flavorful. She took another sip.

"No time for one, since I'm a workaholic," she admitted. "Which is why I need Davis to show his conniving face so I can get back to work."

Caroline nodded. "I'm a veterinarian," she said. "I used to work at the clinic in town before things got a little . . . weird. I miss working with the animals and the variety of the day. So I can understand you wanting to get back to your job."

"When you say 'weird,' is that because you're publicly involved in a ménage relationship?" Kira wasn't the only one who could be candid.

The alpha female arched a brow at Marena's question and then smiled in Caroline's direction.

"Yes, I am in a ménage relationship. Do you think that's strange? Oh, no," she said, tucking her hair behind her ears. "Maybe you think it's a little odd that these very sexy and virile men would look toward full-figured women for their love interests?"

Marena frowned at that odd question, tilting her head to the side as she considered her response. "I've never had a problem with my body and I've been what doctors call 'obese' according to their BMI charts and guidelines since I was seven years old. Yet even now, at twenty-eight years old, I've never been diagnosed with high blood pressure, diabetes, or any other medical condition directly related to obesity. I'm healthy and sexy and don't give a damn who thinks differently. So, the answer to your last question is no, I'm not at all amazed that a group of very attractive men would have the good sense and awesome taste to look to a plus-size woman for their pleasure. Why the hell wouldn't they?"

Kira laughed then. Loud and long, until she almost dropped her half-full glass of wine on the pretty Aubusson rug.

Caroline had smiled as well, nodding her head as she reiterated her first question, "So it's just the ménage thing you find strange?"

Marena shook her head. "Not at all. To each his own. If that's what makes you and them happy, then who am I to have a problem with it? In fact, let's just get this out of the way right now. I don't have a problem with any of you. Feline shape-shifters or lycans or whatever else might be walking this earth. It's a big planet, room enough for all of us in my book."

"If ever we thought of creating a lycan council you'd get my vote as spokesperson," Kira said finally after her laughter had subsided. "I like you, Marena."

"I do, too," Caroline added. "And that's a good thing, especially since Phelan's so taken by you."

"No," Marena replied quickly. "He's not. He doesn't do girlfriends."

"Really?" Kira asked. "He told you that?"

Marena nodded. "Yes. He did."

"When? Before or after he made you scream his name?" Kira continued.

Now that was a little beyond the honest scope and Marena hesitated a moment. That was a mistake.

"No, don't answer that. Tell us this, Marena: Why did you drive all the way from San Francisco to Montana? If you wanted to get back to work so quickly, why go so far?" Caroline asked, this time lifting her own elegantly arched brow.

Her red-painted lips had tilted slightly as if she was enjoying Marena's discomfort.

"I . . . I don't know," Marena replied honestly, thinking back to the afternoon she'd left her condo and climbed into her SUV.

She'd just begun to drive knowing only that she needed to get away from the police who would no doubt show up at her apartment momentarily. Tammi said they were asking about her and wanted to question her. It was only a matter of time and that's why she'd left, but she hadn't thought, not once, of where she was going.

"I just drove until the buzzer went off telling me I was low on gas. I pulled over at the next gas station and got right back onto the road. Continuing nonstop," she finished quietly, her gaze going to the window once more.

She looked out to the dark night with no light in sight. It was an ominous blackness that, for some reason, she felt a kinship to.

"Until Phelan found you in that B and B," Kira finished. "What made you stop there?"

Her fingers clenched the stem of the wineglass until she thought she might actually break it. "I was hungry, I think," Marena started, trying to remember back to those moments when she was in the SUV and she decided to pull off the road. "I wanted to eat and to lie down. I was in so much pain and I felt so sick and then I wasn't anymore. The pain was gone and . . . and Phelan was there."

"Phelan was there because it's where he was supposed to be to save his mate," Caroline told her matter-of-factly.

"His what? No," Marena said, shaking her head. "I'm an attorney. I don't do boyfriends or romantic connections. It gets in the way and I can't . . . I don't want . . . He's not—"

The words she was stumbling over were halted immediately, only to be replaced by a yearning so deep and so warm that she almost buckled with its intensity. That feeling had come as his hand touched her shoulder.

"Are you ready for bed?" Phelan asked.

Marena looked up to see Kira and Caroline smiling knowingly at her. When she looked at Phelan it was to his drawn brows, thin stretched lips, and a muscle twitching in his jaw. He was upset, angry possibly. At her? Or something that had been said? She didn't know and she didn't care. Just as she didn't give a damn what Caroline and Kira had been trying to say. Phelan was nothing to her. None of these people were. No, she acknowledged that they all would be a means to an end once she found Davis. That's all that mattered here. Find Davis, clear her name, get back to her job and her life.

Nothing else.

Not even the sexy lycan who was staring at her while his hand rested on the shoulder where she'd been bitten. Especially not him, Marena thought as she once again attempted to ignore the pulsating of her pussy and the heaviness of her breasts.

CHAPTER 8

His body jolted with the sudden and intense pain ripping like a fresh wound down the left side of his face. Phelan didn't growl, he didn't yell out in agony, but he did reach up grabbing tufts of his hair and pulling until the pain there matched the pain in his face. Angered by that action, he quickly pulled his hands down, fists clenching in his lap as his eyes watered and he opened them to the darkness of his bedroom.

Tossing back the sheets that had tangled between his legs, he rose from the bed, walking steadily toward the patio doors. He'd chosen this back part of the house as his refuge because it wasn't close to the rooms of any of the other pack mates. Blaez and Kira had their own suite on the second level of the house while Channing and Malec were located on the far end of the first level. Here Phelan could be alone with his demons. He could sit in the darkness or out on his small porch with the closest view into the forest and think about the life he'd been given and the burdens he'd been forced to bear. Alone.

Once outside he leaned forward, bracing his hands on the wrought-iron railing. It was one of the few spots where they'd used something other than wood on the house, because Phelan had liked the strength and the clean lines of the black iron. Everything in his world was about strength. A lycan needed inner strength as much as the physical because they were created to sustain whatever came their way. That wasn't entirely correct; they were created out of vengeance and pain and to an extent sentenced to live the same way. It had taken Phelan a while to absorb and accept that fact. His inner strength had been the only reason he'd been able to bear all the disappointments and pitfalls in his life.

Heat fused his face and for a moment Phelan could visualize the moment Eureka had wounded him. It had been a dark night, similar to this one, only there had just been a storm, so the scent of rain, wet leaves, and fresh mud filtered through the air. They'd been standing at the base of a cliff near Mount Elden in Colorado and he'd just finished telling Eureka that their time together was over.

"You are not who I thought you were," Phelan had said, hating the sound of the words as they hit the air. He'd despised the fact that she'd deceived him, lied to him, and most likely used him.

He had been a fool to think there was anything real between them, to believe for one second that a lycan could have the happiness that a normal human did. From the time of his birth Phelan hadn't known that type of happiness. His parents had left him at an orphanage when he was five years old, after they'd taught him everything about the lycans and the world within which they were cursed to live. They'd simply walked away and he'd never seen them again.

Sixteen years later, he'd felt like he was once again experiencing that feeling of desolation, of loss so severe he could barely breathe. He despised that feeling, right down to his very core.

"I am the love of your life," Eureka had replied, coming to stand right beside him, her hand going to his elbow and holding tightly.

A day before, possibly even an hour prior, Phelan would have relished that touch. He would have enjoyed the way it made him feel inside—wanted, needed, possibly loved. But now he knew differently. He'd seen and heard all that he needed to when he was in the Olympic realm. He knew the truth.

"You are a vengeful bitch!" he stated vehemently, pulling his arm away from her and taking a step back. "It is your job, inbred in the very cells of your body. Your main goal is to punish in the name of justice. Instead, you do his bidding, no matter what that is."

"You are wrong," she replied calmly.

"I am right!" Phelan roared, his teeth elongating. "I saw you with him, saw you vowing to kill me and any other lycan that got in your way! You pledged your allegiance to Zeus."

"It is what I am supposed to do," she answered. "You already knew who and what I was when we met. But then things changed, Phelan. You changed them for me, for us."

She looked and sounded sincere, but she had been the same way standing in that garden, surrounded by tall, colorful and exotic plants, looking up at Zeus as if he were her personal savior. The sight was burned into Phelan's memory, as was the rage he'd felt at that moment. He'd wanted to kill the god right then and there for once again wreaking havoc on his life. He hadn't, thanks to Blaez and the intense training they'd undergone for their covert ops team. Phelan knew at that moment that he was in control of himself and his destiny. Even in the Olympic realm, when faced with a fury, he was still in control.

"I was a fool," he admitted solemnly.

"You are my love," she'd insisted.

"No." He'd shaken his head. "I am nothing to you now. And you are nothing to me."

"That is a lie! We are everything. We are the new! We can change everything together. What difference does anything or anyone else make as long as we are together?" she'd continued, her eyes growing brighter.

Phelan had not answered her. He had not told her that the difference was the lycan who had saved his life, the one whom he had vowed to protect until the end of his days. He did not mention Blaez because he no longer trusted that Eureka wasn't sent to kill him.

"I should have known better," was his stilted reply. "I should have known that there was no happiness for us. For any of us. There is only the duty of who and what we are. That's all there will ever be."

"You are wrong, Phelan. There is more. We've had more," she pleaded.

"We've had lies and deceit! You never said that you were directly under Zeus's authority. Not one time did you claim to be one of his pawns."

"I cannot change who and what I am! I am a fury. My family are the justice keepers in the Olympic realm," she argued.

"And in the human realm? What are you doing here? What justice could you possibly dispense on this earth? Or is there another reason Zeus wants you here?"

She'd gone silent then, as did everything else around

them. The wind had stilled and there were no sounds from any other creatures of the night.

"I am going to turn and walk away. Do not follow me. Do not come to me again. This," he'd said with a bitter taste in the back of his throat, "is done."

He'd turned then and taken only one step when the air picked up violently, swirling around him as if he'd walked into the center of a storm. She'd made a horrific sound, somewhere between the deafening screech of a harpy and the wounded call of a bird. When Phelan turned again she was right there, arms stretched wide. Her face had looked thinner, her eyes turned totally black as her long, raven-colored hair blew in haunting tendrils around her face.

"It will never be done!" she yelled, her voice a hollow echo on the strong winds. "You will always be mine!"

She was swinging before Phelan could react, the vicious claws of her right hand slashing across his face.

"No one will want you scarred and broken. No one but me, and I will never leave you, no matter how far you try to run! And you will never find another, never give your heart and soul to a mate. Only me! Only us!"

She'd continued to scream even as her nails had dug deeper into his skin, scorching him with a heat that Phelan swore he could feel in the core of every bone of his body. It had taken all the physical strength he'd been born with and accrued in the military to grab hold of her wrists and to finally pull her hand free of his face. He would never strike a woman; his father had engrained that into his head early on. Then as he'd grown into a man, Phelan had continued to stand by that rule. Still, he wanted her out of his sight before she could tempt his resolve any further. He picked her up from the ground where she'd fallen back and he growled long and loud into her face. He shifted so that she could feel the full rage of the beast within him and then he tossed her away, watching as she tumbled over the cliff. She would spread her wings and fly; of that Phelan had no doubt. He just wanted her to fly away from him forever.

With his face bleeding and his heart seemingly ripped straight from his chest, Phelan turned away. Still in lycan form, he'd run hard and fast, not stopping until he was deep into a forest, not sure in which state or which realm. There he'd stayed for too many days to count. Until he'd known what he must do, how he needed to proceed from that moment on.

The memory was so fresh and so potent, Phelan was now out of breath as he stood on the patio. He gripped the iron railing so hard he could hear it cracking the wood where it was embedded in the floor.

"It's okay now," Marena said from behind him, her voice a husky whisper. "It was just a nightmare. I've been having them a lot myself lately."

She hadn't touched him, thank the gods. Yet she'd stood very close, almost until the skin of her arm could rub along the skin of his. The touch hadn't been necessary and neither had the words, Phelan suspected. The comfort was there in her presence alone. The same comfort he afforded her when she was in pain. It was there between them, as natural as the rising of the sun. Another anomaly he wanted to curse, to rail against in anger. Only at this moment he simply did not have the strength.

"It is painful," he admitted in a quiet voice, a hand lifting to his scar before he knew better and stopped himself.

Marena moved then, leaning closer to him and lifting her arm until her hand covered his on his face. Gently, she pushed his fingers away, letting her own trace the ugly bumps of skin. Phelan couldn't bear to look at her while she did. He did not want to see the pity in her eyes.

"A woman did this," he heard her say softly. "She was hurt and confused and lashed out in anger. Petty and foolish anger that hurt you physically and mentally."

Phelan shook his head. "No. Not inside," he insisted. "I let her inside once, but that was the one and only time. This was not done to hurt me. It was done to dissuade you."

He did look at her then, saw the quick flash of shock and then knowledge in her amber eyes. This was the first time he noticed that her eyes were the color of Kentucky bourbon, his father's favorite drink. Her lashes were long and fanned over her cheeks when she closed her eyes. She was tall, not near his six feet three inches in height, but the top of her head met his chin, so that all she had to do was look up and their gazes were instantly locked. That's how they stood now, as he'd turned a bit when she touched him. Their sides rubbed against the railing, her hand on his face, his fingers clenching and releasing as he resisted the urge to touch her in return.

"I didn't even know you when this was done," she told him. "I had no idea I would ever know someone like you, so how could she want to warn me away?"

"I believe she knew the time would come," Phelan admitted. Everyone had seemed to know a mate would soon appear for him. Everyone but him, of course.

No, that wasn't true. Phelan hadn't doubted there was a mate out there for him. He'd simply refused to take one, and right now, knowing all that he knew, Phelan wasn't certain that he was going to change his mind on that stance.

Regardless of how tempting Marena Panos may be.

"But I don't do girlfriends," he reiterated what he'd already told her, taking a slow step back, until her hand fell from his face. "I don't do relationships or connections of any kind."

"Okay," she replied after a few seconds of silence. Nodding her head, she folded her arms over her ample chest, turning back to lean her bottom on the railing this time.

Tonight she'd opted for shorts, skimpy and flirty with large pink hearts all over the white material. The tank top she wore was pink also, like the flowers that grew beneath his mother's bedroom window. Phelan frowned then, ignoring how delicious the swell of her breasts looked squeezed together by the tight cotton material.

He hadn't thought about his parents in years and in the last ten minutes he'd thought of them twice as he'd looked at her.

"I'm guessing you have a reason for taking that stance. Would you like to share?" she asked.

Phelan's immediate response was, "No."

To that she'd simply raised a brow.

"How do you expect me to take that answer? It could simply be a dare, to see how intent I may be on testing your resolve, or you could be dead serious because you've got some deep, dark past that's scared you way more than she did physically." Marena shrugged. "There are a few other options, but it would be much simpler if you just told me the truth."

He stood a good distance away from her now, testing a theory that had just popped into his mind. Earlier today she'd taken a shower while he'd been in his office and she hadn't complained of any pain. Tonight he'd walked out here and stood for a few moments and she hadn't had any pain. Or maybe she had and that's why she'd come out here looking for him. So he'd walked to the other end of the deck. It wasn't that far, maybe thirteen feet. She hadn't moved, only watched him curiously, no doubt waiting for his response to her question.

The response he didn't want to give but suspected was going to be the only way to end this conversation. He hadn't known Marena long, but what he knew for certain was that she was used to asking questions and getting answers. In fact, he was betting that her mind was whirling right this moment with ways to get the answers from him that she wanted. All of which showed her skills as a talented litigator. For some odd reason, that made him proud.

"I'm not good with connections. My parents left me at an orphanage when I was five years old," he told her, and was surprised at how simple the words sounded to his ears.

The admission had long since lost its initial sting, but normally the afterthought angered him. Tonight, for whatever reason, it didn't. That was just another event in his life, one he'd managed to overcome, much like all the others.

"And for a time you blamed yourself for their decision," she spoke quietly but matter-of-factly. Almost as if she knew the story he was about to tell.

"When did you finally come to your senses and realize you had no control over what they did?" she asked.

Phelan almost smiled at her candor. People didn't always say exactly what they meant, nor did they mean what they said. He was beginning to realize that Marena, however, most likely did both.

"I was ten when I experienced my first shift," he told her,

still keeping his distance but watching her carefully, and attentively.

"It's a little younger than most born lycans, but my father predicted it might happen that way. My parents made sure to tell me everything there was to know about lycans and our origin before they left me. I guess that was a plus for them in the parenting-skills department. Anyway, I grew stronger from that point on, until one day in middle school I actually turned the teacher's desk over because she'd given me a failing grade on a test just because I didn't put my name on the paper. That's when I learned I also had the ability to cross over to the Olympic realm."

"What's the Olympic realm?" she inquired, immediately curious.

"It's where the gods reside, the place from which the lycan curse originated. When Zeus changed Lykaon into a wolf, the change also gave Lykaon the power to move within the realms. Lykaon passed that power along to Nyktimos and I was lucky enough to get that particular slice of DNA through my full-bred lycan parents."

"So you can be here one minute and in another world the next?"

Phelan shook his head. "Something like that, yes."

She was quiet then, the air around them still.

"Is she from that other realm?"

"No," he replied, wondering why when he'd just told Marena about one of the greatest tragedies of his life she was still asking about Eureka.

"You didn't want any connections because your parents left you, so you thought everyone would eventually leave. But then she came along and you let her in, and she hurt you. Physically and mentally."

"She cursed me," Phelan said instantly, and regretted it the moment Marena's eyes grew wider, her brow lifting.

"Cursed? Are you serious?"

He sighed, feeling instantly like he and Marena were not alone. Looking around, trying to see through the darkness, Phelan ignored her question for as long as he could.

"I'm serious about the fact that she tried to curse me. About whether or not the curse is real, I'm not totally on board with that one."

"Good," Marena said with a slight chuckle. "Because I was about to declare you all the way crazy."

"Really?" Phelan replied, taking steps to close the distance between them. She hadn't made any mention of being in pain; for whatever reason he still wasn't sure. Only that it could possibly be because he was in his rooms, so that even though his body wasn't physically close to her, his personal space was.

At any rate, he didn't like not being physically close to her. That wasn't something Phelan had wanted to accept before, but now, tonight, he suddenly wasn't in the mood to deny it.

"You think I'm crazy because I'm a lycan and I live out here in the midst of the mountains with a pack of lycans. But what about you?" he asked as he came closer to her, so close that when he reached out a hand his fingertips instantly brushed over the line of her jaw.

"What about me?" she asked, lifting her chin defiantly, her eyes already tinged with desire.

Phelan absolutely loved that about her. The way she so quickly went from resolute, pissed off, or downright angry to totally aroused. Her long lashes fanned as her blinking came slower like she was already intoxicated, when he hadn't even offered her a drink.

"You're not crazy for working yourself to the bone just to please a family that obviously already loves you?" It was a serious question, part of the things he'd observed about her in the days that he'd known her.

She blinked quickly and almost looked away, but that stubborn part of her refused. "I just want them to be proud of me," she replied. "And how do you know they love me? You don't know anything about me or my family."

"I know that you're willing to face the lycan that took your humanity without a second thought in order to get a job that you may or may not be able to keep in the long run, just to impress them. That tells me that they must mean a lot to you, and as you don't strike me as a woman that would waste her time or emotions on someone that didn't deserve them, I've concluded that you come from a very loving and supportive family. Your parents are probably already proud of you and would be if you were flipping hamburgers at a local McDonald's."

Phelan hadn't realized he'd come to all those conclusions about her until this very moment. Truth be told, he hadn't wanted to admit how much he'd thought about her since the night he'd followed her into that B and B. He seemed to be admitting all sorts of things tonight.

"You don't know me," she said, and this time she did look away.

Phelan caught her chin in his palm, turning her slowly until she faced him. "I know what you're about to become," he told her seriously. "I know how you feel when you're about to climax into my mouth or over my dick." He rubbed his thumb over her bottom lip, pressing inside until the tip of her tongue swiped across his skin. "Oh," he groaned. "I know you very well, Marena. So well, I know exactly what you need at this moment."

She shook her head, even as her body quivered against his. "I don't *need* anything," she told him defiantly.

The words lost a good measure of steam, as when she'd spoken them her tongue had touched his thumb again and her eyes had grown darker. Phelan smiled knowingly and she moved away from him. He watched her walk back into the room and waited a beat before following her.

"You don't need this?" he asked, cupping his already-erect cock.

The entire time they'd been standing outside she hadn't once looked at him. Of course she'd already known he was nude. It's the way he always slept. She hadn't said anything about it when she'd climbed onto the opposite side of his king-size bed, and Phelan hadn't been in the mood to ask her personal preferences. He'd slept naked beside her the night before and planned to do so again, for however long it was that she would be sleeping with him.

She turned to face him, standing on the other side of the bed. Her nipples had already gone hard, poking through the thin layer of that tank top as if they were calling him out personally. His erection throbbed in his hand at the thought.

"I'll say it again," she started, glancing briefly at his rigid length, then lifting her eyes up quickly to meet his. "I do not *need* anything."

When he didn't speak but continued to stroke his length, staring at her knowingly, she huffed.

"Damn! Is that all lycans think about?" she questioned. "Kira and Caroline were talking about it earlier. Malec and Channing both watch Caroline's every move as if they're ready to pounce on her at any moment. And the only reason Blaez's desire for Kira might seem a little on the tame side—even though I saw them in the kitchen, and let's just say if I hadn't walked in they would have been on that counter doing more than tossing the salad we had for dinner—their yearning for each other is almost palpable at any given time. I swear it's like this place should be a brothel instead of a home."

She'd grabbed a pillow when she was done, pounding her fists into its sides, then tossing it down on the bed in frustration. Phelan almost smiled, but he knew better. He knew exactly what Marena needed—a lesson in lycan lust. And he was just the one to teach her.

Moving without speaking, he picked up two remote controls, one he used to switch on the seventy-inch flat-screen television that fit perfectly into the built-in shelves across from his bed. The other operated the Blu-ray player. Opening a black box on the very last shelf, Phelan pulled out a disc and slipped it into the Blu-ray. He stood back then, pressing the PLAY button, and waited for the picture to appear on-screen. He didn't turn to see what Marena was doing because he knew she was still standing, still battling between what her body wanted and what her mind thought was appropriate.

The screen became alight with none other than the full moon and Phelan sensed her body going totally still. The newborn lycan in her immediately coming to attention. Smoke rolled from the bottom of the screen, lifting upward until it almost covered the moon, but the orb grew brighter, getting closer, until it filled the entire screen, its luminescence washing over the room. Phelan felt his muscles tense as he put down the remotes and let his hands fall to his sides. This particular video always affected him in the same way.

Installing the surveillance cameras at Club Entice had been so he could keep an eye on Eureka and her guests. Not along romantic lines, but Phelan wanted to know if she was making any alliances with otherworldly beings or even humans that he should know about. His gut told him he still needed to keep an eye on her, even though over the years since they'd been apart she'd made no attempt to come after him or Blaez.

Marena's gasp echoed throughout the room, but Phelan did not turn to look at her. He continued to watch the scene where the two female lycans had entered the room, naked. One grabbed the other around the waist and leaned in to kiss her mouth. The kiss was heated and wet, the camera zooming in to show the women's tongues dueling with each other. As the kiss progressed, one of the women slipped her hand between the other's thighs, fingering her until the woman was gasping with her own pleasure. This continued for a few minutes more with one woman sucking the other's breast as she continued to thrust her finger deep inside the woman's pussy.

Two male lycans entered the room at this point. Both naked. They stood right beside the women, looking at them for a brief moment while stroking their rigid cocks similar to the way Phelan was now stroking his. When the men moved closer and kissed, with the same intensity that the women had previously, Phelan wondered what Marena was doing and what she was feeling. He did not turn around to see.

After the kiss the men moved to stand behind each woman, grabbing their breasts and pressing their dicks against the women's asses. In the next seconds it became a licking and sucking fest that eventually turned into the foursome fucking like the uninhibited creatures they were.

Another gasp from Marena, this time one that sounded more like a moan, had Phelan finally turning around.

"Why would you do that?" she asked from where she was now lying on the bed, her shorts discarded, legs spread wide, hands cupping both breasts.

Inwardly Phelan smiled. Her lycan was definitely beginning to take over.

"It's what you needed to see, what the lycan in you needed to relate to," he told her as he moved to the end of the bed closest to where she lay.

From there he could see the pretty folds of her pussy and the rise of her ample breasts as she tweaked and pulled her nipples.

"Every kiss, lick, suckle, we feel it all, tenfold," he explained to her, jerking his cock so hard he thought he might actually come simply from watching her. "You felt those kisses, didn't you? When the two women were kissing, you could feel the desire building inside you and you tasted their tongues as if they were in your mouth."

She shook her head then, her hair splayed like dark tendrils along the pillow.

"I'm not . . . I . . . ," she attempted to say, then paused. Her breath was coming in quick pants now, her tongue licking along her bottom lip, then over the top line of her teeth. "I don't do lesbian," she finally managed to say.

"We don't bother to name what we do or feel," Phelan told her, moving closer until he was now standing at the side of the bed, using one hand to rub along her inner thigh.

The skin here was so soft, so pliable. He loved clenching

his fingers, grabbing it as tightly as he could, then releasing it. Marena sucked in a breath when he did that.

"I've never watched porn before, either," she admitted, her brown eyes gazing up at him.

Phelan stared down at her, shaking his head. "Again with the titles and names. That's a human thing," he told her as he leaned down closer to lick his tongue along the top line of her teeth the way she had. "You're a lycan now, Marena. A hot and insatiable lycan that I'm going to enjoy fucking until she can no longer think straight."

"That's not what I'm here for." She whispered her reply, but when he lifted her thigh so that her entire leg was coming up, her foot planting itself firmly on the mattress, Marena did not resist.

No, instead she let her other leg fall farther back onto the bed, until the lips of her vulva were peeling back like a lovely flower, revealing the sweet nectar inside.

"Beautiful," Phelan murmured while staring down at her.

She wasn't cleanly shaved, but her dark curls had been trimmed to a landing-strip patch that was tempting every ounce of his strength. He wanted to lick along that path, straight down to the skin just above the hood of her clit.

"It would be better if you were bare," he said gruffly. "Much, much better."

"Nobody's ever said that to me before," Marena replied.

"Then they were all fools. You'll feel everything from the brush of my breath to the slap of my palm deeper and more intensely when you're bare."

"The what?" she asked, and Phelan knew exactly what part she'd wanted him to repeat.

Instead of doing so verbally, he moved the hand from her thigh, bringing it back slightly before slapping his fingers against her pussy. She jerked off the bed and he did it again. This time she hissed and arched her back. When she settled, looking up at him with pleasure-filled eyes, Phelan did it again, this time keeping his hand on the warm flesh and cupping her tightly.

She undulated her hips, rubbing herself thoroughly into his palm, her hands now gripping her breasts. Her eyes were hot and intense on his and Phelan moved in closer, until his dick was only inches away from her mouth. She blinked and then moved so that her tongue could swipe over the bead of cum that had surfaced at his slit. Phelan moved in closer, until he was all but kneeling on the bed beside her, his hand directing his cock into the warmth of her mouth.

Marena sucked him in quickly and Phelan slipped two fingers into her dripping center. Closing his eyes, he relished the feeling of warmth from her mouth and her pussy, his teeth clenching tightly together as he wondered distantly if he'd ever felt this good with a woman before. He wasn't even fucking her and yet there was this complacency, this comfort zone he felt himself slipping into. It was blissful and satisfying knowing that however he touched her, however she touched and sucked him in return, they would each be satisfied beyond measure. If he had to pull his fingers and his cock out of her right now, Phelan would have known the delectable feeling of her, no matter what.

He had that knowledge or feeling for no other woman. Not even Eureka.

With that thought he wanted to be inside Marena right now. He pulled away from her, hearing her groan of displeasure.

"Don't worry, baby. I've got you," he said, moving her over on the bed.

When Phelan climbed onto the bed he angled his body on top of hers. She gripped his thighs and then his cock, taking him deep into her mouth once more. He stretched her legs wider, diving in with tongue extended to lick her glistening pussy. The more he licked and sucked, the more she did, until their noises were much louder than the television, filling the room with not only their combined scents but also sounds. It was erotic as hell as Phelan clenched her thick thighs between his fingers, while pumping his cock into her mouth.

She was taking him that way without any problem, letting him thrust in and out of her mouth as if it were her pussy. The sweet, wet, and hot pussy that his tongue couldn't get enough of, until his spine tingled, his legs stiffening as he was about to come into Marena's mouth. Pulling out quickly, Phelan shifted on the bed, turning Marena over and bringing her up onto her knees.

He leaned in, nipping her plump ass with his teeth, then kissing the spot and licking it. Over and over he did this until he felt like he'd covered the entire globe.

"Phelan," she whispered his name, poking her voluptuous bottom back into his face.

On a groan, Phelan pulled back, rubbing his hands over her plump ass, opening her cheeks and watching intently as the head of his cock made its way to its destination. The craving was deep and almost debilitating, wrapping around his throat and squeezing as he looked at the lightness of his cock moving between the slightly darker complexion of her ass. She was so wet, the head of his cock slid from her pussy entrance back to her anus and Phelan had to close his eyes to the immediate and intense pleasure shooting through his body as if someone had set off fireworks.

Marena pulled away quickly, her head turning until she could stare at him over her shoulder.

"Shhhh, baby. Not yet, I know," he told her, vowing to himself that he would take her there. He would own her ass before all was said and done.

Not wanting to inquire where that thought of ownership had come from or what the hell he planned to do about it, Phelan aimed his cock and thrust into her pussy with one smooth movement. She bucked beneath him and he grabbed hold of her hips, settling himself deep inside of her. When she was wiggling beneath him he knew she was more than ready and he began to pump, hard and fast, until they were both screaming, both letting loose the most powerful orgasms they had ever experienced.

CHAPTER 9

It was two weeks later when Marena awoke to excruciating pain. She curled into a fetal position at the corner of Phelan's bed resisting the urge to scream out in agony, but slowly losing the battle.

The pain had all but subsided during the last weeks as she and Phelan had remained virtually inseparable. They'd continued to search for Davis, and by "they" Marena meant the other lycans. Channing was steadily contacting other Devoted packs in the California area, asking questions about Davis and anyone he might have been associated with, while Malec, Blaez, and Kira worked to figure out what Davis's endgame might be. They were all certain there would be an endgame, especially Marena.

He'd stayed in her head. Day in and day out she'd heard him calling to her. Only his voice hadn't seemed as loud as it had before in the last couple of days. In fact, Marena had noticed that she wasn't as irritated by his calling to her, declaring her his, and telling her that he was still coming for her. She hadn't told Phelan about this new development. That thought came as a surprise to her, especially since lately she'd been telling Phelan a lot. In fact, she and Phelan had been sharing much more than Marena had ever thought they would.

"You're bonding," Blaez had told her yesterday morning right after breakfast.

It had been one of the first times that she'd been left alone with the alpha and she'd admitted to feeling just a little nervous in the first few seconds of their interaction. Blaez Trekas was a tall and imposing-looking man with his muscled physique, bald head, and thick goatee. The air of leadership was apparent in everything from his walk to the arch of his brow when he watched her as if he were actually looking inside of her, revealing everything he wanted to know about her without asking one single question.

"I know what that means in the human world," she'd said with her back facing the mantel.

They were in Phelan's room and Phelan was in the shower. In the mornings after breakfast she and Phelan had begun going for long walks throughout the forest. There he would explain to her more about the lycan world, the curse, and sometimes what might be coming with tomorrow's supermoon. They did not talk about Davis during these times, which could be the reason Marena hadn't told Phelan about the change in what she was feeling about the other lycan.

This was how she knew that things said in the human world often had different meanings in the lycan one. A huge part of her had begun to accept more openly that there were two worlds, both of which she would now have to deal with.

"It's normally when a new blood begins to cling to the lycan that created it," Blaez answered.

He'd slipped his hands into the side pockets of his black cargo pants that were tucked down into black steel-toed boots. The T-shirt he wore was also black and melded to his broad chest like a second skin. He looked as if he was ready for combat, sans a gun or some other type of weapon. The only other lycan in this house who dressed more like he was still in the marines than the others was Phelan. So Marena was well used to this look. Only on Phelan it had a very different effect on her. Blaez struck her as a commander about to either give an unwanted assignment or unveil an enemy. She wasn't certain which one was about to happen but squared her shoulders and lifted her chin to let him know she was ready for the confrontation regardless.

"He did not create me," she'd replied clearly, as if she needed to reveal this fact to him.

"No," Blaez said with a quizzical tilt of his head. "And that is what's so very interesting about you, Marena Panos. You have been in this house for more than two weeks now and in that time I have been watching you. I've observed you with Kira and Caroline, Channing and Malec, and most certainly with Phelan. We were all shocked the night he brought you here and curious to see how this would unfold."

"Nothing is unfolding," she told him. "You're trying to find a Hunter and I'm hoping that when you do I'll be able to salvage what's left of my career."

The words sounded hollow to her ears and it made her unsteady. Marena had never heard from Gail. Phelan had given her a brand-new laptop to use and a secure Internet connection that would allow her to log into both her work and personal e-mail without being detected or traced. Unfortunately, with that she'd immediately discovered that her work e-mail account had been deactivated. The automated message received when Phelan had attempted to send her a message from one of his many e-mail accounts was that she was no longer with the firm and to contact Tammi Logan to find out which attorney in the firm had inherited Marena's cases.

It had taken her a couple of days to deal with that bit of news, days when Phelan had remained closer to her than ever.

"You will never be able to return to your old life," Blaez said as easily as if he were telling her the time of day. "That time has passed."

No shit, she thought with an inward sigh. Since learning of her seemingly easy dismissal from the firm she'd dedicated countless hours to, Marena had thought long and hard about her next steps. She was still an attorney and still planned to practice, regardless of what might now be inside of her.

"I am still part of the human world. My family is human and there's no way I'm going to walk away from them, or from what I've worked so hard for all my life."

"No one is asking you to do that," Blaez told her. "It will simply be on a different level at this point. As I said, you are bonding with Phelan. That is a very interesting development."

"He's helping me to embrace the change," she stated, just as Phelan had told her often.

"Yes," Blaez said with a nod of his head. "He is doing that very well. And you are adapting. I've seen you reading the books and speaking with the females. I know that you are coming to terms with what we are and what we are facing."

"I'm doing the best that I can," she admitted.

"You are doing a phenomenal job and I believe that is because of your connection to Phelan. I've never seen him this way before. He is different with you."

Now Marena folded her arms across her chest. She did not want to talk about what was between her and Phelan on a personal level with Blaez. Hell, she and Phelan did a damn good job not discussing that particular topic between themselves; no way was she about to let someone else have that privilege.

"He is doing what has to be done," she stated seriously, not liking the emptiness in the pit of her stomach as the words were released.

"Yes, Phelan will always do what has to be done. But with you, he is also doing what he wants to do. I can see it in the way he watches over you, how he protects you. It is the way a lycan looks at their mate," he told her.

Marena didn't openly flinch, but a barrier immediately went up in her mind. She'd heard this word many times since she'd been here. Kira and Caroline were sure to talk about this particular aspect of the lycan life with her as often as they could. So Marena knew how serious it was for a lycan to find and claim a mate. She also knew that this would never happen between her and Phelan because he did not do girlfriends, as she often reminded herself. And Marena was not looking for a boyfriend. It was as simple as that.

"I am not his mate," she replied. "He is not looking for a mate. He doesn't want one."

"We don't always get what we want," Blaez stated flatly.

"Right," she replied. "That's why that bitch of a fury tried to maim him, because she wasn't getting what she wanted."

Since learning about what had happened between Phelan and Eureka, the fury, Marena had begun to despise the woman for being so petty. For days after Phelan had shared the truth with Marena she'd looked at that scar on his face and wanted to yell with how stupid and immature that act had been. Now, however, she really just wanted to slap some sense into the otherworldly bitch but doubted she'd ever have the chance to release that bit of tension.

Blaez arched a brow as if what she'd said had been extremely interesting to him. Marena frowned the second she realized she'd just played right into his hand. He was here trying to tell her that Phelan was her mate and, despite her denial of that connection, she'd just responded like a jealous lover.

"All I'm saying is that she shouldn't have done that. If he didn't want to be with her she should have been mature enough to walk away. Leaving him scarred wasn't going to make him want her."

"Yet you want him even with the scar. Even knowing about his past and why he holds himself at a distance, you want him. You walk beside him every day. You sit with him during meals and sleep with him at night. You two are intimate on a level that he has never been before. I'm betting you haven't been this way with anyone else, either."

"We're not going to do this," Marena stated. "Whatever is between Phelan and me stays between us. It is none of your concern."

Blaez took a step toward her then and Marena let her arms fall to her sides.

"Any- and everything that happens to one of my betas is my concern," he told her.

"I'm not one of your betas," she'd insisted in as respectful a tone as she could muster since the guy was the leader of this pack, even while totally pissing her off.

"You have yet to accept who and what you are," he'd said simply before leaving the room.

Now, as the pain dominated every bone in her body,

Marena wondered if what the alpha had said was correct after all. This wasn't a human pain; she knew that instinctively. The cracking sound she heard each time she moved or even took a deep breath was that of bones breaking. The rapid beating of her heart and the heat soaring throughout her insides were beyond the tachycardia symptoms she knew well from all the medical malpractice cases she'd handled. When she opened her eyes everything around her spun out of control until she was certain she would lose consciousness, but she never did. She felt as if she might actually be dying and if that was true what the hell would she be reborn as? Because even through this heavy haze of pain, Marena knew without a doubt that it wasn't over. It was just beginning.

Phelan heard her moaning. He felt the shift in the bed as she moved and his eyes instantly opened. Seconds later, when he could hear the rapid pace of her heartbeat as if she were hooked up to the surround-sound system in his room, he sat straight up in the bed and looked to where she should have been lying beside him. That's when he'd seen her.

She was curled into a ball in the corner of the bed, shaking and moaning. Changing.

He rolled over and immediately pulled her back into his arms. Cuddled close behind her, he could feel her body trembling and wished like hell he could take this part away. He knew he couldn't; every new blood had to go through it. This was the last stages of their body accepting the lycan. Phelan moved in closer, burying his face in her neck and holding her as tightly as he could, hoping his body heat was providing some sort of solace.

After weeks of being with her, Phelan still had no idea why he was the one she needed to be near, but he'd long since stopped trying to figure it out. To be perfectly honest, he'd stopped thinking on that subject because Kira and Caroline had been so adamant about giving him their reasoning for this occurrence.

"You're her mate," Kira had said bluntly, two nights ago when Channing was just a few feet away explaining something in a book to Marena.

"I am not," Phelan replied tersely.

"You can't fight it," Caroline added.

Phelan had sighed. "I'm not fighting anything. I'm simply trying to keep her comfortable until the change is complete."

"And then what?" Caroline asked.

"You ever wonder why you're the only one that can keep her comfortable?" Kira asked.

Phelan felt like he was in front of a firing squad.

"I found her, so I'm stuck with her. It's as simple as that," he'd replied, and hoped that it would end the conversation.

"Love is never simple," Caroline said with a shake of her head.

Phelan did not hesitate. "I'm not in love with anyone."

Kira patted him on the shoulder. "Maybe not just yet, but it will come."

Phelan had instantly been alarmed. "What did you see?" he asked Kira, hating that he had to at least give her words the benefit of the doubt because she had that sight power. There was a very good chance that she had seen something that substantiated the claim she and Caroline were so adamantly trying to make. He had to admit if that was the case it would explain a lot.

Yet Phelan didn't want that to be the case. Malec had brought this same issue up a couple of weeks ago when he'd asked why Phelan had thought he'd scented a Hunter that night when who he'd really scented was Marena, all on her own. He'd known then that something was up between them, because she did not have a Hunter scent but something definitely different and yet still totally alluring.

He'd thought she was his mate. Then he'd dismissed it. Or rather Eureka had. He'd put that thought in the back of his mind and dared it to resurface, until now, when he was staring into the eyes of the one person who could see if it was actually true. But Kira had only shaken her head.

"I have not seen you claiming her. But you will fight for her, Phelan. You will save her. And why else would you do that if she's not your mate?"

The question had haunted him in the quiet hours of the night, while during the day Phelan had proceeded like there was no change in the situation.

Until now.

Holding her at this moment felt different. There was the need that he hoped he was fulfilling, but there was also something else. Something more.

"I can't breathe," she whispered, snapping Phelan out of his own thoughts.

He turned her quickly so that she was lying on her back. Brushing the hair away from her face, he ran his thumbs over her slightly parted lips. Her eyes were half-closed, long lashes feathering out. She was the prettiest woman in the world to him, even without one ounce of makeup or being dressed in stylish clothes and high-heeled shoes. Lying here with her hair all over the place and nothing on her mind

but the impossible pain, she was the most enticing creature Phelan had ever seen. And all he wanted was for her
pain to go away.

Leaning forward, he touched his lips to hers then. It was
a slow touch and she stiffened, not sure what to expect.
Phelan cupped her cheeks, keeping his eyes open and
trained on hers. He parted his lips farther, tilting his mouth
over hers. He breathed in slowly then, one deep breath at a
time. Her eyes opened wide with the first breath, but by the
third try she'd relaxed and accepted. He was breathing for
her, giving her each breath she needed to make it through
each bout of pain. He had no idea why he'd done that, just
that it had seemed like the right thing to do.

After a few more tense moments Marena's eyes opened
totally, her hand going to her face to push back more of the
wild strands of hair.

"I don't know what's happening," she said when Phelan
pulled back from her.

"You're continuing to change. Your bones are reshaping
and preparing to go from one form to another. It's a painful
process, but you're handling it like a true soldier."

She smiled at that. "Am I going to get an honorary badge
of honor or something like that for my courage in the midst
of crazy-ass lycan gene shifting?"

Phelan smiled and realized that he liked seeing her do
the same. "I'd give you a million medals of honor for all that
you've been through." Then he sobered. "I wish you hadn't
been put in this position."

She blinked a couple of times before finally saying, "If
I hadn't been bitten, I wouldn't be here with you now. Is that
what you wish hadn't happened?"

"No," he replied immediately, Kira's words coming quickly

to mind. "I am not saying that. I want . . . I mean, I am fine with you being here. More than fine, actually."

"In spite of all this," she replied. "I think I'm more than fine with it, too."

With those words and because he wasn't certain what else might come tumbling out of his mouth, Phelan moved on the bed, sliding his arms beneath Marena until she was cradled in his arms. He stepped off the bed and headed to the bathroom.

"We'll shower and then take our walk before breakfast," he told her. "I think we could both use the fresh air this morning."

She nodded, resting her head on his chest.

"You may have to carry me, Phelan. I don't think my legs are in the mood to cooperate."

Entering the bathroom, Phelan switched on the light and dropped a kiss to her forehead. "To the ends of the earth, Marena. I'd carry you there and back if it would make you feel better." And if he could somehow take back what had been done to her.

What made Marena much better was the feel of Phelan's soapy palms rubbing over her shoulders and down to her heavy breasts. As his fingers grazed over her nipples she shivered where she sat in his lap on the bench in the shower. The stall was huge and made her wonder why she didn't have a bigger one in her condo. Possibly because she'd never thought of showering with anyone before. Now, after these weeks with Phelan, who seemed to take particular pleasure in bathing her, she didn't think she'd ever be able to live with a shower-for-one again.

He held each breast, cupping them in his hand, being sure to get soap beneath each mound. Then he was moving down her torso, the warm water and scented soap filling the stall with a steamy fresh scent.

"I'm going to forget how to bathe myself," she said just because he was moving between her legs and she needed to say something to keep from screaming in ecstasy.

"I won't ever forget how good it felt to have my hands on you this way," he replied, and Marena couldn't help but feel a sense of sadness at his words.

He was speaking as if at some point he expected not to have this opportunity. It was a totally logical summation since she lived in San Francisco and he in Montana. Not to mention the fact that they weren't really in a relationship together, no matter how much this situation seemed to contradict that. Once Davis was found this would all be over.

She would never see Phelan again.

He'd moved so that she was now standing, water cascading down the front of her body while his soapy hands ran down her back and over her ass. She was glad for this position, not because she liked how it felt when his hand went between her crease and even farther until he was once again touching her pussy, but because she didn't want him to see how disappointed she was at the realization that she may never see him again.

Thirty minutes later they were walking out the back door, taking the wooden steps from the porch and heading down the now-familiar trek across the length of the grassy property until they entered the thick brush of trees. Marena had been used to walking around the office, around the courthouse when she was in trial, and even a few occasions when she'd allowed Gail to drag her to the gym. She'd never walked through a forest with its uneven terrain, twigs, and leaves and rocks and tree branches hanging low enough to smack her in the face a few times. Nor had she packed for such an endeavor. Phelan hadn't seemed to mind and had immediately ordered her tennis shoes and a number of outfits made of spandex that gripped every ounce of her thick physique. She'd seen the way he looked at her each morning when she'd dressed in one of the outfits, so she knew they'd been selected because he liked them. That made it much easier to put them on each day and she hadn't realized that until this morning.

She liked that Phelan enjoyed what she was wearing. The way he looked at her appreciatively had also put a smile on her face. Albeit a temporary one.

What she still hadn't come around to liking was this walking along the steep inclines and trekking over rocks to cross the creek. It was the same path she'd traveled for days now, and while she'd become accustomed to the sounds of the many animals that Phelan had described as living in this area, she wasn't any more comfortable about being so close to them.

"It's a Black Swift," Phelan said when she jumped once again at a sound from above.

"A what?" Marena asked, folding her arms over her head, wishing she'd had the good sense to wear a hat. She had no idea what a Black Swift was or whether it would peck the head of or poop on the intruder making noise so early in the morning.

"It's a bird. There's probably a nest back there behind the waterfall." He was pointing straight ahead to where Marena knew the jagged rocks would drop down about thirty to forty feet into rolling water that poured from the beautiful waterfall above.

"I'm not a fan of birds," she admitted just as another squawking sound ripped through the air.

This time Phelan stopped. Marena would have bumped into him if she hadn't felt the immediate tension ripple through his body. So she stopped as well, looking up in the direction where she knew she'd heard the noise. For endless moments there was nothing else, not one sound at all, which itself was strange.

"We're not alone," Phelan announced in a tone lower than he had been using.

"More birds?" she whispered as over her head the tallest of the trees swayed.

Any bird or other creature that may have been resting in said trees was now fleeing, without making a sound. Amidst the silence was a quick gust of wind and Phelan moved closer to where Marena stood, reaching out a hand to touch her arm. She looked to him in question, quickly noting the seriousness and also the warning in his gaze.

"The realms are open," he said seconds before they heard the heavy footsteps coming toward them.

Marena only had a split second to react as through the trees to her right came a loud noise. She had no idea what the noise was or who or what was making it; all she knew was that she needed to move. With speed and agility she'd never known she possessed, Marena sidestepped and watched in awe as a huge spike-edged club slammed into the ground, spitting dirt and leaves into the air.

Her heart thumped wildly as she followed the beefy hand that held the club upward, tilting her neck until she stared into the eyes of a man with long, dark hair and a wicked scowl. He was clearly angry that he'd missed his target. He was also very tall and part horse.

"Run!" Phelan yelled when the creature had turned his attention fully on Marena.

She heard Phelan's words and knew they made perfect sense. This was one big bad monster and he was coming right for her. She should run, scream, get the hell out of Dodge. But she didn't.

Instead, something along her spine shifted and tingled. She moved her head, rolling her neck until it cracked, and this time when the creature lifted his arm, yelling some hideous-sounding battle cry as he once again aimed that deadly-looking club at her, Marena opened her mouth and growled right back.

She had no idea where the sound came from but felt it vibrating through her entire body. Still, it did not stop the creature from proceeding with his assault, but this time as the heavy club came barreling toward her Marena lifted her arm, folding it over to block the horrific blow. Her body jolted with the contact, but she did not fall to the ground and she was not clobbered by the club. Instead, she pushed back with another vicious growl sounding through the air.

Above, she saw Phelan in his lycan form jumping down onto the creature's back, straddling him as a man would a normal horse. With his mouth open, sharp teeth protruding, Phelan lifted his arms, bringing both his hands and those long claws down to sink into the creature's flesh. He roared and reared back, but Phelan held on tight.

Marena wasn't certain how long he'd be able to hold on that tight and knew she needed to do something to help him. Without another thought she charged forward, coming to a stop just as the creature's front hooves came stomping down. She was beneath him now and he turned his human head to see where she'd gone. Feeling a sting in her own fingers, Marena looked down quickly, saw that her own set of vicious claws had sprung free. They looked surreal, like a manicure gone hideously wrong, but she didn't think on that too long. Instead, she followed Phelan's lead and lifted her arms, thrusting them deep into the creature's underbelly. When he roared again, coming up on his hind legs, Phelan growled from above. Marena growled as well, sinking her nails into the creature again and this time pulling back so that she was creating long and jagged cuts that bled ferociously.

In the next moments there was more growling and footsteps. Marena couldn't see what was going on from where she still stood beneath the beast, but she'd felt a growing warmth inside of her as the growling had continued. It was a comfortable and expected feeling. Yet she had no idea why she was feeling it in the first place.

The creature began to wobble and Marena knew he was going to fall. He would land directly on her when he did. She pulled her claws from the beast one last time and turned to see which way she could run, but it was too late; the creature was already going down, his dark shadow covering Marena completely.

She screamed when it felt like her arm was being pulled out of its socket, her body sliding roughly over the ground, dirt flying up into her face and mouth. Then she was moving upward, being lifted into strong arms and cradled like a baby.

"I told you to run," Phelan said, his chin resting on the top of her head. "'Run' means 'run,' dammit! It does not mean 'stay'!"

He continued to talk, his arms around her tightly, his head holding hers down against his chest as they moved.

"You weren't ready for that. None of us were, but especially not you," he continued. "You should have run! Hell, you shouldn't have been there. That's my fault. I shouldn't have taken you out. I should have known they'd be watching. That they would eventually come. Fuck! I should have protected you!"

They were moving fast, so fast Marena only felt the brush of wind on her cheeks. Even when she tried to open her eyes she didn't see anything but a blur of movement. Seconds later—or at least that's what it felt like to her—his booted feet sounded on the planked steps and then they were inside. She recognized the scent immediately. They were in Phelan's room.

It smelled like him in here: rich, exotic, masculine. As she inhaled deeply and exhaled slowly, still cradled in his arms, Marena realized with a start that it also smelled like her. The sweet floral scent of her lotion was in the air, and the scent of her clothes, of her body when she stripped naked, it was all here, all circulating, blending to become one heady aroma that had her body immediately reacting.

She squirmed in his arms then, struggling to get free, to stand on her own two feet so that she could think clearly.

"I won't let it happen again," Phelan said, holding her even tighter. "I swear I won't let anything happen to you again."

"Stop," she said, too softly at first, because Phelan simply continued.

He moved until finally he sat on the edge of the bed, adjusting her on his lap. Marena pushed away, using more strength than she knew she had until she was on her feet.

She stumbled so that she wouldn't fall on her ass. Righting herself, Marena pushed back the thick strands of hair that had fallen in her face. Her legs were steady almost immediately, her body extending until she was standing straight up, her gaze zeroing in on Phelan quickly.

"What was that out there?" she asked, her fingers still running through her hair, trying to untangle it.

Phelan looked at her oddly for a few seconds. He was back to his human form, his eyes green again, not that glowing blue she'd seen in the forest. His teeth and nails and the rest of his face were normal. No, she thought with a start, nothing about him was normal.

And now, she thought with a start, neither was she.

"That was a centaur. Most likely sent by Zeus to hunt and kill our pack. He knows that Blaez is close, that we're all protecting him," Phelan said with a shake of his head. "He knows."

Marena shook her head.

"No. I meant what was it that happened to me?" Her hair was fine, Marena decided, and dropped her hands to her sides. "What did I do and how was I able to do it?"

Saying the words emphasized the memory and Marena looked down at herself. She saw the blood from the centaur on her clothes, her arms, her hands. She should be repelled, should run into the bathroom in a hurry to shower, but she did not. Instead, she stood perfectly still, lifting her head to Phelan, the one she knew had answers, once more.

He took a deep breath, his hands and arms covered in blood as well, and leaned forward, his elbows resting on his knees.

"The pain you felt this morning was the last of the physical change your body would make to accept lycan

DNA. Your bones, muscles, every ligament and cell in your body, are now lycan. The first shift will come in the next twenty-four hours, on the night of the full moon. But for now, the strength, the sight, the hearing, everything, will begin to fall into place." He'd been looking down at the floor as he spoke, but now he lifted his head and gaze to her.

"You were able to fight the centaur as a partial lycan using your claws and your strength. Even when Blaez and the others arrived you continued to fight, along with us, against the hideous beast. This is your life now, Marena. This is who and what you are."

She didn't shake her head even though a part of her screamed the word "no" as loudly as it could. Only Marena knew the truth. She knew it because she felt it, moving just beneath her skin, slithering along her spine, and opening her eyes. Phelan was right: she could see differently now, more clearly.

"I am a lycan," she said, tasting the words for the first time.

"You are a lycan," he repeated, and came to stand in front of her.

"I fought as a lycan with you and the others," she said. "Just as I was supposed to because I am—"

"You," Phelan said, catching her chin between his fingers, "are a gorgeous and fearless Devoted lycan. There is no doubt in my mind of that fact now. Not one damned doubt."

"This is my life now," she said, licking her lips and shifting from one foot to the other.

"Your life is what you make of it," Phelan told her. "I could stand here and tell you that only the lycan matters, but I know that's not true for you. I've accepted who and what

I am and now you must do the same. If you're an attorney and a lycan, that's your choice. But there is no more room for denial, Marena. No more time for questions and guesses. Zeus knows we're here. He won't be thwarted again."

"Phelan's right," Blaez said, walking into the bedroom where they stood. "He knew exactly where we were almost as if he'd been tipped off."

The others filed into the room after Blaez, all eyes on Marena.

"She's been right here with us . . . with me this entire time," Phelan said as he moved to stand in front of her, separating her from them.

"But he knows her scent; his DNA is inside her. He would know how to find her wherever she went," Malec stated sternly with his arms folded over his chest.

"Did you know what was coming?" Caroline asked her. "Did you feel it ahead of time, Marena?"

"No," she instantly replied, then frowned as she stepped from behind Phelan. "I did not know who or what was coming and I resent being accused of doing something I wouldn't have known how to do in the first place."

"No one is accusing you of anything," Kira said from beside Blaez. Her hair had been pulled back from her face, her shirtsleeves pushed up over her elbows.

"Bullshit!" Marena snapped back. "You're all standing here accusing me of telling Davis where you were and who you were hiding. It's taken me weeks to wrap my head around all that is going on here and you think the first thing I'd do was run and tell that bastard something like this?"

"We think that we've been safe here in this forest for over a year and now, when you've been here for just about three weeks, the centaur appears," Channing said. "Coincidence?"

It was Marena's turn to stand with one hip jutting forward, arms folded over her chest. "Call it what you want, but if I'm not mistaken, before I arrived—hell, before I was even bitten—a Solo was here and before that her old pack came calling for a fight, so don't act like my appearance is the only questionable one here. Besides, I didn't come here on my own; I was brought here," Marena finished.

"She's right. I found her and I brought her here. This could not have been a setup," he said.

"It wasn't," Kira added. "Not in that way."

Marena and the others looked to her for a more detailed explanation.

"You didn't know she was going to get bitten or that you were going to be the one to find her," Kira said, "but that act alone proved to be the perfect opportunity for someone."

"The harpy," Phelan mumbled, and then cursed. "She set us up. Eureka," Phelan mumbled. "That bitch."

"You think she's somehow involved?" Blaez asked Phelan.

"She has to be," he replied, clenching his fists. "Her allegiance is to Zeus. It always has been. Dammit!"

Marena shook her head quickly digesting everything that was being said. "Eureka being the one that put those scars on your face? The one that's probably still in love with you?"

Caroline made a sound but quickly clapped a hand over her mouth, while Kira stared at Phelan with an expectant look on her face. Marena frowned because if anyone expected an answer from Phelan, it was her. Not because they were committed to each other or anything like that, but because she'd been sharing a bed with him and having sex with him; if his ex was about to make some violent comeback into his life, she damn sure had a right to know.

"I can't prove it," Phelan said tightly. "I just have a feeling."

"A feeling?" Marena asked, not liking the fact that Eureka could still illicit "a feeling" in him.

"We need to figure out if that feeling is true or not," Malec said as if Marena hadn't just asked a question. "Because if it is and she knows of our location, we need to be prepared to fight back when the next bounty hunter shows up."

Blaez nodded, extending his arm so that Kira immediately laced her fingers with his. "We're going to be prepared regardless. We'll go and make plans. Malec and Channing will try to figure out which bounty hunters might likely appear next. You," he said, nodding to Phelan, "get cleaned up and figure out Eureka's involvement, if any. We need to eliminate her from the situation if she's not a threat and look in other directions."

"Like toward Davis," Marena added since they'd all been acting as if she weren't standing right there. It was one thing when they weren't including her in their conversations because they thought she hadn't fully accepted her lycan status, but now, after she'd almost been killed by a beast she was still reeling from seeing right here on earth, she wasn't going to be ignored. She was a part of this battle, whether she wanted to believe or was ready to accept.

"What if he is using his DNA lingering in my body to track me down? Why wouldn't he simply show up at the door? How or why would he summon that thing that was out there? It doesn't make any sense," she said.

They all looked at her then and Marena continued.

"He has to have a stake in this. What is it? Why me? I didn't know any of you before Phelan came into my room at the B and B that night."

"She's right," Kira said, speaking slowly as she continued to stare at Marena. "Why did he bite her now? She said she's known him for years and he's kept his distance? There was no way that anybody could have known that she would end up here, nobody but . . . another being with the power of sight."

The room grew quiet, until Marena asked the question she figured might be on the rest of their minds.

"Who else would have this power? I thought the Moon Goddess gave it to you specifically?" she asked.

"That's true in my case," Kira said. "But others may have been born with their own power. But the way Phelan can cross the realms and Blaez . . . well, Blaez is who and what he is. It could just be in another being's genetic makeup that they can see the future and the past, or maybe just the future. Maybe there was someone that knew this was how things would turn out, that knew this would all unfold on the night of the supermoon."

"It makes sense," Channing added. "Since that's the night when we and every other being within the two realms are at our most powerful. The otherworldly veil over the earth will be lifted and we'll all see equally even though there is no equality among us. Humans will see other beings and we'll see them. We'll walk beside each other and for the first and only time know exactly who and what each other really are."

"The perfect time for a battle," Malec declared.

Phelan nodded. "A battle the other beings are betting on winning."

CHAPTER 10

Marena turned over onto her side, dropping an arm above her head as she slept. Seconds later she turned onto the other side, her mind drifting in and out of sleep with something on the side of slumber pulling at her persistently.

She moved as if in a fog, walking slowly because she wasn't certain what was before her, yet not wanting to turn back because a part of her knew he was there. He had come for her, just as he'd promised. Marena kept walking. She kept looking.

And there was nothing.

Just an ominous darkness and apprehension so thick it threatened to choke her. A cool breeze blew and the long silk nightgown she wore moved with silky smoothness over her bare legs. There were long slits up both sides of the gown, so in a few minutes with another gust of air she would be entering the X-rated department as more of her thigh and probably a good portion of her bare and shaved crotch would be visible.

Still, she moved forward, refusing to be deterred.

He touched her then, a featherlike wisp of his fingers over her thigh, and Marena hurriedly looked down. There was nothing there. She gasped as she felt the touch on her other thigh. Again, there was nothing there.

Then she was falling, hitting a soft surface with a huff of breath as he climbed on top of her. She opened her mouth to scream, but there was no sound. There was only the breeze and the weight of him pressing down on her.

"I told you I was coming for you, Marena," Davis said, his voice raspy and creepy.

So much so she wanted to clap her hands to her ears to keep from hearing it altogether, but she didn't. Marena remained perfectly still, determined to use her brain this time, to think and not react as she did before—the time when she'd shot his sorry ass for trying to rape her. No, this time she was determined to get the answers she wanted from Davis—even if he was only in her dream.

"You shouldn't have been a coward and run the first time!" she snapped back, knowing he would respond.

Davis loved a good argument, almost as much as Marena did. It's why they'd both excelled at their jobs and, sadly, why he'd been drawn to her in the first place. Marena had no idea where that thought had come from, but she instinctively knew it to be true.

"Not a coward," he replied. "Just biding my time."

"For what? A command performance?" Her rapid heartbeat was surely a dead giveaway of her nervousness, thwarting the steady edge of her voice.

"Oh, no, sweetness," he said, and then chuckled. "You think this is about you, don't you?" The sick and demented laughter continued. "You have no idea."

"What's your motivation here, Davis? Make your case and I'll see if you have sufficient evidence to proceed," she said quickly, grasping for the part of him she hoped was at least a bit of the human attorney he'd pretended to be all those years.

"Totally justified," was his response, the sound of his amusement making her stomach churn.

Marena opened her eyes wider, hoping and praying it would help her see through the darkness. Why she wanted to look him in the eye she had no idea; it had been enough seeing his facial expression that night in the hotel.

"Explain the justification," she pushed. "Tell me what the hell I ever did to you, to make you want to put me in this position."

"Oh, that," he said, and then cleared his throat. "Let me see, you walked around that office for years with your head held high as if you were better than every other attorney in that firm and probably in the whole state of California. And then one day I realized you were absolutely right. You were better. You were smarter and stronger and perfect to get me what I needed."

She'd been listening to his every word, trying to decipher what he meant by them, and losing that battle pitifully.

"I don't understand," she admitted, biting back the fear that circled in the pit of her stomach with that admission.

Marena always understood her cases. She knew what her goals in life were right down to the second of each day that it would take her to achieve them. She'd always been superorganized and focused to a fault. Not understanding something was not acceptable, especially not now.

"You don't, do you?" he asked with a laugh.

His hands were on her then, cupping and squeezing her breasts until tears stung her eyes.

"You were meant for this," Davis taunted. "You were

meant to be used to bring about a new leader. The partners all thought you were meant for greatness and when I finally saw it I knew they were right."

"You don't know a damned thing about me!" Marena yelled.

She lifted her knee on pure instinct, hoping like hell it would land in his groin and send the sick bastard's balls straight up to his throat. She had no idea how that worked in a dream with a lycan or whatever the hell Davis was, but she did it anyway and when the weight on her chest lessened she rolled to the side. Her nails extended immediately, scraping over the nothing that seemed to be beneath her, and she heard a growling sound that she thought might actually be coming from her.

Davis laughed.

"Silly bitch!" he yelled. "You have no idea what's about to happen."

"I could say the same for you," Marena said, coming up to a stand, then launching herself in the direction where she thought he was standing.

Eureka rubbed her palms over her breasts. Phelan frowned because they were too small.

She sat atop him totally naked, moving her bare pussy over his thick length. He was hard, that was for sure, but not for her. The thought hit him like a boulder, smacking against his head with such force he actually jerked back.

"What's the matter, baby? Don't you love me anymore?" she asked, her head tilted, eyes gleaming with arousal.

Phelan did not hesitate to say, "No."

She froze, hands still on her tits, hips in mid-tilt, eyes

darkening instantly. Phelan didn't give a damn. He put his hands on her waist and lifted her off him, dropping her to the bed or the chair or wherever they had been lying. He had no idea where they were and didn't care. What mattered was that he was completely over her and totally into someone else. The thought should have made him frown or at the very least bristle at the idea, but it did not. Instead, it gave him a burst of energy, a purpose, he thought with an inward smile.

"Where the hell do you think you're going?" Eureka called from behind him. "Back to her?"

Eureka laughed then, a throaty chuckle that stopped him in his tracks. There was something eerie about her laugh, something he'd never heard before, and it had him turning back to look at her. Still naked, she'd come to a stand, dropping her hands onto slim hips, tossing her hair back over her shoulders.

"You thought you were going to get to keep her, didn't you?" She shook her head making a *tsking* sound as she moved closer to him. "It was all a plan, Phelan. She was the bait and you bit—from the looks of it you bit hard," she said, looking down at his throbbing erection.

His body ached with the need to be inside of Marena. She'd lie next to him already asleep when he'd climbed into bed. How she managed to look so peaceful in slumber after the day they'd had he wasn't able to figure out. They'd spent hours on the computer, searching every lead they could on Davis and wondering how in the hell he could have known that Phelan was connected to Blaez and why he'd wanted to thrust Marena into the equation. That was Marena's scenario, as she'd told him after Blaez and the others had left them alone. It was about her and not in an egotistical way, because Marena Panos was proud and confident, but she wasn't arrogant or conceited by any means. Phelan, on the other hand, hadn't wanted to believe it had been solely about her. He'd been so used to all the fucked-up shit in his life stemming from the day he was born and branching out over the years. It had to be Eureka, he'd thought even while he'd entertained Marena's ideas.

Now, in the depths of his dreams, with Eureka standing just a couple of feet from him, gloating, Phelan knew he'd been absolutely right all along. But somehow, so had Marena.

"Tell me what you've done," he said to Eureka in the most lethal, no-nonsense voice he could muster. "Tell me right now."

"Always demanding," she said. "That's what first attracted me to you. That 'I know what I want' attitude combined with the 'fuck you if you're not willing to give it to me' eyes. I loved it from the start."

"You lied from the start and I'm not in the mood for any more lying!" he snapped.

"You're not in the mood?" she asked. "I'd beg to differ with you."

Again she was looking at his dick, and for the first time in all his life Phelan hated the fact that he slept in the nude. Still, he did not falter.

"What does Marena have to do with any of this? How do you know her?" he asked through gritted teeth.

Eureka shook her head. "Oh, I don't know that damned human, or well, I guess she's not a human anymore, is she?" She lifted a brow as she grinned. "She wasn't my plan, but when they came to me with their thoughts I figured it would work because I knew you and I knew this day would come."

"What the hell are you talking about? What plan?" Phelan asked, rage building steadily inside him.

Eureka had come to stand directly in front of him now, dragging her long, black, deadly nails down his bare chest and over his ribbed abs. He didn't even blink as her fingers went lower, the scrape of the sharp nails moving along the length of his still-rigid cock.

"What. Did. You. Do?" he asked, resisting the urge to grab her by the arms and shake the hell out of her, literally.

"Oh, it's not what I did this time, Phelan my love. This was all you. I wasn't certain you'd walk so blindly into the trap, but you did. They'd already seen the mate in your future; all we had to do was intercede," she said, her voice going to a low whisper.

"Who'd seen my mate? What are you saying, Eureka? Just spit it out, dammit!"

He needed the words, the truth, like he needed his next breath. Because Phelan was absolutely certain that whatever she told him, whatever master plan he'd unwittingly been a part of, was about to get blown straight to hell!

"The Moirai, you goof. They know everyone's fate, remember," she told him as she looked up into his eyes. "They showed Zeus who she was and the rest fell neatly into place." She cupped his balls then and groaned with the weight of them in her hands.

Phelan grabbed her by the wrists, remembering another time that he'd done the same thing. That night he'd thrown her off a cliff. This time he'd felt like ripping her fucking head off!

"Zeus knew about Marena? How could he? She hasn't been a lycan for that long. If you so much as even think about touching her—"

"What's going to happen, oh Phelan the mighty?" a male voice asked from behind where Phelan and Eureka stood. "What are you going to do when you find out I not only bit that bitch, but I claimed her, too?"

Pushing Eureka back with all his strength, Phelan turned slowly to see the infamous lycan he'd spent the last few weeks searching for, standing only a few feet away. Phelan contemplated asking the bastard the same question he'd asked Eureka. Then he considered simply shifting and killing the sonofabitch, but he didn't. Instead, Phelan found himself pausing, listening to a voice he'd never heard in his mind before.

Phelan! she screamed his name as if she was desperate for him to hear her. *Phelan! He's here! Davis is here!*

Marena?

He's here and I know why. I know how. I know what he wants to do. It's been about us all along. You and me and—

She'd stopped talking and Phelan knew why. In the seconds he'd been hearing her mindchat with him she'd come into the area where he stood with Eureka behind him and Davis in his lycan form in front of him. Marena had come in and looked around, not sure what she was seeing and, then again, Phelan thought, perfectly aware of what was going on.

You're mindchatting with me. Only lycans can do that, he told her.

They can't hear us, she said.

No, they cannot. Although he's a lycan, your words are for me.

You're in my dream.

Phelan tilted his head slightly. *You're in my dream. How is that possible?*

Davis turned to her then, his claws elongated, a growl ripping from him as he charged toward her. Phelan didn't hesitate but jumped through the air, knocking the lycan down.

Wake up, Marena. Wake up now! he yelled to her.

But you—

Wake up!

And she did. They both did, sitting straight up in the center of the bed, chests heaving as their hands moved over the comforters until finding each other and twining together. They did not speak this time and did not mindchat, because they both knew. Now they knew exactly what was going on with Davis and Eureka.

"I don't know how that just happened," Marena said, shaking her head. "I was asleep and Davis was there and you were there. Were you there for real?"

She'd looked over to him at that moment and Phelan felt his chest constrict. In her voice he heard trust and expectancy. She expected an answer from him, a truthful one, and what else? What had this really turned into?

Eureka said it was all a part of a plan that Zeus was told by the Fates—that Marena was his mate and therefore would be the perfect one. The perfect one for what? To reel him in? Because damn, that's exactly how he felt right now, like she'd been reeling him in from that very first day.

"It was real," he replied. "Tell me about your dream. Tell me what Davis did and said to you."

The room was dark, but Phelan could see every part of her. He knew it all by memory. The arch of her brows, the sharp line of her nose, the pert shape of her lips, it was all emblazoned in his mind so that, even if he tried, Phelan knew he would never forget her. Not even when it was time for her to go.

She sighed. "He was on top of me, laughing and taunting me, but I wouldn't cower," she told him.

"No," Phelan said then, squeezing her hand in his. "You would never cower." She was too strong for that.

"He said I was meant to be used to bring about a new leader. Like he planned to bite me all along."

Phelan frowned into the darkness.

"I can't believe it; Blaez and the others were right yesterday. I did bring that centaur here. I told Zeus where Blaez was hiding," she stated in a voice that sounded both small and incredulous.

"You did no such thing," Phelan told her. "All you did was live your life. You had no idea what was on the other side or, hell, what was walking right beside you. If you had known you would have gotten so far away from Davis he would have had no choice but to figure out another plan."

"Would I have?" Marena asked him.

Phelan didn't understand her question or, rather, he didn't want to think too hard on what she might be trying to tell him, because it didn't matter. Nothing else mattered but the issue at hand; still he couldn't help but say, "What are you asking me?"

"I'm saying that if I knew who and what Davis really was and what he was attempting to do—become some type of new otherworldly leader—wouldn't I have tried to stop him? I'd like to think I'm a fair person and that I believe wholeheartedly in the little democracy the humans of the U.S. have got going. So I wouldn't be likely to accept someone or something trying to change any of that. That's what

Davis is doing, isn't he? He's trying to become a new leader for the lycans on earth? And he's going to get Zeus's help because Davis is going to give the angry god what he's been searching for—Blaez."

Phelan inhaled deeply, letting each word she'd spoken resonate in his mind. She was probably right. No, he admitted, she *was* right. That had been Davis's plan all along. But how had Eureka been connected to this?

"I've got to go," he said, releasing Marena's hand quickly and moving until he was off the bed.

"What? Go? Where are you going?" She was talking while moving to switch on a light.

By the time Phelan had grabbed his shorts from the chair near his dresser, Marena was up and coming to stand beside him.

"Where are you going?" she asked, touching a hand to his elbow. "Tell me, Phelan. This involves me, too, so I have a right to know."

He thought about her last words long and hard. He supposed she was right; she was involved in this even though she'd never planned to be. And damn, how Phelan hated that they'd sought her out and made her a pawn in a game they knew was going to turn deadly. He wanted to protect her, to keep her as unscathed as possible, considering she would never be the same again and there was absolutely nothing he could do about that fact.

"I'm going to find Eureka," he told her. "She's involved in this, too."

"You think she and Davis were working together, that's why she was in the dream, too," Marena said.

Phelan hadn't realized she'd seen Eureka. He'd pushed her aside before he'd lunged for Davis.

"I think this was a bigger plan than any of us ever realized and now it's time to put an end to it, once and for all," he said tightly, and moved to his closet to get a pair of jeans.

Marena moved, too, going to the other side of the room where the bag she'd had with her weeks ago was sitting on the floor beside the dresser. He'd given her drawers to use for her clothes. She also had things in the closet with his and Phelan touched them each time he went in there to get something of his own. He'd never had a woman's garments near his, never smelled another person's scent in every direction he turned. A scent that with each passing day was beginning to smell more and more like his.

"You can't go, Marena," Phelan said without even turning around to see that she'd begun putting clothes on as well.

He just knew that's what she was doing, that she would be thinking about fighting this battle, too, out of some misplaced sense of duty.

"I can and I am," was her response.

She probably hadn't stopped or even slowed down what she was doing, either. They were just alike in that way, stubborn to the core.

"It's a long ride and it's going to be dangerous," he said as he pulled a shirt over his head and turned to where she was doing the same thing across the room.

He watched as the tight-fitting hot-pink material moved down over her breasts and torso, pressing the breasts he loved touching and licking down. She already had on yoga pants and moved to sit on the side of the bed so she could pull on the matching black-and-pink tennis shoes he'd bought for her. Months ago, when Phelan had walked into the kitchen to see Channing and Kira ordering clothes on-line, he'd sworn he would never do anything as domestic as buy clothes for a female. Just two weeks ago he'd logged on to the same Web site he'd seen Channing and Kira using and he'd selected pieces that he wanted to see Marena in as if she were there for his pleasure. That wasn't the case. Phelan found himself trying to remember that more often than not lately.

"I don't want you to get hurt," he admitted, and her head snapped up as she looked at him in surprise.

"Same here," was her quick response as she went back to tying her shoes. "I don't want you hurt, either. And the best way for both of us to remain safe is for us to remain together."

"Marena—"

"No," she said, coming to a stand and shaking her head. "This is a pointless argument that's going to waste more time than we have. The supermoon is less than twenty-four hours away. All hell's going to break loose at that point, so it makes more sense for us to take care of this situation sooner, rather than later."

She made total sense and she'd already grabbed her jacket and was walking out of the bedroom before it dawned on Phelan that he still needed to put on his boots and get his own jacket. Doing those things, Phelan thought it was best not to try to figure out exactly when he'd lost this ar-gument or what, if anything, he planned to do about it.

CHAPTER 11

The sun had just begun to set as Phelan slowed down. He drove his bike around to what was definitely the back entrance to a building that looked like it had been dropped in the middle of nowhere. Marena kept her arms around Phelan's waist, leaning her body into his as she had been for the past hours since they'd left the lodge.

They'd stopped only once for gas, at which time Phelan had brought her two bottles of orange juice and checked her reflexes.

"Block me," he'd said when they'd stood just a few inches from the bike.

At first Marena hadn't known what he meant, but then he'd hurled a punch at her and instinct had kicked in. She lifted an arm to block him. He'd swung again and again, moving around her, using his leg to try to sweep hers, and she'd combatted him as if she'd been training for this moment all her life. She was moving faster than she ever had before and was as light on her feet as a person weighing half her body weight. When he picked her up and slammed her to the ground Marena bolted up just seconds after her back had touched the dirt ground, pushing him off her and baring her teeth.

She had teeth, sharp and long, pricking against her lips as she attempted to close her mouth. A look down at her hands showed her claws once more, and this time Marena flexed her fingers back and forth to get used to the look and feel of the deadly weapons. Her entire body felt different, rejuvenated and energized as she stood with her legs spread slightly apart, her mind poised for attack.

"You're ready," Phelan had said to her then. "Focus your mind on everything human. The feel of your human hands and feet. The way you talk and walk, sleep and wake. Put your mind . . . and eventually your body back into the human state."

Marena felt her head tilting as she stared at him through a crystal-clear gaze. She could see not only Phelan in his human body but way beyond him to the edge of a cliff. Below the cliff were a town and buildings with lights and cars, people. She inhaled deeply at the sight and picked up several different scents—leaves from the trees near the cliff, cigarette smoke from where she had no idea, and gasoline fresh from the gas station.

"Focus on the human," Phelan said once more. "Focus, Marena. Control the lycan and the shift."

She blinked and inhaled again, this time scenting the air, looking up to the crystal blue of the sky. Her gaze returned to Phelan, to his tall form, the muscled arms stretched down at his sides and strong legs clad in navy-blue cargo pants. His boots were laced tight, the scowl on his face deep and yet relenting—if only to her.

To her, Marena Kay Panos, attorney-at-law. And lycan, she thought with a start. Marena was now a full-fledged lycan, just like Phelan.

There was a sort of deflation at that thought, a physical

one that continued as her nails and teeth retracted, her face felt less full, her shoulders less broad. Marena stared at her hands, lifting one slowly up to her face to feel her human teeth and cheeks. Human, she thought with a sigh, human once more.

"It gets easier," Phelan told her. "Over time you won't feel the shift as definitively. Each move will be as natural and seamless as breathing."

"But I was one of you," she said. "In those last moments I was a lycan just like you and the others."

Phelan nodded. "You fought like a lycan—a newbie, of course, but good enough. You're a quick learner, so the shifting will come to you in no time."

Marena took a deep breath and released it. "Right, I'll get used to it, just like I got used to the idea of being bitten in the first place," she said.

Because she had no choice. There had never been a choice for her in this new development of her life. She didn't know how she felt about that much control being taken away from her and didn't have time to consider it now, as Phelan had come to stand in front of her, putting his hands on her shoulders and shaking lightly until she looked up at him.

"We need to get going," he said. "It'll be dark soon and we should be there before then."

She nodded her response.

"You can do this," Phelan told her. "I know that you can go in there and handle yourself like any seasoned lycan. I believe in you."

Marena blinked at his words, warmth spreading quickly through her body because nobody had ever said those words to her before. Sure, she'd believed in herself all these years, working toward a goal she knew without any doubt she would someday reach, but nobody had ever told her they believed she could do it. Not her parents, her siblings, no one. Until Phelan.

She'd followed him back to the bike, taking the helmet he'd given her at the lodge and placing it over her head once more. Phelan had laced and secured it tightly, keeping his gaze on hers as he did. Then he climbed onto the seat and waited while she did the same. When she slipped her arms loosely around his waist, he grabbed her wrists, pulling her so that her body was flush against the back of his, her arms even tighter around him. She'd stayed that way until this moment, until the bike came to a complete stop and Phelan sat straight up, staring at the building in front of them.

"She's in there," he said solemnly.

"And so is he," Marena replied. She wasn't totally sure how she knew, but she did know. Davis Sumpter was in that three-story building with its large tinted windows and straight line of flashing lights around the rooftop.

"This could be a setup," she continued, her mind thinking and seeing more clearly now that they were here. Now that she was a full-fledged lycan. "The two of them are devious. They've concocted this scheme in the hopes of getting you, Blaez's most powerful protector, away from him. They'll have someone ready to attack him while we're here dealing with them."

That was the endgame, she thought with a start. Divide and conquer had long since proved to be an excellent strategy.

Phelan looked over his shoulder at her, unable to hide the surprise on his face. "They may be devious, but I think they've sorely underestimated me." He cleared his throat then and said, "They've underestimated us."

There was no time to feel any special way about how Phelan had looked at her. It was definitely not the most opportune time to wonder if that burst of hazel in his green eyes was the start of something more than just the duty he'd figured he owed to her in these last weeks. Why she wanted it to be more Marena wasn't sure. No, that was a lie: she was certain why she wanted it to be more; only now was not the time to explore any of this.

Now, she thought as she stepped off the bike and removed her helmet, was the time to make things right.

They'd walked the few feet to a back door that was already open and Phelan stepped inside as if he'd done this on a regular basis. Marena wondered at that. How many times had Phelan been here with Eureka?

It was dark inside and Marena had to blink a few times before her eyes adjusted. Phelan, however, moved with fluency. He'd been here a lot, she surmised with a frown as she walked behind him. They took the steps one at a time, coming to another door, this one a glistening silver that glowed in the dark stairwell. Phelan paused for a second, turning to say over his shoulder, "Stay right behind me," before he touched the knob and pulled the door open.

Marena didn't have a moment to take the next step before Phelan was pulled forward and that silver door was closed tight, leaving her in the darkness alone. Instinctively she reached out, letting her palms fall flat on where she knew the door had been. She pounded against the flat surface, yelling, to no avail, for it to open. The cold air came next, sweeping over her back, then coming in such a strong gust that it turned Marena around so that her back was now flat against the access. She gasped at the strength with which she was held to that spot, wrestling with her mind and her gut on what she should do next.

Get through that door and find Phelan, was the first thought.

Stand tall and fight whatever the hell was at play here, was the next.

The sound of nails scraping along the wall and the click of heels along the concrete floors turned out to be the deciding factor. At her sides Marena clenched and unclenched her fists, rotating her neck until it cracked as she stood up straight. She was ready for whatever was coming in the dark.

"Well, now, let me get a good look at my Phelan's chubby little mate," the female voice spoke just seconds before a ball of fire appeared to illuminate the area.

The fire was held in the pit of her hand, casting an eerie gaze to her long, black-colored nails.

"And you must be Eureka," Marena said slowly, taking in every detail of the witch . . . or, rather, the woman.

"So he told you about me, huh? Guess that means I made a lasting impression," she said with her dark as coal eyes, pulled so tightly into points at the ends that it looked painful.

Her hair was dark and long, Marena thought as it fell behind her back. Her breasts and waist, hell, her entire body, was small, model thin, and clad only in a black leather bra and skintight leather pants.

"The scar you put on his face speaks volumes of the relationship, without Phelan ever saying a word," Marena replied.

She'd taken a step away from the door, moving closer to Eureka. The fury expected her to be afraid. Eureka had anticipated the human female to still dominate Marena's presence and in fear of the unknown being in front of her taking control. She was dead wrong.

"Oh, he told you about that, too," Eureka replied with a shrug. "Well, you know what you humans like to say, 'all's fair in love and war,'" Eureka quipped.

"No," was Marena's response. "All I know is that I'd never hurt the one I professed to love. I'd never damage him in such a way that he'd remain in conflict even through the days that I was not with him. In other words, I'm not a sore loser like some of us . . . ah . . . beings tend to be."

Eureka tossed her head back and laughed. "'Sore' being the operative word," she said seconds before tossing that ball of fire directly at Marena.

Marena was moving before thinking, her legs lifting from beneath her as she jumped upward, her nails grabbing on to the walls, feet doing the same. That ball of fire whizzed past her back, slamming with a burst of new flames against the door. Jumping down, she landed in front of Eureka and without hesitation reached out a hand to clasp around the fury's neck. She squeezed tight, pushing Eureka back until she slammed into another wall, the cinder blocks cracking and crumbling with the motion.

"You need to learn that when someone doesn't want to play with you anymore it's time to pack up your toys and go home," Marena said, tightening her hold on Eureka's neck.

Eureka's eyes bulged fleetingly before she was sinking those vicious nails of hers into Marena's arms. Marena growled, her grip lessening on Eureka's neck momentarily.

That was long enough for the fury to shake herself free and send Marena falling down that last flight of stairs at the same time.

The tumble was brutal against Marena's body, but she still managed to jump up at the landing, squatting down so that her nails now rested on the floor, her head lifting to stare up at Eureka, who stood at the top of the stairs. In seconds the fury jumped down and Marena leapt forward, catching her in the air. They tussled and banged against the walls, going down another flight of stairs and slamming hard against the floor at the bottom. Eureka came out on top and was poised to scratch Marena the same way she had Phelan, until Marena grabbed both her wrists.

"You think you can defeat me because you're a new lycan?" Eureka asked with a sickening smirk across her burnt orange–toned face. "You think you've won because you turned out to be his mate and you're not repulsed by his face or his demons? You're not shit!" she yelled into Marena's face.

Marena didn't cower from the flames that had appeared in the center of Eureka's eyes; nor did she give a damn what the fury was saying to her. All she knew was that she needed to get this bitch out of her way so she could go and find Phelan, because they were definitely working the divide-and-conquer angle. She knew that now without any doubt.

Pushing back with all her strength, Marena bent Eureka's wrists until she heard cracking and Eureka screamed out in pain. Marena was fast when she released her wrists, reaching around and gripping her by the hair. Jumping up, Marena swung the fury to the side, slamming her against the wall once more.

"I'm a lycan, bitch!" Marena spit as she felt herself shifting, her teeth elongated, strength multiplying.

She slammed Eureka into the wall again. More concrete rained around them at the force and Marena released the fury, loving the sound of her howling in pain.

"That's what I want you to remember," Marena said, looking down at her. "That I'm the chubby new lycan that took Phelan away from you," she told her finally before grabbing her by the neck and turning until there was another cracking sound.

In the next moments there was quiet. The cold ceased, the fire was gone, and Eureka lay dead on the floor. She remained still until her body shriveled up and turned to a pile of dark ash. Marena backed up then, her hands shaking, heart throbbing, at the realization that she'd killed her.

She had actually taken a life.

The building vibrated around her once again, giving Marena something she'd have to ponder over later. Phelan was up there alone. She had to get to him, had to help him, if it was the last thing she did.

Phelan had turned to the closed door, cursing because Marena was left on the other side of it. That was only allowed to last for a second, because in the next moment he was grabbed from behind by thick claws digging into his back.

The pain had the beast within him breaking free instantly and with it all the strength of the lycan Phelan normally tried to restrain. With arms outstretched he bent slightly, then lifted back with a horrendous growl that shook the walls and released the hold of the beast behind him.

Phelan turned quickly, knowing exactly what he would see at this point. Davis Sumpter with his distorted lycan face, marred by black tarlike marks. His nails were long and jagged, his body thick and solid.

"So you're the bastard that's taken my scent away from her," Davis said, balling his fists and growling back at Phelan. "She's mine to claim!" he yelled.

Phelan only shook his head, not the least bit intimidated by the lycan's growl or his words.

"She was never yours," Phelan replied. "They knew that when they enlisted your help. Just like they knew how your part in this would play out."

Davis shook his head, long strands of wispy hair shaking at his shoulders. His eyes were the same lycan blue as all the others', but they were marred by thick black stripes, ones Phelan had seen before.

"They set you up the same way you thought you were setting me up," he told Davis. "You were a pawn and now it's time for your part in this to be over."

"Fuck you!" Davis said, tilting his head back to growl once more.

Phelan knew what was happening. If he did not kill Davis, the hounds of Hades that were already in his blood would. He must have been bitten himself at some point, probably how Zeus had gotten the lycan's attention in the first place. The god would have had his brother's hounds inflict the wound, then shown up and appeared to save Davis from it. Not only rescuing the lycan but offering him a chance at leadership as well. Davis, the greedy, self-absorbed bastard, would have fallen for the lure like a pro. He would have done Zeus's bidding without question, biting Marena and making it all but impossible for Phelan not to find her.

She was his mate after all; the Moirai had told Zeus that, so he knew that the two would be united eventually.

She was Phelan's distraction. His mate would be the only one to draw him away from Blaez, the only connection strong enough to make him leave the alpha he'd pledged his life to.

"It worked," Phelan said. "I'm here and so is Marena."

"You dare to bring my beta to me. You are more stupid than Eureka said," Davis taunted, believing he had the upper hand.

If Phelan were another type of man or lycan, he might have felt sorry for the poor bastard. As it stood, he was neither and so, running toward Davis, Phelan struck out with his strong fists, taking the lycan off guard and knocking him to the floor.

"You're the stupid one if you believe I'm going to let you keep calling her your beta," he told Davis before kicking his body across the floor.

To his credit, Davis did make it up on to his feet, but then he keeled over, vomiting thick dregs of black tar as he coughed over and over again. They were killing him from the inside. It had to be painful and dreadfully dark where he was right now. Still, Phelan had no pity. He walked over to Davis then, grabbing him at the neck by his nails. The lycan howled in pain as Phelan was sure to thrust his nails deeper as he lifted Davis off the floor.

"She's nothing to you, now or ever," he told Davis. "She is her own lycan, her own woman."

"She's a bitch in heat!" Davis continued. "I can smell her ripe pussy right this moment and I want it," he said. "I want her, all of her. I can claim her tonight. This night I can claim that bitch and make her mine forever! I can—"

With his free hand Phelan thrust his nails into Davis's gut, taking any other words the lycan dared to speak from him immediately.

"Your forever is gone," Phelan said with a growl. "Dead and gone!"

With all his might he threw the lycan so far and so fast that when he crashed through the windows and out of the building there was a huge flash of light. The building shook again and this time the floor threatened to crumble beneath Phelan.

"Phelan!" he heard Marena yelling. "Phelan! The building's going to collapse!"

He was turning toward her voice, watching as she came running through the door he'd witnessed close on her face. Never in his life had he been so happy to see someone. She was safe. Thank everything he knew, she was safe and alive. Phelan was just about to run to her, to grab her up in his arms and swear to never let her go, when there was another glittering bolt of lightning and a familiar voice yelling from behind him.

"Go, Phelan! This is my fight, my life."

It was Blaez.

Kira was standing right beside him, Channing, Malec, and Caroline behind them. Marena had run across the room, grabbing hold of Phelan's arm, watching just as he was, as the roof of the building was ripped free. In the center of the dark night sky was the supermoon. Big and bright, draped in a haze of red, dominating the space as if it had every right. Between it flashed another bolt of lightning, and when that bolt disappeared the god emerged.

"The lycan demigod," were the words spoken from the great god Zeus as he walked along that lightning bolt with ease, eventually stepping down into the center of the room.

"You've gone through a lot of trouble to find me," Blaez said, taking a step away from Kira.

"To kill you," was Zeus's quick reply.

"But you can't kill me," Blaez told him. "That's why you had to go to such great lengths to find me. You cannot take my life."

"Insolent child!" Zeus roared, lifting his hand until another sizzling lightning bolt appeared.

He hurled it at Blaez, who then shifted into his full wolf form. Next to him, Phelan heard Marena gasp, and he reached for her hand, intertwining his fingers with hers. Although she knew that Blaez was half demigod and half lycan as a result of his mother, Kharis, being a child of Artemis and his father, Alec, being a direct lycan descent of Nyktimos, she did not know, however, that this power meant Blaez could turn into a full-grown black wolf.

The wolf dodged the bolt and then leapt forward, landing directly in front of Zeus. Blaez howled, with his neck bent back toward the moon, and rain immediately began to fall. A few feet away from Zeus and the wolf, Kira's eyes glowed a bright white, her arms lifting up from her sides, hair blowing in the cool breeze.

Out of nowhere came another blinding light that swirled around the room like a gusting storm, until finally settling into a small female form.

"Selene," Zeus gasped. "You are meddling again."

"I am protecting them," the Moon Goddess said, her voice like a litany of chimes in the air. "They are my creation, Zeus. They have my power. A power that even you in all your mightiness cannot destroy."

"They are mine!" Zeus yelled. "All of the packs belong to me, as I created them. I started this with Lykaon."

"And I ended it with the Selected and the demigod lycan," Selene countered calmly. "They are mine and their peace will be so."

Zeus pulled another bolt, this time slamming it into the ground beneath his feet, causing what felt like the biggest earthquake in the world to erupt. The Moon Goddess lifted a hand, sending her golden beams along the floor and up the walls. They even stretched up to the red of the supermoon, dripping down over the orb in brilliant white.

"Their peace will be so!" she yelled louder and louder, until the shaking stopped and Zeus backed away with a vicious curse.

"You will regret this, Selene! You all will!" were the god's last words as he disappeared in a roll of thunder amidst the falling rain.

"I think," Marena whispered, "on some level he already regrets it."

Phelan held her hand tighter, pulling her closer to him. "I think you're right, baby. I think you're absolutely right."

CHAPTER 12

It was late and rain still fell in a soft, steady drizzle that made a tapping sound against their helmets. The asphalt was one shining stretch of black in front of them with only the beam from the motorcycle's headlight to guide the way.

Marena held on tight ignoring it all and relishing the warmth of Phelan's body against hers.

She'd thought they were going to die. Each of them as they stood in the face of Zeus's human form. He was the most powerful god; surely he could kill them all without blinking an eye. She should have known better. Or at least should have thought that little scenario through a little further. If Zeus could have killed them all so simply, what had stopped him from doing so all this time? If it were simple, why had it been so hard for him to find Blaez and to take care of the loose thread he'd felt as though he'd left dangling all those years ago?

Because it wasn't that simple and the Moon Goddess had shown up to make that point perfectly clear.

"I knew she would come," Kira had said when they'd all finally made their way out of the building.

They stood beside Blaez's black Escalade only minutes

after the Moon Goddess's bright beams had carried her back to her realm.

"You knew she would rescue us and save Blaez?" Marena had asked.

Kira shook her head. "She appeared in my dream telling me to be strong, that the moment she'd created me for was at hand. I knew then that there was nothing that could defeat us," Kira spoke as she held Blaez's hand tightly in hers.

The alpha had come down the stairs with them in his wolf form. A huge, gorgeous black wolf with startling blue eyes that had actually produced enough light to guide them through the dark stairwell. Once at the truck, Channing had opened one of the back doors and the wolf had climbed inside, coming out moments later as a fully dressed man.

"Then this definitely was all a part of their plan," Marena added. "I mean the part up until the Moon Goddess appeared. Zeus had used Davis and Eureka to get Phelan away from Blaez. They thought he was the strongest and most protective of the betas, but they hadn't counted on a Selected being in the picture."

"They hadn't counted on all of us working together to keep Blaez alive," Malec added. "It didn't take us long to figure out their strategy after you left. That's why he quickly got on the road behind you and came out here."

Phelan nodded. "I was wondering how you made it here so fast without me having a chance to call to you."

"It all made sense. The only thing strong enough to take you away from Blaez would be your mate," Caroline said, looking from Phelan to Marena.

She'd felt uncomfortable with the knowing gazes but was no longer alarmed at the sound of that word. Caroline and

Kira had been saying it for weeks. Blaez had even approached her about the situation. But it was the moment Eureka had the audacity to speak about her supposedly being Phelan's mate that Marena had finally grabbed ahold of the word and hung on for dear life. If that powerful and vengeful fury was irritated enough to come after her with her deadly nails and fireball palms, there must have been some truth to the word. It must have meant she was definitely a threat to the woman and her revenge against Phelan for leaving her. And if that was the case, then Marena was without a doubt Phelan's mate. Regardless of the fact that a mate was exactly what Phelan didn't want.

"We shouldn't stay out much longer," Blaez had said then. "It's not safe out tonight, not for any of us."

In the distance there were howls and eerie sounds that had Marena moving closer to Phelan. He wrapped an arm around her waist and Marena resisted the urge to smile. She did, however, lean into him, accepting his protection and his warmth. He walked her over to his bike, telling them all he'd see them back at the lodge. Then he'd put her helmet on and helped her onto the bike. She'd waited expectantly while he put his own helmet on and climbed on in front of her and she quickly leaned into him once more.

This was the most comfortable and complacent she'd ever been and it hit her, much like that lightning bolt that had brought Zeus down from the sky, that it was so because this was where she belonged. Phelan was the one she was meant to be with. She was destined to be a lycan and his mate.

Now, after hours of riding, she was still wondering how she was going to convince Phelan of that fact. He'd never wanted a mate, because another connection meant someone else could walk out of his life taking a chunk of his heart with her.

Marena would never hurt him that way. She knew that for a fact because just the thought of leaving Phelan had gripped her heart like a vise, spikes of pain already radiating throughout her body. She shivered with the thoughts, burying her face farther into his leather jacket and holding on to him as tightly as she could.

Seconds later Phelan was turning off the road. There was no exit sign and no asphalt to make the drive smooth as it had been. Now they were bumping over dirt and grass wet and slick from the rain. She had no idea where they were going and was going to ask, but they moved into a clearing where Phelan brought the bike to a stop. He took off his helmet, hanging it on one of the handlebars, and sat there for just a few more seconds.

Marena sat up straight then, pulling her hands back from around his waist, until Phelan grabbed her wrists, holding her still.

"I've been bound to you from the very start," he said so softly she almost didn't hear him. "From the very first moment on that dark highway. I picked up your scent and there was no turning back. No walking away.

"I don't do girlfriends," he said matter-of-factly, and Marena frowned at his back. "I don't have romantic connections or entanglements and I don't make promises." He stopped talking and took a deep breath. "Not ones that I don't intend to keep."

With a quick motion Phelan had kicked the stand on the bike down and hopped off, leaving Marena to stare at him in question. His hands were on her next, grabbing her by the waist and lifting her up off the bike, setting her feet down on the damp ground, her backside leaning against it.

"I promise I won't give you a reason to leave me," he started, cupping her face in his hands. "I promise to let you be whatever and whoever you want to be in this world and to stand right by your side while you do so. I promise that everything that has happened in my past will stay there. I promise to be whatever and whoever you need me to be as long as you're happy. As long as you're . . . mine."

She didn't have a moment to speak before Phelan's lips were on hers, his tongue pressing hungrily inside her mouth and taking charge. Marena gasped and slipped her arms beneath his jacket to wrap around his waist, pulling him closer while tilting her head further into their kiss.

"I promise, Marena. I promise," he was whispering, his hands moving quickly over her body.

Marena felt his hands at her waist again, reaching up beneath her top to grab hold of the band of her pants. He pushed them down roughly, dragging her underwear with them until they were pooled at her ankles. In another quick motion he was turning her, pressing her down so that her stomach lay over the seat of the motorcycle and then his fingers were sliding down the crease of her ass.

He rubbed down until he was parting the tender folds of her pussy, circling his fingers around her clit until her essence began to flow from her much like the rain pelting against her bare skin. Marena held on to the leather seat, clenching her teeth as the feel of his fingers on her drove her slowly insane.

When he thrust a finger deep inside of her she gasped, bucking back against his hand and begging him for more. "Phelan, please."

"Always," he sighed, using his other hand to squeeze her ass. He released that cheek and slapped his palm over it until it began to sting and Marena moaned.

"Always for you, I promise," he told her while working his finger in and out of her pussy.

She was wet, probably more so than the ground after it had been raining for hours now. The slick sound of his fingers on her skin moved from one hole back farther to another where he circled and petted, teasing and prodding. Marena sucked in a breath and shook her head, yelling, "Phelan!"

He moaned from behind her. "Yes, my mate," he said. "My. Mate."

Marena loved the sound of those words from his mouth, almost as much as she loved the touch of his tongue on her ass cheek, when he kissed her there. He bit her and stroked his tongue over the throbbing area, then went lower, until his tongue was licking up and down her swollen lips, just a breath away from her clit. Marena was throwing her ass back into his face, screaming for him to take more, to lick harder, faster. She wanted to come. Damn, she wanted it more than she'd ever wanted anything else in her life. She wanted to come all over his face and then ride his dick until she came again.

Her mind was full of all the lascivious things she wanted to do with Phelan and that she wanted him to do with her. It was the full moon, she knew, sending their sex drive to higher heights and threatening to strangle them if they didn't act on it. Then there was something even more powerful. Something that exacerbated her need for Phelan, creating a burning ache in the center of her stomach. She needed Phelan to give her more.

And that he did.

Coming to his feet, Phelan had at some point released his throbbing erection and then pressed the bulbous head of his cock against her dripping wet entrance. He thrust in so fast Marena almost slipped off the bike. The feeling of him filling her completely was so good she'd opened her mouth and screamed at the contact.

His palm was on the center of her back as he pounded into her mercilessly. The cool of the rain mixed with the heat of her arousal had Marena moaning in ecstasy. She thought surely that the way her body was bouncing over that motorcycle they were both going to hit the ground at any moment, but they didn't. Instead, Phelan's dick moved in and out of her with expert precision, hitting her G-spot over and over again until her thighs shook with her release.

He leaned over her at that very moment, ripping her shirt from her shoulder and sinking his teeth into her bare skin. It was the exact spot where Davis had bitten her and it had hurt like hell. This time it didn't, yet Marena yelled out anyway. She realized she was yelling because as Phelan bit into her he also licked over the wound, sealing it with his saliva at the same time as his dick pulsated inside of her, spurting his hot cum deep inside of her.

She felt it in that instant, the connection between them being bonded and strengthened. He was right; it had been there since day one. It was what had kept them together, the fact that she had remained in pain until he was near. He'd been her relief and her comfort immediately, while it had taken her time to become his solace, his safe place after all the pain and disappointment he'd endured.

Now, on this rainy night of the supermoon, they had become one. He was her mate and she was his. And when his still-rock-hard dick slipped from her pussy to press slowly against the tight bud of her anus, Marena yelled out, "I love you, Phelan. I love you so much, my mate!"

He moaned her name as he pressed deeper inside her. "Marena, my mate. I so love you. I am so fucking in love with you."

He pumped her slowly, deeply, over and over again until the point where neither of them could have resisted no matter how hard they tried. She lifted her head the second she felt him releasing into her one more time, and Phelan leaned forward, touching his hand along the line of her neck as they both howled their love and claimed the supreme power of the supermoon.